Praise for the novels of
New York Times bestselling author J.T. Ellison

"Well-developed, multidimensional characters and an exceptionally strong plot power bestseller Ellison's eighth Taylor Jackson novel... The characters' humanity and the gut-wrenching problems they face in life-and-death situations put Ellison in the top rank of romantic suspense novelists."
—*Publishers Weekly*, starred review, on *Field of Graves*

"Followers of this series will relish the revelations of how Ellison's protagonists first connected. New readers of this page-turning, suspenseful thriller will want to catch up on the author's other books."
—*Library Journal* on *Field of Graves*

"As always when it comes to author J.T. Ellison, this book is a creation of fear, suspense, with even a little humor thrown in... Ellison shows a skill and talent that is more than exceptional at laying out a fresh path leading to a murderer that readers will not believe!"
—*Suspense Magazine* on *Field of Graves*

"Everyone should already be reading Ellison, but those unfamiliar with her work could start here."
—*RT Book Reviews* on *Field of Graves*

"A genuine page-turner... Ellison clearly belongs in the top echelon of thriller writers. Don't leave this one behind."
—*Booklist*, starred review, on *What Lies Behind*

"Thriller fanatics craving an action-packed novel of intrigue will be abundantly rewarded!"
—*Library Journal* on *What Lies Behind*

"Fans of forensic mysteries, such as those by Patricia Cornwell, should immediately add this series to their A-lists."
—*Booklist*, starred review, on *When Shadows Fall*

"A gripping page-turner...essential for suspense junkies."
—*Library Journal* on *When Shadows Fall*

J.T. ELLISON

FIELD OF GRAVES

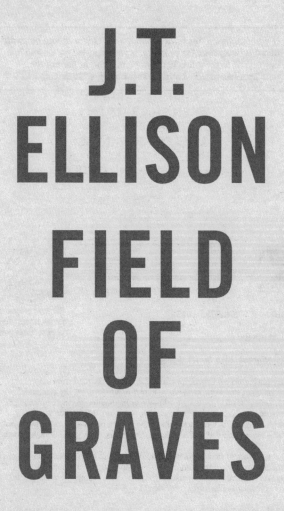

MIRA

ISBN-13: 978-0-7783-3053-0

Field of Graves

Recycling programs
for this product may
not exist in your area.

www.MIRABooks.com

Printed in U.S.A.

For Joan Huston,
who championed this book way back when,
and assured me it stood the test of time.

And, as always, for Randy.

FIELD
OF
GRAVES

When the Lamb broke the fourth seal, I heard the voice of the fourth living creature saying, "Come." I looked, and behold, an ashen horse; and he who sat on it had the name Death; and Hades was following with him. Authority was given to them over a fourth of the earth, to kill with sword and with famine and with pestilence and by the wild beasts of the earth.

—Revelation 6:7–8

PROLOGUE

Taylor picked up her portable phone for the tenth time in ten minutes. She hit Redial, heard the call connect and start ringing, then clicked the Off button and returned the phone to her lap. Once she made this call, there was no going back. Being right wouldn't make her the golden girl. If she were wrong—well, she didn't want to think about what could happen. Losing her job would be the least of her worries.

Damned if she did. Damned if she didn't.

She set the phone on the pool table and went down the stairs of her small two-story cabin. In the kitchen, she opened the door to the refrigerator and pulled out a Diet Coke. She laughed to herself. As if more caffeine would give her the courage to make the call. She should try a shot of whiskey. That always worked in the movies.

She snapped open the tab and stood staring out of her kitchen window. It had been dark for hours—

the moon gone and the inky blackness outside her window impenetrable—but in an hour the skies would lighten. She would have to make a decision by then.

She turned away from the window and heard a loud crack. The lights went out. She jumped a mile, then giggled nervously, a hand to her chest to stop the sudden pounding. *Silly girl*, she thought. *The lights go out all the time. There was a Nashville Electric Service crew on the corner when you drove in earlier; they must have messed up the line and a power surge caused the lights to blow. It happens every time NES works on the lines. Now stop it. You're a grown woman. You're not afraid of the dark.*

She reached into her junk drawer and groped for a flashlight. Thumbing the switch, she cursed softly when the light didn't shine. Batteries, where were the batteries?

She froze when she heard the noise and immediately went on alert, all of her senses going into overdrive. She strained her ears, trying to hear it again. Yes, there it was. A soft scrape off the back porch. She took a deep breath and sidled out of the kitchen, keeping close to the wall, moving lightly toward the back door. She brought her hand to her side and found nothing. *Damn it.* She'd left her gun upstairs.

The tinkling of breaking glass brought her up short. The French doors leading into the backyard had been breached. It was too late to head upstairs and get the gun. She would have to walk right through the living room to get to the stairs. Whoever had just broken through her back door was not going to let her stroll on by. She started edging back toward the kitchen, holding her breath, as if that would help her not make any noise.

She didn't see the fist, only felt it crack against her jaw. Her eyes swelled with tears, and before she could react, the fist connected again. She spun and hit the wall face-first. The impact knocked her breath out. Her lips cut on the edge of her teeth; she tasted blood. The intruder grabbed her as she started to slide down the wall. Yanked her to her feet and put his hands around her throat, squeezing hard.

Now she knew exactly where her attacker was, and she fought back with everything she had. She struggled against him, quickly realizing she was in trouble. He was stronger than her, bigger than her. And he was there to kill.

She went limp, lolled bonelessly against him, surprising him with the sudden weight. He released one arm in response, and she took that moment to whirl around and shove with all her might. It created some space between them, enabling her to slip out of his grasp. She turned quickly but crashed into the slate end table. He was all over her. They struggled their way into the living room. She began to plan. Kicked away again.

Her attacker lunged after her. She used the sturdy side table to brace herself and whipped out her left arm in a perfect jab, aiming lower than where she suspected his chin would be. She connected perfectly and heard him grunt in pain. Spitting blood out of her mouth in satisfaction, she followed the punch with a kick to his stomach, heard the whoosh of his breath as it left his body. He fell hard against the wall. She spun away and leapt to the stairs. He jumped up to pursue her, but she was quicker. She pounded up the stairs as fast as she could, rounding the corner into the hall just as her attacker reached the landing. Her weapon was in its holster, on the bookshelf next to the pool table, right where she had left it when she'd gone downstairs for the soda. She was getting careless. She should never have taken it off her hip. With everything that was happening, she shouldn't have taken for granted that she was safe in her own home.

Her hand closed around the handle of the weapon. She pulled the Glock from its holster, whipped around to face the door as the man came tearing through it. She didn't stop to think about the repercussions, simply reacted. Her hand rose by instinct, and she put a bullet right between his eyes. His momentum carried him forward a few paces. He was only five feet from her, eyes black in death, when he dropped with a thud.

She heard her own ragged breathing. She tasted blood and raised a bruised hand to her jaw, feeling her lips and her teeth gingerly. Son of a bitch had caught her right in the jaw and loosened two molars. The adrenaline rush left her. She collapsed on the floor next to the lifeless body. She might have even slept for a moment.

The throbbing in her jaw brought her back.

Morning was beginning to break, enough to see the horrible mess in front of her. The cat was sitting on the pool table, watching her curiously.

Rising, she took in the scene. The man was collapsed on her game room floor, slowly leaking blood on her Berber carpet. She peered at the stain.

"That's going to be a bitch to get out."

She shook her head to clear the cobwebs. What an inane thing to say. Shock, she must be going into shock. How long had they fought? Had it been only five minutes? Half an hour? She felt as though she had struggled against him for days; her body was tired and sore. Never mind the blood caked around her mouth. She put her hand up to her face. Make that her nose, too.

She eyed the man again. He was facedown and angled slightly to one side. She slipped her toes under his right arm and flipped him over with her foot. The shot was true; she could see a clean entry wound in his forehead. Reaching down out of habit, she felt for his carotid pulse, but there was nothing. He was definitely dead.

"Oh, David," she said. "You complete idiot. Look what you've made me do."

Now the shit was absolutely going to hit the fan. It was time to make the call.

THE
FIRST
DAY

1

Three months later
Nashville, Tennessee

> *Bodies, everywhere bodies, a field of graves,*
> *limbs and torsos and heads, all left above*
> *ground. The feeling of dirt in her mouth,*
> *grimy and thick; the whispers from the dead,*
> *long arms reaching for her as she passed*
> *through the carnage. Ghostly voices, soft and*
> *sibilant. "Help us. Why won't you help us?"*

Taylor jerked awake, sweating, eyes wild and blind
in the darkness. The sheets twisted around her body
in a claustrophobic shroud, and she struggled to get
them untangled. She squeezed her eyes shut, willed
her breathing back to normal, trying to relax, to let
the grisly images go. When she opened her eyes,
the room was still dark but no longer menacing.
Her screams had faded away into the silence. The

cat jumped off the bed with a disgruntled *meow* in response to her thrashing.

She laid her head back on the pillow, swallowed hard, still unable to get a full breath.

Every damn night. She was starting to wonder if she'd ever sleep well again.

She wiped a hand across her face and looked at the clock: 6:10 a.m. The alarm was set for seven, but she wasn't going to get any more rest. She might as well get up and get ready for work. Go in a little early, see what horrors had captured the city overnight.

She rolled off the bed, trying hard to forget the dream. Showered, dressed, dragged on jeans and a black cashmere T-shirt under a black motorcycle jacket, stepped into her favorite boots. Put her creds in her pocket and her gun on her hip. Pulled her wet hair off her face and into a ponytail.

Time to face another day.

She was in her car when the call came. "Morning, Fitz. What's up?"

"Morning, LT. We have us a body at the Parthenon."

"I'll be right there."

It might have become a perfect late-autumn morning. The sky was busy, turning from white to blue as dawn rudely forced its way into day. Birds were returning from their mysterious nocturnal errands, greeting and chattering about the night's affairs. The air was clear and heavy, still muggy from the overnight heat but holding a hint of coolness, like an ice cube dropped into a steaming mug of coffee. The sky would soon shift to sapphire the way only autumn skies do, as clear and heavy as the precious stone itself.

The beauty of the morning was lost on Lieutenant Taylor Jackson, Criminal Investigation Division, Nashville Metro Police. She snapped her long body under the yellow crime scene tape and looked around for a moment. Sensed the looks from the officers around her. Straightened her shoulders and marched toward them.

Metro officers had been traipsing around the crime scene control area like it was a cocktail party, drinking coffee and chatting each other up as though they'd been apart for weeks, not hours. The grass was already littered with cups, cigarette butts, crumpled notebook paper, and at least one copy of the morning's sports section from *The Tennessean*. Taylor cursed silently; they knew better than this. These yahoos were going to inadvertently contaminate a crime scene one of these days, sending her team off on a wild-goose chase. Guess whose ass would be in the proverbial sling then?

She stooped to grab the sports page, surreptitiously glanced at the headline regaling the Tennessee Titans' latest win, then crumpled it into a firm ball in her hands.

Taylor didn't know what information about the murder had leaked out over the air, but the curiosity factor had obviously kicked into high gear. An officer she recognized from another sector was cruising by to check things out, not wanting to miss out on all the fun. Media vans lined the street. Joggers pretending not to notice anything was happening nearly tripped trying to see what all the fuss was about. Exactly what she needed on no sleep: everyone willing to help, to get in and screw up her crime scene.

Striding toward the melee, she tried to tell herself that it wasn't their fault she'd been up all night. At least she'd had a shower and downed two Diet Cokes, or she would have arrested them all.

She reached the command post and pasted on a smile. "Mornin', kids. How many of you have dragged this crap through my crime scene?" She tossed the balled-up paper at the closest officer.

She tried to keep her tone light, as if she were amused by their shenanigans, but she didn't fool anyone, and the levity disappeared from the gathering. The brass was on the scene, so all the fun had come to a screeching halt. Uniforms who didn't belong started to drift away, one or two giving Taylor a sideways glance. She ignored them, the way she ignored most things these days.

As a patrol officer, she'd kept her head down, worked her cases, and developed a reputation for being a straight shooter. Her dedication and clean work had been rewarded with promotion after promotion; she was in plainclothes at twenty-eight. She'd caught a nasty first case in Homicide—the kidnapping and murder of a young girl. She'd nailed the bastard who'd done it; Richard Curtis was on death row now. The case made the national news and sent her career into overdrive. She quickly became known for being a hard-hitting investigator and moved up the ranks from detective to lead to sergeant, until she'd been given the plum job she had now—homicide lieutenant.

If her promotion to lieutenant at the tender age of thirty-four had rankled some of the more traditional officers on the force, the death of David Martin—one of their own—made it ten times worse. There were always going to be cops who tried to make her life difficult; it was part of being a chick on the force, part of having a reputation. Taylor was tough, smart, and liked to do things her own way to get the job done. The majority of the men she worked with had great respect for her abilities. There were always going to be detractors, cops who whispered behind her back, but in Taylor's mind, success trumped rumor every time.

Then Martin had decided to ruin her life and nearly derailed her career in the process. She was still clawing her way back.

Taylor's second in command, Detective Pete Fitzgerald, lumbered toward her, the ever-present unlit cigarette hanging out of his mouth. He'd quit a couple of years before, after a minor heart attack, but kept one around to light in case of an emergency. Fitz had an impressive paunch; his belly reached Taylor before the rest of his body.

"Hey, LT. Sorry I had to drag you away from your beauty sleep." He looked her over, concern dawning in his eyes. "I was just kidding. What's up with you? You look like shit warmed over."

Taylor waved a hand in dismissal. "Didn't sleep.

Aren't we supposed to have some sort of eclipse this morning? I think it's got me all out of whack."

Fitz took the hint and backed down. "Yeah, we are." He looked up quickly, shielding his eyes with his hand. "See, it's already started."

He was right. The moon was moving quickly across the sun, the crime scene darkening by the minute. "Eerie," she said.

He looked back at her, blinking hard. "No kidding. Remind me not to stare into the sun again."

"Will do. Celestial phenomenon aside, what do we have here?"

"Okay, darlin', here we go. We have a couple of lovebirds who decided to take an early morning stroll—found themselves a deceased Caucasian female on the Parthenon's steps. She's sitting up there pretty as you please, just leaning against the gate in front of the Parthenon doors like she sat down for a rest. Naked as a jaybird, and very, very dead."

Taylor turned her gaze to the Parthenon. One of her favorite sites in Nashville, smack-dab in the middle of Centennial Park, the full-size replica was a huge draw for tourists and classicists alike. The statue of Athena inside was awe-inspiring. She couldn't count how many school field trips she'd been on here over the years. Leaving a body on the steps was one hell of a statement.

"Where are the witnesses?"

"Got the lovebirds separated, but the woman's having fits—we haven't been able to get a full statement. The scene's taped off. Traffic on West End has been blocked off, and we've closed all roads into and around Centennial Park. ME and her team have been here about fifteen minutes. Oh, and our killer was here at some point, too." He grinned at her lopsidedly. "He dumped her sometime overnight, only the duckies and geese in the lake saw him. This is gonna be a bitch to canvass. Do you think we can admit 'AFLAC' as a statement in court?"

Taylor gave him a quick look and a perfunctory laugh, more amused at imagining Fitz waddling about like the duck from the insurance ads quacking than at his irreverent attitude. She knew better, but it did seem as if he was having a good time. Taylor understood that sometimes, inappropriate attempts at humor were the only way a cop could make it through the day, so she chastised him gently. "You've got a sick sense of humor, Fitz." She sighed, turning off all personal thoughts, becoming a cop again. All business, all the time. That's what they needed to see from her.

"We'll probably have to go public and ask who was here last night and when, but I'm not holding my breath that we'll get anything helpful, so let's put it off for now."

He nodded in agreement. "Do you want to put up the chopper? Probably useless—whoever dumped her is long gone."

"I think you're right." She jerked her head toward the Parthenon steps. "What's he trying to tell us?"

Fitz looked toward the doors of the Parthenon, where the medical examiner was crouched over the naked body. His voice dropped, and he suddenly became serious. "I don't know, but this is going to get ugly, Taylor. I got a bad feeling."

Taylor held a hand up to cut him off. "C'mon, man, they're all ugly. It's too early to start spinning. Let's just get through the morning. Keep the frickin' media out of here—put 'em down in the duck shit if you have to. You can let them know which roads are closed so they can get the word out to their traffic helicopters, but that's it. Make sure the uniforms keep everyone off the tape. I don't want another soul in here until I have a chance to be fully briefed by all involved. Has the Park Police captain shown up yet?"

Fitz shook his head. "Nah. They've called him, but I haven't seen him."

"Well, find him, too. Make sure they know which end is up. Let's get the perimeter of this park searched, grid by grid, see if we find something. Get K-9 out here, let them do an article search. Since the roads are already shut off, tell them to expand the perimeter one thousand feet outside the borders of the park. I want to see them crawling around like ants at a picnic. I see any of them hanging in McDonald's before this is done, I'm kicking some butt."

Fitz gave her a mock salute. "I'm on it. When Sam determined she was dumped, I went ahead and called K-9, and pulled all the officers coming off duty. We may have an overtime situation, but I figured with your, um, finesse…" He snorted out the last word, and Taylor eyed him coolly.

"I'll handle it." She pushed her hair back from her face and reestablished her hurried ponytail. "Get them ready for all hell to break loose. I'm gonna go talk to Sam."

"Glad to serve, love. Now go see Sam, and let the rest of us grunts do our jobs. If you decide you want the whirlybird, give me a thumbs-up." He blew her a kiss and marched toward the command post, snapping his fingers at the officers to get their attention.

Turning toward the building, she caught a stare from one of the older patrols. His gaze was hostile, lip curled in a sneer. She gave him her most brilliant smile, making his scowl deepen. She broke off the look, shaking her head. She didn't have time to worry about politics right now.

2

Taylor approached Sam cautiously, making sure she followed the ME's path to the body. They wouldn't be able to blame any loss of evidence on *her*. Pulling on her latex gloves, she tapped Sam lightly on the shoulder. Sam looked up. Anticipating Taylor's first question, she shook her head.

"There's no obvious cause of death—no stab wounds, no gunshot wounds. Evidence of rape. There's some bruising and tearing, a little bit of blood. He got her pretty good. There's some dirt on her, too. Wind probably blew some stuff around last night. I'll get a better idea when I get her open."

She rocked back on her heels and saw Taylor's face for the first time. "Girl, you look like crap. When's the last time you slept?"

"Been a while." The sleepless nights were catching up with her. She was almost thankful when a new case popped like this; the past slid away briefly when she could focus her attention elsewhere.

Sam gave her one last appraising glance. "Hmmph."

Dr. Samantha Owens had shoulder-length brown

hair she always wore back in a ponytail, feminine wisps she couldn't control framing her face. She often joked that she'd rather look like a girl than a ghoul when she met someone new so the first impression wasn't one of horror. Taylor was always amused to see people scatter like rats when they found out the beautiful and composed woman was a professional pathologist. Most run-of-the-mill people didn't want to hang out with a woman who cut up dead bodies for a living.

Unlike many of the women she and Taylor had grown up with, Sam didn't join the Junior League, have beautiful babies, and lunch at Bread & Company. Instead, she spent her time perched over Nashville's endless supply of dead bodies, a position she was in much too often. She was also Taylor's best friend and was allowed liberties where others weren't.

"I've been telling you, you need to get some help."

"Hush up, Sam, I don't want to hear it. Tell me about our girl." Taylor let the knot in her stomach and the ache in her temples take complete hold. She had warmed up in the early-morning heat, but looking at the dead girl was giving her the chills. "Fitz said she was dumped?"

Sam traced an invisible line around the body with her finger. "Definitely. She wasn't killed here. See the livor pattern? The bottom of her legs, thighs and calves, her butt, the inside of her arms, and her back. The blood pooled in those areas. But she's sitting up, right? The lividity wouldn't present this way unless she had been chilling out on her back for a while. She was definitely dead for a few hours before she was dumped."

Taylor looked closely at the purplish-red blotches. In contrast, the front of the girl's body looked as pale and grimy as a dead jellyfish.

"No blood either. Maybe he's a vampire." Sam leered briefly at Taylor, made fangs out of her fingers, hissed. Her morbid sense of humor always popped up at the most inappropriate times.

"You're insane."

"I know. No, he did her someplace else, then dumped her here." She looked around and said quietly, "Seriously, this feels very staged. She was put *here* for a reason, posed, everything. He wanted her found right away. The question is, why?"

Taylor didn't comment, but tucked Sam's remark into the back of her mind to be brought out and chewed on later. She knew it was worth thinking about; Sam had sound instincts. She turned back toward the command center. Seeing Fitz, she peeled the glove off her right hand, put two fingers in her mouth, and whistled sharply. He turned, and she shook her head. The helicopter definitely wasn't going to be needed.

Taylor looked back at the girl's face. *So young. Another, so young.* "Give me something to work with. Do you have a time of death?"

Sam thought for a moment. "Looking at her temp, she died sometime before midnight. Let's say ten to twelve hours ago, give or take. Rigor's still in, though she's starting to break up."

"Gives him time to kill her and get her here. Okay. Semen?"

"Oh yeah. It's all over the place. This guy really doesn't care about trying to be subtle. Not terribly bright. It shouldn't be too hard to match him up if he's in CODIS. He's certainly not holding anything back." She laughed at her pun, and Taylor couldn't help a brief smile.

"How about under her nails? Did she fight back?"

Sam lifted the dead girl's right hand. "I looked pretty closely, but I didn't see anything resembling skin or blood. I'll have them bag her hands and do scrapings back at the shop, but it doesn't look like she got hold of anything. We didn't find any ID with the body, so we'll print her and send them over to see if you can find a match. They'll be clear enough to run through AFIS."

Taylor was hardly listening. She stared at the girl's face. *So young*, she thought again. Man, there was going to be major fallout when they held this press conference. The statement started percolating in her head. *At six o'clock this morning, the body of a Caucasian female was discovered on the steps of the Parthenon...*

She looked back to Sam. "So no idea what killed her, huh?"

Sam relaxed, sitting back on her haunches. She stripped off her gloves and watched Taylor leaning in on the body.

"Hell if I know. Nothing's really jumping out at me. Give me a break, T, you know the drill."

"You'll get me all the pics yesterday, right? And do the post right now. I mean—" she attempted a more conciliatory tone "—will you do the post right now?"

"I'll bump her to the top of the guest list. There's something else… Do you smell anything?"

"Just your perfume. Is it new?"

"See, that's the weird thing. I'm not wearing any. I think the smell is coming from the body. And I'll tell you, Taylor, this would be my first sweet-smelling corpse, you know?"

Taylor *had* noticed the scent. She inhaled sharply through her nose. Yes, there were all the usual stinks that came with a dead body: the unmistakable smell of decay, the stink of fear, the tang of stale urine and excrement. But overlaying all these olfactory wonders was a tangy sweetness. She thought hard for a moment, searching for the memory the smell triggered. The scent was somehow familiar, almost like— That was it!

"Sam, you know what this smells like? The spa across the way, Essential Therapy. Remember, I gave you a gift certificate for a massage there for your birthday? They have all those lotions and soaps and essential oil candles…"

"Wait a minute. You're right. She smells like incense." She stared at the body. "What if… Okay, give me a second here." Sam reached into her kit and extracted a small pair of tweezers. She bent over and started picking through the dirt on the body.

"What are you doing?" Taylor watched Sam put

a few pieces of leaves and sticks into a small white paper bag. Somewhat disgusted, she watched Sam shove her nose into the bag and breathe in deeply. "Ugh, Sam."

"No, here." Sam's eyes lit up, and Taylor was tempted to back away. But Sam grabbed her hand and shoved the bag toward Taylor's face. "Really, smell."

Taylor wrinkled her nose, swallowing hard. It was one thing seeing the body and smelling it from a few feet away, but sticking her nose into the detritus that came from the body itself was totally gross. Grimacing, she took the bag and inhaled. The scent was smoky and floral, not at all unpleasant.

Sam's eyes were shining in excitement. "This isn't dirt, Taylor. These are herbs. She has herbs scattered all over her body. Now what the hell is that all about?"

Taylor shook her head slowly, trying to absorb the new discovery. "I don't know. Can you isolate which herb it is?"

"Yeah, I can let a buddy of mine at UT in Knoxville take a look. He's head of the university's botany department and totally into all this stuff. I don't think it's just one herb, though. The leaves are all different sizes and shapes. Oh man, this is too cool."

"Sam, you're awful." Taylor couldn't stop herself from smiling. "You like this job too much."

"That's why I'm good at it. Tim's our lead 'gator today. I'm going to get him set up here to bag all this stuff, and I'll have a runner take it up to UT

ASAP. You know, it would be a lot simpler if that idiot mayor would help us get our own lab capable of handling this kind of stuff. Hell, it'd be nice if we could even do tox screens in-house."

Sam continued grumbling under her breath and stood up, signaling the end of the conversation. She waved to her team, calling them over. The body was ready to be moved.

"Wait, Sam. Did Crime Scene pick up anything else? Clothes, jewelry?"

"Not yet, but you're in their way. She's got enough of this crap on her that it's gonna take them a while to collect it all. Why don't you go back and try to find out who this girl is for me, okay? Y'all need to catch this guy, 'cause once the press gets ahold of this, they're gonna freak the whole city. It's not every day I have to come to the middle of Centennial Park to collect a body, much less for a staged crime scene. Look at the vultures hovering already."

She swept her hand toward the media trucks. Their level of activity had picked up, excitement palpable in the air. Techs were setting up lights and running around on the street by the duck pond, with cameras and portable microphones in tow. The news vans were lined up around the corner. Taylor watched Fitz and the patrol officers struggle to keep the reporters from rushing the tape to gather their precious scoops. Nothing like murder in the morning to start a feeding frenzy.

"Seriously, Taylor, you know how they are. They'll find some way to spin this into a grand conspiracy and warn all the parents to keep their girls at home until you catch whoever did this." She started grumbling. "It should be frickin' illegal for the chief to have given them their own radios. Now every newsie in Nashville hovers over my shoulder while I scope a body."

Taylor lowered her eyelids for a second and gave her best friend a half smile. "Well, honey, if it makes you feel any better, all the talking heads and their cameramen are squishing through goose poo trying to get their stories. Guess Lake Watauga has its purposes after all. Call me as soon as you have anything."

Sam laughed. "Yeah, yeah. Split. You're making me nervous."

3

Taylor made a last slow circuit around the crime scene. The techs were carefully moving about, photographing the site from every possible angle. She half noticed them brushing fine black powder in the areas surrounding where the body had been found, looking for latent fingerprints.

Why the Parthenon? Why would the killer dump a body in the middle of West End? You couldn't look in any direction without seeing students jogging from the gates of Vanderbilt, trendy yuppies coasting through the gourmet restaurants and bars, hippie granolas Birkenstocking their way to the natural food and clothing stores. It was a risky venture, even in the overnight hours.

She made a few notes, thinking about Sam's comments. *Staged. Huh.* The scene wasn't terribly gruesome compared to many she'd seen, but it did have a more organized feel to it—after all, he had made himself very vulnerable coming out in the open with a dead girl slung over his shoulder, risking the time to arrange her and scatter herbs on her naked body. He'd spent at least a few minutes setting things up. A huge chance to take that no one would be around. Even teenagers who were supposed to be in bed were out cruising through the park all night.

Taylor headed in the direction of her car and passed Sam's lead investigator, Tim Davis, as he started up the stairs.

"Later, 'gator," she called out.

Tim gave her a dirty look. "That joke is really getting old."

She gave him her sweetest smile. "Tell that to Sam. She's the one who christened you guys *'gators*. Besides—" her voice dropped two octaves "—'Death Investigator' just sounds so, well, depressing."

"Death is depressing, Taylor." He smiled and turned away.

Taylor felt a brief qualm of conscience. Tim was one of the best 'gators the medical examiner's office had and was deadly serious about his work.

She stopped walking and turned around to look at the Parthenon again. She stood quietly, staring at the huge structure. What the hell was this guy up to? A sacrifice to the goddess Athena, who guarded the murky interior of the building? She laughed, startling a goose ten feet away. It waddled off, honking in annoyance. *Yeah, take that theory into the squad room. The boys would love it.* She shook the image of the goddess out of her mind.

It was time to get to work. Taylor picked her way through malodorous fowl dung scattered all over the ground back to the phalanx of police cars. She needed to talk to the young couple who'd found the body before they were brought in to give their formal statements. She walked out into the control center and found Bob Miller, the first officer on the scene. He was short and stout with a bristling black mustache and impossibly white teeth.

"Officer Miller. Where do you have them?"

He flashed her a brilliant smile. "Hey, LT. He's in my car, and she's over with Wills." Keith Wills was Miller's partner and was becoming a specialist in handling witnesses of the female persuasion. "She's still crying, but she's calming down. Name's Catey Thompson, he's Devon Post. They got engaged last night, messed around until nearly dawn, then went out for a *rrrromanteek* sunrise stroll." His dreadful Italian accent got a quick laugh and a headshake out of Taylor.

"Had they been drinking?"

Officer Miller returned to his normal southern twang. "Yeah, champagne. But they knocked off the heavy celebrating a few hours ago. They were pretty straight when they set out, and now...well, they're scared sober, if they weren't already."

"Thanks, Miller. Will you stick around and make sure the scene stays sealed up tight for me? Fitz already has a grid search going on, and I don't want anyone messing it up." She clapped him on the shoulder. "Sorry, pal, it's gonna be a long day."

He smiled and strode away. Taylor approached Wills, who was holding Catey's hand and offering her a box of tissues.

"Hello, Officer Wills. Miss Thompson? I'm Lieutenant Jackson from the Homicide Division. I'm the lead detective investigating this murder. I'd appreciate it if you could give me your account of what happened this morning."

Catey might be pretty, but Taylor was having a hard time seeing it at the moment. Long brown hair escaped the clip that held it back, and her brown eyes were bloodshot. Her perfectly petite nose was cherry red, and her face was swollen and blotchy from crying. She looked up, took a deep breath, and spoke in a soft, hesitant voice.

"We were walking through the park, waiting for the sunrise. We walked right up to her. I was actually annoyed that we weren't alone. She was sitting on the top step, leaning back against the gate. I thought she was watching us. Her eyes were open, and at first I didn't realize…" Her voice began to waver. "I thought maybe she was there to watch the sun come up, too. But she was naked and just sort of sat there, and I realized she was dead." She began to cry again. "I started screaming, and Devon pulled me away. He took my cell phone, and I heard him calling for help, then I threw up. It was horrible. Is she really dead?" The girl was preparing to get hysterical again.

Taylor ignored the question. "Miss Thompson, this is very important. I know it's difficult to revisit the memory, but if you could try for me, hold yourself together for a little longer?"

Officer Wills pushed the entire box of tissues into the girl's hands, and Taylor continued. "Think very carefully. Did you see anyone else around? Maybe someone walking in the park at the same time? Did you hear a car?"

She snuffled into a new tissue. "No. I'm sure we were the only people here. It was so nice, so peaceful. My God, what happened to her? Are we safe? What if he saw us? Oh my God, oh my God, ohmyGod…" She began bawling in earnest, and Taylor patted her on the shoulder.

"I'm sure you're perfectly safe, Miss Thompson, so don't worry. I seriously doubt whoever killed her was hanging around. Thank you for your help. Officer Wills is going to take you downtown to make a formal statement, and then you and your fiancé will be free to go. If you remember anything, anything at all, even if you think it doesn't matter, I want you to call me. Okay?" She handed her a card with her office and pager numbers on it. "You can call me day or night."

Catey sniffed, trying to regain some semblance of control, dragged the tissue under her eyes, spreading raccoon rings of mascara. "Thank you, Lieutenant Jackson. Can I see Devon now?"

"We'll get you two together downtown, all right? Thank you for your help."

Catey nodded. Taylor stepped aside with Officer Wills.

"Do their stories match?"

"Yeah, to a tee. They're really shook up. Do you want to talk to him, or can I take 'em now?"

Taylor felt the headache deepen. She rubbed her forehead. "Go ahead, get them out of here. Better if the cameras don't get a shot of their faces. Thanks, Wills. You did a good job here this morning. Can you leave a copy of your report on my desk as soon as you get it done? And gather up everyone else's, too?"

"Sure thing, LT. I'll bring them up ASAP."

Looking around, she corralled Fitz and told him to get back to the squad as soon as he could get away. The boys from the ME's team had bagged the body and were rolling the stretcher toward their plain white van. Though most people wouldn't give a medical examiner's vehicle a second glance, the van's circumspect attempt at discretion didn't fool the media, who followed every movement with their cameras, even running after the van as it pulled away. With some good B-roll filler on tape, they turned for another source. Taylor was fifty feet away, walking with her head down, ostensibly looking to avoid the muck left behind by the ducks and geese. The yells started.

"Lieutenant!" screamed Channel 5.

The NBC affiliate chimed in. "Who is the victim? What was cause of death?"

Their onslaught beat in time with the throbbing in Taylor's head. It wasn't unusual for her to make statements at a crime scene; normally she was fine with the cameras. Taylor had striking good looks that she worked to her advantage when necessary. Huge gray eyes—the right slightly darker than the left—shifted between clear smoke and stormy steel, depending on her mood. Lips just a touch too full encased orthodontically enhanced straight white teeth, and a slightly crooked nose gave her countenance a vaguely asymmetrical aspect. She was nearly six feet, blond and rangy, with a deep voice, husky and cracked.

This particular morning, though, with dark smudges under her eyes, a hasty ponytail, and a nasty headache, she looked slightly less than ethereal.

"No comment, guys. I'm sure we'll have something to say later on."

"C'mon, Taylor. You need to let us know so we can make the noon report." A flaxen-haired beauty from Channel 2, her rectangular tortoiseshell glasses sliding down her well-done nose job, stuck a mic in her face. "Just give us something," she pleaded.

Lee Mayfield of *The Tennessean* gave Taylor an inquiring smile. Taylor shook her head; she'd be damned if she gave the paper's crime reporter anything. Besides, the woman would spin it her own way and distort the facts anyway. Let her do it on her own.

"You have to give us *something* to go on, Lieutenant," the latest talking head from Channel 17 admonished.

Taylor whipped around, her limited patience worn through. Spotlights glowed in her eyes, blinding her for a moment. Blinking back into focus, she said, "I said we'll have something for you later. Now quit lurking around my crime scene. You're making my team's work difficult."

Taylor turned her back on them, hurried across

the small parking lot in front of Lake Watauga, jumped into her unmarked squad car. Wow, she'd let them get to her. Not very professional. It seemed every little thing got to her these days. Oh well, it would give them something fun to work on for their precious stories: Lead Investigator Loses Temper.

"Jerks," she said vehemently, rubbing her temples. She watched the press milling around their trucks, each trying to find a spin on her blatant and sarcastic remarks.

One by one, she saw the cameras start to point at the sky. A banner day for Nashville's reporters. A murder and an eclipse, all tied up in one tidy little package for them. The noon broadcasts really were going to be chock-full of fun.

She pulled to the east entrance of the park, noticing the Park Police weren't letting anyone in, on foot or by car. At least they were making themselves useful.

She stopped at a light and briefly closed her eyes. The body of the dead girl was stark against her eyelids. Taylor couldn't help but think of the terror she must have felt as her life was stripped away, and wasn't surprised to feel the anger come. It had been like that lately.

Over the years, she'd learned how to detach herself from crime scenes. She had to; it kept her sane. After a time, she'd grown relatively numb to the atrocities she saw. Lately, though, her armor had developed cracks.

Giving the Parthenon one last glance, she realized the vibe surrounding the scene was making her very uncomfortable. She had the feeling she'd missed the message the killer was trying to send.

She turned left onto West End Avenue and registered the slow burn that had started. "I'm gonna catch you, you son of a bitch. You just wait. I'm coming."

4

The sky darkened. The moon moved before the sun, blotting out the sunlight in momentary increments until the world became a shadowy place, darkness scarring the light.

He gazed at the miracle, oblivious to the scene in front of him and the frenzy he had created. He had been so patient. So focused. He'd interpreted the signs correctly, and now he was being rewarded.

He murmured at the sky, *"...And the sun became black as sackcloth of hair, and the moon became as blood."*

Then it began to pass, and the man felt his heart stir once more. So many things to do.

He left the parking lot. No one noticed him.

5

Taylor followed the streets back to headquarters, swinging down Church Street toward Hooters, turning left on Second, circling the courthouse, driving past the front entrance of the Criminal Justice Center. She frowned at the attempt to modernize the architecture of the building. Someone had gotten the idea that they could take a squat, brown brick square and fancy it up with a courtyard full of benches and a rounded portico over the main doors. A nice idea, but the bevy of criminals scurrying in and out of the doors of the CJC ruined the effect.

Adding to the atmosphere was the close smell of river water, which made Taylor wrinkle her nose in disgust. The water level of the Cumberland was low, and the fetid reek didn't help the depression of the area.

It was a busy morning. It took five minutes to find a spot. After circling twice, she finally slid into a space on Third by the back door to her offices.

Taylor went up the flight of concrete stairs leading to the side door entrance, stepping carefully around the overflowing bucket of cigarette butts in the corner of the landing. Swiping her card to gain access, she pulled open the door and made the short walk to the Homicide office. Her team was already assembling, putting together the necessities to start the murder investigation.

"Are y'all up to speed?" There were nods all around.

"Okay. I'm gonna check in with Price."

Taylor hadn't missed a stride as she crossed the room. Though the door was uncharacteristically closed, she walked into the captain's office without knocking.

Captain Mitchell Price was a small, generally happy man in his early fifties, nearly bald, with an impressive mustache he took great care to groom. As the head of the Criminal Investigative Divisions, he oversaw Homicide, Vice, and all the other investigative departments. Price was on his phone when Taylor barged in, but quickly placed his finger over his mouth, hit the speaker button for her to hear, and set the handset quietly back in the cradle. He ran his hand over his shiny scalp, pushing away the last few stray strands of faded red hair, and motioned to the door, rolling his eyes at the voice now emanating from the speaker. Taylor closed the door silently behind her and took a seat across from his desk.

"Damn it, Price. When are you going to have some answers for me?" Mayor Meredith Robbins was yelling loud enough that even with the door closed, Taylor knew the rest of the squad could hear her strident voice. "When are your people going to get their asses in gear? A girl shows up dead in the middle of Centennial Park, which is going to be closed for God knows how long while your teams wander around, and we've got the Arts and Crafts Fair this weekend. There are trucks full of crap ready to get in there and unload, and I'm the one who has to smooth out all the granola-filled feathers. It's too late to cancel this thing now. There's going to be hell to pay if you can't get the park open immediately. And all you can tell me is 'you're working on it'? I want some answers, and I want them now!"

Taylor mouthed the word *bitch* to Price, then turned away, smiling. Meredith Robbins was a thorn in the department's side. The woman was a self-serving, nasty politician whose only concern was making herself look good, the citizens of Nashville be damned. How she got elected in the first place was still a mystery to Taylor.

Turning back to Price, she twirled her finger around and raised an eyebrow. He smiled and nodded, interrupting the tirade.

"Um, Mayor, we're working things as fast as we can. I'm sure we'll have some answers for you very soon. And the sooner we can get off this call, the sooner I can get the details from Lieutenant Jackson."

"Fine. Get back to me the moment you have some new information. And get the damn park opened back up. If the vendors start canceling because of this, I will hold you personally responsible."

Price sighed loudly for effect and said, "If anything, Meredith, I'd assume the curiosity factor is going to *draw* people to the park, not drive them away." The comment hit its mark, and she backed down a bit.

"No more excuses. Get the park open. And tell that lieutenant of yours to be nicer to the media." She hung up the phone with a bang, and Price slowly clicked off the speaker. He looked at the phone with distaste, and then raised a hairy red eyebrow at Taylor.

"Well, that was fun. She is such a pain in the ass. Ignore her—I'll deal with it. But tell me you have something for me."

Taylor took in a deep breath. "Sam thinks the scene was staged, and I have to agree. She's going to get the girl's prints over here ASAP. As soon as they show up, we'll start looking for a match. That's my number one priority. I want to give this girl a name, and find out where she's from."

"What other thoughts did our intrepid ME have?"

"There was plenty of semen for a sample, so I'd like to ask Sam to send it over to Private Match instead of TBI. I want to see if we can get a quick hit in CODIS."

"You don't think it's this yahoo's first rodeo?"

"I don't. The whole thing felt off to me."

Price sat back in his chair. "How off?"

"I wouldn't be surprised to see more. The scene was definitely staged."

"Great. Just what we need."

"No kidding. So are you cool with me sending the DNA to Simon Loughley? The tox screen will go to him automatically anyway. This way, he can handle the whole case."

Partly because of Meredith Robbins's actions over the past three years in office, the MNPD still didn't have their own forensics lab. She had suggested that if the department wanted their own lab, they could cut employees to get the necessary budget requirements, and Metro had no intention of cutting their officers. So they were beholden to other official labs for results. They hated sending high-profile DNA to the FBI labs for comparison, because even with a push there could be a wait of a year or so. The TBI, Tennessee Bureau of Investigation, was the next best bet, but they too could drag out the final results over several months. Their only choice for fast-track cases was private labs. It wasn't standard operating procedure, but there were times and cases that necessitated a quick turnaround. Private Match had done work for them in the past. Taylor trusted them, and trusted Sam's abilities to finagle the work quickly. Plus, Simon Loughley had been a friend for many years. He could be counted on to do the work fast, and get it right.

Price played with one end of his mustache. "No, I think we'll be able to handle it. If this is going to be as high profile as you think, we can't afford any bureaucratic funding roadblocks. You heard the mayor. I'll pin it on her if I can't make it happen. Surefire way to get it through. This may be a great opportunity to hit her again with the new forensic lab proposal…"

"Good idea. I'll let you handle that," Taylor said. "Getting back to reality… Our witnesses aren't going to be much help. They didn't see another soul. We're hoping that will change when they get a chance to calm down." She gestured toward the ceiling. A huge, dark brown watermark in the corner caught her eye, distracting her for a moment. Her voice trailed off, then she addressed him again.

"Price, there's something else. There were some sweet-smelling herbs scattered on the body. Sam's sending samples to a buddy to get a quick ID, but this changes the complexion of this case. They have to be part of the staging, because I doubt some drunk wandered by and threw a posy on her."

"Herbs? What kind of herbs? What the hell is that about?"

"I have no idea, but we'll have to keep a tight rein on that little tidbit. It could be a signature, and we really don't want it getting out."

"This place is leaking like a sieve, Taylor. You keep that deep, okay? Nobody hears about it outside of your detectives." He leaned back in his chair. "So how do you want to run this? You've got a few open cases on your plate right now, but this should take priority."

"Yeah, we have several that are on the burner, and two very active. I can offload them on Fitz, let him run them, and if this pops, we can pull him back in. He can manage things out of here for me if anything happens. Plus, I think it would be good to bring Marcus Wade in to back me up on this. He needs the experience."

"Works for me. Which cases do you want to give Fitz?"

"The Lischey Avenue murder from last week. The one the paper picked up and ran with? Little Man Graft murdered Lashon Hall, Terrence Norton saw the whole thing, but he's not talking. That one."

Price groaned and Taylor grinned. Anytime the news got involved in their cases, something was bound to go wrong.

"Mayfield didn't do us any favors, did she?"

"No."

"Little Man and Norton are getting to be frequent fliers with Metro." He shook his head, frowning. "Think you can nail them for this one? I'm getting tired of their antics."

Taylor barked a laugh. "It's not me, Price. Blame it on their peers. I made a solid case two months ago on an assault charge against Terrence, and the jury acquitted him in forty-five minutes. Anyway, I haven't been able to shake anyone loose on Lischey Avenue. There *is* a fourteen-year-old kid who witnessed the murder, but his mom has him in hiding and won't let him make a statement. I begged and pleaded, but she said no way. I don't blame her—these guys are absolutely ruthless. There's a better than even chance he'll get himself killed if he talks."

"So what do you want to do?"

"I want Fitz to work his magic on Terrence. See if he can scare anything out of him. Lashon was supposedly his best friend, so maybe Fitz can appeal to the kid's conscience. If not, we don't have enough to charge Little Man with this murder, but he is on probation. If Terrence will give it up, we can get him on a weapons charge at the very least. And then charge Terrence as an accessory. Like I said, it's a mess."

"Let Fitz go to town. He'll nail one of them on something, and the rest will topple like dominoes."

"That's what I'm hoping. I was gonna pull him in on this anyway." She got quiet for a minute. "There is one that I wanted to handle myself, but I can turn it over if you want. Suicide last week, seventeen-year-old boy. There's something way hinky about this one. Rescue got the call that a kid committed suicide. They responded and found the boy shot in the bathroom, but he'd been dead for a few hours. The father made the 911 call. When the officers arrived, he told them he and the boy were sitting side by side on the bed in the father's bedroom, having an argument. He claims the boy reached over him to the bedside table, pulled the father's .44 out of the drawer, stood up, walked three feet to the bathroom door, put the gun to his right temple, and pulled the trigger. Sort of an *I'll show you* gesture.

"When I got on scene, the father had hidden the gun in a basket across the hall from his room. His kid was lying there in a mess of blood and brains, and the dude asked me if he could step out for a bite to eat. I almost shot him myself. I think the father shot the kid, set the whole scene up."

"Anything to back up your theory?"

"Instinct. Plus the wound didn't have any contact burns, but it was such a mess that we're waiting for the autopsy to come back to get the trajectory. The father has a record of domestic assault—the mother disappeared three months ago. I can't shake the feeling that he's lying to us. I'd like to find the mother. May be more than one murder there."

"Are you comfortable handing it over to Fitz?"

"Yeah, he can handle it fine. I just want the bastard nailed." She stood, swiping her hands down her thighs to smooth out the invisible wrinkles in her jeans. "I'll pull the files and brief Fitz. He's already familiar with both of these cases." She started for the door, but Price held up a hand.

"Hey, sit back down for a minute."

She did, wary. "What's up?"

He swiped back another rather invisible strand of hair. "Julia Page called from the DA's office. The Special Investigative Grand Jury has scheduled your testimony on the remaining charges of the Martin case. You're on call to appear sometime Wednesday or Thursday, depending on how things are progressing. Julia is pleased with the state of things so far. She wanted me to let you know."

Taylor was astounded that Price could call it "the Martin case" with such nonchalance. Four CID detectives, three in Vice and one in Homicide, had been complicit in one of the largest and most professionally run methamphetamine labs the state of Tennessee had ever seen, and in the death of a twelve-year-old girl. Not to mention Taylor's own involvement in the case. She had uncovered the scheme. And ended it with a finality that was unmatched.

Testifying in front of the special grand jury was no big deal, especially now that she'd been cleared. She'd be asked detailed questions, and she'd give detailed answers. It was David Martin who would haunt Taylor for the rest of her life. *Detective* David Martin. He wouldn't be arrested, indicted, or even charged with running the scheme. Because he was dead, and Taylor had killed him. But that had been self-defense. The grand jury said so.

She smiled at Price. "Thanks for the heads-up."

"Taylor, I think—"

"Price, it's all good. Really. I'm all set to testify against Martin's partners. I have everything laid out. As for the rest of it—" she sighed "—I'm doing my best to put it all behind me. The shrinks cleared me. Internal Affairs cleared me. The DA's office and the GJ cleared me. It is past, gone, forgotten." *That's it, girl*, she thought to herself. *Keep up a brave front. He doesn't need to know about the whispers from the other officers, the panic attacks, that you can't sleep without horrific nightmares.*

Price stared at her for a split second longer, and she wondered if he knew everything she'd been thinking without her saying a word. But the moment passed and he nodded.

"Then go find me a name for our Parthenon girl."

6

Taylor closed the door quietly behind her. She took two steps and tripped over a ream of paper. She fell into her desk, banging her leg on the corner of a half-opened drawer. She bit back a curse, rubbed at the bruise. Surveyed her kingdom.

The Homicide squad was crammed cheek to jowl into a crappy forty-by-forty-foot bull pen. The close quarters meant no privacy and constant distractions. At least there were fewer bodies to deal with. Six months earlier, the decentralization of Violent Crimes had created several distinct Homicide Units. Each city sector now housed a grouping of general detectives who handled everything from fistfights in bars to aggravated assaults to murders in the projects. In Nashville, Homicide covered the full gamut of physical crimes.

Taylor's group was unique. She ran an elite squad of detectives nicknamed "The Murder Squad." They were the most successful shift in the CID. What made Taylor's team different from Nashville's other homicide detectives was the element of mystery in their jobs. If a violent crime occurred that resulted in a death, and there was no suspect, they caught the case. If the trail went cold after twenty-four hours, it was theirs. If another shift didn't want to deal with a case, it fell into their laps.

Taylor was proud of her team of detectives. They had an incredibly high close rate, nearly 86 percent, which had its good and bad points. It got them excellent press and made the department look good, which meant perks all around like interesting cases, less scrutiny, and more freedom for outside work.

But success was always tempered with a desire to see failure. There were the detectives who dumped their loads simply because they wanted to see her fail. She hadn't made a lot of friends when she'd killed David Martin, even though he was as dirty as they came. There were grudges aplenty among the detectives who'd worked with him. In some minds, if she'd just come forward with what she suspected, Detective Martin could have been charged and tried with his partners instead of killed. No one wanted to see a cop dead, even if he was a bad guy.

Which would have been fine by her, if Martin hadn't tried to kill her first.

She was on shaky footing. Her once-carefree demeanor had changed. Her actions were tempered with caution. Her words more measured and thought out. She was on edge all the time, though she thought she was doing a pretty good job of hanging in there. At least in public.

The news that she would testify again this week was actually welcome. She just wanted to get it over with so she could put it all behind her. Though she knew as soon as the grand jury handed down the indictments, the plea bargaining would start, then the trials. It wasn't going to end, not really, for a very long time. And there was nothing she could do to erase the memory of David Martin, dead on her billiards room floor.

None of it mattered. She had a job to do, and she was going to do it.

Fitz came into the squad room, whistling.

"Ahh, Mr. Fitz. Thank you for joining our little party."

"Don't mention it. I strive to achieve perfect timing."

"And so you have." She sat on the edge of her desk. "Okay guys, let's get started."

Marcus Wade, her wet-behind-the-ears rookie, and Lincoln Ross, her seasoned computer expert, faced her expectantly. Fitz took a seat across from her. He was her veteran; they'd been together for years now. Between the four of them, Taylor was pretty certain they could crack any case that came their way.

"What's happening at Centennial?"

"There's nothing turning up on the grid search," Fitz said. "And we haven't found any witnesses. Even Adidas claims to have been asleep on his personal bus bench, like a good little boy."

Adidas, so named for his labeled gym bag from the sporting goods company, was one of Nashville's many homeless citizens and a well-known fixture around the park, but not a threat to anyone but the pigeons. "Was he sober?" Taylor smiled to herself. Fat chance of that.

"Naw, he was reeking like a distillery. He must have lit it up last night. Didn't even hear the sirens this morning."

"Too much to ask to have a witness, I guess. Okay, boys. Here's what's going to happen. Price and I decided Fitz is going to take over some of my cases so I can focus on our murder this morning. Is that cool with you, Fitz? I'm going to keep you in the loop on everything that happens, and if we need to pull you back in full-time, we'll do it. I'm hoping we can wrap this up quickly, but if not…"

"Fine by me. You gonna let the kid here run with you?" He pointed at Marcus Wade, who sat up straighter in his chair. This was the highest-profile case he'd ever been tapped to work.

"Yep, that's the plan. If you would be so kind as to wrap up the park and file your report, I'd appreciate it. Then you can start messing around with my stuff."

"Sure thing." He gave her a smile, and Taylor thanked whatever being had sent Fitz her way. Any other detective would have gotten snotty or hurt by the request to stand down, but Fitz knew enough about the politics not to worry. Taylor knew he would never suspect her of cutting him out of a case to take the glory for herself. He had told her from the beginning that her move to lieutenant would cut back some of his responsibilities and allow him the space to prepare for a graceful retirement from the force in a few years. Taylor returned the smile with gratitude.

She turned to Marcus. The kid was handsome, with long brown hair and puppy-dog brown eyes. He made a good impression to the outside. Taylor knew under his happy-go-lucky exterior, he was smart, and despite his lack of experience, she was happy to have him. Eagerness was sometimes a better quality in a detective than years on the job; people got staid and used to their own methods. Taylor liked Marcus's fresh perspective in her investigations.

"Marcus, you work with the Metro spokesman, Dan Franklin. He needs to be briefed so he can give a statement. I want to be in complete control of all the info before we talk to anyone. So no leaks about anything, okay? Hopefully we'll have an ID on this girl and can inform her next of kin, maybe even a cause of death, and we can release it in the statement. The mayor's pressing for something official ASAP." Taylor snorted through her nose. "She's pretty fired up. The big arts and crafts fair starts Friday, and she's pushing to get the scene cleared and the park open."

"Got it."

"And, Marcus? I know you and Lee Mayfield have been seeing each other. No preferential treatment, and no pillow talk. Okay?"

Marcus turned three shades past eggplant and looked at his desk. It wasn't a huge secret that he had been dating the crime reporter for *The Ten-nessean.*

"Umm, actually, I broke it off. She's not very cool. I'll talk to Franklin."

"Oh. I'm sorry. Well, maybe I'm not. Forget about her. You're right, she isn't cool at all."

She felt badly that Marcus had been forced to air that tidbit in front of everyone, but such was life. Lee Mayfield was a bitch, and Taylor was happy Marcus had gotten her out of his system. She would sink her claws into any man she thought would give her some scoop. At least the kid learned his lesson early.

She focused on Lincoln. He was wearing a beautiful blue suit, white shirt, and purple tie today.

"Linc, I want AFIS set and ready. Number one priority is putting a name on this girl."

AFIS, the Automated Fingerprint Identification System, would run the dead girl's prints through the local fingerprint database. If there wasn't a match, the prints would go into the huge national AFIS database.

"Will do."

"If we get a hit, I want you to track down where she's from so we can go check it out. Go through the whole drill. I want you to run everything through the computers. Go up to the Intelligence Unit, log into the ViCAP database. Upload our details, and check for any similar MOs." ViCAP, the Violent Criminal Apprehension Program database maintained by the FBI, would look for any similar crimes that matched the description of their murder.

"Cover the gamut. Look for killings with and without rapes, and unsolved violent rapes. And we have something unique to run through ViCAP. Check for herbs or dried flowers found at murder scenes."

Eyebrows rose all around.

"Sam noticed a sweet smell coming off the body. She bagged a whole bunch of leaves and stems, though we don't know what kind of herbs they are yet. We need to keep this real quiet until we know what's going on, so Marcus, keep Franklin out of the loop, too. It may end up being nothing."

"Or everything," Lincoln chimed in.

"Or everything. So no leaks. No one outside this office knows about this but Sam. Keep it that way. There's also DNA to plug in. I want you to search through the sexual offender database, too, see if someone's done anything similar in any of the nearby jurisdictions. Check on the guys convicted of sexual crimes before, only on a smaller scale. Peeping Toms, our friendly flashers. Remember we had a rash of those last year in Bellevue? Pull any of the files that look good. Also, monitor the missing persons listings. If he's snatched anyone else, we need to be ahead of the game. Any calls with young women missing, I want to hear immediately. Drag me out of whatever I'm doing."

"Gotcha, boss. I already started running the missing persons list to see if anyone matching her description has popped up. So far, nothing, but I'll keep looking."

Lincoln's deep, velvety smooth voice made Taylor take a deep breath and blow it out slowly. She gave him an appraising glance. He had the most beautiful skin she had ever seen, a shade somewhere between caramel and mocha latte. His straight nose led to sensually full lips. He was sensitive about the gap between his front two teeth. Taylor thought it only added to his charm.

"Lincoln, are you wearing another new suit? You're going to go broke here soon." Taylor loved to tease him about his obsession with clothes. He was always dressed impeccably, favoring Italian suits and couture ties. He bought his shoes from New York, beautifully worked leather that seemed to mold to his feet. He was single and spent all his money on his wardrobe.

"Well, I may have had a purchase arrive yesterday. Gotta keep looking sharp for the ladies." He gave her a huge smile, and Taylor smiled back fondly. She privately thought he looked like Lenny Kravitz sans nose rings, and could easily understand his appeal to women of all ages and races. Maybe in another life…

"So if you're done raggin' on me… I've got ViCAP running already, but I'll go plug the herb thing in. I've also pulled our open case files that have a sexual component, in case one looks remotely like this. I just want to see if this guy may have been working before. When Sam has a DNA sample, I'll get together with the TBI and take a run through CODIS, see if there are any matches to the semen."

All of the acronyms the Feds came up with amounted to alphabet soup as far as Taylor was concerned. It seemed every day the FBI or the law enforcement community came out with a new acronym for the tools they used. A new database, neoteric scientific tests, flowchart, and task forces—none were immune to the alphabet game. The standard joke was that the acronyms were formed before the official names so the higher-ups could make sure the nicknames "worked." They got so busy digging through the bowl trying to see what they could put together they often fell in and drowned.

Taylor smiled at her crew in appreciation, and told them to scatter. "Rock and roll. Keep checking in with me. Fitz, let me run those files by you real quick." She turned to her desk, then swung back. "Gentlemen? Let's find this jerk. Now."

7

Taylor took the long way when she headed out to Sam's office. Flying by the exit that would lead her to the morgue, she turned north and felt herself relax as she drove up the interstate, letting the wind from the open window blow her hair around. Thirty minutes of head-clearing drive time wouldn't change anything. The girl would still be dead. And Sam would probably applaud her taking a few minutes to herself.

She settled into the fast lane and started passing cars, pushing eighty. Cruising mindlessly, she jumped when her cell phone chirped. She let out a deep sigh, moved over three lanes, and pulled onto the shoulder.

"Yeah, Jackson."

"Hey, LT, it's Marcus. We got a hit on the prints."

"That was quick. Who's our girl?"

"Shelby Kincaid. She's a student at Vanderbilt. She doesn't have a record, but we got lucky. She was printed for a job she applied for at a day care center on West End."

"Damn it," Taylor said with heart. "A student at Vandy, and no one reported her missing?"

"Nope. At least there's nothing official. Want me to call the school?"

She thought for a minute. "Tell you what. Let me get over to Sam's and see what she's found from the autopsy. We're going to want to tread lightly. Vandy won't cooperate with us without some paper. Go ahead and get a subpoena started for Kincaid's records. Besides, I don't want to start a panic if we can help it. This is going to be the lead story on the news. It was sensational enough that she was found at the Parthenon. When the media finds out she was a Vandy coed, they're going to go nuts." She ran a hand through her hair, unconsciously combing out the windblown tangles. Catching a knot, she looked in the mirror in aggravation and struggled to put it into a ponytail while holding the cell phone. She lost the whole mess, hair and phone alike, and cursed. She grabbed the phone from between her legs and brushed her hair out of her eyes impatiently.

"I assume there was contact information with her print card?"

"Yep." She could hear him shuffling papers in the background before the roar of an 18-wheeler passing much too closely drowned him out.

"…Kentucky. Want me to—"

"Wait, wait. Say that again. Couldn't hear you over the traffic."

"Where are you?"

"I'm pulled over to the side of Interstate 24. Where's she from again?"

"Bowling Green, Kentucky. The contacts are Edward and Sally Kincaid. I assume they're her parents. We need to get them notified."

Taylor rubbed the back of her neck. "Go ahead and call Reverend Spenser. I always like to have him around when I have to do a notification. He can get in touch with the Bowling Green police, see if their chaplain's available to do the notification. Ask him to arrange to have them driven down here, too."

"Will do. They're going to want to talk to you, I'm sure."

"Yes, but I don't want to talk with them until Sam has more definitive results. I'd like to be able to give them her cause of death, if we have one. Damn, this really sucks. Get the family notified, then we'll go ahead with Vandy. Be delicate, Marcus. This is going to be beyond difficult for them."

"Yeah, I imagine it will ruin their lives. I'll talk to the chaplain and get it all arranged."

"Thanks, man. I'll be back after I see Sam."

"Um, Taylor, before you go?"

"What?"

"Your dad called."

Her father. Her chest tightened. Oh man, talk about something she didn't need.

"Did he say what he wanted?"

"No, just that he needs to speak with you. He said it was important."

"Yeah, it always is," she muttered.

"What?"

"Nothing. Go on and get in touch with Shelby Kincaid's parents. I'll talk to you later."

She hung up, pushing thoughts of her father away and getting her mind back on the case. There was nothing worse than having to tell parents they'd outlived their child. She was more than a little relieved Marcus was going to handle the notification.

She pulled back out on the interstate and took the first exit leading her back into the city. She tried not to think and, instead, enjoy the few moments of freedom she had left. A pointless endeavor. She gave up and gunned the car.

The late-afternoon traffic was terrible, and it took her twenty minutes to plow her way through to Gass Boulevard. The State of Tennessee Center for Forensic Medicine was run by a private group contracted with the city. Their brand-new, twenty-thousand-square-foot building looked more like the local offices of a corporate giant than a morgue.

She pulled into the parking lot, more than a little jealous of Sam and her new realm. It sure beat Homicide's crappy little office. Then again, they didn't have dead bodies next to the break room.

She was buzzed through the door into the spacious lobby. She was facing the family viewing room, where family members of the deceased could identify their loved one's mortal remains on closed-circuit TV.

She was thankful the new system had been put into place. It was easier for the family not to go through up-close-and-personal body identification, or deal with photographs of their dearly departed. They had a quiet, nicely furnished room, professional support, and some distance from their deceased family member. It was a good system.

One of the grief counselors would eventually be back there with Shelby's parents, ready to bolster and guide the family through their worst nightmares. Taylor felt chill bumps on her arms. She was glad she didn't have to come back and deal with them tonight. Loss wasn't something she was ever comfortable with.

Despite the constant flow of people who entered and exited the building throughout the day and night, there was never a magazine out of place, nor a small piece of trash sitting on a side table. Taylor secretly thought members of the cleaning crew lurked in the hallways, ready to sneak into the foyer unseen to straighten and sanitize at a moment's notice.

She waved to the receptionist, Kris, and entered the door leading to the autopsy suite. The odor hit her: in contrast to the sweet, clean smell of the open foyer, this area was antiseptic and metallic, overlaid with chemicals, like a hospital corridor. And it was colder, sterile and overtly hygienic. The smells weren't unpleasant. They were simply what she always associated with death.

The odd reek settled in her sinuses. Taylor tried to concentrate on other things as she walked in. She knew that within a few minutes she'd get used to it. She always did.

Stopping briefly in the biovestibule, she changed into a pair of disposable scrubs and went inside.

The main autopsy suite held four fully functioning workstations, two on the wall facing Taylor, and two on the opposite wall. Sam was at the far table, the natural sunlight from the huge skylight above streaking her hair with rosy highlights.

"Sam."

Sam turned toward Taylor with a look that said, *Go away, I'm trying to work.*

"Sorry, Sammy, I need to talk. We've got an ID. Her name's Shelby Kincaid. Went to Vanderbilt. We're notifying her parents right now, so I wanna see what you have."

Sam actually looked at her this time, blinked, finally realized who was there, and said, "Oh, hey. Gear up. Vanderbilt, huh?" There was almost no inflection in her voice. She was lost in her work.

Taylor pulled on the remaining protective gear and gloves gracefully, the motions born of too many repetitions. She donned her eye shield and joined Sam at the table. Lying on a tan plastic washable coating covering an icy, stainless steel slab were the remains of Shelby Kincaid. She didn't look like a sleeping child anymore. The huge Y-cut, actually shaped like a deformed U, cut from her sternum to her pubis, exposing her internal organs, which Sam was in the process of weighing. She set the mud-colored liver in the scale, dictating the weight into the microphone clipped to the front of her smock. She handed it to her assistant, who wandered off to busy himself with something. He knew Taylor and was more than a little afraid of her. Sam watched him go, chuckled, then became all business again.

"Ventricular fibrillation. And something's hinky with her liver." She didn't elaborate.

"Okay. Wanna expound on that? I don't know if *hinky* will stand up in court."

Sam's forehead wrinkled. "That's the problem. On the surface, I can't tell you what's wrong. I sent off the tox screen, so we should get that back quick enough. But they can't look for anything but the obvious, and the way her organs look…my gut tells me we need to look deeper. I sent a runner with all kinds of samples to Simon's lab—blood, urine, tissue, the works. I asked them to do a more comprehensive workup than the normal drug and alcohol screen. I'm hoping they can isolate something off the standard panel."

"Like what?"

She waggled her head casually and shrugged, like a child with an important secret. "Oh, I'm thinking poison."

"No way. Poison? Cyanide?"

"Not cyanide, I didn't get an almond smell when I opened the body. I don't know what we're looking for, but I definitely think she ingested something, and it didn't sit right with her system."

"Ingested something like what?"

Sam gave Taylor a sweet smile. "Honey, that's what we're going to find out. Back to business. She was raped repeatedly. Even more bruising and tearing than I'd thought, lots of semen. We're going to have to wait for the labs on that, too."

Taylor's shoulders knotted up. "How long's it gonna take?"

"Well, it won't be overnight. I'll try to talk Simon into dropping all his other fascinating cases and handle the toxicology right away, but I can't promise anything. As far as the semen is concerned, I can send it up to TBI with a push and have them do the rapid DNA, or I can throw it to Simon and ask him to handle it as a personal favor. We haven't talked in a couple of days though, so he may blow me off." She busied herself with a scalpel.

Taylor waited for a more detailed explanation, but seeing none forthcoming, decided not to voice an opinion on the rocky relationship's latest turn. "I already ran it by Price. It won't be a problem. Go ahead and give it all to Simon. If you don't want to call in one of your own, tell him it's a favor for me, and I'll owe him one."

"Got it." She gestured toward the computer screen behind her. "The rest is basics. Height, one hundred seventy-six centimeters, weight, forty-seven kilograms. Blond hair, blue eyes. Maybe a little anorexic. No distinguishing characteristics, no tattoos, nothing out of the ordinary. Doesn't look like she's had any surgeries except a tonsillectomy." She looked up, gave a wan smile. "Sorry, Charlie. Right now we've got a run-of-the-mill dead girl. Little Shelby didn't put up much of a fight, nothing under her nails, no defensive wounds. That's about as exciting as it gets."

Taylor sighed. She knew the drill. Nothing else

could be done here until they had the lab results back. "Can I give her parents a cause of death?"

Sam thought quietly for a moment. The parents would want every detail, and there weren't a lot to give them. She shrugged. "Tell them we're doing more tests and hope to have an answer for them quickly."

"Great, that helps a lot. All right, keep me in the loop on anything you find. And I mean anything. I don't care how obscure it is. I can deal with Simon if you don't want to do it yourself." It was a dig for information, but Sam saw right through it.

"Yeah, I may do that."

Taylor knew discretion was the better part of valor when it came to Sam and Simon. "Okay, then. Play nice with Simon. I think he likes you." She grinned and walked out of the room.

Taylor pulled out on Elliston Pike and started back downtown. As the skyline came into view, she was overcome by exhaustion. She had planned to go back to the office, maybe take the warrant over to Vandy, but it was late; their offices would be closed until the morning. There was nothing she could do tonight. She decided to hit a drive-through and go home. She called Marcus, gave him the update from Sam, told him she was out for the night, and suggested he and Lincoln should do the same.

She stopped at the Taco Bell near her house. Eating her dinner in the car, she finished before she hit her driveway. She stumbled into the house, set her holster and gun on the coffee table, gave the cat a rub on the head, fell onto the couch, and crashed immediately.

Again, there was a field of graves, stretching out before her. A large statue shadowed the land, covering waves of ripe wheat in sheaves, and the path forward was littered with body parts, arms and legs bent in imitations of crosses, bones shaped into grave markers. The sky was red with angry storms, and the wind whipped her hair around her face. Flowers pushed dead from the earth, black and rotted, their scent overwhelming. She walked toward the monstrous statue, the grave markers waving in synchronous motion, reaching out to touch her, strange dead hands and legs and arms draping against her body, grabbing her legs, holding her back, pulling her to the earth...

Taylor woke with a cry, sweating, her breath coming in jagged gasps. She wiped the tears from her face. She groaned when she looked at the clock on the mantel, which read 4:15 a.m. The nightly ritual was fulfilled. She wouldn't be able to go back to sleep. She hit the shower and headed into work.

THE
SECOND
DAY

8

He watched the body drift away slowly, bumping into driftwood as the current caught it and dragged it toward the shore. He felt a brief pang of sorrow. The woman had been beautiful, perfection in dimension and proportion. Until the end.

Still, she was a worthy sacrifice. She had brought him much joy, much pleasure. It was her own fault she was dead. Dead and gone. No longer.

9

Marcus and Lincoln were futzing around in the captain's office when Taylor walked in. When Price went out and things were slow or on hold, the squad had a habit of congregating in there to watch TV.

Lincoln vacated Price's chair for Taylor to sit in. She did so gratefully. It was the one chair in the squad that was remotely comfortable.

"Where's Price?"

"Ran down to talk to the chief." Marcus rolled his eyes. "Old windbag wanted to have another press conference so he can look like he's actually being a cop."

Taylor laughed. Their chief of police was about as popular as the mayor.

"Did you find Shelby's parents?"

"Yeah. Reverend Spenser talked to the Bowling Green police chaplain. They did the notification, and BG's chaplain is driving them down this morning. They're pretty upset. Her dad's a Baptist minister. The chaplain knew Shelby, too."

"Great. Lincoln, any luck on any of the databases?"

"Nothin' yet. Hit a dead end after her prints popped. Sam have anything new?"

"Outside of the possible poisoning? No. She sent everything over to Simon. It'll be a day or so before we know what the poison might be."

"If only we could identify the poison, I could plug it into ViCAP, maybe broaden the scope a little." Lincoln's eyes were shining. He loved playing with the technical stuff.

"Once we have it identified, you can put it in the system, but not before. We need to keep it quiet, like the herbs. Especially with her parents." She looked pointedly at Marcus, a silent warning to keep his own counsel outside of the squad room.

Price's phone rang, and Taylor picked it up. "Homicide... Okay, thanks." She cradled the phone. "Marcus, Shelby's parents are here. Wanna go out and get them?"

"Damn, they're early. I'll meet you in the interview room." He stood, brushing invisible lint from his pants. Taylor could see the air of discomfort that washed over him; facing grieving family members wasn't his favorite thing to do either. He squared his shoulders and walked out. Taylor gave Lincoln a small smile.

"Do we have any coffee or anything we can offer them?"

"I'll go make some."

"Thank you. If the chaplains are out there, see

if they want some, too. I'd best go save Marcus. Bring the coffee when it's ready."

He smiled in acknowledgment and left the office. Taylor pulled her hair out of its ponytail, unsuccessfully attempting to smooth it down. Impatiently reholstering the unruly mess, she squared her own shoulders and marched the short distance to the interview room in the hall. Marcus already had Mr. and Mrs. Kincaid inside. A box of tissues had miraculously appeared at Mrs. Kincaid's elbow.

The Kincaids were small, unassuming people, easily in their late fifties. Mrs. Kincaid's eyes were rimmed in red, but there were no tears threatening to overflow. Mr. Kincaid had a vacant look on his face but seemed to be holding up. Marcus introduced Taylor. She pulled up a chair.

"Mr. and Mrs. Kincaid, thank you so much for coming down. I am so sorry for your loss." Her cliché was worn but sincere. Mrs. Kincaid nodded and sniffed. Shelby's father took control of the meeting.

"Where is our daughter, Lieutenant? We want to see her."

"Could we get you anything to drink? Coffee, water…"

Mr. Kincaid cut her off sharply. "No. Where is our daughter?"

Taylor looked at Marcus, signaling him to tell Lincoln to forget the coffee. He stuck his head out the door, gestured to Lincoln, then stepped back in and shut the door behind him, lounging quietly against it.

Taylor took a deep breath. She had a feeling this

wasn't going to go well. "She's still at the medical examiner's office, sir. We had to do an autopsy to see…"

Mrs. Kincaid lost it. "You cut our baby open? How could you do that?" She started crying. Her husband put a hand on her arm. She immediately quieted.

"I'm sorry, ma'am, but her death was ruled a homicide by the medical examiner at the scene. We're required by law to conduct an autopsy." Taylor hated having to give that pat line to a child's parents, but there was no way to cushion the blow. "There was no identification found with the body, so in order to obtain an identification we had to follow protocol. That's how we found out who she was. I'm so sorry," she repeated.

Mrs. Kincaid reached for a tissue and buried her face in it, dignified sobs leaking out. Again her husband squeezed her arm. Taylor didn't think it was meant in a kindly way. She got the impression he was uncomfortable with open displays of emotion, which seemed interesting for a man of the cloth.

"Lieutenant, Detective Wade said Shelby was murdered. Who did it? I want to know who killed our baby."

"We don't know yet, sir, but we're doing our very best to find the killer and arrest him. We have some evidence that will be helpful…"

"DNA?"

The advent of TV cop shows made every layman an expert in criminal investigations.

Taylor nodded. "Yes, sir, we do have some DNA evidence."

The light went out of his eyes, and he rubbed his chin. "Was she raped?"

Taylor didn't want to go into detail. "We believe that may be the case, sir, but we won't have any answers until the laboratory results come back."

"How was she murdered, Lieutenant?" Mrs. Kincaid had finished crying. Taylor could see the steel creeping back into her eyes. When Taylor didn't answer immediately, the woman's voice softened. "It's only fair that we should know. Was she shot? Strangled?"

"No, ma'am. There were no obvious signs to tell us how she died. The medical examiner is doing a number of tests to see what killed your daughter. We won't know anything until the toxicology reports come back."

Mr. Kincaid jumped in again, cutting his wife off. "You don't know what killed her? Then how do you know she was murdered?"

Taylor decided honesty was the best policy. "Shelby was found at the Parthenon, sir, with no clothes on and signs that she'd been raped. The scene felt staged. Until the tests are back, I'm afraid that's as much as I know at this point. You'll be the first to hear when we find something conclusive. Can you tell us a little bit about your daughter?"

Mr. Kincaid gave her a dirty look. "There's nothing to know. Shelby was a good girl. She didn't drink. She didn't do drugs. She worked hard for her grades. She was on scholarship. What exactly are you asking?"

In spite of his escalating tone, Taylor gave him a reassuring smile. "Sir, I meant nothing by the remark. The better I know your daughter, the quicker I can find her killer. Do you know if she was seeing anyone, had a boyfriend at school?"

Mr. Kincaid jumped in quickly. "She didn't have time for a boyfriend."

His wife looked at Taylor and said softly, "She would have told me. We are—were—very close." She swallowed hard, forcing herself to stay in control. "When can we see our daughter, Lieutenant? When can we take her home?"

Shelby's parents weren't going to be much help. She got the feeling that even if Shelby did have a boyfriend, Mr. Kincaid wouldn't know about it. Though she may have confided in her mother… Taylor made a mental note to follow up with her privately.

"I'll have an officer take you to the medical examiner's office. They won't be able to release the b—Shelby until there is a definitive cause of death, but there are things that need to be taken care of. Marcus? Could you arrange to have Mr. and Mrs. Kincaid taken over to the ME's office?" He nodded and left the room silently.

Taylor pulled a card out of her wallet. "I'll probably need to speak with you again, at a more appropriate time, of course. In the meantime, if you think of anything that may be helpful, please call me." She started to hand the card to Mrs. Kincaid, but Mr. Kincaid reached out and grabbed it.

"Thank you for your help, Lieutenant. We'd like to see our daughter now."

"Of course, sir."

Marcus stuck his head in and nodded. "I have an officer ready to escort you there."

Taylor stood and put out a hand. Mr. Kincaid looked past it, but Mrs. Kincaid reached out, barely touching her fingers to Taylor's. They were shaking.

"Thank you, Lieutenant." She followed her husband out.

Taylor sat back at the table, cradling her head in her hands. Marcus came back in and sat across from her.

"So, what do you think?"

"Well, I think Mrs. Kincaid knows more than she's saying. Maybe we should take a run at her without her husband."

"I agree," Taylor said. "He shot the boyfriend issue down awfully quick. Maybe Shelby confided in her mother and left Daddy out of the loop. Let's give them a few days. It's possible Mrs. Kincaid will get in touch with us."

"So what now?"

"What now? Let's take the subpoena on over to Vandy and see what we can dig up about Shelby."

10

Marcus was quiet on the drive to the campus, and Taylor let him stew in his thoughts until they reached the parking lot.

"What's on your mind, Marcus?" There was no answer. "Helloo. Earth to Marcus." She poked his knee and he jumped.

"Oh, I'm sorry, Taylor. Lost in my own little world."

"And what's happening in your little world?"

"I don't know. I'm getting a weird vibe."

"That narrows it down. Care to explain?"

He sighed and looked out the window. "I don't really know. When we talked to Shelby's parents, they seemed rather emphatic that she was all work and no play. Seems to me a preacher's kid away from home for the first time may have gotten herself into a little bit of trouble here or there."

"You're probably right. Let's go see if she's really been their sweet little girl."

The campus was lit with the colors of fall, fallen leaves strewn across the quads. It seemed serene, tranquil, untouched by the tragedy. Boys played football, and coeds watched them in admiration; students rode their bikes down the street, calling to one another. It was so bucolic, it almost made her nervous. Picture-postcard perfect—the calm before the storm. Clearly news hadn't spread about the murder. Taylor didn't know if she'd rather they panic or be unaffected.

They got out of the car and walked to Kirkland Hall, the college's administration building. Sitting on a stone bench in front of the edifice was a man in his early forties. He had a thick mustache, matching light blond hair, and a shiny badge pinned to the front of his pristine tan uniform. Taylor groaned aloud. The man smiled and gave them a little wave. He didn't get up, just sat with his legs spread wide in front of him, a small manila folder sitting quietly next to him.

Taylor tried for politeness. "Chief Graber. How are you this fine morning?"

"Not well, not well at all. I assume you're here because one of my students is dead, and you've come to give your condolences. To apologize that no one from Metro bothered to contact me when you discovered the Parthenon girl was a Vandy student. To ask for any and all cooperation my police force can give to your investigation. That about sum it up?"

Taylor didn't know whether to laugh or cry. Graber wasn't going to make this easy. She softened her tone.

"Chief… Charles. You know that the past twenty-four hours have been a madhouse. We've only known that Shelby Kincaid was a Vandy student since—"

"Since you ID'd her body, yesterday. For God's

sake, Taylor, did you think I wasn't going to find out?" Graber jumped up and started to pace the portico. He had a strange gait. One leg seemed to snap in front of him as he walked. Taylor saw Marcus staring and decided it was the perfect moment to introduce him.

"Marcus Wade, I'd like you to meet Charles Graber, chief of the Vanderbilt Campus Police. And a royal pain in my ass."

"I guess you two already know each other?" Marcus asked.

"Since ninth grade. She dated my little brother at Father Ryan. Broke his heart, too."

Graber's tone wasn't lost on the young detective, and Taylor went crimson under Marcus's grin.

"Charles, please. Now isn't the time. We need to focus on Shelby Kincaid. We have a court order for her records. I figured the school's administration wasn't going to be terribly cooperative, so we've preempted them."

Graber picked up the manila folder. "And I figured you'd be thorough enough not to show up empty-handed. Here, I'll trade you." He handed her the folder. Taylor nodded sharply at Marcus, who pulled out the legal documents from his inside coat pocket. He handed them to Graber, who didn't even glance at the paperwork.

"I can save you some time, Taylor. I know my way around this campus better than you do. I'm happy to help."

Taylor caught the note in his voice, and couldn't help but feel for the man. His campus police were much more than glorified security guards. They had all the powers of a metro police force, only with a smaller area to govern. But he had no jurisdiction over this particular crime. Taylor knew he didn't want the glory. He was genuinely sorry that one of the school's students had been murdered. But it was her case, and she wanted to run it her way. And she owed him nothing but civility. He still held a grudge, about his brother, and other things, and she tired quickly of his relentless barbs.

"Tell you what. If we run into trouble, I'll give you a call, have you smooth the road. Sound okay?"

"Hell, Taylor, when have you ever had any trouble smoothin' the road? You've got a gun. You can shoot your way clear. You do it enough. I'll be in my office if you need anything."

Taylor bit her lip, forced herself not to respond. He gave her half a smile, turned his back, and walked away. The hitch in his walk was more pronounced from behind.

Marcus looked at Taylor. "Another friend of David Martin?"

She shook her head. "Yeah."

"Jerk."

She wanted to smile, but opened the folder in front of her and read quickly, pleased her voice didn't waver.

"Okay, Marcus, she was in Carmichael Towers East. The roommate's name is Vicki Chen. Let's go have a chat with her."

They set off across the quad, leaves crackling

beneath their feet. Shaking off Graber's comments, Taylor looked around at the young and carefree as they simply existed. They had nothing more serious to worry about than their next test, their next meal, their next party. No dead bodies lined up in rows at the morgue, no bugs crawling through eye sockets, no sense of their own mortality. Maybe they didn't watch the news, or if they had heard that one of their own was cooling rapidly in a coffin-sized refrigerator, they simply didn't care.

Taylor sensed the anxiety creeping up her spine. There was nothing she could do to keep any of them safe. She couldn't stop the rapes, the murders, the abuse. The thematic judgments began rolling through her brain. *I can't help. I can't stop them; when one goes down, another meaner and uglier one pops up in its place. Why am I doing this anymore? Why, why, why do I even want to be a cop anymore?*

She was starting to hyperventilate. Marcus was looking at her strangely. She felt light-headed, but refused to make an ass out of herself in front of her youngest detective. She bent down, looking to anyone who cared as if she were tying her shoe.

"Too bad cowboy boots don't have laces," she murmured. She sucked in a couple of breaths, felt her heart slow. Looked up at Marcus, gave him a halfhearted smile. He smiled back quizzically, but didn't ask if she was okay. She wasn't, but she'd never admit it to him. She wouldn't admit it to anyone.

11

Shelby Kincaid, by all accounts, was the good girl her parents insisted she was.

Her roommate, Vicki Chen, met them in the dorm room they'd shared. Chen was pretty, with long, dark hair; small, rectangular glasses; jeans tucked into a pair of brown UGGs, the tops of which were turned down to show the interior fleece. She looked like every other student on the Vanderbilt campus.

And she was devastated by her friend's loss.

"I just don't understand how this could happen. She was happy, she was working hard, we had tickets for R.E.M., for God's sake. You know how quickly that show sold out? She had no reason to wander off."

Taylor had asked Marcus to talk so he could get more interview experience. With a nod from her, he kept pushing.

"Wander off?"

Chen waved a hand in the air. "She must have, to cross paths with a killer. This is Vanderbilt. It's

Nashville. It's safe here. That's why all of our parents want us to go to this school, because it's so safe."

Taylor wanted to tell her it wasn't true—there were no safe schools, safe places. Death could strike anywhere, anyone. But she bit her tongue.

"Tell me more about Shelby's personality, Vicki. What was she like?" Marcus asked.

"Shy. Quiet. She spent most of her time in the library. She was an engineering student, a damn good one. Straight A's every semester, carrying a 4.0 GPA. She had to keep the scholarship—her parents can't afford to send her here."

"What is tuition now?" Taylor asked.

"We're at thirty-one thousand, and that's only tuition, doesn't include books and meals and housing. It's gotten very expensive to attend Vandy, and the scholarship kids depend on the help. Shelby had a full academic ride, and she wouldn't do anything to jeopardize it."

"So she's a good student," Marcus said. "What else?"

Chen played with the tips of her hair. "Shelby was popular with her teachers, and she seemed happy most of the time. Content. She was pretty homesick, though. She called home several times a week. No car, so she couldn't head back there on weekends like some of the local students do."

"How'd she get around?"

"The kindness of strangers. Oh my God, I didn't mean that. I meant friends. I'm sorry, she just kept to herself so much, didn't let people in. Even me. She wasn't super close to anyone here."

"What was she doing in the days leading up to her disappearance?"

"Nothing. The girl led a pretty dull life. She stayed on campus for the fall break, but most of us do, it's party time for four days straight. For Shelby, it was extra time to study. She had exams coming up, and preparing was her main focus for the weekend."

Marcus took a note. "And when was the last time you saw her?"

"Friday night. I talked her into coming to dinner at Willy's Diner. You know the place, right? It's easy to walk to, cheap, pretty popular. I practically dragged her kicking and screaming—she didn't want to waste the cash. But she'd been working so hard, I knew it would be good for her to get out. We hit Willy's at 6:45 p.m. Around eight, I noticed Shelby hadn't come back to the table after a bathroom break. I didn't think much about it—we'd already paid, were just hanging out at that point. I actually laughed it off, figured she'd gone back to the room." She bowed her head. "I am such a jerk. If I'd paid more attention, maybe she'd still be alive."

Marcus soothed her. "You can't think like that, Vicki. It sounds to me you were doing all you could to look out for your roommate."

A few tears trickled down her face. "Yeah, well, it wasn't enough, was it? I got back at eleven thirty or so. Shelby wasn't here, so I assumed she'd gone back to the library. In the morning, no Shelby, and her bed was untouched. Around lunchtime, I went to the library to check on her, wondering if she'd fallen asleep in the carrels. She wasn't there. I called Metro, but they told me she'd have to be missing for at least twenty-four hours before they could get involved. I didn't want to call her parents—I was afraid I'd freak them out. She could have been anywhere, you know? By the time Metro would talk to me about filing a report, you'd already found her."

"What about a boyfriend?" Taylor asked. "Was she seeing anyone?"

She could see the hesitation on Chen's face, though she answered quickly. Too quickly.

"Are you kidding? Shelby wouldn't have any time for a boyfriend. I've never seen her in the company of any of the men on campus."

The answer was so pat, so confident, so final, Taylor didn't buy it. Especially when Chen started to cry in earnest, almost as if she wanted to distract them.

"You're sure about this? Is it possible she was seeing someone and simply hadn't told you?"

Chen shook her head, wiping the tears from her face with a red bandana. "No. No way."

Taylor gave Marcus the whirlybird finger. Time to wrap it up.

He stood, handed the girl a card. "Thank you for your time, Miss Chen. Please call us immediately if you remember anything relevant."

Taylor and Marcus left the sobbing Chen and

wandered back into the quad. Taylor spotted two boys smoking, walked over to bum a cigarette. Marcus watched her with concern, and she gave him a wink. The only time she smoked anymore was when she was really stressed out, but she tried to give him a carefree attitude as cover. Quitting was awful. She felt bad enough about her occasional slips without disapproving glances from her teammates.

She walked back to him, knew he'd seen her slide the spare behind her ear. Appreciated the lack of comment.

"Anything stand out from Chen's interview?" she asked.

"She was evasive about the possible boyfriend. We need to pursue that angle if at all possible. I think Shelby was seeing someone and didn't want people to know. Her dad, especially."

She rewarded him with a big smile. "Excellent. Exactly right. So who was Shelby seeing when she was supposed to be studying at the library? And why was it so important to keep the relationship secret?"

Before he could comment, her phone rang.

"Jackson."

"It's Fitz."

"Thanks for that. I do have caller ID on this thing. What's up?"

"We're opening the park back up. Crime Scene got exactly squat, no trace, no worthwhile prints, no ID or clothes. She may well have flown there and landed on those steps."

Taylor laughed. "That's about the best logic I've heard today. What's Sam up to?"

"She wrapped things up about an hour ago. She said she's sending over the autopsy report. Everything's square with Loughley, too."

"Hmm. Did you call him?"

"Nope, she did it all by her pretty little self. Why?"

"Nothing, just curious. We're not getting too much over here either, other than the distinct impression Shelby Kincaid has a secret lover. We're on our way. You need anything while I'm out?"

"If you get by Jack's Bar-B-Que, you could grab me some pulled pork, buns, and a Bud," he said hopefully.

"Mmm, sounds good. Skipping the beer, though. Sorry." She clicked off her phone and snapped it back onto her waistband.

"Okay, Marcus, let's get some lunch and head back to the office."

Taylor took a last drag on her cigarette and flicked it away into the bushes. Saw a figure over Marcus's shoulder. Chief Graber was standing by Carmichael Towers. He wasn't smiling. Taylor ignored him, turned her back, and they started walking back to their car.

Taylor's cell phone rang again as she touched the handle to the driver's side door. "Yes?"

"Hey, T, it's Fitz again. You're gonna have to skip the food. How about meeting me at the sidewalk behind the River Stages."

Taylor rolled her neck to the left with a loud pop.

"And I'm hungry too. What's so interesting behind the stage, Fitz?"

"How's about another dead girl?"

Her heart sank.

"Oh no. We're on our way. Give us five minutes." She clicked off, looked over at Marcus, who was lounging with his arms across the top of the car, watching the coeds.

"Get in, slugger. We've got us another body."

12

Taylor and Marcus drove back downtown in silence. Riverfront Park was only a few blocks from police headquarters. The body had conveniently washed up in their backyard. They parked and walked toward River Stages, a popular summer concert venue. Fitz waved cheerily at them.

"Come on down and meet our next contestant." He led them down to the river.

Taylor shook her head and smoothed a stray hair behind her ear. As they neared the water, she saw the tarp over a lump on the riverbank. Marcus stayed a few feet behind her.

"Okay, Fitz, what do you have?"

He pointed unnecessarily at the body. "Well, there we have another dead girl. Boat passin' by saw something in the weeds, came by for a closer look. She was facedown—they used a grappling hook to turn her over, called 911."

"Who got here first?"

"Who else? Officer Wills. Happened to be on

Second Avenue when the call came—he was here within a minute."

"Good, good. At least we know he didn't screw anything up."

Marcus was shifting from the ball of one foot to another like a small child who needed to go to the bathroom. Taylor caught the movement.

"Okay, Marcus?"

"Yes, ma'am. Though two girls in two days is a little creepy for me."

"Yes, it is. But that's what you get when you work Homicide. Let's go take a look, shall we?"

They made their way to the water's edge. Taylor leaned in and pulled the tarp back from the body, grimacing at the smell. She hated floaters.

A young woman's ruined face stared back at her. "Damn," she said softly. She pulled the tarp the rest of the way back, careful not to disturb anything lying beneath it. The girl was naked, bloated with the buildup of gases that had brought her to the surface. There were five distinct stab wounds on her torso. At least it would be a little simpler to determine what killed this one.

She started to replace the tarp when she heard Sam a few yards away.

"Go ahead and leave it off, Taylor. I need to take a look." She tripped on some unidentifiable piece of trash and she fell into Marcus, cursing under her breath. He grabbed on for dear life to the first available appendage. It happened to be her left breast. She barked a laugh and gave him a smile that only deepened his blush.

"God, Sam, I'm so sorry."

"That's okay, cookie. Nice catch." She winked and he recovered nicely, giving her a charming smile back.

"Hey, T. You're keeping me a little busy, ya know?"

"Yep." Taylor stepped back from the body to give Sam room to set up. She did so quickly, knelt next to the girl's body, poking and prodding.

"Stabbed a few times, huh? She hasn't been in the water too terribly long, maybe a week." She picked up one of the girl's white, puffy, wrinkled hands. "Washerwoman's hands. There's probably enough skin left for prints. We'll see. She's not too old either—I'm guessing between eighteen and twenty-two." She reached around and rolled the girl onto her left side, picking at the detritus stuck to the girl's limp body. She scraped some of the dirt into a bag and stuck the bag into the pocket of her jacket. "Hmm." She rolled her into her previous position carefully and stood up. "Was anything found with her?"

Officer Wills tripped down the bank to join the party. "No, ma'am. We've been searching up and down the bank, and there's nothing out of place."

"Okay. Let's have one of the 'gators take a look around. Hey, Taylor?"

"Yup?"

"I'm going to get her back to the office, see if I can get anything to ID her with. And I'm going to post her now, instead of waiting until the morning. Come with?"

"Guess I should. Marcus, head back to the office and tell Lincoln to start another round of database searches. Since she's been dead awhile, there may be a missing persons report on her. If we get any prints, I'll bring them over."

Marcus nodded and headed away purposefully. Taylor shot Sam a knowing look. Poor kid just didn't like dead bodies. He'd have to get over it if he wanted to survive on her team.

"Fitz, do me a favor, stick around in case they come up with anything."

"Righto. I'll ring if anything shows up."

"Thank you, sir. Sam? Let's do this."

Forty minutes later, Sam had the body zipped into a bag and loaded into the back of the unmarked ME van. A small crowd had formed at the top of the hill, and Officer Wills was roping the area off to keep out the curiosity seekers. Taylor followed Sam up the hill, got into her car, and moved out, lost in thought.

Her cell phone rang. She was going to have to turn the thing off; she'd never get anything done if she spent all her time answering calls. She stifled the thought when she saw the caller ID. Sam's personal number. She clicked on the Talk button.

"I'm right behind you. What's up?"

"I didn't want to announce it in front of everyone. I took samples of the muck on her back. Smelled it when I got into the car. There was no unique scent, but the composition looks similar to the herbs we picked off of Shelby."

Taylor's heart skipped once, then started again in a rush. "You're telling me this is the same guy?"

"I definitely don't want to go there yet. I need to have this analyzed and do the post. But two girls in two days, with similar presentations? Taylor, this isn't good."

"No kidding. I'll see you in a minute." She hung up the phone and looked at the car passing her on the left. A harried mom with three kids in the back, all laughing and making faces at her as they blew past. They had no idea what waited for them when they got older.

Taylor felt the sadness well up inside her and tears prick her eyes. She shook it off and concentrated on an image of the dead girls.

13

Taylor patiently watched Sam gently slice and dice their floater. Once they had retrieved some messy but usable prints and sent them to Lincoln, she'd decided to stay out of the way. Sam was working fast, looking for any similarities inside the two dead girls while she went through the remaining steps of her post.

Taylor's phone rang again, and she decided to take a breather and answer it outside. It was Lincoln.

"Hey, Taylor, how's it going over there?" The scratch of a match and a quick breath out gave her away. "Smoking again?"

"Let me worry about my own lungs. What's up?"

"I've got an ID on the floater."

"Whoa, you are good. I didn't know if the prints were going to be usable at all. So who is she?"

"Her name is Jordan Blake. But I don't think you're going to want to hear the rest."

Taylor sank down on the steps, pulling hard on the cigarette, as if a lungful of carbon monoxide would lessen the blow from whatever bad news Lincoln was about to spring. "Shoot."

"I played a hunch, started with our local AFIS database. It kicked back several possible matches. I eyeballed them to see if we were close. One was."

"Oh, God no, don't tell me."

"She's a junior at Vanderbilt, Taylor. We have a serious problem on our hands."

Taylor began to pace the sidewalk in front of Sam's building, her mind churning. Two girls dead, both murdered, both from the biggest local college campus? This was going to bring everyone out of the woodwork.

"Lincoln, get your butt into Price's office. Let him know what you've got. Has anyone filed a missing persons report on her?"

"I haven't found one yet. When Sam gives me a solid time line, I'll be able to get more specific, but I've gone through the past month's reports and haven't found any matches, which is totally bizarre. I mean, a Vandy student not being reported missing for this long, by anyone? Something's not jibin' here, LT."

"None of this is jibin', Lincoln. Go on and tell Price what's up, let him decide how to proceed. Sam should be done with the post soon, so I'll come in the minute I have the preliminaries. And, Lincoln? Don't tell anyone about this. Fitz and Marcus are fine, but no one else. Price is going to call the shots from here, okay? We're going to have media crawling all over us, and we don't want to make a misstep."

"You think it's the same guy?"

"I don't know. Until Sam finishes the post and we run all the evidence, there's no way to know. But the posing, the staging, the sexual assault—we may be dealing with more than a simple predator."

"A serial," he said, and she heard the teeniest bit of excitement in his voice.

"Possibly. And that, my friend, is top secret information. I'll be there shortly. Be good."

"You, too. Oh, hey. There's a big front headed our way. We're supposed to have bad weather for the next few days. Be careful."

Taylor clicked off the phone, tossed the cigarette under the wheel of a relatively new Mustang convertible. Lincoln wasn't kidding. The sky was darkening, and she could smell the storm; the dry tang of rain getting stronger by the minute. She looked to the west, saw the first lightning strike. Maybe the storm would improve her mood; she always loved a good rain.

Knowing she could put it off no longer, she headed back in to give Sam the bad news.

14

Sam was stripping off her gloves and shield when Taylor walked back in. Her heart reached out to her friend. Taylor was exhausted—that much was readily apparent. Her hair was spilling down from her ponytail, her shoulders were slumped, and there was no bounce in her step. Her eyes were so gray Sam thought rain could pour out of them at any moment, and the smudges underneath were getting worse. She looked as if she had a cold starting on top of it all; she'd been sniffing for most of the afternoon. Sam went to her and surprised her with a quick hug. Taylor hugged her back, quick and hard.

"You look like crap, Taylor. You need to get some sleep and some sinus medicine."

"Thanks, Mom." She gave her a halfhearted smile. "I don't have good news."

"Neither do I. You want to go first?"

"You go on ahead."

"Well, this one's cause of death was definitely from the stab wounds. There were two deep ones, got right into her heart. She didn't suffer long.

The other wounds are perimortem, and different. They're vicious, ragged wounds with notches, two more in her chest and one right in the gut. Just missed her liver. From the clean stabs, it looks like he used a regular knife with a serrated blade; the flesh on one side of the wound is torn."

"And the others?"

"Same knife, I think, but he turned it after it went in. Spun it around. A little extra to make it hurt worse. There's no way to know for certain which were first, but there was a lot of bleeding. She was alive for the torture, unfortunately."

Taylor blew out a breath. "You're saying 'he' a lot."

"She was raped, repeatedly, over a length of time. There was enough tissue left to show healed tears on both her vagina and anus. There were also fresh tears. Couldn't get any semen—it was washed away by the river—but she was being roughed up for a while before she died. And…"

"And?"

"She may have been poisoned as well. She looks a lot like Shelby on the inside. Her liver has the same characteristics. I took all the samples and had them run over to Simon. I asked him to drop everything and analyze them."

"Sam, this isn't good. Same guy, same point of origin? I'm praying we don't have a serial on our hands."

"You had news to share, too. What was it?"

"Lincoln got an ID. Her name is Jordan Blake. She's a junior at Vanderbilt."

Sam was quiet for a moment, then whispered under her breath, "Damn."

"Yeah, damn is right. Do you have any idea when she was killed?"

"She hadn't been in the river for more than a week. Four or five days would be my guess. He could have tossed her in anywhere south along the Cumberland, and it took her this long to float upstream, or she was weighted and broke free. My bet is the latter. He threw her away like a piece of trash, Taylor. There wasn't any of the reverence or—" She paused, bit her lip. "I don't want to say *gentleness* of the other kill. But Shelby's death didn't seem as careless. This one—Jordan—she pissed him off."

"Was she killed before Shelby?"

"I don't know. I can't say for sure, not with the water damage."

"What about the herbs?"

"Like I said, I can't be sure whether they were herbs, though the stuff I scraped off looked similar to what we got off Shelby. The thing is, if the composition is the same, he was with the body *after* she washed up on shore. Further proof he weighted her, then let her come to the surface to be found."

"Or...wherever he had her, he unweighted her, scattered the herbs on her back, and let her float in."

Sam thought about that for a minute. "Okay, that works for me, too. If he had spread them after she was on the bank, they wouldn't have been wet, and these were definitely mucky. But recent, the water would wash them away quickly. He was right there, Taylor."

Sam watched Taylor fiddle nervously with a ring on her right ring finger. It was a thin silver band, very plain. She'd picked it up in Hawaii on a brief vacation and hadn't bothered to take it off since. It held some symbolic meaning to her. One night, when they'd been very drunk, she told her it was a circle of life and a circle of death. Sam was aghast when Taylor said she didn't want to take it off, that it was a constant reminder of her failings. Sam had to resist the impulse to reach over and wrench the ring right off Taylor's finger and throw it in the trash. Taylor Jackson had no failings that Sam could see, other than caring too damn much about her job.

"Taylor, there's one other thing."

"More? What?"

"She was pregnant. About six weeks along."

Taylor could do nothing but stare. The thoughts were flying, bouncing off each other like bumper cars. None were coming together.

Sam continued. "It's possible some of the tearing and damage I found could have been inflicted that long ago. It's possible that whoever killed her was the father of the child."

"You're reaching there, Sam."

"I know. But it could be. You can't rule it out. If he was the father, it's possible he didn't know about the child."

"Or he did, and that's why she ended up in the river, viciously stabbed. Ah, hell, Sam, this is just too much. Can you run the DNA you collected from Shelby against the fetus?"

"I can, yes, but it isn't going to happen as fast as you'd like. Simon's already dumped a couple of high-profile private cases he's working on—he's not going to want to jump through this hoop again immediately. Besides, I'm only bringing it to your attention. It's possible we have two different killers, despite the similarities."

Taylor stood for a long moment, staring at her best friend. Tapped a finger along her leg. "I understand, but I want it done. Please ask Simon to drop everything and work on this, okay?"

"All right. I'll ask. I may go over and help him run some samples, speed things up."

"That would be incredible, Sam. Thank you. I'm heading back downtown. We need to get a game plan together, find this girl's family and give them the news before we release any information. You'll get to me the second you hear from Simon?"

"I will. Hey, I heard about the grand jury. Are you okay? Do you need anything? I know revisiting all of it won't be easy."

Sam was possibly the only person on earth Taylor had been completely honest with about that night. Oh, she'd told the truth, she'd just left out the parts that made her look weak and stupid for falling for Martin's rap. She'd never forgive herself for hesitating. If she'd only gone straight to Price the moment she found out, none of this would have happened.

She hugged her best friend, long and hard. "Thank you for caring. I'm fine, I promise. It's only a recitation of the facts, and I want to see his partners go down."

"It wasn't your fault, Taylor. Not one ounce of it. Don't you ever forget it."

Taylor smiled sadly. "If you tell me that often enough, one day, I might start to believe you. I gotta run."

"Do me a favor? Stop by the drugstore and grab some Advil Cold & Sinus. We can't have you getting sick on us."

"Yeah, yeah, yeah," she said, waving good-bye.

15

He stood in the shadows, watching, felt the breeze kick up, smelled the fire coming from the sky. It was time. He said the words quietly, hands raised.

"'And after these things, I saw four Angels standing on the four corners of the earth, holding the four winds of the earth, that the wind should not blow on the earth, nor on the sea, nor on any tree.'"

His voice rose, the ecstasy of the moment driving him. "But I am the fifth angel. And I call upon my brothers to unleash the winds of wrath upon us. Blow away the sins of our people, take those undeserving of my love. Ruin the nonbelievers, allow my vision to caress those worthy of my divinity."

In answer, the wind blew harder, and he knew he was blessed.

16

The rain was coming down hard by the time Taylor rolled into headquarters. She was fervently hoping the captain had a plan.

The squad room was unnaturally quiet, so Taylor wandered out into the hall, looking for her people. Lincoln was walking toward her with a pot of coffee, gesturing to the conference room. She followed him in to find Price, Fitz, and Dan Franklin sitting around the table. Marcus had pulled out a whiteboard; a thick black line drawn down the middle separated it into two columns. She'd have to hold off telling them about the possible herbs Sam had collected from Jordan Blake's body. She didn't want Dan Franklin to have that information until they were ready to use it.

One of her quick-thinking detectives had scrounged up a picture of Jordan Blake. She hung on the left side, and a picture of Shelby Kincaid was taped to the right. It was the first real look she'd gotten at Jordan. There was absolutely no comparison to the ruined body they'd found in the river.

While Shelby was pretty in an unassuming way, more cute than beautiful, Jordan Blake was stunning. Take-your-breath-away, movie-star, attention-getting gorgeous. How in the world a girl like that could have disappeared unnoticed was a real mystery.

"You guys have been busy," Taylor said.

Fitz shot her a smile and Price nodded a hello.

"Hi, Taylor. Grab a chair. We're going through our next steps and putting together all the info we've got so far. We're short on Jordan, obviously. You and Marcus are going to Vandy when we finish, and dig up everything you can find on her." Price was smooth and in control, just the opposite of how Taylor was feeling inside. "In the meantime, Lincoln is looking for the girl's family. There was none listed on her print card, so he's called over to Vandy to get her personal information."

"If they give you crap, let me know," Taylor said. "They can get prickly about releasing student information without a court order."

"I went the back route." Lincoln grinned at her, and almost on cue, the phone on the table rang. Lincoln checked the caller ID, then picked it up. "Lincoln Ross."

He hadn't answered with the standard "Homicide." That must be the people from Vandy. Taylor was glad to see things were being handled so delicately. He jotted down a few notes and thanked the person on the other end of the line warmly. Taylor raised a brow at him. Wondered who he had called in the favor from.

Lincoln had the decency to blush. "Old friend," he muttered.

"So what's the deal?" Price obviously wasn't in the mood to play "tease the detective" at the moment.

"Jordan is from Houston. I'm going to go call the chaplain, see if he can start working his magic to get her parents notified." Lincoln rose and headed back into the warren to make the call.

Price watched him go, then turned back to Taylor. "What did Sam have to say?"

"Her sense is we may have the same killer. On the surface, it looks like two totally different suspects. Jordan had been raped over a period of time and stabbed five times, two that caught her in the heart and killed her pretty quickly. But Sam saw the same liver necrosis as Shelby, the indicator of possible poisoning. She's sent everything to Simon Loughley with an emergency push. One little snag. Jordan was six weeks pregnant. We could have a set of coincidental deaths here, two different men entirely."

"Or we could have one man who's ridding himself of dead weight." Price stroked his mustache. "I don't want any talk outside this room about serial killers, series killers, or mass murderers on the loose with a hard-on for Vandy coeds. Dan, we need a press conference. We'll need a very succinct and brief statement for the late news. I'm talking bare bones here. And I want Taylor to be there with you to take a few questions."

Both Franklin and Taylor opened their mouths

to protest. Price held up his hands. "We've had quite enough controversy in this shop, and enough media attention to last a lifetime. Putting Taylor on camera will show we're back to normal. She is in charge of investigating these homicides, and I want a female face on the case. It will make the coeds listen. And it will help after yesterday morning's little snafu."

Taylor closed her mouth and narrowed her eyes at Price. He simply smiled.

"Now, Taylor, get a subpoena for Jordan Blake's records, and do it fast. I want you and Marcus to go back to Vandy and check things out. Be a little discreet. This is eventually going to get out, and I don't want it to look like we've stepped on anyone's toes. Fitz, I'm pulling you back in full-time. You head over to Private Match and sit on Loughley until he comes up with the results."

Fitz shrugged. "It's not going to happen tonight, Cap. It takes time to run all those little tests."

"I don't care how long it takes. Just go over and help him out. Y'all are dismissed. Dan, stay behind—we'll work on the statement. You can call Taylor later with the time she needs to show up."

They stood, and Fitz said, "Taylor, can I have a second?"

"Sure. I need to check on Lincoln anyway." They left the room, Price still barking instructions to Dan Franklin in the background.

Lincoln was hanging up the phone when they walked in. "Here's something interesting for you. The chaplain called his counterpart in Houston, who knows Jordan's family. They ran out to the house—apparently the parents don't live far from their HQ. Jordan's parents have been in Europe for the past month. They've got another month planned, and their maid didn't know how to reach them. She said the dad calls into his office every once in a while, so we called over there to have him call as soon as he gets a message. The maid gave them the number of a sister who lives in Washington, DC. They're trying to get in touch with her, see if she can reach the parents." He shook his head. "Some family. No one seems to talk to anyone else."

"Very sad. Keep after them, Lincoln. If we're having a press conference tonight, I'd like to be able to use Jordan's name. Fitz, let's go in Price's office."

They went in and Fitz closed the door. She saw the look of concern and steeled herself.

"You okay, sweetheart?"

"Of course I am."

"Hey, little girl, this is me you're talking to. Marcus told me about your panic attack over at Vandy."

She felt her chest tighten. "Great, now he's tattling on me?"

"No, no, no, he didn't know what happened, exactly, only said he thought you were feeling sick. Lucky for you, you do look like you're coming down with a cold. That's what I told him. I'm the one who put it together."

She laughed. "Why does everyone think I have a cold? I feel fine."

"You don't look like you feel fine. You look

stressed and strung out and ill. What's up? Are you worried about the grand jury?"

"Fitz, honey, I love you to death, but I'm fine. I just got a little hot and stopped to catch my breath. Maybe I *am* catching something. So stop worrying about me. We've got two very dead girls and a city that's going to go into panic mode when they hear the connection. More important things, you know? Sam may have gotten some herbs off Jordan Blake's body. Tell Price and Lincoln for me, okay? I didn't want to mention it in front of Franklin."

Fitz nodded but still looked doubtful. He knew about the dreams. He knew about the panic attacks. He knew she'd been riding the edge. He had tried to talk her into taking some time off after the shooting. She'd bullied her way back and hadn't stopped. She was finally starting to show some cracks.

"You got me worried, little girl."

"Fitz, I'm fine, I swear. I haven't been sleeping, that's all. We solve this case, I get my testimony over with, and I'll take a few days off. Promise. But right now I have to scoop up the puppy and go over to Vandy. Okay?"

He leaned over and put a hand on her shoulder. Squeezed, then got up and left without saying another word.

Taylor took a deep breath. *Shit.* If Marcus was noticing she wasn't 100 percent right, the others were, too. She needed to get herself in check, and fast.

David Martin just wouldn't let her go, the bastard.

17

Taylor and Marcus took the familiar route to Vanderbilt's administrative offices. Chief Graber was nowhere in sight. Taylor didn't complain. They caught a plump, grandmotherly woman holding a clear plastic umbrella just as she was locking the doors to leave.

"Excuse me. I'm Lieutenant Jackson and this is Detective Wade—"

"Detective Wade. I remember seeing you yesterday. I'm Gladys Thorton." She gave Marcus a sweet, inviting smile. He coughed and looked at the ground. "You were here about Shelby Kincaid. I saw you talking to Chief Graber right after he came and got the Kincaid girl's records. I heard more about it on the news. Poor little lamb."

"Yes, ma'am, it is a shame. We need a favor, though. Would you mind letting us in and looking up another record for us? I promise it won't take long."

"Well, I've got my book club in an hour. If you can be quick…?" Taylor nodded and Gladys turned the key, unlocking the door, happy to chat despite her rush. "Have you ever read *Middlesex*? I just couldn't seem to get through it. I'm embarrassed, really, I'm sure they're all going to think I'm some sort of dummy, but it just didn't capture my interest. These big books..."

Taylor smiled at Marcus and let the woman prattle as she led them into the office. Maybe they'd get lucky and she'd be too distracted to question their motive in pulling another record. News of Jordan Blake's death wasn't out yet; they needed to be careful.

"Whose record did you say you wanted?"

Marcus finally spoke. "Uh, we didn't. But we need Jordan Blake's file."

Gladys stopped. "Jordan Blake," she said disapprovingly. "Do you have a court order for the records?"

Marcus waved the blue-backed paper in front of her.

"You're supposed to go give that to the counsel's office first, but since Chief Graber took responsibility for the last one, I'm sure he'll do the same for this. He knows you're here?"

Taylor shifted uncomfortably and told a tiny white lie. "Um, no, ma'am. I wasn't able to reach him before we got here. He may have gone home for the day."

Gladys clucked, "That poor man. His leg pains him something awful. You just leave the court order with me, and I'll make sure it's all taken care of. Jordan Blake. My, oh my. Did she kill the Kincaid girl?"

Taylor froze. "Why would you say that, ma'am?"

Gladys was bumbling around the office like a bee in search of honey, smiling over her shoulder at Marcus all the while. "Oh, the Blake girl, she's a bad apple, if you ask me."

Bingo, Taylor thought. Gossip was as good as anything right now. Taylor leaned in confidentially to give the woman more comfort to spill the beans. "She is? Can you tell me why, Gladys?"

"Well." She directed her scandal-laden voice at Marcus. "Jordan's been trouble since day one. Always getting herself in scrapes. Drunk driving, wild parties, missing classes. She's on academic probation again this semester. If I were the dean, I would have kicked her out long ago."

"Why hasn't he?"

"Why, because she's a Blake, dear. Jordan is Gregory Blake's daughter."

Marcus looked blank, but Taylor suddenly understood. She mentally kicked herself for not putting it together sooner. The Blake family was one of the largest benefactors to Vanderbilt. Gregory Blake was an incredibly successful oilman from Texas who had attended Vanderbilt for undergrad and law. He'd made a lot of money and wanted to give it back. He'd done his best to get his name on Vanderbilt's new library, but the honor had gone to Alexander Heard and his wife, Jean. Heard was the ex-chancellor of the university and had much more clout than the oilman from Texas.

But it all made sense now. Out of the country, no contact with their wild child, just throwing money at the situation rather than dealing with it. It was going to take some tightrope walking to keep this from becoming a huge mess.

Taylor grabbed Marcus's hand to keep him from talking any further. Gladys had led them into the records room and was riffling through the cabinet marked *B–2006*. Graduates scheduled to receive their wings in 2006. Girls and boys ready to take on the world, unknowing and untried. Innocent. Taylor felt the old familiar worthlessness creeping up, but shut it away firmly.

Gladys was still talking. "So did that girl get into trouble again? I can see her getting involved with the wrong crowd, one that could hurt the Kincaid girl. I swear, one of these times she's going to get herself in some real trouble. Such a shame, too, because she's a smart girl. If she just applied herself... Here's the file." She looked at her watch. "Oh my, I really do have to lock up and get to my book club. The rain makes the traffic so awful. Why don't you just take it with you? You can bring it back in the morning. Leave the subpoena on my desk. I'll deal with it tomorrow, too."

As she spoke, she ushered them out the door, locking it behind them. "See you in the morning." She gave Marcus another smile and hurried off, humming quietly to herself.

Marcus was still speechless. Taylor started laughing, then found she couldn't stop. The fit of hysteria was catching, and they ended up sitting on the steps of the building, trying to catch their breath. The rain had calmed to a heavy mist, and the overhang of the ornate edifice gave them enough shelter. Taking advantage of the dry spot, Taylor groped in her pocket and came up with a wrinkled pack of Camel Lights. She offered one to Marcus, who accepted sheepishly. "You're a bad influence."

"If the whole squad hadn't decided to quit smoking at once, it would be a lot easier to cheat."

They lit up, sat companionably for a few moments, smoking, not speaking, lost in their own theories about Jordan Blake. Without warning Taylor burst out laughing again. She stood and started to the car, giggling as Marcus walked slowly after her, impervious to the rain.

"All right, puppy. Let's go talk to some of Jordan's classmates. Give me a second, I've got to grab my phone—I left it in the car."

Dan Franklin had left a message on her cell while they were in with Gladys. The press conference was in an hour.

All the humor fled. Just what she wanted—to face the cameras again.

18

Captain Price was getting ready to walk out the door when his phone rang. He hesitated; it was late, and he was caught between the desire to just clear the hell out and the knowledge that he had to take the call. He let out a huge sigh and walked back to his desk.

"Price."

"Hey, man. How goes it in the land of make-believe?"

"Garrett Woods. How the hell are ya? It's been a while. You in town?"

"Don't I wish? No, I'm sitting here underground at Quantico, as usual. I think I'm becoming a vampire. The light hurts my eyes when I get outside."

"Sorry to hear that. You still running the BSU up there?"

"Behavioral Science… Investigative Support. They can't decide what they want to call us. Yeah, I'm still running it. Isn't all it's cracked up to be these days. Too many crazies and too little time.

Speaking of which, I hear you guys are having a little fun down there yourselves."

Price caught the note in his friend's voice. *Uh-oh.* He really liked the man, but he didn't relish the thought of the FBI trailing around his cases. He'd had many good experiences with them, but he'd also found when profilers get on the case, things could go a little astray.

"Fun times, always," he said cautiously. "It's been a while, Garrett. To what do I owe the pleasure?"

"Can't a friend call and say hi?"

"Not when that friend is with the FBI and I've got a popping case."

Garrett started to laugh. "Okay, okay. I'd like to ask a favor."

"Shoot."

"Word on the street is you may have a serial on your hands."

"We have two dead girls in a short time span, both of whom attended the same college, but we have nothing tying them together outside of proximity. It's probably too early to start bantering around the serial theory, you know?"

"Yeah, I do. This isn't an entirely official inquiry. But you know the drill. If you do have a serial, I'll have to pull a field profiler in who has too damn many things going on with his own stuff to be a huge help, yada, yada, yada. I was thinking perhaps we could approach things a little differently."

Price sat back in his chair. This was going to

be interesting. He'd known Garrett for years, and trusted him. His instincts caught a little note of desperation in his old friend's voice, which intrigued him. Garrett wasn't a man who flustered easily.

"Go on."

"I have an agent there in Nashville who's not working right now. He's been on a temporary sabbatical. I was wondering if you'd be willing to let him come in and consult, on my dime."

"Why do I get the feeling there's more to this?"

He heard Garrett heave a sigh. "Can't put anything past you, huh? It is a special situation. His name is Dr. John Baldwin. He's one of our best and brightest. He got himself in a little trouble here a few months ago, and it kinda screwed him up. He headed home to Nashville to sort out his head, so to speak."

"What kind of trouble, Garrett?" Price's tone was obvious.

"Nothing illegal or improper. He was involved in a shooting. Three of his teammates were shot and killed, and he's been putting the blame on himself, big-time. I'm not sure I'll ever get him to come back to the FBI. But I want him back, Price. He's a damn good cop. One of the freakiest profilers I've ever had. He's got this sixth sense that's busted open a ton of cases when no one else had a clue. Really intuitive, on the ball..."

"So why's he so torn up? He knows the risks."

"It's a long story, but not a new one. He feels he got them killed. One was a junior agent on his first case. He hasn't been able to shake the guilt.

I'm hoping a taste of the real world will bring him back to life, so to speak."

"Why don't you just pull him back in on one of your cases?"

"Because he refuses to leave Nashville. He claims he's planning to quit the FBI for good. He may refuse to talk with you, I don't know. But I need to try, Mitch. I don't want to lose him, in any sense of the word."

"Do you really think he's going to be any good for us if he's not any good for you?"

"Point taken. I think if he feels useful but isn't in charge, it may shake something loose. Maybe we can even convince him it's his civic duty to help out in his hometown. I'd consider this a personal favor, man. Nobody up here knows I'm doing this, so I may get my own ass in a sling."

"I suppose you already know about my LT and her shooting?"

"Jackson? Yeah, I heard about it. Sounds like she got jammed up good. I did hear she was back on the job. She doing okay?"

"Far as I can tell. Shrinks cleared her, department cleared her, and she's back and rolling. Like your guy, she's a damn good cop. I would have hated to lose her."

Garrett was quiet while Price thought it over. Finally, he asked, "You think Baldwin will do it?"

"I haven't talked to him about it. I wanted to clear it with you first. If you give the word, I'll call him right now and run it by him. He may tell me to go to hell. He's already done that a few times.

But I have some new information pertaining to his case. It might help pull him back in."

"Loose cannons aren't always the best people to have around a delicate situation, Garrett. I'd need your personal assurance that you'll keep up with him, make sure he's not going yahoo on me."

"You have my word. I wouldn't even think about asking for this if I thought it would backfire. He'll either say yes or no. If he says no, well…"

"All right, man, if he'll talk to me, I'll talk to him. Though if I get any indications he's not working out, I'll be the first to cut the strings."

Woods heaved out a sigh of relief. "I owe you one. If I can talk him into it, I'll have him call you tonight to set things up. I'll make it clear it's only a consulting role. If there's a problem, you let me know."

"Will do, Garrett. You owe me more than a beer this time."

After a few pleasantries and promises to keep in close touch, Price hung up the phone. He didn't want to mention the call to Taylor just yet. He thought he'd see if the man called in first, then deal with the fallout. He shut off his office light and went home.

19

Dr. John Baldwin sat on the easy chair in his living room. The room was devoid of light except the flickering of the television, tuned to the local CBS affiliate, but muted. On the table next to the chair was a half-empty pint glass of Guinness and a Smith and Wesson .38 Special snub-nosed revolver.

Baldwin stared at the television, eyes unfocused. He was very drunk. Drunk enough to play the game. He was ready. With any luck, he'd have a little accident and there would be no more guilt.

Baldwin had been a handsome man once. He stood six foot four, had jet-black hair graying slightly at the temples, lively green eyes that could look into the very soul. But now he looked ten years older than his thirty-seven years. He had a week-old beard shot through with dense silver the color of moonlight that barely filled in the gaunt lines of his face. His eyes were shrouded with guilt.

He had been forced out of his job at the FBI six months earlier. Not by his bosses. By his own conscience. Six months to relive the shame, the embarrassment, the knowledge that he had caused three deaths. Six months of replaying the case. Reliving his actions. He had been the head of the Investigative Support Unit, thriving in the shadowy world of psychological profiling. Was the darling of the BSU. He had the book smarts, of course: PhDs and a law degree, and the years of field experience. He was a good cop. Used to be a good cop.

Then Harold Arlen had rocked his world.

Arlen, an inconspicuous mechanic in Great Falls, Virginia, had killed his career, definitely, but he'd also taken a chunk of Baldwin's soul. Baldwin had seen so much in his years at the FBI, but Arlen went to new heights of hideousness. Once a week for six weeks, like clockwork, a young girl had been found in the woods near Great Falls, Virginia.

Every law enforcement officer, every neighbor, every member of the media, everyone thought Arlen was responsible. But they had no proof. Not a single hair, a minuscule fiber, a shred of mitochondria. Nothing.

Baldwin knew in his soul that Arlen was guilty. It was the way he acted in his interviews, playing, laughing. How he only truly came alive when they showed him the crime scene photos. It was all there. But there was no evidence.

Their last-ditch attempt to pin the murders on Arlen proved fatal. The evidence they'd been searching for finally appeared, stuffed into the back of an underwear drawer. Arlen had come home and found them rooting through his house, and had gone wild, whipped out a gun and started shooting.

All the agents were caught by surprise. Baldwin's bullets were the only ones that found their mark. He'd killed Arlen, but Arlen had gotten enough shots off before he was hit to kill the other three agents.

The guilt Baldwin felt was overwhelming. He'd lost three good men for no reason other than his own desperation to solve an unsolvable case. Arlen was dead, the case was done. Then another little girl turned up dead. They'd found hairs on her body, and a DNA comparison didn't link them to Arlen.

There was an inquiry. Baldwin could see the judgment in the eyes of the agents around him. Getting scum off the street was one thing, and Arlen had been scum: a purveyor and seller of child pornography. Losing, no, sacrificing three good men, though, in the guise of taking down a killer? No one accused him directly, but he felt the eyes on the back of his neck. He sat with the ghosts of his friends every night. It was too much, and he left.

By the time he'd arrived at his boyhood home in Tennessee, Baldwin was already too far gone to save. A life sentence for murder would have been easier than a death sentence of freedom. He'd had no contact with his old life for six months, except the occasional phone call from his old boss, which never went well. He'd wallowed in guilt, drank to excess, popped every pill he could find. Anything that would make him numb.

He soon realized that there was only one way out. He didn't have the balls to get it over with himself, didn't quite have the nerve to meet his maker straight out. So for the past few weeks, every night, he sat in his chair, playing the game according to his own set of rules.

Baldwin pulled himself back to consciousness. He'd given himself permission to relive the fateful mea culpa, to flog himself for his stupidity, just as he did every night he was sober enough to think. He'd asked forgiveness of his dead friends once more. He wanted to put an end to his overwhelming guilt, to serve his time in hell. He figured it couldn't be much worse than what he dealt with every minute of every day. That's where the game came in.

He forced the thoughts away. Took a last gulp of his beer. Palmed the small gun, his throw-down weapon from the old days when he was a decent cop. It was ready to go, like a roommate begging to leave on the ultimate road trip.

He lifted the revolver to eye level. Read the words *Made in the USA* engraved on the side. It gave him a sense of pride—wouldn't do to play with anything foreign, despite the supposed origins of the game. He leaned back in the chair and gave the cylinder a spin. One spin, one try. If it didn't happen, he'd put the gun away until the next night. The ratcheting noise comforted him, and as it stopped he took a deep breath. Put eight pounds of pressure on the trigger pull and pointed it at his temple.

The staccato tones of Wagner's "Ride of the Valkyries" filled the silent room, startling the gun from his hand. Baldwin grabbed for it and got a grip on it, then groaned and set the weapon in his lap. His fucking cell phone was ringing. Loudly. Insistently. He choked back a laugh. He'd forgotten to turn it off.

Ignore it! He raised the weapon again. *Just do it. You won't be able to sleep if you don't play the game.* But a thought niggled in the back of his mind. Who the hell would be calling? No one had called in weeks. They'd tried, at first. "Take a leave of absence, Baldwin. We'll be in touch." And after the first month, they had been. But the calls inviting him back hadn't been returned. When the case ultimately resolved, they'd sent him a letter giving him a year's leave, left him alone to battle his demons.

Shaking his head, the curiosity got the better of him. He had all night to kill himself. Hell, he had the rest of his life to do it. He picked up the phone.

"What?" he barked.

"It's Garrett."

Baldwin sighed and gently set the gun back on the side table. Maybe it wasn't his night to die after all.

20

Baldwin didn't know exactly how to respond to the man on the other end of the phone. He opted for the truth.

"I'm kinda in the middle of something, Garrett."

"Baldwin, I wouldn't bother you if it wasn't important. I'm sorry it's been so long. After our last conversation, I thought you'd rather not hear from me."

Baldwin listened with half an ear to the platitudes from his former boss. His thoughts kept drifting to the gun next to him. Hopefully, this was a last-ditch mercy call and he could get back to the game. His attention gradually drifted back to the phone when he heard the word *killing*.

"Huh? What was that again?"

"The Nashville police are working two murders. Coeds from Vanderbilt. There are some bizarre aspects to the deaths. I think they may have a serial on their hands. I just talked to the captain down there. He's an old friend of mine. Your name came up. Do you feel up to doing a little consulting? Or are you still messing around with your gun?"

Baldwin gave a little laugh. How nice to be so predictable.

"'Fraid I'm a little tied up at the moment, Garrett. With my stellar reputation and all, why the hell would they want me? Let me guess—you didn't tell him the whole story?"

"Like I said, Mitchell Price is a friend. He knows what went down. He's a big believer in second chances. So am I. I'm not asking you back to the Bureau. I'm asking you to talk to a friend of mine. Maybe give him a little advice. Maybe sign on for a while to see if they can get this guy who's hunting young women in your backyard. That's all."

"Why don't you send one of your people?"

"Because this is right up your alley. You're already on-site. You're familiar with the territory. And despite what you seem to consider your little fuckup, you're still one of the best in the business. C'mon, Baldwin. Humor me. Get out of the house for a while. Maybe do some interacting with the rest of the world. It might pull you out of the funk. You have been in a funk, right, Baldwin?"

Therapy. Yeah, he was falling for that.

"I don't think this is such a good idea, boss."

"Well, I do. They need another brain, Baldwin, and I don't have any to spare. Since you're probably not real up-to-date with the program, we're losing people right and left. Big bucks on the mashed potato circuit, everybody wants to be a consultant on cable TV. We're low on resources, and all the remaining personnel are in Minnesota, working a skinner case. Guess you haven't heard about that either. Never mind. Will you do it? It's only a conversation."

"I didn't ask for any favors, Garrett."

"This isn't one for you, Baldwin. It's a favor to me. Just call Price, go in and see him. You can make the decision from there."

"Hold on," Baldwin said as he pulled the phone away from his ear and reached for the TV remote. He turned up the opening of the local ten o'clock evening news. A pretty blond anchor in tortoise-shell glasses, with a long nose and the requisite overbite that reminded men of what a mouth like that could do, spoke quietly, with the intonation of doom only a TV person could muster. Two female students from Vanderbilt University had been found brutally raped and murdered, their bodies left at two of Nashville's very public sites.

"The press has it."

"Hard to keep it away from them."

He stared up at the ceiling, willing the report to go away. He heard a woman's voice fending off detailed questions nicely. *Quelling the panic,* Baldwin thought to himself. Shaking his head, he turned the TV up to listen.

"…Shelby Kincaid, of Bowling Green, Kentucky. She was a sophomore at Vanderbilt, and was reported missing several days ago by her roommate." The woman cut off a question: "No, John, we're not releasing the name of the roommate. Get real." There was a ripple of laughter throughout the room. "The second victim is Jordan Blake, of Houston, Texas. She was a junior at Vanderbilt. Yes, she is the daughter of Gregory Blake. We don't have any indication this crime is in any way related to her father's business." There was a flurry of sound, voices, papers, phones. The woman ignored it and pressed on.

"We want to pass a message to all students in town. Don't go out alone. Stay with friends if possible. Keep your doors and windows locked at all times. Go to class in groups. Don't put yourselves in any compromising situations, especially with alcohol and drugs. We're doing our best to find the suspect. Thank you." The shouting started again, but she turned and walked out of the room. A man the TV screen named as Dan Franklin approached the podium. Baldwin wasn't paying attention anymore.

Man, the chick was pretty. He thought he knew her from somewhere, though she looked a little older and worn a little thin. They'd picked the right woman as their PR spokesman. Spokeswoman. She obviously knew everyone there, had kept them under control.

As he came back from his thoughts, the female anchor threw it to her co-anchor. The story was over. Then it hit him. *Taylor Jackson.* That's who she was—they'd gone to Father Ryan together. He'd always thought she was hot as hell, but she was more into the popular crew's scene than he had ever been. He'd never pursued the matter, and he'd bet a million dollars she'd never remember who he was.

Besides, she was a couple of years younger, and he hadn't been on the A-list on the private school circuit. Nashville really was a small town.

Baldwin switched stations and watched as another distraught female anchor gave the details of the rape and murder of the two girls. He was able to get a little more information before they cut away to the footage of the press conference. The rest of the story was a simple reprise. There was no new information coming out tonight.

He knew the cops had much more detail, but there was only so much the public could handle, much less understand. Without realizing he was doing so, Baldwin mentally began forming a profile of the murderer, murmuring to himself.

"Guy's white, around thirty, complete sociopath. He's killing in a private place, probably has some menial night job that gives him free movement during the day. Lives with someone who can support him, had a crappy childhood, domineering mother, distant father, yada, yada, yada. Killing girls with similar characteristics of someone close to him, probably has a record, these aren't his first crimes. Has kept souvenirs, is keeping clippings from the paper and watching the media coverage. Doesn't date, very organized, stalking the girls. Wants the police to see what he's done, so he's dumping in a public place. Lives in the area, has means of transport…" He trailed off. The typical profile of a serial killer.

It was getting redundant, and some of the profilers he knew had been sloppy lately, often throwing the same categories at all the killers, lumping them together. Granted, killers weren't terribly original, but the complacency that came with dealing with these men was beginning to show. There were "former" profilers all over the cable news networks anytime a series of killings started, and even when there was only one violent crime to go on. They needed to be a little more careful. The word was out that they hadn't been completely accurate in a few cases. He'd heard a former cop bluster his way through a television interview a few weeks before, saying, "Profilers don't put cuffs on the criminals." That could start some trouble.

Baldwin came back from his thoughts to hear Garrett yelling at him. "Sorry. What?"

"God, man, where'd you go?"

"Just watching a little TV."

"I have something else I need you to know. It's about Arlen."

Baldwin tensed. "I don't want to talk about him, Garrett. All bets are off if you bring him up again."

"But, Baldwin, there's new—"

"That's my deal, Garrett. No Arlen, and I'll think about talking to your friend. Are we clear?"

"You're not exactly in a position to make demands on me, Baldwin. Just let me tell you what's happening."

"No."

Garrett was silent for a moment. "Fine, have it your way. Will you call Price?"

Baldwin gave a last longing look at the gun. "Yeah."

He clicked off the phone and gently set it down on the table beside him. Went into the kitchen, fetched another Guinness. Poured it into an ice-cold mug from the freezer. He'd always preferred it cold, rather than the correct British lukewarm.

The gun wasn't calling as loudly now. He'd felt a small adrenaline rush at the news reports. Maybe it wouldn't be such a bad idea to talk to the captain. He could pull out at any time and come back to his miserable little existence. Maybe fate was dealing him a new hand. He guzzled half the beer, called Price at home, and set an appointment for eight in the morning.

He sat back in the chair, took a smaller sip of the beer, picked up an empty notepad from the coffee table. Began writing out the thoughts in his head. Time to trade the mind of one madman for another.

21

Taylor was wide-awake. She had gone home after the press conference and hit the bed completely exhausted, hoping a good night's sleep would help her think clearly in the morning. Instead, she kept reviewing the facts of the case. The whiteboard from the squad room shone brightly in her mind's eye, the faces of the dead girls running over and over through her head.

After an hour of tossing and turning, she finally accepted sleep wasn't going to come anytime soon. She got out of the bed and made her way to her pool table, flipped on the TV as she walked by for noise.

Racked the balls. Took the break. Smoothly cracked the balls into their respective pockets. She felt the tension go out of her shoulders as she finally started to relax. The rain was still coming down. The local weather station had broken into the late-night feed to give radar warnings for the severe thunderstorms moving through the area. Tomorrow's storms were supposed to be even worse.

Taylor kept a small refrigerator in the back

corner of the room. She made her way there and grabbed a bottle of ice-cold Miller Lite. She sipped and mused, expertly sinking ball after ball, reracking, breaking, playing eight ball against herself.

With a delicate meow, her cat jumped up on the table and began batting at the balls. Taylor couldn't help but laugh. The kitten adopted from the local shelter and named Jade for her green eyes was at the very least Taylor's best confidante. She had adopted her on a whim. She'd gone into the animal shelter to serve a warrant, saw the scruffy kitten sneeze, and fell in love. She was surprised to realize that she never felt alone when the cat was around.

She racked the balls again, shifting her thoughts to the weird aspects of the case at hand. She hadn't given the drug angle too much thought. These were college kids, who did stupid things like drink and do drugs to excess. Was it possible straitlaced Shelby had decided to lighten up a little bit, and fell in with the wrong crowd? According to Gladys, Jordan was a habitual user, but no one from her crowd knew Shelby.

The limited connections bothered her. The beer and fatigue were dragging her mind into Park.

Getting more in depth with Shelby's background had been hard; there was little new information to be gained. Calls around campus had given them a few answers, but left more questions in Taylor's mind.

She was sure the girl was seeing someone. They hadn't found any kind of birth control in her things; the campus clinic had no record of her being a gynecological patient with them; they only had a single record on her—she'd received antibiotics for a bout with bronchitis earlier in the semester. No one else had been able to confirm or deny her out-of-class activities—apparently even the students in Shelby's program didn't know her well. Her advisor had lauded her with praise. Taylor sensed it was heartfelt, not just laurels for the dead. Her parents obviously cared for her. She was a hardworking scholarship student who seemingly kept her nose clean. So why would someone want to rape her, leave her body at the Parthenon, and cover her with herbs?

The herbs told Taylor that whoever had killed Shelby cared about her, in some sick, twisted way. Even though her body had been abused, she had been given some kind of tender send-off, a show of reverence.

She racked up the balls again.

Jordan Blake was a different story. Her file made much of the tale self-evident. Jordan was out of control. She'd been on academic probation since she arrived freshman year. She'd been booted out of her sorority pledge class, was in and out of the health clinic for three pregnancy scares. Nobody they talked to could give them any definitive ideas on where she had been in the days before her death. It seemed Jordan Blake was friends with everyone and no one.

Irrefutable fact—the girl was pregnant when she was killed. She'd been stabbed and thrown in the river. Even if the detritus on her body comprised the same herbs they'd recovered from Shelby, this wasn't a crime of love. It was a crime of hate. Or passion.

Sam's comment about the killer being the baby's father rolled through her head.

Good girl, bad girl. Angel, devil. How could the same man have so much love for one and so much hatred for the other?

Taylor put up her cue and perched on the edge of the table. There was a thought niggling in the back of her mind, but she was too tired to gain access to it. She gave up for now, hoping it would rear its head in the morning. Maybe she could sleep her way to an answer.

Tossing the empty beer bottle away, she made her way back to her bed, hoping she was foggy enough to escape the nightmares about dead girls begging for her help to find them justice.

She wasn't.

Bullets were flying in the darkened sky. She heard them whizzing by her head, felt the heat as they ripped through her hair. She saw him go down. She was screaming, clawing at him, trying to get away from the hand that reached up and grabbed her by the throat. She fell beside him. He was dead. She could see the entrance wound, glistening silver in the moonlight. Her hands were slick with blood: It covered all of her, drowning her in its viscous blanket, dragging her down into the weeds as they curled and spread over her body. There was no hope. There was no pain. She gave up her struggle and lay serenely next to the empty soul beside her, waiting for the strangling vines to drag her into the earth to decompose along with him. She heard a voice, turned to hear better. Jordan Blake's empty eyes stared back at her. She jumped, and tried to roll away, but the vines held her tight. Only her head could move, and she turned away, not wanting to see. When she opened her eyes again, Shelby Kincaid lay beside her, wearing a crown of thorns, hands reaching for Taylor's face, silently mouthing, "Please..."

Taylor rolled out of bed, heart kettledrumming in her chest. Her Glock was in her hand; she was panting in fear.

She tried to control her breathing. Put the gun back under the pillow.

The dreams were getting out of control. She had lost her edge completely; the ghosts of her failures were dragging her down, haunting her every moment.

A thought—indistinct, clouded with fatigue. She needed to find a way to help the girls, but it was too late. They were all dead.

She lay back down, head against the pillow, eyes wide, too tired to even cry anymore.

THE

THIRD

DAY

22

Taylor was knee-deep in the squad's squalor and on her third Diet Coke. She'd come in before five, unable to stay alone anymore. At least there was activity at all hours at the CJC.

She was skimming the ViCAP files Lincoln had pulled when she noticed a tall, good-looking man walking toward Price's door. She didn't recognize him as department material, figured he was a politico, maybe from the mayor's office. Dismissed him with a distracted nod. She'd learned long ago when to keep her head down.

Half an hour later, she was combing the autopsy reports when Price opened his door and said, "Taylor, could you come here for a minute?"

Taylor grabbed her piles of information, assuming he wanted to see where she stood, though she didn't have anything new. She realized she hadn't noticed the handsome guy leave, and sort of laughed at herself. Oh well. There were plenty of decent men out there, should she want to take the time to find them. Who was she kidding? She'd learned her lesson. She was married to the job now.

She was surprised to see the man sitting in front of the captain's desk, went on guard immediately. What the hell was this? Was he a lawyer? A new Internal Affairs transfer?

The man didn't make a move to greet her. He was staring at the floor with his shoulders slumped. His hair was standing on end, as if he had been running a comb soaked in egg whites through it to stiffen it into a modified Mohawk. He reached up with his right hand and scrubbed at his hair, leaving it even more disheveled. *That explains that*, she thought.

"Price?" She turned to her boss, the question lying heavily between them.

"Dr. John Baldwin, meet Lieutenant Taylor Jackson." He nodded toward the man, who gave her a brief, surprised glance and a grim smile. Taylor caught a glimpse of green eyes surrounded by impressively deep-set smudges, as if he hadn't slept in a week.

"Nice to meet you, Dr. John Baldwin. No offense, but who exactly are you?"

A deep baritone startled her. "A washed-up drunk who has no business being here." He stood, nodding at them both. "Thank you, Captain. I do appreciate the offer, but I think your case is in capable hands." He inclined slightly at the waist, and Taylor was taken aback yet again. Baldwin was at least six foot four, but so thin his clothes drooped from his shoulders as if on broken hangers. When he walked through the door she'd seen vestiges of what would have been, with a little TLC, a very good-looking man. Up close, he looked as if he'd been on a weeklong bender. She made his age as late forties.

"Whoa, Baldwin, sit back down." Price had come around from behind his desk and was ushering the man back into his seat. Baldwin didn't resist, but sat heavily, expelling a long sigh. He resumed his mournful glare at the linoleum.

"Taylor, Baldwin is with the FBI's Behavioral Science Unit. He…"

"Was," said the skeleton in the chair. "*Was* with the BSU. Get the details straight, Captain."

Price took a long look at Baldwin, then continued. "Dr. Baldwin worked with the BSU for many years, and has taken a leave of absence to pursue a few personal matters. I would like to see him act as a journeyman to your case, Taylor, in a consulting role. He has…"

"Had," came the flat voice.

"*Has* immeasurable experience in sexual murders. I believe he can be of help."

Taylor was swinging her head between the two men, confused. This Dr. Baldwin certainly didn't want to be here. What was Price up to, assigning her a babysitting job for some suit from the FBI? She opened her mouth to protest, but the captain interrupted.

"Dr. Baldwin, would you mind stepping out for a moment? I'd like to speak to Lieutenant Jackson privately. And don't leave. Please."

Baldwin sighed noisily. "I need caffeine. Soda machine in the hall? I'll help myself." Without waiting for an answer, he saw himself out of the office, shutting the door quietly behind him. He was quite sure Captain Price was going to fill Taylor in on all his dirty little secrets. Good. The details should seal the deal. She wouldn't want him on the case, and he could go back to his dank chair in the darkened living room and get on with, well, whatever.

He didn't know why he'd even bothered. Price's eyes weren't exactly accusing, more appraising, almost compassionate, but he'd felt them bore into him. That's how they would all be. Humoring him, but watching closely to see he didn't botch anything. *Screw it,* he thought. He'd rather have the judgment.

But his feet didn't follow his brain. He didn't leave. He got his soda, and for reasons he would never be able to understand, he went back into the squad room, sat at the nearest desk, and waited for Judgment Day.

23

Taylor sat in the newly vacant chair, fidgeting with her hair. "Price, who the hell was that?"

"That, my dear, was one of the most talented profilers the FBI has ever seen. The man's a legend, or was. MD from Johns Hopkins, double doctorates in psychology and criminology, a law degree, the best close rate in the business. There are rumors that he's psychic, if you like to believe that crap. But our good doctor has fallen on some hard times."

"That's an understatement. He looks like he's been out trolling Dickerson Road."

Price raised his eyebrows and sighed. "Yeah, well, as far as I know, he has been."

"Then what in the world is he doing *here*? He doesn't look like he could read a full file without landing face-first in it."

"He had a bad experience a few months ago. Pulled himself out of the field, then out of the Bureau altogether. He's been hermiting down here in Nashville for months. His boss was giving him some space, but thinks it's time for him to get his feet wet again."

Taylor was already shaking her head. "Not on *my* case. I don't need some middle-aged drunkard trailing around with us, getting in the way or stopping off for a drink while we do the work."

Price steepled his hands in front of him, elbows on the desk. "I understand your reservations, I do. But this is a special favor for an old friend. Baldwin's a good cop, and despite his current appearance, I can assure you he won't be a hindrance."

"You can assure me, huh? I'm not sure this is such a great idea, boss. Why doesn't he just go on back to Quantico and bury himself there?"

"He won't. They've been begging him for a while. He's done nothing but shut them out. Garrett Woods—my friend, his boss—thinks it's imperative he gets back on the horse, and he thinks doing it here as a consultant would be the best way to get him out of his funk."

"Funk? I'd be more inclined to label it clinical depression."

"You may be right. And if that's the case, working can only do him good. We're throwing him a lifeline here, Taylor. Don't think he doesn't know it. He may be a wreck, but he still has a bit of pride left. Give him the files and let him look them over. Encourage his ideas. I don't want you babysitting. We can toss him the life preserver, but if he won't hold on, it's not our fault. Got it?"

She huffed out a sigh in silent protest. "Got it." She grew quiet for a moment. "This doesn't have anything to do with the Martin case, does it? Oversight until the rest of them are on trial?"

Price looked at her in surprise. "No. Why would you think that?"

"I just didn't want there to be any confusion. In the squad, I mean."

Price gave her a gentle smile. "I understand. No, we can't have it look like you're being undermined in any way. Don't worry about it. I'll make sure everyone knows that this is a deal for me. No one will think he's being brought on to watch your back."

She waved the comments away, embarrassed to have even brought it up. One day, she'd stop thinking everyone, even those who'd been her biggest supporters, like Price, was holding the shooting against her.

"I was just asking. Forget I mentioned it."

"Taylor, I know things aren't easy for you right now. Just be secure in the knowledge you did the right thing. I wouldn't have you on my team if I didn't think you had."

Taylor blushed. It was amazing how Price could read her mind.

"Back to Baldwin—what is the problem that's driven him into this state?" she asked.

Price looked around the tiny office, trying to make a decision. Finally, he said, "Look, Taylor, I think that's going to be his story to tell you. He may or he may not, so I wouldn't push it."

"What about the boys? What am I supposed to tell them about this?"

"That we are honored to have one of the FBI's best on our side."

"Oh, come on, Price. You really want me to pretend in front of them? They'll pick it up quick enough that the guy's on the edge. They're cops— they've seen it before."

"Yeah, well, give them some credit. They've got softer hearts than you."

She forced out a smile. "Gee, thanks. Nicest compliment I'll get all week. Cold, heartless bitch, that's me."

"I can't imagine anything further from the truth."

"All right, I'll give this a shot. But I'm not promising anything."

"Good girl. I appreciate it."

"Sexist." She grinned at her boss, then left the office, wondering what had driven John Baldwin to her doorstep.

And what, exactly, he had been told about her.

24

Retrieving a Diet Coke, Taylor came back into the squad room to find the man in question sitting on the edge of her desk, his own soda in hand, looking slightly more awake than fifteen minutes prior. The rest of the detectives were giving him a wide berth, neither threatening nor welcoming. They looked at her with ill-concealed curiosity on their faces.

"Okay, pals, Fingerprints-R-Us is on the case." Her attempt at levity made Baldwin cringe, but she ignored it. He'd have to get used to it; they rolled hard on her team.

"This is Dr. John Baldwin, late of the BSU in grand ol' Quantico. He'll be joining us as a consultant to work the murders of Shelby Kincaid and Jordan Blake. Let's make him some room, get him briefed, and let him look over the files. Cool with you, Doctor?"

He shot her a look she couldn't quite define but didn't take as kindly. He took a deep breath and half smiled. "Please, everyone calls me Baldwin."

"Baldwin, then. Let's get you acquainted with

the rest of the team. Lincoln Ross, our resident computer geek. AFIS, ViCAP, CODIS, any database you want, he's your man." Lincoln nodded graciously.

"Pete Fitzgerald, forensics. He only answers to Fitz, isn't that right?"

"You got it. Welcome aboard." He stuck out a hand, smiled genially, but Taylor could see him coolly appraising their newest member.

"Marcus Wade, our rookie. He's only been with the team for a few months—he's still getting his feet wet."

Marcus smiled hugely. He was a good-looking kid, innocence and sensuality rolled into one. He could probably get information out of people no one else could. Charm and good looks could be disarming.

"I'm wet behind the ears, too. It's nice to meet you."

Baldwin felt odd being the center of attention. It had been a long time since so many people were staring at him as if he held the Rosetta stone in his hands. "It's good to meet you all. I promise not to be in the way."

Marcus suddenly lit up like a streetlamp at dusk. "Wait a sec. Are you *the* Dr. John Baldwin? The atypical sexual sadism guru? You worked the case in Virginia last year, the child killer who kidnapped and murdered six little girls, right?"

Taylor noticed Baldwin's briefly pained look. Her curiosity piqued; whatever happened to drive him away from Quantico must have been pretty bad. The profilers up there were tough as nails; they saw horrors she could only imagine. What had happened to this man? Was it something to do with the case Marcus had mentioned?

Baldwin tried a smile. "Yeah, I did. Pretty brutal stuff. It's good to meet you."

"Maybe we could talk about the case over lunch. I'll buy."

Taylor took pity on Baldwin. Marcus may have hated dead bodies, but he was fascinated with sexually motivated killings. Given half the chance, he would forget everything he needed to do and sequester Baldwin in an interview room to talk shop the rest of the day. She jumped in before Marcus could secure his date and start his interrogation.

"One thing at a time, puppy. Let's give Dr. Baldwin a little space to get started. Baldwin, tell me what you'll need to do your initial assessment."

Baldwin squared his shoulders. He didn't want to be here. Lieutenant Jackson was humoring him, but he had a headache, and he really wanted a beer. Meeting her oddly colored eyes, somewhere deep inside he felt a spark of pride stir. It may goeth before his fall, but he didn't want to embarrass himself in front of her, or the rest of her team.

"I'd like to start with the crime scene photos and the files you've compiled on each girl. I need the autopsy reports, and I'd like to speak to your ME a little later on. I assume you've run the databases. I'd like those results as well. If I could, I'd like a quiet place where I can look over the files. Alone, preferably. I'll need some mental space to come to any conclusions."

Taylor looked surprised but quickly covered it with a cough. If he was going to make an effort, she could try as well.

She gave the necessary directions. Baldwin was escorted to the conference room across the hall from the squad room. Taylor started to follow him in to get him settled, and he stopped her.

"I know you have questions about me, but I promise you, I'm going to stick close to home, read these over, give you an opinion, and be out of your hair. That should satisfy everyone involved, don't you think?"

Taylor saw nothing but pain in his green eyes, and something told her to keep trying. "How about this, Dr. Baldwin? You go over those files. See if you come up with anything interesting. Then we'll talk about your imminent dismissal. Okay?" She turned and shut the door behind her before he had a chance to respond.

"Great," he said to the blue wall. "Just fucking great. Fine, I'll look. I'll give them some suggestions, they can go track them down, and I'm out of here." He sat angrily at the table. He realized it was the first emotion he'd felt in months, but he pushed it to the back of his mind.

25

Baldwin ran his fingers through his hair, making the too-long strands spike like porcupine quills. He'd read the files on the dead girls twice, and didn't remember a word. He stood and wandered around the conference room, looking idly for something to play with. He found only a handful of paper clips and a tape dispenser. They'd cleaned out the cell of the condemned. Back at the table, he half smiled to the wall, picked up a clip and started prying the wire apart. When he finished, he picked up another, then another, until a ramshackle chain-link fence formed itself on the table in front of him.

Who was he trying to kid? He didn't have any business being here. Garrett and Price knew that, yet they were pushing him to come back to the land of the living, something he wasn't sure if he was willing to do. Yet here he was, files spread before him, two beautiful girls dead, and he had only the simplest curiosity about how they'd gotten there. In his old life, he would have already taken each word of each file apart, would have a sense of whom they were dealing with. He'd be formulating plans on how to stop the killer from striking again. Now, well…

He struck the table with his fist, scattering the barricade of paper clips all over the table. He impatiently brushed them aside, watching them scatter in random patterns on the floor. He stared, trying to find some clue in the metal outline, but saw nothing. An appropriate reaction for one whose mind was a jumbled blank.

He was out of practice.

With a sigh, he pulled the file of Jordan Blake toward him, and started again.

The door to the conference room opened, light spilling in from the hall. It was the woman, Jackson, the light haloing around her head. She looked like an avenging angel.

"Mr., ah, Dr. Baldwin? Fitz and I are getting something to eat. Would you like to join us? Samantha Owens, our ME, may come with the results of the tox screens on our two murdered girls. You said you'd like to meet her."

Baldwin glanced out the window, surprised to realize it was dark out. He'd been cloistered in this room all day with no break. Checking his watch, he saw it was past seven. In response, his stomach growled. He looked at Taylor sheepishly.

"Sorry, time got away from me. Are you sure it's cool if I join you?"

Taylor smiled. "Everyone has to eat. Besides, you look like you could use a square meal. We're going to Mulligan's Pub down on Second. Come on. A walk will do you good."

Baldwin considered for a moment. Why not? He had nothing better to do, and no place better to be.

"All right. If you're sure." He followed her out the door, then stopped and went back into his new office, grabbing the files and shoving them in his tattered leather backpack, shaking his head as he did. The case had its claws in him, and he didn't want to let it go so quickly. Nor did he want to leave his notes behind.

Taylor watched him closely. He was disheveled, his hair standing on end, unshaven, clothes wrinkled. He almost looked dangerous, and much more engaged than he had earlier. She was surprised to feel a moment of longing in her stomach. There was something about him that intrigued her. She'd spent all afternoon wondering what he was up to.

Stop that, she snapped to her mind. *You have enough problems of your own without taking on his, too.*

26

A traditional Irish green-and-gold sign framed the wooden doorway over Mulligan's Pub, holding the promise of the real deal. Quartered windowpanes gave it an inviting, homey look. Upon entering the warm, smoky foyer, there was dining to the left and a cozy bar situated straight ahead. A moth-eaten ibex, stuffed and smiling benevolently, presided over the deep walnut bar with a benign billy goat grin.

Celtic music played quietly. The weekends featured excellent live Irish music, boasted a loyal clientele braying drunkenly for their favorites and always finding succor in the generosity of the band. A plaque on the bar wall claimed the pub's distinction as the first bar in the state of Tennessee to pour a pint of Guinness draught.

Taylor and Baldwin arrived first. They'd walked to the restaurant in silence. She'd been at an unaccustomed loss for words, and the uneasy silence had enveloped them in a fog. After putting their name in for a table, they hit the bar for a beer. Taylor wondered for a moment if it was smart to let him drink, then decided she wasn't his mother. She didn't know how to approach the situation, anyway. They ordered, then she excused herself to go to the ladies' room to regroup.

She washed her hands and looked long and hard in the mirror. She wasn't happy with the face staring back at her. Her hair had come down from its ponytail. She quickly wrestled it back into place. She had dark circles under her eyes. Her face was pale. She looked like hell, but she felt worse. Maybe she *was* coming down with something. Maybe she just needed some sleep. She splashed some water on her face, dried off with a scratchy towel, and forced a smile at the wraith in the mirror. A little better.

Back at the bar, Baldwin had an empty pint glass in front of him, was started in on another.

She sat next to him. "Um, listen, Dr. Baldwin, take it easy, okay? We need to get our ducks in a row. This is a business dinner, and I need you clearheaded."

Baldwin squinted at her, drained the second pint, turned to the bartender and asked for a double Glenfiddich. Drink in hand, he turned toward her as if about to say something, then bit it off and looked away. He didn't taste the Scotch.

"Baldwin," she said, softly. "What's up?"

"Nothing. The lighting in here is nice. I haven't been here in years."

Taylor looked around and had to agree. The gas lanterns glowing softly over the brick and walnut were soothing, much more comfortable than the harsh lights they'd worked under all day. She imagined him sitting alone in the dark in an anonymous room and realized he probably hadn't been socializing very much. But she wasn't his keeper, and she didn't want to start anything.

The hostess signaled the table was ready. "Are you coming?" she asked.

"I'll just…get the tab."

Taylor sighed and turned away, leaving her errant charge behind with his Scotch. Fitz came in the door, flirted happily with the hostess while they assembled around the table. As Taylor and Fitz sat down, the door opened and Sam breezed through.

Taylor saw her friend come in and gave a jerk of her head toward Baldwin, who still stood at the bar. Sam gazed sharply toward him, spotted Baldwin leaning against the wooden counter and made a beeline for him.

"Hi. Sam Owens. I'm the ME." She stuck out her hand. Taylor could have sworn she saw Sam's eyelashes bat. She glowered at her. Sam returned the look with an innocent smile.

"Do you care to join us, or are you going to drown your sorrows at the bar while we watch and make bets on when you'll fall down?"

Baldwin's eyes went wide in shock, and he barked out a laugh of surprise.

Taylor stifled a giggle. Baldwin certainly wasn't aware of Sam's inability to use the smallest measure of tact.

"Sure, what the hell. I've got nothing better to

do." He signaled for another whisky, but Sam shook her head at the bartender and said loudly, "Water."

Taylor watched the exchange with interest. Baldwin was meekly following Sam to the table, looking distinctly uncomfortable and nursing his chilled glass. It looked like Sam may have tamed the beast.

Once settled with drinks and food ordered, Fitz sat back in his chair, rubbing his tummy. A hint of malice gleamed in his crooked smile. "So, Baldwin. You spent all day with the files. Got any answers yet?"

"I'm not really ready to talk about any of this. I mean, I haven't had enough time to formulate an opinion, and it would be best—"

Taylor cut him off. "Why don't we share some of our thoughts with Dr. Baldwin first, instead of putting him on the spot right out of the gate." She stared pointedly at her second. Fitz choked back his smile and assumed a more serious face.

"Oh, of course. Sounds good. Okay, Dr. Baldwin. Here's what we know. Got us a couple of dead lookers who happen to go to the same school. One's dumped in the Cumberland, one ceremoniously placed at the Parthenon. Both were raped and scattered with herbs. You following, *Doctor*, or do I need to use smaller words?"

Taylor leaned back in her chair, crossed her arms over her chest, and cleared her throat. "Fitz," she grumbled, the name coming out as a distinct word of warning, but Baldwin rose to the bait alarmingly fast.

"Sounds like you've got it all figured out, *De-*

tective. You really don't need me for this. I'll just head on home now. Here you go." He reached under the table for his backpack and pulled out the files, tossed them on the table. The contents spilled everywhere. Baldwin stalked out the door.

Taylor didn't try to follow him. She raised a hand to Sam, who was rising from her chair, and shook her head. Sam sat back down, puzzled.

"Why'd you let him run out of here like that?"

"Don't look at me. Fitz is the one who chased him off."

"Didn't take much, did it?"

Sam shook her head. "I can't believe you two. What is this, some sort of club initiation, and he failed?"

"No," Taylor said. "Dr. Baldwin has some demons. He'll have to put them to bed if he wants in on this case. I told the captain I'd play ball but I wasn't going to babysit. If Baldwin wants to, he'll be back."

Sam was still glaring at Taylor.

"All right, all right. Fitz, that wasn't very nice of you. Behave next time you see him. If we ever see him again. In the meantime, Sam, can I have a bite of your stew?" Taylor had already speared a piece of beef.

"Yes, you can have my dinner. What demons does Baldwin have?"

Fitz eyed Taylor, who nodded imperceptibly. "News reports say the doc got a few of his men killed on an operation up in Virginia. Nasty case, child murderer. They went in with a warrant, and the guy came out shooting. Caught three feebies before Baldwin took him out."

Sam had stopped eating and glanced sideways at Taylor, who hadn't moved. "Well, we all know it can happen. If he's really messed up about it, who are we to judge? *Right*, T?"

Taylor sighed deeply and ignored the jab. "No one's judging. And that's not the end of the story. After they cleaned up the mess, another girl was taken and killed. He'd pegged the wrong guy, and they lost three men needlessly. So yeah, I can understand. Probably not enough, though." She resumed eating Sam's stew.

They were all quiet while they finished their meals. Fitz gallantly asked for and paid the check. He bid them a good-night and left the two women to their conversation.

Taylor leaned her chair back on two legs and put her arms behind her head. She knew what was coming.

"I expect better of you two. The man was clearly hurting, and you pushed him away. Now what are you going to do?"

"Sam. That man is well beyond any help I could give. And what do you mean, what am *I* going to do? I'm not doing anything. He's not my responsibility."

"Not your responsibility? Price asked you to bring him on the team, didn't he? You're the team's leader, aren't you? You sound pretty responsible to me. And you've both been through similar incidents."

"It's not the same thing."

"Oh, bullshit, Taylor. You've been dragging around enough guilt for ten men. You have more in common with Baldwin than you think."

"Sam, knock it off, okay? I don't have time to get into someone else's nightmares right now. We've got a nasty killer out there that I'd like to catch. By the way, did you get any more info on the girls' tox screens?"

"Not yet, but you'll be the first to know. Simon said they'll be back to me tonight. I'll call you as soon as I have them. And no, I won't knock it off. It's time you got back to your life. It wasn't your fault you had to shoot Martin. He attacked you, for Christ's sake. It's not like you were in love with the guy—"

"That's enough!" Taylor was flushed and angry. She didn't have time to rehash her own nightmares either, and she didn't like it when Sam preached at her. She rose and put on her coat.

"I'm going home. Call me if you hear anything."

Sam's phone rang. She held up a finger. "Hold on. Let me get this first." She put the phone to her ear. "Sam Owens… Yeah… Mmm-hmm… You're kidding… Really? That's great, thanks so much. I'll call you back in the morning."

Taylor had her arms crossed on her chest, breathing heavily through her nose. "What is it?"

Sam raised an eyebrow. "You may change your tune about talking with Dr. Baldwin when you hear this."

27

"Garrett, I'm out. These Nashville people don't need me—they know what they're doing. Please, just...don't call me again."

Baldwin hung up on his former boss's voice mail. He threw the phone toward the couch, where it bounced off and lay prone on the floor. He'd been fuming around his house for the past hour. He was as pissed at himself as he was at the damn homicide team. He knew Fitz had been baiting him, trying to see if he could be taken seriously. He'd shown them, with no questions, he couldn't. He was even more furious with himself that he gave a crap.

He reached for another beer and started to gulp. He finished in record time, even for him, the now-professional drinker. He stared at the bottle, willing it to fill itself so he could just drown in it. It didn't. He threw it across the room, satisfied when it shattered against the wall.

He felt the familiar calm sweep over him. He luxuriated in it. This wasn't drunkenness; it was the finishing point. He'd felt it before, and knew what he needed to do.

He went back to the bedroom. His gun was on the nightstand, right where he'd left it. He picked it up, caressing the steel. Having it in his hand made him feel better, calmer. He'd made this decision before, when he started the game. He'd always given fate a little room for chance. Now he was acting on sheer, reckless bravado. He would no longer allow himself to be steered off course.

He walked with purpose back to the living room. He tidied up a bit, but left the broken shards where they were. Looking at them helped his tranquility; knowing he might be scattered carelessly over the wall above them gave him comfort.

Baldwin sat in his favorite chair, and didn't waste any time. Tonight would be different; he could just feel it. He checked the speed loader to make sure the bullet was in place, leaned back, and gave the cylinder a vicious spin.

Put the gun to his head.

Pulled the trigger at the very same moment someone started knocking on his door. The noise startled him, and the gun jerked. A bullet flew out of the two-inch barrel of the Smith and Wesson at full velocity, grazing his cheek. He heard shouting and thought he recognized the voice. God, was that Taylor Jackson? What in the hell was she doing here?

His door crashed open, and the homicide lieutenant flew into the room with her weapon drawn, looking around wildly.

Baldwin drew down on her purely by instinct. A worthless move on his part, considering the solitary Winchester .38 bullet that had lived in his gun for the past few weeks was now lodged in the wall of his living room. They faced each other, guns sighted point-blank between the other's eyes.

Taylor was the first to flinch. She slowly holstered her weapon, never letting her gaze stray from Baldwin's face.

"Why don't you put the gun down, Baldwin?" she said softly. "I'm not here to shoot you. Or to get shot. Come on, put it away. Christ, you're bleeding." She started toward him, still mindful of the gun trained at her head.

Baldwin started laughing. Taylor was caught short, then smiled cautiously. He lowered the weapon, and she quickly took it from his hand and tossed it into the kitchen. He was doubled over by now, hysterical with laughter.

"Baldwin, I think we need to get you to a hospital. You're bleeding badly."

He hiccuped, still snorting with mirth. "No, Taylor. No hospital. What in the name of all that's holy are you doing here?" He was calming down, but still held his sides as if he would explode.

"I wanted your opinion on something. And I wanted to apologize. We treated you badly today, and I'm sorry." Her gaze took in the room, noting the disarray, the broken bottle, the phone lying askew on the floor. Her eyes trailed to his face. "Really, Baldwin, you're bleeding. Let me fix it up for you."

"Leave it." His voice was sharp, and Taylor froze four feet from him. He turned toward the kitchen, then spun back and landed awkwardly on the couch. Taylor could see exhaustion shadow his face. She dared a step, and another, then sat quietly in the chair, looking at the fireplace while he composed himself. Damn, she had barely gotten here in time. Maybe she hadn't been in time at all; she didn't think a quick chat was going to change the man's mind. She decided to try anyway.

"You wanna tell me why I saw you through the window with a gun to your head?"

Baldwin shook his head, smiling at her. "Seems I just can't win. I've been working this little project for a while now, and I keep getting interrupted." He leaned back into the couch, covering his eyes with his crossed arms. "Every time I'm all set and ready, the fucking phone rings, or someone knocks. Really, Taylor, it would have been better if you'd come five minutes later. You'd have assumed I wasn't home, and seeing as the shot went off this time, I'd be out of this hell."

This time. Oh boy. She knew she'd have a job in front of her with Baldwin, just didn't realize it would entail dragging him out of the jaws of Cerberus. She was shocked to see tears roll down his face.

"I'm kinda glad I showed up when I did. You'd have been a hell of a mess to clean up." Her tone was light, but the look she gave him wasn't.

"Well, thanks, I guess." He gave her the first genuine smile she'd seen since she met him that morning. God, it had only been a day, but she felt as if he'd been under her skin forever. She let out her breath, suddenly aware that she had been holding it.

She gave him a small smile back. "Seriously, let me clean you up a little bit."

He brushed a big hand across his face, clearly embarrassed. "No, let it be. I'm fine. I want to know why you really came over here."

He was staring at her so intently that she felt a shiver run down her spine. "To be honest, Sam had some news at dinner I thought you might be interested in. Some results came back from the tests on Shelby Kincaid and Jordan Blake."

Baldwin looked at her with doubt. "And why do you think I'd be interested in any of it? I quit tonight, remember?"

"You can't quit something you never started." She was surprised at how bitter she sounded. Not exactly the tone to be taking with someone who looked as though he had been prepared to kill himself a half hour prior. "I mean..."

Baldwin's face had hardened. "I know what you mean, Taylor. You're right. I didn't want to be there, I didn't want to work this case, and I certainly don't intend to start now. Why don't you take your do-gooding ass out of here?" He got up quickly and headed for the bedroom.

Taylor didn't hesitate, ran after him, heart pounding. If he had a second weapon in there and was intent on finishing the job...

But Baldwin had only gone in the bathroom and opened the medicine cabinet. She let out a breath. Good. If he was going to tend his wound, he wouldn't be trying to shoot himself at the same time.

"Baldwin, I…"

"I thought I told you to leave," he said, not turning from the mirror, where he was gingerly dabbing alcohol on his cheek. "Damn," he hissed.

"Come on, man, let me do that." Taylor pushed her way into the bathroom and grabbed the cotton before he could resist. She felt all the fight go out of him as he slumped against the counter. He didn't resist when she finished cleaning the cut, pulled out a bandage, and gingerly placed it over the wound. On impulse, without thinking, she reached in and kissed it.

Baldwin jumped and grabbed her wrists. "What did you do that for?"

Taylor was at a loss for words. She mumbled something and backed away. He let her go.

Baldwin turned and stared in the mirror. He shook his head, snapped off the light, and followed Taylor's trail. He could hear her in the kitchen, messing with ice. He sat on the couch and said nothing.

She came out of the kitchen with an improvised ice pack. She handed it to him with a shrug. He took it and set it carefully on his face. The cut was starting to throb. Taylor stood with her arms crossed, looking at him as if he were a ticking bomb that would go off at any moment. He met her eyes and gave her a weak smile.

"There's Advil in the cabinet next to the refrigerator. Will you get me four?"

Taylor nodded. She needed to get out from under that gaze. She took her time finding the pills. She didn't know what the hell she was doing, but as long as it kept the gun out of his hand, she'd keep doing it. She spied the revolver under the kitchen table. Picking it up gingerly, she checked the chambers, found them empty, and stuffed the gun in the back of her jeans.

Baldwin's eyes were closed when she came back in the room. She thought maybe he'd gone to sleep, but jumped when his deep voice softly rumbled, "Thanks."

"Sure." She got the feeling he was thanking her for more than the painkiller. She handed them to him and backed away again, stationing herself against the mantel of the fireplace.

"You can't understand," he said. "You've never been in a place like this. A place with no hope."

"Yes, I have."

Baldwin's eyes shot open, and he saw her staring at the marble inlay at the base of the hearth. He felt the sadness radiate from her. He started to ask, stopped himself. He didn't like to talk about his demons; he couldn't imagine she would either. He was surprised when she answered the unspoken question.

"I shot a fellow detective a few months ago. Killed him. Let's leave it at that for now, okay? So yeah, I've been there. It's not a nice place to be.

Besides, I don't think talking about *my* problems will help you right now."

Baldwin was intrigued, but didn't push it. His natural inclination was to fall back onto his training and try to draw her out, but he laughed instead.

"Sure thing. Neutral ground then. What was so important to bring you over here at midnight to interrupt all my grand plans?"

Taylor was suddenly serious, all business. A spark flashed in her eyes, and she grinned.

"Aconite."

28

Baldwin sat up in surprise, wincing as the ice pack smacked hard against his cheek. He leaned back slowly. "Aconite? They were poisoned with aconite?"

Taylor was happy to see she'd captured his interest, the investigator in him coming to life. At least for the time being.

"Yep. Sam noticed that the panels for both girls showed a high level of alkaloids in both the kidneys and liver. She had her buddy test for poisons, and aconite showed up in lethal doses. Some way to go, huh?"

"What exactly does aconite do to the system?"

"That's the bad part. According to Sam's crash course, it's a central nervous system depressant. Vomiting, flushing, blurred vision, dry mouth, lowered body temperature. Severe burning sensation in the mouth—tongue, lips, and throat. Also causes paralysis and intense pain. Could have taken up to six hours to die. It's not a pleasant death.

"Sam also confirmed Jordan had the same herbs

scattered on her body as Shelby and got an ID on them. It's a real mishmash." Taylor pulled her notebook out of her coat pocket.

Baldwin realized she still wore her suede coat, and figured she must be getting hot. "Take off your coat and stay awhile?"

"Ha." She hesitated a moment, then shrugged out of the coat, tossed it on the back of the chair, and sat down, reading off the list.

"Rosemary, sage, sandalwood, basil, pennyroyal, bay, white sage, anise, chamomile, clove, fennel, and lavender. All can be grown in the garden, or bought in a million places."

"And the aconite? Can it be grown or bought?"

"Both. Sam had one of her guys pull it up on the internet. There are a billion websites that sell it, and it can be grown in someone's backyard."

"So perhaps we're dealing with a gardener of some sort."

"Sam also found that there are specific uses for all of these herbs. The Wicca websites give a lot of information on what to use when, for ceremonies, celebrations, holidays, burials." Taylor used the last word lightly.

Baldwin raised an eyebrow. "Wiccan burial rites, huh? Or it could be some kind of cult. Herbs and poisons. Think finding the girl at the Parthenon has anything to do with this?"

"Oh yeah, definitely. We're going to have to do some in-depth research on the uses of the poison, see if there's anything that ties it to the locale. I don't know what the relationship is, but it's too kooky not to be a part of the pattern."

"And Jordan had the poison in her system, too?"

"Yes. Her COD was the stab wounds to her heart, but she'd ingested the aconite prior to the kill shot."

"Maybe it didn't work quickly enough and he stabbed her to finish her off?"

"Could be."

"So where do you go from here?"

Taylor eyed him coolly. "I don't know, Baldwin. That's why I came over here tonight. I thought maybe you'd seen this kind of stuff before, because I sure haven't. Thought maybe you'd like to help us find out what it all means. Help us find this asshole before he kills another girl."

Baldwin was looking into space. "Sacrificing. Not killing. He's sacrificing them. The question is, why?"

Ah, she had him. She knew that look. Anyone who got a theory, a glimmer of an idea, got that spaced-out look of being lost in his or her own mind. She'd been like that enough times herself to recognize the cause. She decided to take the chance.

"So, are you in?"

Baldwin shook his head. "Huh?"

"I said, are you in?"

Baldwin tried to look her in the eye, but failed. This woman had witnessed the most desperate act of his life, and in essence, saved him from himself. Would he be able to work with her day after day to find a madman? Would she be able to work with him, knowing he wasn't altogether stable?

He dragged his eyes back to hers.

"I'm in."

29

Taylor was reluctant to leave Baldwin alone, but she knew he needed some time to process what had happened over the past few hours. She'd laid out a few ground rules, including not playing Russian Roulette until the investigation was closed, which he snickered at but nodded gravely in agreement. She had cautiously offered the name of a good friend who happened to be a psychotherapist, and was shocked when Baldwin hadn't brushed her off. He hadn't jumped up, shouted for joy, and demanded the number to make an appointment on the spot, but at least he had taken the suggestion. She left her friend's number on his kitchen counter. The next steps were up to him.

She pulled into her driveway and was amused to see a little face staring out the window, eyes in slits of bliss at the sight of her mommy finally making it home for the night.

She turned the key in the lock and could hear the disgruntled mewing from outside. She pushed open the door and laughed when the cat flipped onto her back, desperately begging for a tummy rub. Taylor was only too happy to oblige.

"There's my little baby. I'm so sorry I had to leave you for so long. Were you lonely? Did you miss your mommy?" She'd long since given up feeling embarrassed about talking baby talk to a cat. She rubbed and scratched the cat's ears and was rewarded with a long, rumbling purr, then a quick nip on the top of the hand as a reminder not to do it again.

"Ouch, brat, that hurt." Taylor stood up, sucking the tiny puncture on her hand. "Fine then, see if you get any loving. Interesting day today, though? Did you have any visitors? Did Greg the bunny come see you?" A rabbit had taken up residence on the side of the house, and came to feast on the bird food scattered on the ground in front of Jade's favorite window. "Maybe we should put out some food for him in the morning."

Taylor wandered into the kitchen, grabbed a Diet Coke from the refrigerator, and made her way back to the couch. She picked up the remote and put it down. She wasn't in the mood to surf for an old movie or other distraction. She was thinking about Baldwin.

Jade followed her to the couch, jumped up into her lap, kneading her way to Taylor's shoulder, where she settled in with her nose pressed into her neck.

"Oh, sweetie, that tickles." She stroked the cat, lost in thought. "You know, John Baldwin is a com-

plete mess." The purr in response was the only en-
couragement she needed.

"He's as screwed up as I am. He lost three of
his men and feels totally responsible. He may be,
for all I know. But wow, he's on the edge. I found
him getting ready to shoot himself tonight. I can
identify with that. I mean, there were a few times
there when I didn't think I was going to make it."
The feelings she'd been bottling up all night over-
came her, and she choked back a sob, her shoulders starting to shake. Jade didn't seem to mind,
and kneaded a little more, settling in closer, giving her a hug. Taylor squeezed back, trying to get
herself under control.

She took a deep breath, holding it for a count
of thirty then letting it out slowly. It was a trick
her therapist had taught her, and it did work. She
felt much calmer when she let it out. She thought
she had finished the self-flagellation. She had been
cleared in David's death. Been put back to work.
She'd dealt with the looks, the whispers. Went on
with her life with a small empty spot gnawing quietly at her heart.

"Baldwin seems like a decent man. He could be
handsome if he got himself back together. I'm telling you, cat, I may be in the business of saving people, but I really didn't know what to do when I saw
him with that gun. I just reacted, like I would do
with anyone I found like that. It seemed to work—I
think he may be okay. But it scared me."

Jade gave Taylor one of those unnerving stares,

holding the eye contact until Taylor scratched her on the nose and she settled back in.

"Yeah, you're right. Maybe I want him to be okay. Sam seems to like him, and she's a pretty good judge of character. We'll see." She shrugged, too hard, and the cat dug in her back claws and leapt off her shoulder.

"Damn, girl, why do you do that?" Taylor peeled back her shirt and saw the long scratches on the top of her arm. "I swear, you do that again…"

Jade sat calmly on the rug, washing her front paw. Confession time was over. "Fine." Taylor drained the Diet Coke. "I'm going to bed."

Exhaustion hit her like a brick as soon as the word *bed* came out of her mouth. She made her way up the stairs with Jade galloping ahead of her, sounding like an elephant on a tear. She made it to her bedroom and to the bed, lying down fully clothed, and was asleep within minutes, a purring bundle of fur curled up behind her legs.

THE

FOURTH

DAY

30

Taylor was dreaming again. She knew it was a dream this time, but couldn't drag herself out of it. It wasn't exactly the same dream; it was a more tailored nightmare. Only the worst parts replayed themselves: the yelling, the heat of the bullet as it flew, the look of absolute shock on her face when she realized whom she had killed. It replayed slowly, inexorably, as all tragedies do. She could see every detail as if it hadn't been dark. The tiny spot of blood from a shaving cut mingling with the blood pouring out of his head, the gel he applied to the cowlick on his forehead making each strand of hair glow and shine, the blue fleck entrenched in the brown of his right eye. And then it all sped up, and she was standing over him, the cold steel smoking, a smile on her face.

She woke with a start, tears wet on her cheeks yet unable to open her eyes, her brain lingering on the final scene. It was different this time. Before, she'd never been able to stop before she died along with him. She didn't feel the gut-wrenching pain that usually accompanied the dream. In fact, she felt almost peaceful. She concentrated for a moment, trying to relive the last moments. She could have sworn she'd heard a word just before she came to, but her rapidly awakening neurons forced it away, and the word slipped from her grasp as quickly as it came.

Taylor opened her eyes to the sun streaming through the window. Jade was still zonked out at the foot of the bed, a surprise. Usually when she had the dream the cat was right next to her face, her piercing emerald eyes full of concern, as if she shared in her pain. She mustn't have shouted out this time.

She got up, peeled yesterday's clothes off, and jumped into the shower. While she washed her hair she tried to recall the element of the dream that had changed, but still couldn't put it into words. She gave up, finished her shower, dried and dressed and headed to the kitchen, the thought of a fizzy jolt of Diet Coke pushing everything else out of her mind.

31

Baldwin hadn't slept, but the constant nagging voice in the back of his mind had blessedly shut up. He wasn't sure what was going on. Eight hours before he'd been loaded and cocked, recklessly imbuing fate with chance. Now he felt a strange sort of hope, almost as if he had absolved himself of something.

After Taylor left, he'd sat in the dark the rest of the night, thoughts turning, cascading waterfalls of feelings through his head. None made much sense, but when the sun came up, he was determined to help Taylor Jackson.

He arrived at the station before she did, felt a vague sense of disappointment. He shook it off, got buzzed in through the back door, helped himself to a soda, and sat down at Taylor's desk in the squad room. He caught the curious glances from the night shift as they bundled up and went to live their lives for the day, and was sure the word had gone out the lunatic ex-agent was on the grounds.

You're being paranoid, Baldwin. Stop it.

Ringing chatter came down the hall as Taylor and Fitz shared insults to begin their day. They entered the room laughing hard, and Baldwin was surprised to realize he wanted in on the joke. But they stopped when they saw him, the mood sobered. Taylor greeted him warmly. Fitz stood to the side, still eyeing Baldwin as if he smelled like a piece of moldy Limburger cheese. He chose to ignore him.

"Morning, Taylor." He saw her eyeing him, could see the thoughts running through her head. Yes, he was still in one piece. Yes, he had made it in to help them work the case. No, he didn't look all that great, but at least he was still with them. He subconsciously touched the bandage on his cheek and gingerly gave her a smile.

"And to you, Baldwin. I trust you slept well?" He was taken aback. He'd assumed his actions of the night before had been duly reported, but it looked as though she hadn't filled Fitz in at all.

"Like the dead." He was rewarded with an ear-splitting grin. He laughed, feeling the tension in the room melt away. A brief glance at Fitz brought it all back.

"So, Baldwin, Taylor told you about the poison?"

"Yes, she did. I'm anxious to hear more."

"Ain't we all, son. Taylor, where's Sam?"

A voice rang out from the hallway. "Right behind you, old man."

Fitz jumped, then turned and bear-hugged the ME. He drew her off the ground and swung her around, outwardly annoying her to no end, but

Baldwin could tell it was just an act. Again the feeling of being an outsider crept in, and he looked away. This was more than just a team of cops, they were a close-knit family. He hadn't felt as if he belonged to a family for a very long time.

"Damn it, Fitz, put me down. You're gonna make me hurl my sausage biscuit all over you."

He obliged and backed away, smiling. "Don't you go doing that now, sugar! We can't have the ME puking all over the squad room this early in the mornin'. Might start a few rumors, ya know what I mean?"

Sam guffawed. "Very funny, Fitz. Taylor, help me."

"Oh no, Sam, looks like you're the one who opened that door."

"Gee, thanks. Some friend you are." She turned to Baldwin. "Dr. Baldwin," she sang out gaily, "you look like crap."

"Thank you. I think."

"Don't mention it. Taylor, where's Lincoln? I asked him to do some research on aconite for me."

"I don't know where he is. Probably up to his ears in ViCAP. I'll go hunt him down." She left the room, and Baldwin felt distinctly uncomfortable again. Taylor was his link into this group, however tenuous that might be. He only had his intellect to go on, and he suddenly wanted to prove himself to these people.

You're insane, they don't care, why are you bothering? But when Sam looked him up and down and said, "Baldwin, who looks like crap, care to give your thoughts on our little case?" he settled down and waded in. He couldn't help himself; Sam's enthusiasm was infectious.

"The aconite is one of the strangest things I've ever seen. It is a very uncommon poison in the criminal canon. Plus, poisoning homicides are usually perpetrated by women, which doesn't fit, since obviously Jordan and Shelby were with a man before their deaths. Because of this, we can't rule out a team, though I'm inclined to think we're dealing with a sophisticated male suspect."

"Go on," Fitz said.

"Jordan's murder seems like overkill to me. She'd already ingested the poison. The killer intended for her to die in the same fashion as Shelby. To stab her after the fact was violent, personal. I'd guess she pissed him off after he gave her the poison, mouthing off, perhaps, maybe even trying to escape. He needed to stop her, grabbed the knife and started swinging. It would explain the differences in the way the bodies were discovered as well. He was furious with Jordan, so he discarded her, tossed her in the river like a piece of trash.

"On the other hand, Shelby was treated with respect. She was loved, revered. Given an honorable burial in his mind. Scattered with herbs... I think we may be looking at some sort of ritual, maybe even an offbeat religious faction. The aconite itself strikes me as almost cultish."

Sam and Fitz were paying total attention to him now. "What doesn't fit is the herbs Sam found on Jordan," Fitz said.

"Right. Even though he killed her in a rage, he took a moment to throw some herbs on her body before he cut her loose. Conscience got the better of him, maybe? The herbs are definitely important to him. It has to be part of his ritual. They aren't a clue left for us—there was a good chance the wind or the water would wash the herbs away before we got to the body. They're strictly a device for his own peace of mind. And then we have the aconite angle, which is also quite odd."

"You can say that again." Lincoln and Taylor came back into the room, arms loaded with a stack of papers half a foot high.

Taylor was shaking her head. "You're going to love this. There's some really weird stuff out there relating to aconite. Witches and warlocks and pagans. It's on all the lists of poisonous plants on every botanical website. It's an alkaloid and will kill you pretty darn quick, but the homeopathic sites list medical uses for it. The Chinese use it for pneumonia and rheumatism. There's a well-documented history of its use through medieval times, and it was used in Greek and Celtic practices and pagan burial rites. You can get it anywhere, too. The homeopathic websites actually sell it."

Lincoln jumped in. "Here's more fun stuff. According to some of the sites I accessed, aconite was often mixed with belladonna, which produced a kind of delirium akin to flying. Pliny the Elder sanctioned its use for euthanasia. When he wrote *The Natural History*, he gives a whole history of the squabbles of the Roman emperors and their families. They used aconite to get rid of enemies of the state. The Romans used aconite to poison rivals because accusations of murder by poison were incredibly hard to prove. You could get it from any drug peddler on the street, hence the custom of the royals having food tasters. I can go on and on—there's a ton of stuff out there—but I also came across one interesting tidbit on one of the Wicca sites. Aconite's magical properties include protection and invisibility."

Baldwin was intrigued. "Protection and invisibility. Huh. I like the protection angle. Maybe this guy thinks he's shielding these women from something? Then he scatters them with burial herbs to complete the ritual. Interesting. Toss the Parthenon as a dump site in there, and we've got ourselves a real throwback to the ancients."

Taylor took a seat next to Baldwin. "We could trace all the purchases of aconite over the past month, but I don't think it will do any good. It can be grown in a garden in the backyard." She consulted one of the sheets. "'An absolute must for every witch's garden.' It would be a waste of time looking for the source. We'll have to trace the killer through the evidence we have, and take Jordan's and Shelby's lives apart. There has to be some connection between the two besides Vanderbilt. I don't think this guy just spotted them on the street and decided to grab them. Something in my gut tells me this was planned, that they were chosen for a reason. We just have to figure out what the reason is."

"I think you're right, Taylor. The organization

of the scene at the Parthenon shows quite a bit of thought. If we were talking a normal serial killer, one who escalates in violence, the poisoning would come before the stabbing, instead of the other way around." Baldwin ran his hands through his hair, a gesture Taylor was starting to recognize. "But I don't think we're dealing with any kind of serial or series killer who would fit a standard profile. Stabbing and poison as MOs are very different pathologies, and these deaths aren't indiscriminate. We're dealing with a man with a purpose, a reason. Whether he's sending us a message or doing it for himself is the puzzle. Unlike the usual killer who stages a crime scene, I'm willing to bet our involvement is secondary to his primary goal. In other words, he's not leaving them for us to find. He isn't showing off."

The group digested this idea, and Taylor was the first to speak. "Okay, where do we start?"

"You have the files on the girls from the university? Let's start there. There has to be an overlap between these two girls. It's a liberal arts school, so there has to be a curriculum they have to follow before they declare a major. Let's go back through their records and start looking at any classes they may have had in common."

Taylor started giving assignments. "Lincoln, get back online and see if you can find anything else on the aconite. Toss in the herbs, the Parthenon, anything you think could be related. Baldwin and I are going to start working through the records."

The phone rang on Fitz's desk, and he answered

it gruffly. "Homicide… Yeah… Shit." He banged the phone down and started rubbing the lower half of his face.

"What's the matter, Fitz? You look like you've seen a ghost. Is everything okay?" Taylor looked spooked. There was something in Fitz's eyes that was freaking her out.

"That was Missing Persons. They just got a report of a girl named Jill Gates, who's been missing for the past few days."

Taylor sat down slowly. "Spit it out, Fitz."

"She's a student at Vanderbilt."

32

The flurry of activity died down as the news sank in. Two dead, another missing. Taylor sat with her head in her hands, and Baldwin tried not to show how shaken he felt. This suspect was moving too damn quick for them to get the slightest idea of what he was trying to do.

Taylor stood, shaking her head. "I need a smoke," she said to no one in particular. Everyone watched her stalk out. Baldwin half rose in his chair, indecisiveness painted all over his face. He looked to Fitz first, almost asking his permission to try and reach out to Taylor. Fitz nodded imperceptibly. Baldwin gave a relieved sigh and headed out to the landing where he had seen all the cigarette butts.

What the hell are you doing, man? He barely knew Taylor, but for some reason felt protective of her. Even through his own pain he could see she was suffering, and he felt it was more than just this case. From her simple statement last night, telling him she'd shot a fellow detective, he assumed it was a case gone south, but perhaps there was more. He'd overheard Fitz and Marcus talking in the hall yesterday, caught Taylor's name, but they'd clammed up the moment they realized he'd walked up to them. Something was up; both men looked earnest and concerned, but they had switched gears and welcomed him, asking if he wanted coffee or anything. He'd refused and continued down the hall, curiosity draping him in its mantle.

He let himself out of the door quietly, as if she wouldn't notice the beep on the lock as it disengaged. Taylor didn't turn, just shifted her weight to her other foot. He didn't know what to say, but she took care of that.

"What's up, Baldwin?" she asked. He didn't know how she knew it was him, but was grateful she had initiated the conversation.

"I had a feeling you might want to talk."

She whirled around, and he could see she had been crying; her nose was red and her eyes puffy. He felt a pang of relief. This gorgeous woman wasn't perfect; she looked like hell when she cried.

"Talk about what? That this case is getting to me? That I'm feeling overwhelmed and pissed and utterly incapable of stopping this predator? That I'm having panic—"

She stopped herself, and Baldwin realized she must feel she was letting way too much information out. He didn't blame her. He was a stranger to her. But she'd said enough to let him know she was in pain, and it broke something inside him. He just wanted to reach out and help.

With a last deep inhale, she flipped the half-smoked cigarette out in the street and pushed past him to the door. Baldwin reached out and grabbed her hand.

"Don't, Taylor. Talk to me."

She gave him a puzzled look. "What do you want me to say? I don't know you, Baldwin. I don't know if I want to. Every time I look at you I get the feeling…ahh, screw it. I don't need this right now." Yet she didn't move to grab her passkey. Baldwin seized the moment, spoke quietly, still holding her hand.

"Taylor, circumstance has brought us together in a pretty bizarre way. A couple of days ago, I was willing to be gone from this world, and the next thing I know I'm working a case with a bunch of people who would probably prefer I head back to Virginia and leave them alone. I can't get a handle on what's happening either. Maybe I'm running from my own problems by trying to help you with yours. I don't know. I don't know anything anymore. But I'm here for you if you want me."

"You're here for *me*?"

He could see he'd said the wrong thing. Her eyes were blazing, her face suddenly transformed into anger. He locked in on her eyes, and felt himself lost in her internal storm. *They are the most peculiar shade of gray*, he thought to himself. They looked just like the storm clouds that had been rolling through the sky for the past few days. He heard her voice from a distance, and drew himself out of his momentary trance.

"What do you think you can do, *Dr*. Baldwin?"

The sarcasm was biting, and he involuntarily winced. "You think you can ride in here on your white horse and make everything right? You can't. There are some things you have no idea about, and my life is on the top of the list." She whipped her hand out of his and drew the passkey through the lock. The door almost struck him as a gust of wind blew it back on its hinges. He watched Taylor stalk down the hall, shoulders straight, back strong.

He smiled ruefully to himself, and looking back over his shoulder at the sky turning black, he whispered, "My white horse? You were the first one in the saddle."

33

Father Francis Xavier was tired. He'd been hearing confessions for the past three hours, absolving his flock of their daily sins. A mundane bunch today: The most heinous thing he'd heard was from a young woman having lustful thoughts for her boyfriend. At least she'd come to confession. In this day and age, the modernization of the Church sometimes seemed to undermine the very morality its young members were taught to practice. He doubted he'd made much of an impression. He'd probably hear from the same girl next week, asking forgiveness for going through with the act. Oh well. He was doing the best he could.

He emerged from the confessional, stretching his tired back and deciding what to do for dinner. He removed his stole as he walked toward his office. He was expecting a student from Aquinas, Mary Margaret de Rossi, for a quick tea and chat in an hour. Maybe he'd convince her to head up to Starbucks and have some coffee instead. It would be quiet enough to talk and maybe cover some of her Latin language work. He had been tutoring her for several weeks. Her enthusiasm to learn the dead language heartened his soul, and he was thrilled that his young friend wanted to understand more of the ways of the Church. After coffee, he could pick something up on his way home, or run through the buffet line at Belle Meade Cafeteria, get a real meal. *One advantage to living in the South*, he thought wryly. *Meat and threes.*

As he turned the corner into the hallway to the administrative offices, he caught a movement out of the corner of his eye. A man had entered the church and was making a beeline for the confessionals.

"Sir, I'm done for the day. I'll be hearing confessions again tomorrow morning at ten. I'd be happy to hear your confession then."

But the man ignored him and ducked into the rosewood box, quickly shutting the door behind him. Father Xavier sighed. Perhaps the man hadn't heard him. He made his way back to the confessionals, slipped into his side, and repeated his statement. There was no sound from the other side of the box.

"My son?" he asked.

"You will hear my confession now, Father. I have no time left."

The voice was low, so soft that Father Xavier could barely hear him. There was something in the tone that scared him. He felt a chill snake down his spine. He sat down, draping his stole over his shoulders.

"I am here, my son."

The stranger bowed his head and made the sign of the cross. "Bless me, Father, for I have sinned. It has been two years since my last confession."

The young priest's words were automatic. "The Lord be in thy heart and on thy lips, that thou mayest rightly confess thy sins. In the name of the Father, and of the Son, and of the Holy Ghost. Amen."

The man paused a moment, then started to speak, the words spilling out faster and faster. "I confess to Almighty God, to blessed Mary ever Virgin, to all the Saints, and to you, my spiritual Father, that I have sinned. I am the angel of the power of God, the angel of judgment, the angel of truth. I and I alone am responsible for creating the One who will save all of us. It is too late for me, but my legacy will be fulfilled. This will be hard for you to hear, Father. But it is time, and I must be absolved for my sins and the sins of my unborn son."

Father Xavier sat upright in his seat. Oh Lord, this one was crazy. What a capper on the day. "Go on."

"Father, I am a scholar—a student of life—a practiced apprentice of love and death, the twin sides of a coin where one cannot exist without the other. I seek to help my disciples into a perfect state of being. Ideal beauty and absolute goodness. I am truth. I am their deliverance. I am the sun, essential to the creation and sustaining life of their world. I am the archangel, forced into their corporeal bodies, fighting to pilot their souls to the radiance of me, where they and I, together as one, can achieve the ultimate bliss."

"My son, I do not understand you. Perhaps you need to speak with…"

"No!" The voice roared from behind the screen. "I will speak to you, to our God. He knows what I say is true, and has told me I am the truth behind the light. That's why I killed them. To save the One who is the light."

"Killed them? Who have you killed?" Father Xavier felt a small bead of sweat roll down his temple and brushed it away in annoyance.

The voice was suddenly rational, coy. "We are under the seal of confession here, Father. I trust I needn't remind you that you cannot go to the police and tell them what I have said here."

Father Xavier leaned back against the wall of the confessional. He'd heard stories of murderers coming to confession, placing their confessors in such awkward positions that there was no clear way out but copious amounts of prayer. His designs on a quiet evening bled away.

"Go on, my son."

"Thank you, Father. You see, I've studied them as they march through their mean exile, looking for the One, the One who will understand and accept my thesis without complaint. I test each one I find worthy, forcing enlightenment into their beautiful heads. I comment on their words, trying, always trying, to help them focus on the light. My disciples flow into my life, anxiously awaiting another of my lessons—to drink in the exquisiteness of my words, to seek sustenance among my phrases, anything that will allow them to flow along their menial course throughout the rest of the day.

"At last, I found the perfect vessel for my substance, one who has allowed me to unfold my wings, force my soul into hers. She carries the One, Father. Our salvation lies in the womb of a woman near here. I fear I may have become lost in her—despite my intentions. I too am not immune to the corporeal sins of the flesh. It has been a true awakening of the small spirit within me. The others were necessary. I had to hedge my bets, as it were. If several were impregnated, it only increased my chances to father the One."

Father Xavier felt dizzy. What in the name of God was this man talking about? He was obviously suffering from some sort of delusional messiah complex. The rational tone was gone again, he was rambling on and on, and Father Xavier did his best to decipher the meaning of the man's prophetic speech. He definitely seemed to have a God complex, but what did he mean about impregnating women to create the Messiah? Did he actually think he had that kind of power?

"…they were given the most spiritual of deaths. They were the catalysts, the ones who came before, the ones who fulfilled the prophecies. And with each death, another cycle was completed, another step toward the coming of the One was fulfilled."

Though he knew the answer, the priest asked, "What cycle are you speaking of?"

"Don't be dense, Father. The End of Days. The coming of our Lord is preceded by a series of events that portend His coming. The winds blow from the four corners of the earth, the seas die, and the rivers turn to blood. The Apocalypse, Father. I have set in motion the creation of our Apocalypse, the actions necessary to clear the way for our son to enter the world absolved. As soon as the prophecies are fulfilled, the One shall make himself known to the world."

34

The reality of the situation sank in for Father Xavier. This was the killer the press had been reporting on. "You're the one killing the Vanderbilt girls," the priest spat out in horror.

"Oh, Father, I am not killing them. I am releasing them from their earthly bonds, allowing them to walk in the light of our Lord while the rest of the world awaits His coming."

"You're crazy. I suggest you leave now." He wanted to get the man out of the confessional and out of his church.

"They were disposed of lovingly, Father." The man continued as if he hadn't heard a word the priest said. "Admittedly, I did lose my temper a few times. But they were given a clean and spiritual release. And it is time for me to have my absolution, for the sins I have perpetrated on these women and the ones to come.

"For these and all the sins of my past life, I ask pardon of God, penance and absolution from you, Father."

Father Xavier sat frozen, his mind racing. He didn't hear the man ask for his absolution. All he could focus on was his statement. *The ones to come.* He had to find a way into this man's soul, try to stop him somehow. He'd heard the news, knew there were two young innocents dead. *The ones to come.* If this man could be believed, there would be more innocents dying, and maybe, just maybe, he would have a chance to stop this monster. Evil incarnate had landed right here on his doorstep.

"My son, I believe in order to have complete absolution, you must tell me everything. God can absolve you only if you speak aloud your sins."

There was silence from the other side of the screen, and Father Xavier was frightened he'd lost the man, said the wrong thing. But the man cleared his throat and began speaking, lucid and clear again.

"If you want all the gory details, Father, then I'll be happy to indulge you. I have created our Messiah. In order to do that, I needed a woman to plant my seed in, to carry our Savior. A modern-day Mary, a mother of the One.

"But there have been complications along the way. I chose three worthy women, but I was wrong about two of them. One went crazy when I explained her role in the future of mankind, and threatened to tell. The other was impregnated by another source. Both of these women failed me, and had to be destroyed, sacrifices to our apocalypse. They were responsible for their deaths, but I purified and cleansed their souls with an ancient and precious ritual, allowing them safe passage to the afterlife. They are in heaven now.

"There is one left, and she carries my son. Our son. She understands and loves unconditionally, both myself and our God and our Messiah. She is safe from me, but others must suffer to complete the path. It will be finished soon, Father.

"There was another chosen for her role in this world. A woman no one would miss, and she proved herself worthy and became one with our Lord."

My God, Father Xavier thought. *He's actually killed* three *women so far.* He decided to try a different tack. "I think you have proven yourself, my son. I believe you have taken enough lives. This has to stop now. I can absolve you of these sins, but I cannot protect your soul if you plan to sin so egregiously again and again. There will be no true absolution for you."

A shifting behind the screen, and Xavier sensed the man was smiling. "Ah, but there will be. I am at one with our Lord. Through His love and guidance I have been acting, and I must follow the path of righteousness in order to fulfill my quest. The signs have not been satisfied, not yet. Soon, it will be done. So very soon."

"But why now? Why the suddenness of your actions? Do you not need time to reflect upon your sins, to understand why what you are doing is wrong in the eyes of our Lord? He does not want—"

"Yes, He does! He has told me I am the Chosen One, the only one who can carry out His plan. And there is no more time, Father. My time is running out, and I must finish before I die. Not only has He granted me the wisdom to create, but also He is taking my life in return. In less time than you can imagine, the One will be amongst us.

"Let me try this again. For these and all the sins of my past life, I ask pardon of God, penance and absolution from you, Father."

Father Xavier couldn't think—he couldn't breathe. This nightmare must be stopped, and he did not have the power to do so. He needed to find a way to leave this man, to pray and reflect, even to break the seal of confession if it would save more lives. He decided to go on with the observance of the confession.

"For your penance, my son, I cannot imagine there are enough Hail Marys that can be said. You must find a way to make reparations, to cleanse yourself of these thoughts and continue down a different path that will end this quest without more killing. Turn yourself in to the police, and all will not be lost. Please, I beg of you, do these things and…"

The man started on his Act of Contrition, as if he'd heard nothing the priest had said. "O my God, I am heartily sorry for having offended Thee, and I detest all my sins because of Thy just punishments. But most of all because they offend Thee, my God, who art all good and deserving of all my love. I firmly resolve, with the help of Thy grace, to sin no more and avoid the near occasions of sin. Amen."

Father Xavier couldn't help it, the words came

before he could stop himself. "*Ego te absolvo a peccatis tuis in nomine Patris, et Filii, et Spiritus Sancti*. I absolve you of your sins in the name of the Father, and the Son, and the Holy Spirit."

The man replied, "Amen."

"Give thanks to the Lord, for He is good."

"His mercy endures forever."

"*In nomine Patris et Filii et Spiritus Sancti*, my son."

He heard the man stand and open the door. He jumped to his feet; though the confession was traditionally an anonymous process, he felt he must see the man. He needed to see what the face of evil looked like.

By the time he opened the confessional door, he caught only a glimpse of the man's back, retreating so quickly from the room that he was a blur.

Father Xavier sat down hard on the seat of the confessional. He heard a rumble of thunder, as if the heavens were displeased.

"Oh dear God, what have I done?"

He got up and rushed to his office. He needed to pray and consult with the bishop. Perhaps he could find a way to break the seal of confession; surely it would be allowed if it meant saving lives. He put on a pot of tea and sat in his most comfortable chair, thinking hard. He had no way to identify the man who had just left. He'd never seen his face, only heard his sinister, low voice.

He could hear the storm raging and looked out the window. The wind had picked up, thunder was roaring closer, and lightning began flashing every few seconds. He took it as a sign. He needed to talk with the bishop immediately.

He reached toward the desk to pick up the phone. The lights went out in the church. He managed to fumble and grasp the phone receiver, but there was no dial tone. The storm had knocked out the electricity and the phones. He was left to sit in the darkness and pray for guidance. He started to do so with fervor.

35

The rain came down hard enough to leach in through the windowsill. Droplets formed a tiny river, slipping down the wall to puddle on the shiny hardwood floor. Jill lay on her right side, watching the progression. She figured it had been pouring for hours now. Wave after wave of thunder and lightning had been rocking the small room. At one point, she thought she heard tornado sirens blast.

She wasn't sure how long she had been locked in the room. She remembered very little of what had happened over the past few days. At least she thought it had been a few days. She'd studied sensory deprivation in a psychology class and figured her perceptions could be completely off the mark. The continuous rain wasn't helping. She knew for a fact she'd eaten three meals: two cheese omelets and one hurried bowl of macaroni and cheese. The urge to sleep had overtaken her before the meals were finished. When she woke each time, the food had been cleared away, only a glass of water left behind. She was glad of the emptiness; she was feeling sick to her stomach.

Standing shakily, she tried to get her bearings. She went to the window, but the shades were permanently drawn within the windows. Double glass, no cord. She wandered to the door, but it too was locked, just as it had been the past fifteen times she'd tried. The only other furnishings in the room were the double bed she had been rumpling, a bedside table, and a small lamp giving off the dimmest glow.

There were no noises except the vicious storm. She jumped as another flash of lightning hit, close enough to make her hair stand on end. The meager light from the lamp was extinguished. The electricity had gone off. Backlit by the violent flashes, she made her way back to the bed.

She was so tired, too tired even to cry. She lay facing the window, wondering what in the world was happening to her. She wasn't panicked; she was simply curious. She should be scared, she should be freaking out, but everything was softly glowing—*drugs*, she told herself, *you're being drugged*.

At least she knew there would be people trying to find her. The father of her child, for one. Gabriel wouldn't let anything happen to her. He had been so good to her, so sweet. An angel. Their affair had been going on for only a few weeks when she'd gotten pregnant. He was thrilled. She'd expected screams and threats, begging to end the pregnancy coupled with "I'll always stand by you." But he was as excited as a new puppy. She wasn't two months along before he started coming up with names. Boys' names. He was absolutely positive that Jill was giving him a son.

The time had flown so quickly. Though she wasn't completely sure it was the right thing to do, she'd agreed to keep the baby. She'd shared the news only with the doctor at the health clinic at Vanderbilt. She hadn't gotten up the guts to tell her parents, nor had she told her friends. She hoped they just thought she was putting on weight. Though she was getting so big now, she supposed it wouldn't stay secret for much longer. Baggy clothes only hid so much.

The lightning was so close, the thunder simultaneous, filling the room with light and shaking the walls at the same time. She hid beneath the covers, praying for the storm to end.

Jill awoke later with a start, crying out, choking. She looked around wildly. The same room, the same bed. She tried to gather her breath. She had dreamed of trees bending unmercifully in the wind, lightning crashing, and drowning in a river of blood.

"It was only a dream, Jill, it was only a dream."

The arms reached her out of nowhere, and she realized Gabriel was holding her, whispering in her ear, soothing her with nonsensical murmurs. Was she dreaming? She didn't have the energy to fight, didn't protest when he laid her back onto the bed gently. She didn't have the ability to shout when he rose and went to the door. Her screams merely echoed in her head as she heard the door lock behind him.

36

The thunder and lightning were moving in, the rain pouring in sheets against the windows of the squad room. The storm was unsettling; the squad room was filled with the smell of anxiety.

Price stuck his head out of his office. "Strategy meeting, conference room, fifteen minutes. And be aware, we're under a tornado watch. Have your stuff ready in case we need to hit the basement."

There were groans and shuffling. Marcus stopped typing and logged off his computer. Lincoln made a slow circuit around the room while Fitz flicked his lighter ever closer to his emergency cigarette. Taylor shifted her boots off her desk but didn't get up. She stiffened as she saw Baldwin step back in, windblown and remorseful.

Price had seen Taylor slam back into the squad room, noticed her body language change when Baldwin came in. He gave her a surreptitious glance, thinking she might have had time to cool down from whatever had pissed her off so badly. No, she was still simmering, nearly giving off smoke from the fires lit inside her. He sighed. He needed his best detective back, all the way. He didn't have time for a turf war.

He walked to her desk, eyebrows raised.

"Everything okay there, sugar?"

She gave him a small smile. "Right as rain."

"Ha-ha." He looked at her closely, started to speak, then decided to leave it alone. She was a big girl. He didn't need to fight any battles for her.

Taylor watched Price's receding back. He was hollow eyed, tired, and obviously just as shocked as his detectives that another Vandy student had disappeared. She felt a pang of remorse. He was a good man; she admired him. She resolved to pull it together, yet again. Mitchell Price was one person she never wanted to disappoint.

Price called, "Okay, everyone, screw fifteen. Let's go ahead and chat about our next moves now. We can do it right here. We have a case to solve. Let's try to get it in before the storm really hits."

As if to answer him, the lights went out, plunging them into darkness.

"The generators are going to come on, right?" Marcus's voice had a little waver in it, the perfect tension releaser. The group fell back on the tried and true: Take it out on someone else.

Fitz called, "Hey, Marcus, you afraid of the dark?"

"No, you big, old, fat fool, I'm just asking if we have generators for this shithole."

Price started to laugh but covered it with a cough. But Taylor didn't hold back. Her giggling was infectious. They were all roaring with laughter when the tornado sirens went off.

Taylor grabbed a Maglite from her desk drawer. Suddenly sober, she instructed, "Everyone to the basement." They all got up to follow her out.

Baldwin felt bad. He hadn't meant to fight with Taylor, just to help somehow. She'd reached out to him when he was at his lowest point. He wanted to give something back. He'd rushed in without taking the time to figure out if Taylor would accept any overtures from him. He was a complete stranger, shoving his way into her case and into her life. No wonder she didn't want to have anything to do with him. He felt the despair creeping up his spine but shoved it away. He couldn't fold this easily, not yet. He needed—well, he didn't know what he needed, but it was something he knew only Taylor Jackson could give him.

He caught up to her on the steps. "Are those the new tornado sirens going off?"

"Yep. After that one hit downtown a few years ago, they put 'em in. This is the first time I've heard them go off downtown, though. Kinda wild, you know?"

Her voice had lost its earlier edge. She had extended the olive branch. He accepted it with open arms.

"It is. I hope this is a false alarm."

They set up shop in the basement, taking cover from the malicious winds tearing at the building. Taylor's voice rang out clear and sharp.

"Might as well have that status meeting now. Here's where we stand. Jill Gates is a junior at Vanderbilt. She's from Huntsville, Alabama; a blonde, like Shelby and Jordan. Her parents reported her missing this morning. They say they haven't spoken with her in four days. Four days, people. He could have snatched her up before he killed Shelby."

"Shelby had been missing for how long before she was found?" Baldwin asked.

Taylor flashed the light at him. "Three days, as far as we know. Her roommate Vicki last saw her Friday night. We found her body Monday morning. If MP had taken the report Saturday instead of assuming it was a college kid doing their thing over the weekend, we might have been able to save her."

The bitterness in Taylor's voice broke his heart. He knew why she'd attacked him now. She was blaming herself for this whole mess. And he finally realized how he could help: Solve this damn case, and give her some peace of mind.

"Let's try to establish a time line here. When does Sam think Jordan was killed?"

Taylor looked to her second. "Fitz?"

"Let me see that flashlight." He shuffled some papers and pulled out the autopsy report on Jordan Blake. "Sam estimates she wasn't in the water more than five days or so." He thought for a moment, counting on his fingers. "With that time frame, she could have been killed on Wednesday or Thursday, then dumped into the river."

Marcus reached over and flipped the page. "So

he kills Jordan on Wednesday night or Thursday morning, then immediately grabs Shelby?"

Baldwin started nodding. "Okay, if that's how it went down, he killed Shelby sometime on Sunday night and dumped her at the Parthenon. Jill's parents report her missing today and say they haven't talked to her for four days. That means the last time they talked to her was Saturday?"

"Yeah, that's what the report says. That means he took Jill before he killed Shelby." Taylor was getting upset. "We should have another body showing up here anytime, huh?"

Baldwin was sitting close to Taylor in the dark room. He gave her what he hoped was an encouraging smile. "Not necessarily. Don't give up just yet. What else do we know about Jill?"

"I got off the phone with Jill's parents right before we got stuck in here," Lincoln said. "They're heading up from Huntsville. They're just blown away by all of this."

"Did they give you any other information?"

"They said she was seeing someone, but they don't have any idea who it could be. She never confided in her parents about that kind of stuff, but they said she was being especially secretive lately. She didn't go home over fall break and told them she was going to stay on campus to get ready for exams. They called her on Saturday, but she was in a rush and got off the phone real quick, said she had to meet a friend for dinner. That's the last they talked to her."

"Good, that's good. Taylor, didn't you say you

had the feeling Shelby had a boyfriend, but her roommate wouldn't give you anything on him?"

"Yeah, I got the sense she was keeping something from me. With Shelby's background, I felt it might be a secret affair."

Price finally spoke. "And we know for a fact Jordan was involved with someone, willingly or unwillingly. Her pregnancy confirms it. If Jill Gates also had a mystery lover, we're getting somewhere here."

Marcus and Fitz spoke at the same time. "Same boyfriend."

Baldwin gave them a big smile. "Same boyfriend. We find him, and maybe we'll find the killer."

37

Mary Margaret struggled with her backpack and umbrella, her glasses sliding down her nose. She was trying to make it to St. Catherine's to meet Father Xavier before the storm hit full force. The sky was a deep green; she'd seen tornado skies before and was certain that the fierce swirling winds were bearing down on her as she ran. The hairs stood up on the back of her neck, and deep chills ran down her spine. She shook off the unsettled feeling. The lightning was close. It was simply static electricity making her hair bush out and stand on end.

A huge gust of wind caught the umbrella and tore it out of her hands. "Damn it!" she screamed, watching it fly away. It was the worst curse she allowed herself to say aloud, but the guilt of losing her temper hit her immediately. Another Hail Mary from Father Xavier. There was no way she was going to be on time for their scheduled meeting. She thought longingly of the warm fragrant tea he would be brewing in his cozy office. She never ran late for their sessions. She hoped he wasn't worrying about her.

Mary Margaret loved her theology classes at Aquinas College. It was a relief for her to be in the company of so many young students who shared her beliefs. When she found her way back to the Church, the doors swung wide and welcoming for a young woman in search of herself. There was no judgment, no dirty looks. Of course, no one knew her background. Mary Margaret had confided in only one person about her past.

She'd met Father Francis Xavier a few months back. He was new to Nashville, too, a young, principled, and compassionate priest. She felt an immediate connection with him and started going to Mass at his home church, St. Catherine's. He was a stranger in town, a little lonely, and always willing to discuss the mysteries of theology with his new friend. One night, she asked him to take her confession. It was the only way she could think of to share her pain and humiliation with another person without repercussion.

She'd told him her whole story. Mary Margaret's family lived in Atlanta and had left the Catholic Church before she hit her early teens. Her grandmother, a full-blown, off-the-boat Italian Catholic, had converted to Baptist for an unknown reason and harangued the family until they switched as well. The main force of her argument was her fear that if they were not saved, she would never see them in heaven.

Mary Margaret had never been terribly religious.

As she entered her teens she found many more exciting things to do than going to church four nights a week and spending weekends in revivals. She fell into a group of misfits who got her drinking, then using drugs. Ultimately, she began having sex with the boys in the group. Atlanta provided many excitements for a rebellious teenage girl, but she soon grew bored of her life and wanted to strike out on her own. With one hundred dollars in her pocket, she left town.

She made her way across the country, hitching rides with strangers, working for cash in small-town cafés, trading herself if she got too low on cash to purchase drugs. She made calls home to her parents, but they were so upset with her that they wouldn't talk to her. She wasn't happy living on the edge. She was lonely, run-down, and a little sick of herself and her behavior. She began having thoughts of returning home. And then it had all caught up with her.

Somewhere in the backwoods of Colorado, she'd hitched a ride with the wrong man. He'd beaten her and raped her, then dumped her in a campground. A church group on a day hike found her bloodied and bruised, but alive. They'd taken her to the nearest hospital, a small community endeavor run by the Catholic Church.

It was the words of succor from the nuns that had brought her back to life a changed woman. One of the nuns told her of a college in Nashville, Aquinas College. It was a perfect place for her to start over. The nuns allowed her to live with them for a time, helped her study for and acquire her GED. They celebrated her triumph when she was offered a small scholarship to Aquinas. With their meager savings, they got her on a plane to Nashville and paid her first year's rent on a small apartment across the street from the school. This setup made it simple for her to walk to class and placate her caffeine addiction at the local Starbucks. She took jobs on campus to pay the rent and worked as hard as she could to begin a new life. Her faith in her rediscovered religion had become the cornerstone to a whole new world.

When she'd finished her confession, Father Xavier found he had even more respect for his young friend. He convinced her it was time to let her parents know where she was. They didn't welcome her back with open arms, but their relationship began to mend. She had been to Atlanta a few times to visit, and was calling dutifully once a week.

She was healing.

As the wind lashed her face and the rain plastered her hair to her skull, she ran across the parking lot and was almost hit when a car screeched around the corner and pulled up beside her. The passenger door swung open, and she was overcome with relief. She knew this car, and the man driving it. How had she gotten so lucky that he was driving by as she was struggling to get out of the storm? It must have been divine intervention. All she saw was shelter and, hopefully, a ride to St. Catherine's. He was yelling at her to hurry up and get in, and with a quick prayer to Mary to keep her safe, she did.

Fighting with the door, she finally managed to slam it behind her. She was soaked to the bone, shaking with fear and cold. For a brief moment, silhouetted against the storm, he was hidden in shadows, his hair standing on end, his eyes blank, ghastly holes in his face.

Then the light went on in the car, he gave her a huge smile, and she saw he was just the ordinary, handsome man she knew. She laughed at herself; it was just the storm spooking her.

"Thanks so much. I almost blew away there."

"I saw under the altar the souls of them that were slain for the Word of God, and for the testimony which they held."

"Pardon me?"

Mary Margaret's internal alarm bells went off, but before she could do anything, she heard the locks on the doors snap closed. The man said nothing more, just smiled and put the car into gear.

38

The storm worsened, and conversation drifted off, the detectives lost in their own thoughts about the case or the storm or what to have for dinner. Taylor sat on the floor under a small stack of blankets, feeling incredibly foolish. She'd been through many storms before, but this one had a different feeling about it: a malevolent, evil oppression. She shook her head, trying to get the feeling of doom out of her mind. How silly was she? Thirty-four years old and afraid of a little storm.

Thunder shook the building, and they heard a rushing noise like a freight train getting ready to ram through the walls. There were a few nervous laughs from the darkness, but everyone was listening to the rushing wind intently.

Baldwin reached over and touched her shoulder to get her attention over the noise of the storm. "Were you here the last time the tornadoes came through downtown?"

His voice gave her a little comfort. Strange, it seemed to be hours since their spat on the stairwell. But Taylor was used to that. She didn't lose her temper often, but when she did, she did it thoroughly and without thought. Once it was over, it was over. She did feel a little embarrassed by her outburst, but she was too worried about the storm to deal with it at the moment. *Besides*, she thought, *fear makes strange bedfellows*. She blushed in the dark at the fleeting image that came with the thought, cleared her throat, and replied to Baldwin's innocuous question.

"No. I was on vacation and saw it on the news. I'm glad I wasn't here. Sometimes I prefer to watch the wrath of God from afar."

"Wrath of God, huh? Think it's that bad out there?"

She gave him a sidelong glance, trying to decide if he was mocking her. She had the distinct impression he wasn't talking about the storm.

But Baldwin sat calmly, legs drawn up and hands dangling loosely in between.

"You never know," she said lightly. "How are we going to find the boyfriend?"

"The moment we're cleared to get out of here, we drive to Vanderbilt and take the place apart. Someone knows who these girls were seeing. From all you've told me, Shelby Kincaid didn't necessarily confide in her parents. She could easily have been seeing someone as well. Three girls seeing the same man? If we're right, now we have a suspect and a possible motive."

"You mentioned cults earlier when we talked about the aconite. Do you think the girls were aware of each other, that the relationship with this man was open, so to speak? Or done in a group? You know how kids love to experiment. If they had a charismatic leader pushing them into a group situation..."

"It's entirely possible. It all depends on our suspect. But I'm inclined to say no, simply because of the timing. It feels like he's snatching and dumping, going through some sort of ritual sacrifice. But I've been wrong before."

"I want to talk to Shelby's mother again. I did get the sense there were things left unsaid during the interview."

"You have good instincts. Follow them."

"So do you," she said, surprised how pleased she was by the compliment. "The problem is, we're three steps behind this creep. I have the worst feeling, like he's out there on the storm's winds, doing something right now. Silly, I know."

"It's not silly at all. It's how I always feel when I'm working a serial. Completely out of control, and every step I make could be the wrong one and cost a life. It's the chance we take, working these cases, knowing no matter what we do, we might be too late."

He said it without artifice, and she realized, for all the seriousness of the conversation, she enjoyed talking to him. *You're out of your mind, Jackson.*

"Something else is bothering me," she said. "They're all so different. I mean, Jordan Blake was supposedly trouble on a stick, and her parents are quite absent. Shelby Kincaid was the extreme opposite, with overprotective parents and a reticent personality, super focused on her studies. Jill Gates is in between, and her parents certainly sound like they're attentive, at the very least. Would one man be drawn to three wildly different personalities? I thought serials went for the same type."

"The different personalities are interesting to me as well, but they all have similar physical characteristics. I think what makes them alike in looks attracted this man, not what made them different. What's bothering me is the mixed presentation. Leaving semen and fingerprints tells me this is a disorganized killer. Multiple victims in a short time frame, staged scenes, the herbs, all point to a very organized offender. In other words, these could be his first crimes and he doesn't know any better, doesn't know how to clean up after himself. Or he could be very much in control, is building up to something bigger and splashier, thinks he's smarter than us and will get away with it, or doesn't care if he's caught. Because he's exhibiting hallmarks of both, that tells me he's decompensating. He's making mistakes now. I'm inclined to think he's a disorganized offender, and there's something else going on."

"How do you do this? Profile, I mean. Quantico is on everyone's radar right now. What y'all do up there is fascinating. Everything you just told me makes perfect sense, but how does it help us catch him?"

He tensed, and she mentally kicked herself. When he answered, his voice wasn't as easy.

"There's a science to it, no doubt, but for most of us, it's the ability to trust our gut. We rely on experience and instinct. Years and years of instinct. If you're a good investigator, it rarely leads you wrong, until…" The unspoken words hung in the air. *Until it does.*

He was no longer relaxed, stood and started to pace. Taylor sighed to herself. *And you were doing so well. Good job upsetting him.* Another thought hit her, this one more immediate.

"Hey, Price? Do you think the generators came on in the jail?"

She could barely see the alarm on her boss's face; the batteries were running down in their only flashlight, and the light was fading quickly.

"We'd better hope so. All of those locks are electronic—the doors would have swung open if the power was off for more than five minutes. Last thing we need, a bunch of half-cocked prisoners wandering the streets. How long have we been in here anyway?"

A small light glowed on Fitz's wrist.

"'Bout a half hour, Cap. Think it's cool to get out of here yet? I'm getting a little claustrophobic."

"I think we're good. Let's go see what's happened."

39

Mary Margaret was sitting on her hands, which were tied low behind her back. She had managed to scoot around a little in the confines of the confessional, but only enough to wedge her fingers under her butt.

The events of the past hours were all a blur. She remembered the man picking her up, their quick exodus to St. Catherine's Church. She was so relieved to be indoors, away from the fury of the storm.

Father Xavier had greeted them, obviously relieved to see she was okay and thankful that her friend had delivered her safely to his door. He guided them into his office. The man she was with asked for something to drink, and the priest poured them steaming cups of his aromatic tea. She could vaguely recall the taste of the tea: amazingly bitter, despite the three spoonfuls of sugar she had dumped in. Regardless, it was warm, and she was safe within the confines of her mother church.

Almost immediately, her mouth had gone numb and her stomach felt violently upset. She vaguely heard Father Xavier remark that he wasn't feeling well either, and then all was black.

It seemed like hours later when she came to. She didn't know immediately where she was. Her stomach felt as if it was filled with knives; her hands were going numb. She thought hard and realized she was still in the church. In fact, she could tell that she was inside the confessor's side of the confessional.

She had no idea how long she'd been stuck in here. The gag in her mouth was cutting off her breath, and she figured if she breathed slowly through her nose she didn't feel she would suffocate immediately. Her stomach heaved violently. Her whole body was going numb; she couldn't feel her limbs anymore.

She heard footsteps and listened intently. They grew closer. She could tell there were two people coming toward her. One was shuffling; one was marching with purpose. She heard muted voices, muttering and moaning. She tried to scream, but the only sound she could manage was a tiny whimper. She felt ashamed. At the moment of her death she should be full of grace, praying to the mother Mary to give her strength and acceptance. She didn't doubt for a minute she was dying; she felt as if she'd left her body already. Her mind was able to register what was happening, but her body was slipping away and wouldn't respond. She couldn't feel them, but the tears began to roll down her face.

The door to the priest's side of the confessional was thrown open. The box shook with the force of a body hitting the wall inside. Mary Margaret could see a man's face, dim and veiled through the partition screen. The door to the confessional slammed again. They were left in darkness.

Mary Margaret could barely make out the white collar around the man's throat. Something told her it must be Father Xavier. She whimpered again, trying to get his attention. His head lolled to the side. She wondered briefly if he was dead. When a moan escaped his lips, she breathed a slow sigh of relief through her nose. Neither of them were dead yet.

She tried to speak through the gag in her mouth, which had loosened.

"Futther," she whispered. "Futther, ere ou kay?"

She was rewarded with a moan, and barely made out the word "devil."

"Futther, ere oo okay?"

She watched him carefully through the screen. His breathing was labored; he was not gagged. Mary Margaret could see a trickle of blood flowing from the side of his head. She could tell his lips were moving, though no sound reached her ears.

The footsteps came again, and the door to the confessional was thrown open briefly. A hand snaked in and ripped the gag from her mouth. She heard the voice, disembodied, as if she were hearing the Holy Ghost speak aloud.

"Confess your sins, little one. Confess and be shriven, go to your heaven with an unsoiled soul."

The door slammed shut again, but before she could cry out, she smelled gasoline. Heard the flick of the match. Felt the heat as the flames exploded around her.

"Father," she screamed, somehow finding the strength to cry aloud. "Father, forgive me, for I have sinned." The flames grew around her, scorching her hair, filling the tiny grave with smoke. She began to cough, knew she would speak no more. She prayed silently.

As Mary Margaret lost consciousness, she heard one last word. A strangled whisper. She didn't know if it was from her God or the priest being immolated with her, but the word filled her with peace, and she stopped struggling against her earthly bonds.

"Forgiven," the voice said.

And the flames took them.

40

He stood watching the flames, a small smile playing on his lips. He raised his eyes to the dark and boiling skies. *"And when he had opened the seventh seal, there was silence in heaven..."*

41

The skies were still roiling with gray and black clouds, and rain continued to pour down. Lightning reached out a fiery hand toward the earth. Nature wasn't finished with her punishment, but the winds had lessened.

Downtown Nashville looked like a war zone. Trees, trash, metal—all were strewn around in the streets like litter after a celestial concert, carelessly dropped by receding waves of humanity. People were venturing into the streets to survey the damage, their eyes wide with the excitement and fear that accompanies every natural calamity. The sense of awe was palpable; it was dazzling to be involved in something that they had no control over.

Workplaces were left with flickering lights or no electricity at all, so many had shut down for the rest of the day. It was better for the people not directly involved in the cleanup to get out of the way. The tornado had cut a swath two hundred yards wide right down the main downtown streets of Nashville, but most of the outlying areas had only suffered superficial damage. There were no reports of deaths.

Fitz, Marcus, and Lincoln had sneaked off to their respective homes to see if they had taken a hit from the storm. Price had to deal with the law enforcement aspects of helping with the cleanup. He wasn't very popular with the rest of the detectives in the CID at the moment. After a brief meeting with the chief of police, he'd called in all the off-duty detectives. They weren't happy to find they needed to go help Patrol work the roadblocks that had been put up around Nashville to help NES get the power back on.

With everyone gone, Taylor finally felt as if she had some breathing room. She and Baldwin stayed in the Homicide office, planning their next steps. They were still on generator power, working under odd, not quite bright lights. The storm damage was impeding their ability to cross town to Vanderbilt to interview everyone again, and the phones were all down. As with most of the downtown businesses, it appeared the school had been closed down, so the students and administration were scattered.

After a frustrating hour of waiting, they gave up, decided to take a break and get some food. She was glad for a momentary respite from the case to clear her head and recharge her batteries.

As they drove out on Interstate 40, circling around downtown, they were impressed at how quickly the cleanup was progressing. Many of the streets had already been cleared. The damage was not as severe as it had initially looked, but many trees were uprooted, and power lines were strewn across the streets.

Taylor decided it would be best to get out of the way, so she suggested they head back to her side of town to get some dinner. She lived in Bellevue, a small community just west of Nashville. It didn't take them long to make the drive. The tornado had been confined to downtown. Once past the exits for West End, the streets were relatively clear.

She pulled into a neighborhood restaurant called Jonathan's, and they went inside. The place was packed, a beehive of activity. It seemed no one wanted to stay at home; they'd all come out to share the day's excitement. They made their way through the throng of people waiting for tables at the front door and went into the back bar.

They'd been making desultory chitchat on the ride over, mostly about the weather. The memory of her outburst had faded away. More comfortable together now, they ordered beers. Taylor brought out a pack of cigarettes and offered one to Baldwin.

Baldwin gave her a grateful grin. "I'd love one, but I quit a few years ago."

Taylor gave him a smile and lit the cigarette. "So did I." She took a couple of drags, crushed it out, and rose.

"Will you order me some fried clams? I need to go to the bathroom."

"No problem." He watched her walk away and saw many heads turn as she pushed through the crowd. He started berating himself. He knew now why he was interested in staying on this case, and it wasn't only the murders themselves.

Taylor wove her way to the bathroom, grateful to find it empty. She stood in front of the mirror, pretending to smooth down her hair. She could have easily let Baldwin head to his own home, but instead she'd invited him to dinner. There was something about him that made her want to stay in his company. She'd lashed out at him earlier more from fear than anything else. When he'd offered to be there for her if she needed him when they were out on the steps, she'd had a yearning so strong it felt like a blow to the chest. Something about Baldwin had gotten under her skin, and she was furious at herself for letting that happen.

At the same time, she wanted to fall into his arms, cry on his shoulder, try to explain the frustration, the pain she was feeling. She was lonely. He was the nearest attractive warm body, even if he was screwed up.

She gave herself a once-over in the mirror. *Knock it off, Taylor. This isn't right.* She nodded to herself in reluctant agreement and went back to Baldwin.

The kitchen had worked quickly; there was a plate of fried clams in front of her seat. She sat, noting that Baldwin had not started eating his cheeseburger. *Manners. Hmm.*

Suddenly shy, she dug into her food. The clams were perfect, crunchy and smooth. She hadn't realized how hungry she was. She noticed Baldwin was eating his burger like a man condemned, enjoying each bite as though it were his last. It brought her up short, and she started laughing.

"You know, they'll make you more if you want."

"I feel like I haven't had a chance to relax and eat in months. You know, the other night at Mulligan's was the first time I'd been in a restaurant for almost six months. I thought I'd savor the moment."

Taylor saw the opportunity. "I've been wanting to ask how you were feeling. You seem to be— What's a good way of putting it…?"

"Better?"

"Yes. Better."

He took a careful bite of his burger, giving himself a moment before he had to answer. "I guess you could say this case has caught my interest. I have a gut feeling it's not over by a long shot."

"The case. Of course."

He gave her a long look, and her stomach tightened. What the hell was she doing?

"Or maybe I felt like you saved my life, and I owed you one." He looked straight into her eyes, marveling at their chameleon qualities. In the darkness of the bar, they were lavender, her pupils dilated. She had a sexy, come-hither quality that he was having a hard time denying. He'd never seen anything so exquisite in his life. Realizing his interest probably showed on his face, he hastily turned away and shoved some fries in his mouth.

But Taylor had caught the moment of unguarded emotion. She didn't know if it was gratefulness or attraction, but she reached over and touched his arm.

"I'm glad you stayed with it." She left it at that and finished the rest of her meal.

They sat quietly, not feeling the need to talk. They'd come to some tacit agreement in their silence. Yes, the attraction was there. Yes, they both felt it. No reason to push anything.

Taylor ordered another round of beers. As they were set in front of them, her cell phone rang. She looked at the caller ID and frowned.

"Price," she told Baldwin, who nodded. He knew their brief idyll was just that, though he was sorry they couldn't spend a little more time together away from the case. Maybe they'd found Jill Gates.

"Hey, Captain." He could see the muscles in her shoulders tense. "Where? Okay, we're on our way. Yeah, I've got Baldwin with me. He'll come along." She hung up, took a last swig of her beer.

"Price wants you to come with me to a scene." She was frowning, her attention already pulled away, and he felt the lack of it keenly.

"What scene? Did they find Jill?"

She shook her head. "I don't know. St. Catherine's Church caught on fire. They thought it was a lightning strike from the storm until the firefighters found two bodies shoved into a confessional. They were burned to death."

42

They pulled into the parking lot at the church, weaving their way through the fire engines. Large crime scene spotlights showed the church exterior. It was made of harled white stone and had suffered only superficial damage, but curls of smoke were still drifting through the air, a smoldering perfume clinging to the parking lot. Taylor saw Sam standing by the entrance of the church. She looked grim, was giving directions to two men with a heavy gurney between them. They went to join her.

Sam gave the two a sideways glance. "What took *you* so long?"

"So long? Price only called me ten minutes ago. We came immediately."

"Oh. Sorry." She frowned, nodding. "I've already pulled them out, and we're taking them back to the office."

"Want to fill me in? Price didn't give me any details."

Sam kept nodding. She was smudged with soot and had a faraway look on her face. "Yeah. Let's go over there." She pointed to Taylor's car and started walking. Taylor and Baldwin followed. "Sorry to be short, but this is freaking me out."

"Sam?" Taylor said sharply. She was getting a little freaked out, too. Sam never got flustered at a scene.

"I'm okay, T, just a little rattled. Baldwin, are you Catholic?"

"No. I'm Episcopalian. At least I used to be. Why?"

"Just wondering. I'm Catholic. This isn't the way I'd like to go. I don't think I'll make it to confession for a while. Taylor, do you have a cigarette?"

"You're going to smoke at a fire?"

"Hey, give me a break, okay?"

Taylor gave her one and lit it for her. "You mind filling us in?"

Sam took a long drag and coughed slightly. "Fire department got the call right after the storm rolled through. Everyone figured a lightning strike started the fire. The guys went in full bore with the hoses, but it wasn't too bad. Seemed to be confined to the nave and chapel. They put it out, but there was that smell, you know?"

They did know. The unmistakable sweet, sickening smell of burnt flesh had invaded their nostrils as they'd drawn close to the doors of the church.

"So they get the flames put out relatively quickly and start looking around. They followed the burn pattern to the confessionals and found them inside. The woman was on one side, the priest on the other.

They're pretty charred—it looks like the fire was started in the confessional, or damn close to it."

Taylor was running through the scenarios when Baldwin jumped in. "So it appears intentional? They were murdered?"

"Seems that way. They have an ID on the priest. Father Francis Xavier. He wasn't burned as badly— his wallet made it through pretty much unscathed. The bishop confirmed he was doing confessions today. He told me he was new to the church, recently moved here from Boston."

"What about the woman?"

"She's a mess. It looks like she was bound, her arms were behind her back, and there was a little bit of cording around her wrists that made it through the fire. But there's nothing on her as far as ID. They searched the church. There's no purse or anything that looks like it would belong to a woman."

"Are you going to try and do a dental on her? Match it to our missing girl?"

The question was lingering in the air around them. No one wanted to say the name out loud in case it would become truth, crystallized by meeting the air.

"I'm going to have to. She's burned up pretty badly."

"I'll call and see if her parents are already up here. They'll need to get her dental radiographs for us ASAP."

"Thanks, Taylor. I'll post her first thing in the morning."

Sam reached over and gave Taylor a hug. "I'm sorry," she whispered, and turned back to her van.

Baldwin turned to Taylor, who looked stricken and suddenly very tired.

"Do you think it's her?"

Taylor sighed. "Yeah." She pulled out her cell phone and speed dialed. "Fitz? It's Taylor. Just wanted you to know. We may have found Jill Gates."

43

The parking lot was full, people rushing about, yelling, panicking. The air smoldered, the scents of smoke and death lingered. A shiver of excitement went through him. It was happening, just as he planned, as he'd been told.

"And the angel took the censer, and filled it with the fire of the altar..."

He turned away. So much left to do.

44

Jill woke when the needle pricked her arm. She shook her head, trying to clear her vision, focusing on the stinging in the crook of her elbow. She started to cry, then felt herself melt away into the darkness again.

She knew the drugs were making her hallucinate. She thought she was sitting in a massive green courtyard, even though she knew she was in the bed. She tried to get her bearings, looking first right, then left, but her head felt as if it was tethered in place. Her arms were bound at her side. She could only look ahead, to the expanse of green grass in front of her. There was a shadow there, a woman swaying like a cobra mesmerized by an unknown song. She tried to speak, to ask where she was, but no words came out. The shadow shifted, slowly, so slowly, side to side, and Jill heard the sound of sobbing. The woman was sad. So very sad. And suddenly she was gone, and the shadows lifted, leaving only a blank wall of green in their place.

Jill heard a voice in her head. She knew it came from the woman. She was angry now, crying and yelling. Her voice faded in and out, and Jill tried so hard to hear what she was saying, but only snatches of the woman's voice came to her. "I will tell," said the voice. "I will tell them what you've done."

Another voice joined the mix, this one somewhat familiar, deeper, comforting. Was it soothing the woman, trying to calm her? The voice of the woman grew fainter, and Jill could hear the gentle voice, quieter this time. "You will be honored."

THE
FIFTH
DAY

45

Taylor and Baldwin shivered in the parking lot of the church. It was barely morning and exceptionally cool, overcast, and breezy. A few times through the night, hot cups of coffee appeared magically at their elbows, borne in on a tray by a young man Taylor didn't recognize. Despite her distaste for straight coffee, Taylor had accepted the steaming foam cups gladly, holding on to the precious warmth and choking down the bitter liquid. Baldwin had been sucking down cup after cup and was jumping around like a child on Christmas morning.

Taylor took in his appearance with a smile. "Baldwin, you're a mess."

He gave her a hurt look and bent to examine his reflection in the side mirror of her car. He took a halfhearted swipe at his hair, which was standing on end and pointing off in every direction like a broken compass needle. He had two days' worth of stubble darkening his jaw and cheeks, and his eyes were bloodshot from the smoke and lack of sleep. He hadn't felt so alive in months.

"Yeah, well, you look great."

Taylor blushed and turned away. She knew he was full of it, but didn't argue. The mark of a true southern belle: Never put aside a compliment. She ran her hands through her hair, smoothed the mass into a messy ponytail. Gave him a smile.

Though it had been several hours since the fire, the reek of burnt flesh was pervasive, even without the bodies present. Taylor had been smoking all night trying to get the smell out of her nose. She'd succeeded only in giving herself a sore throat. Her voice had lowered an octave. The chill, the smoke, and the slight cold were catching up to her. She popped two Advil Cold & Sinus pills out of their blister pack and swallowed them down with the remnants of coffee sloshing around her cup. She wrinkled her nose; it had gone cold.

Baldwin rubbed his hands together and shoved them deep in the pockets of his jeans. "Do you think they're about done in there? I'm getting hungry."

"They should be. Let's go check with the chief, see what's keeping them." They started toward the entry of the nave, but the fire chief walked out before she could reach the doors. He greeted her with a tired smile.

"Lieutenant Jackson. Long night. You've been freezing your tush off the whole time?"

"Yep. Fire Chief Andrew Rove, meet Dr. John Baldwin, FBI. He's working the case with us."

They shook, and the chief said, "FBI, huh? Well, you'll want to know this is, without a doubt, arson. The combustible gas detector found gasoline was used as an accelerant near the confessional. Jackson, your Crime Scene techs are trying to lift some prints from the priest's office; it looks like there were people in there before the fire started. Tea for three, laid out on the coffee table. How very civilized."

"Tea for three. But only two bodies. The victims knew their killer," Baldwin said.

"Could be. We didn't find anything leftover, no gas cans, no rope, nothin'. Place is clean as a whistle except for the office. We're pulling out now, there's nothing more for us to do."

"Thanks, Chief. I look forward to the report."

With a nod and a small salute, he went to his truck.

Tim Davis, Sam's death investigator on the scene, walked out of the church with several bags in his hands. Taylor jogged over to him. "Anything worthwhile?"

"I managed to pick up prints off two of the teacups. Unfortunately, the third was clean, still full of tea. Untouched. There was some liquid left in the two that I printed. I'll run it through the mass spectrometer and see what turns up. And I'll get these prints over to Lincoln. If I were a betting man, I'd wager they belong to our vics, so there may be nothing to compare them to if we can't lift something off their hands. Third cup was probably the person who set the fire. Didn't want to leave any traces behind."

Taylor chewed on that for a minute. Baldwin was silent. She could see the wheels turning in his head.

"Good work. Get out of here, Tim. Thanks for everything."

He waved his bags at her and walked away. Taylor turned to Baldwin, confusion settling in her eyes. She needed some time to think about what had happened. "Wanna get some breakfast?"

He looked deep into her eyes, recognizing the frustration she was feeling. "Yeah, let's do that. I'm starved. My mama always told me, 'When in doubt, eat.'"

They made their way to the car and headed out. They took the back roads past the huge homes in Belle Meade into Green Hills, skirted the morning traffic down Hillsboro Road, and pulled into the parking lot of the Pancake Pantry, a well-established staple for breakfast in Nashville. The restaurant was so popular that an hour wait was not uncommon, but on this brisk morning, the line was blessedly absent. They had to wait ten minutes for the doors to open, both standing with hands in their pockets against the cold. Baldwin moved closer to shelter her from the worst of the breeze. Taylor leaned against him gratefully, happy for the contact as much as the warmth of his body.

When the hostess finally came to unlock the doors, Baldwin held the door for Taylor. Inside, she caught a glimpse of a flyer in the window. The poster featured a large picture of a smiling

Jill Gates. The headline read *Have You Seen Jilly?*
Under her picture were her vital statistics, what she
was last seen wearing, and the phone number to
the tip line. Taylor felt all the breath being sucked
out of her body.

Glancing up and down the street, Taylor realized
there were posters tacked in all the store windows
and stapled over the latest band announcements on
the telephone poles. She felt sick to her stomach.
She'd just seen Jill Gates, and she didn't look anything like the smiling woman in the picture.

She didn't know how she managed to make it to
the table; her legs were wobbly, her vision black-
ening. She felt the chair slide in under her, heard
Baldwin order her a Diet Coke, but nothing was
registering. She tried to breathe, but the panic attack was on her. She bent at the waist, trying not
to faint.

She had no idea how long it took her to get it
back together. She heard Baldwin muttering softly
in her ear and realized he was sitting in the chair
next to her, holding on for dear life. She was mor-
tified to have fallen apart in front of him, not to
mention in such a public venue. She drew in a few
gulps of air. Her head started to clear, and she sat
up. Baldwin let her go and leaned back into his
chair, his eyes full of concern.

"You okay?"

She nodded. Her breathing was returning to normal, and she opened her eyes, shocked to see how
scared Baldwin looked. She gave him a weak smile
and tried to make a joke.

"You've never seen a southern belle have a fainting spell?"

"That was no fainting spell, Taylor. You had a nice, full-blown panic attack. This happen a lot?"

"Can we not talk about this here? I'm fine." She'd recovered enough to take a drink of the soda in front of her. Great, the waitress had seen the whole thing too. But when she looked behind her, the woman was standing at the kitchen door cracking jokes with the dishwasher. Thank God.

"You don't look fine, Taylor."

"Baldwin, let it go, okay?" Her voice rose and she sounded ridiculous to herself. Of course he'd recognize a panic attack; he was a psychiatrist after all. Which meant he'd want to get to the bottom of it. She just wasn't up for analysis right now. She gave a conciliatory smile. "I'm fine, really. Just too much caffeine, not enough sleep, and I'm coming down with something. Inner ear's all messed up. I need to get some antibiotics or something. Don't worry about it, okay?"

He still looked doubtful, but took a deep breath and backed off. She'd talk about it in her own time. "Okay. What do you want to eat?"

"A lot. I'm starved."

The waitress came back, and Taylor thought she could see concern on her face, but she was all business, taking their orders and bustling off.

Baldwin wanted to defuse the moment, so he tried a different tack.

"I knew you in high school, you know."

"What?" Taylor was shocked. She knew most

everyone she'd attended school with. And she'd figured Baldwin was in his late forties. She gave him a good once over, and decided he was definitely younger than that. Years had melted off in the past few days. She could now see he was much closer to her own age.

"I transferred in to Father Ryan my senior year. You were a sophomore, I think. Pretty little thing."

She blushed. "I can't believe I don't remember you. I always hung out with the older crowd. Sam was dating Simon Loughley. He's the guy that runs Private Match. He was a senior when we were sophomores. Did you know him?"

"Knew of him. I kept to myself a lot."

"Why'd you transfer in so late? Where were you before?" Taylor realized she was anxious to learn more of Baldwin's background. She blamed it on simple southern nosiness, but knew she was trying to get closer, to figure him out.

A brief look of pain shadowed his face. "My folks died my junior year. Car accident. We lived over by Old Hickory Lake. My aunt was on the west side of town. She took me in and moved schools on me. I wasn't too thrilled about it, but I didn't have much of a choice. She was trying to do what was best for me." He took a long drink of water, and the smile returned. "She was a crazy old bat, kept after me constantly. I loved her, though, and respected her wish to see me complete my education, just like my parents wanted. She pushed me from Father Ryan into a college in Virginia, Hampden-Sydney."

"I know of it. All boys, right?"

"Yep. I met a psych teacher there I liked, and he suggested I go on to med school. So I hit up Johns Hopkins, they accepted, then I got the JD to go with the MD and the other degrees, and here I am."

"Where'd you go to law school?"

"George Washington. That's how I got into the FBI, actually. I met Garrett Woods, my old boss, at a symposium on campus. He recruited me hard, and it seemed like it would be fun. So I joined up, did my fieldwork, and he pulled me into the BSU after a few years. That's where it all went downhill." He realized he'd been babbling, so he tried to turn it around. "What about you? Where'd you end up?"

"Criminal justice at University of Tennessee in Knoxville. My parents were so proud." Her sarcasm wasn't lost on him. "Having their only child run off to be a cop was the last thing they wanted. Oh my God, I completely forgot."

"Forgot what?"

She shook her head. "Oh, it's nothing. My father called me a couple of days ago. With the case and all, I managed to block it out."

"You don't talk with him much?"

"Nope. Win isn't…well, we had a falling-out a few years back. When I said that my parents weren't thrilled I wanted to be a cop, I wasn't kidding. He was never around, anyway, like he could have influenced any of my decisions." She was pulling away again, back into her protective shell.

"It mustn't have been easy to be Win Jackson's daughter."

She looked up and laughed. "So you know all about it, huh?"

"Not all of it. Some. I was out of state when he was indicted."

"Such a proud day for me. Four counts of interference and tampering with an election of a circuit court judge. God, I thought I was going to die. I saw it all on the news. They didn't even have the decency to let me know what was happening until it was all over. My mom divorced him while he was inside. She remarried and moved to Aspen with her new husband, who's some sort of ski gigolo. We don't have much in common anymore, you know?

"But good ol' Win spent his three years at the Club Fed, came back all changed. Righteous, full of remorse for all those years he'd ignored his only child. Decided if I was going to be a cop, damn it, I was going to be chief of police. Starts calling around, trying to find ways to get me into plainclothes. Can you imagine? A convicted felon trying to call in favors? I could have died."

Baldwin almost laughed. The thought of Taylor Jackson needing Daddy's help to make it on the force struck him as patently absurd. "I assume you got wind of it and shut him down?"

"With a vengeance. Had to make sure everyone I had ever come in contact with knew it, too. I was getting shit from every corner. I was very nearly forced to quit, had to stay in uniform an extra year, which really pissed me off. The worst thing about it—I *was* getting promoted. I'd passed the sergeant's exam right when he decided to help my career along. He set me back instead. So we don't have a lot of father-daughter time, if you know what I mean."

"Why do you think he called now?"

"God only knows. Probably heard the director of the FBI was leaving and wanted to let me know he's trying to get my name in the hat."

Baldwin's face darkened, and Taylor knew she had tripped right into his own nightmares. She decided she needed to change the subject, get back on safe ground.

"Anyway, I wanted to go to UT. Sam went there to be with Simon, so I went there, too. Familiarity, you know? Only I'm not half as smart as Sam. She went on to med school, and I came back here and joined the force. That's it."

"Are Sam and Simon still together?"

"Yeah. They have been taking it very slowly. Every time I think they're going to take the next step, something always comes up. Sam's become the master of relationship procrastination. I think settling down scares the crap out of her. Simon gets so upset with her. He wants kids yesterday, and she won't marry him until she's ready to do that. They love each other, so they'll work it out. Eventually."

They were silent for a moment, each reveling in their new information on the other.

"So what happened with your shooting?" Baldwin asked.

Taylor was caught off guard. She stared at him blankly, visions of bullets and blood dancing through her brain. She immediately went on the defensive. "Why do you want to hear about it? Has Price said something to you?"

Baldwin shook his head. "No, no. Sorry, it's none of my business. I've just been wondering what happened, that's all. I haven't heard the story, and I'd rather get it from your mouth than the rumor mill."

Taylor was bristling like a cornered cat. "There's no story to hear. We had a cop who was dirty. I found out. He tried to kill me. I shot him. That's it." She stopped herself before she told him everything. *I killed a man who at one time I thought was my friend. And more.*

Taylor's cell phone chirped. She answered it with relief.

"Jackson… Yeah?… Okay, we'll be there in a minute." She clicked off. No more intrusions into her private world. All business, that was the way she needed to keep things with John Baldwin. He could be more dangerous than a loaded pistol pointed at her forehead. She felt a pang of sadness; she had enjoyed their breakfast, minus her little panic attack. She stood and gestured for him to follow.

"That was Price. Jill's parents brought in her dental records. Time to go to work."

46

The squad room resembled a horror flick, with zombies dominating the room and halls. It had been a long couple of days for everyone.

Jill Gates's parents had arrived from Huntsville. They called and talked with Taylor from their downtown hotel, which had luckily made it through the storm unscathed. She told them they had found a body. Jill's father immediately made the short trip back to Huntsville, retrieved his daughter's dental records, and had driven the radiographs back to Nashville. He and his wife had taken Taylor's advice to stay put in their hotel until some sort of identification had been made. They'd agreed and seemed rather calm for the circumstances. Jill's mother was absolutely convinced that the body they had found at the church was not her daughter. She claimed she would know in her heart if her Jilly had died, and she just didn't think it was her child dead in the morgue.

Taylor didn't try to dissuade her. Let Sam do a positive ID, then they could deal with the fallout.

Lincoln had been on the computers all night, searching through ViCAP and the regional missing person databases while Taylor and Baldwin oversaw the investigation at the church. He greeted them with sleep in his eyes, his suit rumpled and hair flattened on one side from where he had rested his head in his hand for the better part of the night.

"You find anything?" he asked.

"Nothing yet. There are missing person flyers all over town for Jill. Someone mounted a pretty big campaign. How about you?"

"We've been getting calls all night about possible missing women," Lincoln said. "Four different women, three of them Vandy students. We had to chase them all down. Two were from parents who hadn't talked to their daughters in a couple of days. Happily, both of them called back to say they'd gotten in touch. One was a roommate who'd gotten concerned when her friend didn't come home, but that one showed up drunk and sound asleep at the Pi Kappa Alpha house this morning."

"That takes care of the three Vandy girls. Who's the fourth?"

"Pro who calls herself Mona Lisa. She's working with that program over at St. Augustine's, what is it, Magdalene House? She's got some sort of medical condition and hasn't shown up for her treatments in a week. Magdalene's worried she may have gone back on the street. I threw it to Vice. They'll be able to track her down better than we can."

"Good call. What else?"

"Other than our MP report rate is skyrocketing?

I guess you haven't seen the news yet this morning, or the paper? Mayfield's on another witch hunt." With that warning, Lincoln threw her a copy of the front page of *The Tennessean*. She saw the huge headline, groaned, and settled in to read, with Baldwin looking over her shoulder.

Metro Police Baffled at Murder Spree

BY LEE MAYFIELD, CRIME REPORTER

Sources within the Metro Nashville Police Department confirmed early this morning that the body found last evening in the burned-out husk of St. Catherine's Catholic Church in West End are the remains of Vanderbilt student Jill Gates. Gates was reported missing only yesterday. Despite the attempts of the Metro Police and the lead investigator, Lieutenant Taylor Jackson, to find her before she suffered the fate of students Shelby Kincaid and Jordan Blake, the University Killer has struck again.

The story continued, but Taylor threw the paper on her desk without reading the rest of it. She started swearing under her breath. "Of all the damn fool things to print above the fold, for God's sake. That woman is going to be the death of me. Is she sleeping with Franklin now? I swear to God, I'm going to kill that man with my bare hands if I find out he's even helped her across the street. The 'University Killer'? Who decided to give him a nickname? I'm going to charge that woman with obstruction one of these days, watch me…"

Baldwin was enjoying the rant. "I assume you have a problem going with this Lee Mayfield?"

Taylor huffed out a breath. "No. Well, yes. I mean, it's her problem, not mine. A few years back, she misquoted me in an article that nearly got us sued. She had to print a huge retraction. She's had it in for me ever since. She's been eating up the Martin case. Tearing me to pieces for months."

Fitz had entered the room as she was finishing her tirade. He patted her on the arm. "Don'tcha worry about it, darlin'. She's a full-blown, grade-A idiot, and everyone knows it. Just let it go."

He turned the volume up on the TV. The Channel 5 anchor wore a knowing smile. Taylor was struck at how the media always seemed to enjoy reporting on a tragedy. She turned away, fuming, but looked back when she heard what the anchor was saying.

"Despite the article printed in *The Tennessean* this morning, our sources have confirmed that there has been no identification of the female body found overnight at St. Catherine's Church. According to a spokesperson from Forensic Medical, the male victim has been positively identified as Father Francis Xavier, a recent transfer from the Boston Archdiocese."

"Go, Sam!" Taylor threw her pen at the TV. She picked up the paper and stuck her tongue out at the headline. The tension dissipated for a moment.

Price chose that moment to return to the office to find his detectives laughing their heads off.

"I'd really like to know what's so damn funny," he said indignantly. The tone of his voice was too much, and the gales of laughter started again. Price tried to look stern, but giggled a bit himself; they were all getting punchy from the lack of sleep and the pressure of the case, but he quickly sobered them up.

"Okay, kids, knock it off. Has anyone slept?"

There were headshakes all around.

"Taylor, are you heading over to the ME's office for the post of our burn victims?"

"Yep, I'm going now. Baldwin, do you want to come?"

"Yes, I'd like to be there." He stood up and grabbed his coat.

"Wait," Price said. "Baldwin, I'd like to speak to you, if I may."

Taylor and Baldwin shot each other a look, and he put his coat back down. She gave Baldwin a smile, and a look he read as *see you later*. He nodded back.

"Absolutely, Captain." They went into Price's office, the door closing behind them.

Taylor stared at the door for a moment, chewed on her lip, then turned and grabbed Marcus by the hand.

"C'mon, puppy, let's go see Sam."

Marcus said, "I'm sure Fitz would rather go on out there with you, Taylor. I probably should man the desk for all the missing person calls. Or maybe head home and take a shower?"

Taylor looked at Fitz, who yawned widely and smiled at her. "Sure, love, whatever you need."

Taylor saw the strain on their faces, how tired they all were. They were no good to her like this. "Okay, change of plans. Lincoln, Fitz, Marcus, I want all three of you to go home and get a few hours of sleep. Nothing is going to happen until we find out if this is Jill Gates's body. Report back at one."

Marcus looked as if he was going to kiss her. "Thanks, LT. I could swing by your place and pick up something for you, bring it back when I come in, if you want."

His subtle hint that she needed to clean up wasn't lost on her. She looked down at her smoke-smudged shirt and jeans, smiling ruefully. "That's sweet of you, Marcus, but I've got a change in my locker, and I'll grab a shower at Sam's. Go on now, before I change my mind."

47

Sam fiddled with a scalpel, turning the blade over and over in her hands. She sat in her office with the sunlight streaming through the window, a cup of cold tea at her elbow. She'd been so lost in thought she'd forgotten to drink it. The sun was a welcome respite after the days of rain the area had been flooded with; the water tables were dropping and the minor floodwaters receding. Nashville would heal itself. She hoped she could do the same.

She had gone home the night before feeling overwhelmed and a bit lost. The scene at the church had gotten to her more than she wanted to admit. She figured a hot bath and a glass of wine would settle her nerves.

But when she opened the door there was soft music playing, roses on the table in the foyer, and a delicious smell coming from her kitchen. Smiling, she followed her nose and found Simon Loughley standing in the middle of the kitchen, wearing an apron and conducting the symphonic CD playing with a spatula. The scene was so absurd she burst out laughing. He started, then smiled sheep-ishly and gave her a hug. He was tall and thin, and she could feel his collarbones poking her in the cheek. His sandy hair was too long, his glasses were askew, but his blue eyes sparkled, showing the depths of his patience and good humor. She didn't think she'd ever seen anyone cuter.

"I hope it's not too late for you?"

"I'll take midnight margaritas with you any-time."

"It's wine, does that work?"

"Of course. Let me change and we can dig in."

Though the house technically belonged to them both, Simon generally didn't show up un-announced. Despite the fact they had bought the house together nearly ten years ago, he kept his own apartment on West End. Hypocrite that she was, Sam freely gave him her body, but wouldn't agree to officially "live together" until they were married. It was supposedly a nod to her Catholic roots, but if she were honest with herself, she was just scared of settling down. It had always seemed so permanent to her. After the past few days she'd had, the loss and senselessness of the murders, a domestic commitment was something she was will-ing to think about. She was tired of fighting it, and tired of being alone.

Once she'd freshened up, they sat down to the meal, opened a bottle of wine, and Sam told Simon everything. It felt so good to talk with him, to get all her worries off her chest. He was one of the few who could understand what she went through day in and day out, and she loved him for it. They'd been bickering lately, and she hadn't had his shoulder to cry on for a few weeks. She spilled all the worries that had built up since they'd last spoken: her fears for Taylor and her surprise at the attraction between her and Baldwin. Simon thought of Taylor as a little sister. He shared Sam's concern, but assured her Taylor would land on her feet. She always did.

He'd cleared the table and gotten Sam settled in the living room. He came back in the room with a nervous smile playing on his face. Before she knew what was happening, Simon was kneeling in front of her, pulling out a ring box.

"No midnight margaritas, but how about some diamonds, instead? I can't wait anymore, Sam. I want to marry you. I want a family with you. I want to spend the rest of my days making you happy. Will you marry me? Please?"

She was so shocked that he was actually proposing she barely registered what he was saying. Before she could stop herself, she'd said yes, and the ring was on her finger.

She looked down at her hand again. The diamond was huge, set in platinum and bordered by diamond baguettes. She was still trying to remember exactly what Simon had said, but all she could remember was saying yes, and he swept her off her feet and made love to her the rest of the night.

The phone rang, startling her from her reverie. She dropped the scalpel in her lap and caught it between her knees. An absurd memory flooded her mind—her father, lecturing on the virtues of abstinence when she was a teenager getting ready to leave on her first big date. He had handed her an aspirin as she was going out the door. She looked at him quizzically and asked what it was for. He replied in his booming voice, "If you sit all night with that balanced between your knees, young Simon here won't be able to make any moves on you." He'd dissolved into laughter, and Sam and Simon, both blushing furiously, had scurried away as quickly as possible. Her father would have been proud; she hadn't given in to Simon's relentless begging for another two years, the night of their senior prom.

Shaking her head and giggling under her breath, she answered the phone.

"Dr. Owens, it's Tim. Thought you'd want to know I'm bringing in a body. Female pulled out of Old Hickory Lake this morning by a couple of fishermen."

Sam drew in a quick breath. She hadn't even started the autopsy of the girl they'd found in the church. She was waiting for Taylor to bring over the dental X-rays from Jill Gates's father. Another body could be another chance of finding Jill. Damn.

Tim read her thoughts. "It's not her, Doc. Sorry, I forgot to tell you, she's black. Looks like a drowning."

She blew out a breath. "Well, at least the break in the pattern means this victim isn't part of the Vanderbilt series. No ID?"

"Actually, yes, there is. An ID card that says her name is Tammy Boxer."

"ID card? Like a license, but not a license to drive?"

"Yep. Address is over on Dickerson Road."

"Working girl?"

"Could be. I don't know. Looks like she's been under the water for a while."

"Thanks for the heads-up. I'll see you soon."

She clicked off, shaking her head. Dead prostitutes weren't a rare occurrence in Nashville. The police had actually built a database specifically for their postmortem identification. Since many of the girls went by aliases, the midnight shift patrolled their most common hunting grounds, pulling over to chat and check them out. Dickerson Road, also known as Hooker Alley, was an area with the worst offenders. The officers would go over the girls' information and run their sheets, then take Polaroid pictures and fingerprints and note any tattoos or characteristics. They got as much contact information as they could glean from the girls, though most of it was bogus. They'd use it to track down family, or pimps, should the need arise.

This information was fed into the database, and when a girl showed up dead, she was much easier to identify. Sam had ridden along when they first implemented the program, amazed at the lack of concern the prostitutes showed when they went through the process. It seemed they didn't realize, or care, that the police were doing this so they could identify them when they were pulled out of a Dumpster the next morning.

Sam picked up the phone again and placed a call

to Lincoln. The database had been his idea and was still his baby. He picked up on the first ring.

"Hey, Lincoln. How's it shakin' over there?"

"Shaking and baking, sister. Taylor is heading your way. I'm getting ready to go home myself, get a couple of hours' sleep."

"Good, you guys need a break. I wasn't calling about Taylor. I just got a call from my 'gator, Tim. Looks like they may have pulled a working girl out of Old Hickory. We'll send over the information to see if you can lay out a positive ID."

Sam could hear him clicking away on his keyboard in the background and smiled; he was already loading the database. "Any chance you have a name? I have an MP report on a lost soul from Magdalene House."

"Actually, she had an ID card on her, but who knows if it's really hers." She looked at her notes. "Tim said the name on the card is Tammy Boxer. Ring any bells?"

"Yes, damn it. That's the name they gave me last night. Hadn't seen her in a week, said she missed a couple of med checks. This is really going to make their day."

Sam gave a big sigh. The Magdalene House was one of Nashville's jewels. A minister at Vanderbilt's St. Augustine's Church had developed the program. It was designed to get girls off the street, cleaned up, give them some education and skills, and help them back out into the real world. It was a huge success, and Sam remembered reading that they were opening a second house because the demand had grown so large.

"Will you give them a call and let them know we may have found her? If they can send someone over this afternoon to ID her, we'll try to get things moving over here."

"Yeah, I'll do it. Thanks, Sam, that's one less thing I need to worry about."

Sam wished him well, told him to get some sleep, and hung up. As she did, she heard Taylor in the hall talking with Kris, their front desk attendant. She walked out of the office and nearly collided with her best friend in the hall.

Sam clucked at Taylor disapprovingly, a mother hen unhappy with one of her brood.

"T, you look absolutely awful. You didn't go home last night?"

Taylor did, in fact, look awful. On cue, she sneezed and gave Sam a sheepish grin.

"Naw, I didn't. Thought I'd clean up over here once we're done. Do you have any sinus medicine? I'm out. I think my allergies are getting to me."

"Your allergies, my ass. You have a sinus infection. Why do you always pretend you're not sick when you are?" Sam headed back into her office and opened a cabinet by the door. She pulled out a box of Advil Cold & Sinus and gave it to Taylor. Like most longtime Nashvillians, she always had some on hand. It was a bizarre phenomenon that so many people in the city suffered from some kind of sinus problems throughout the year. The joke was if you didn't have allergies before you moved to Nashville, you would within a year.

Taylor broke two pills out of their blister pack and offered the box back to Sam, who shook her head.

"Keep it. You're going to need it worse than me. Do you have the radiographs?"

Taylor held up a large manila envelope and sneezed again. Sam shook her head, handed her a tissue, and said, "Follow me."

48

They went through the biovestibule and started the changing process that would turn them into medical butterflies.

"I talked to Lincoln a little bit ago. Looks like we have the body of his missing Magdalene woman."

"You're kidding," Taylor replied, arms lost in a smock. "Where'd she turn up?"

"Couple of fishermen pulled a body out of Old Hickory this morning. Her ID card had the name Tammy Boxer on it, and Lincoln said that's the name he was given on the report."

Taylor shook her head. "Another body. It never ends. Sam, what's happening to our city?"

"Let me cheer you up. I heard a great one the other day. This chick suspects her husband is cheating on her. One day she calls home and a strange woman answers. She asks who it is. The woman on the other end of the phone says, 'This is the maid.' The woman's confused. 'But we don't have a maid,' she says. The maid tells her the man of the house hired her that morning. 'Well, I'm his wife,' she says. 'Is my husband there?' The maid gets quiet for a minute. 'He's upstairs in the bedroom with a woman I assumed was his wife.'

"The wife is livid, gasping for air. She says to the maid, 'Listen, would you like to make $50,000?' The maid asks what she would have to do. The wife tells her to go to the top desk drawer, get out the gun, and shoot him and the woman he's with. The maid puts the phone down. The wife hears footsteps, gunshots, and then more footsteps. The maid picks the phone back up. 'So what do I do with the bodies?' The wife tells her to take them outside and dump them in the pool. 'But ma'am, there's no pool here.' There's a long pause. 'Uhhh, is this 494-2873?'"

Taylor guffawed and Sam grinned, pleased with her cleverness.

"Jeez, Sam, that was awful. You're awfully chipper this morning. You make up with Simon last night?"

"Taylor, how come anytime I'm in a good mood, you automatically assume I got laid?"

"Because nine times out of ten, you did."

"Fine. Yes, we had a very late dinner. And drinks. Then a few more drinks. Happy now?"

"No, I want to hear the details. I have to live vicariously through your sex life, remember? Really, Sam, are you ever going to marry that guy?"

Sam got a sly look on her face. "Yeah, I think I might." She held out her hand.

"Whoa, lookie there. Now that's a rock! Are you serious? You guys really got engaged?" Taylor was hopping up and down, pulling Sam in a hug up and down with her.

"Yep. Last night. He finally asked. Properly, I mean."

Taylor couldn't stop grinning. Maybe the planets were finally aligning. "Oh God, I am so excited. Ooooh, and we get to have a bachelorette party! When are you going to do it?"

Sam was laughing. "God, T, I have no idea. One step at a time, you know. I gotta get used to the idea of being engaged first. It was so sweet, though. He actually got down on one knee. You'd think after all these years of saying we should get married, he'd toss a ring at me and say, 'Come on, we have an appointment at city hall in thirty minutes.' But he had a whole speech prepared and everything. Most of which I can't remember. Roses, wine… I'm telling you, he really surprised me. And I just said yes before I had a chance to think. Something in my heart just told me it was time to quit thinking and start doing."

"Oh, Sam." Taylor had tears in her eyes. "It's about time. I don't think I can remember a time that Simon wasn't head over heels for you, and you for him." She started jumping up and down again. "Ahh, man. I gotta give that boy some shit. Let's call him."

"Let's not. We have to get to work. Bodies are a-calling."

Their joking ended abruptly and Taylor gave a huge sigh. "You had to remind me, didn't you? Kill-joy." She handed Sam the manila folder with the dental X-rays nestled inside. Sam took them and started across the room.

"By the way, I almost forgot. I ran blood work on Jordan's baby. I figured it would be easier to see if the blood type from the fetus was compatible with the semen before we went to the trouble and expense of having Simon run DNA. Quicker, too."

"And?"

"Whoever raped Shelby wasn't the father of Jordan's baby. Statistical impossibility."

Taylor tucked this morsel into the ever-growing database in her head on the murders. "Maybe he killed her because it wasn't his baby," she said softly.

"It's a thought."

They entered the autopsy suite. One of Sam's assistants had already placed the burned-out husk on a stainless table, and was ready to start with the X-rays. Sam nodded to him, and he got to work.

Taylor went to the phone on the wall and dialed Price's office. She was surprised when Baldwin picked up the line. "Captain Price's office."

"Baldwin. It's Taylor. Why are you answering the phone?"

"Well, I'm sitting in his office doing nothing. Price got called out to a meeting for something or other, and no one else is here. I just figured…"

"No, that's good. I was calling to talk to you anyway."

"Oh." He sounded faintly surprised. Taylor thought she heard a note of pleasure in the single word. She blushed. Sam, who was watching, raised an eyebrow. Taylor turned away from her, embarrassed to no end. She quickly became all business.

"Sam ran the blood type of Jordan's fetus against the semen from Shelby. It wasn't a match."

Baldwin was silent a moment. "Maybe he killed her because it wasn't his child."

"Funny, I said the same thing. Listen, I've got to go. Sam's signaling, she has the radiographs ready. I wanted you to know."

"Thanks, Taylor. I'll think on it. Let me know what you find out, okay? Wait a second, Lincoln just walked in, and he wants to talk to you." He handed the phone over.

"Taylor?"

"I thought you were going home?"

"I know, I am. Real quick, though, I talked with the people at Magdalene House. They said Tammy Boxer was HIV positive. Will you let Sam know?"

"Ah. Will do. Thanks for everything, Lincoln. You've been a lifesaver. Bye."

She hung up and turned back to Sam, expecting a chastising or brutal tease. Instead, Sam was standing in front of the radiograph view box, shaking her head.

"Heads up, Boxer is HIV positive. What's wrong?"

Sam pointed at the radiograph. "I've got good news and bad news. Which do you want first?"

"The good news."

"The good news is this isn't Jill Gates."

Taylor stood frozen, immobilized by the finding. "You're sure?"

"No doubt about it. These dentals aren't even close."

"What's the bad news?"

Sam turned to her friend, her mouth a grim line slashing her face. "The bad news is this is not Jill Gates." She turned back to the view box. "Who are you, sweetheart?"

She and Taylor stared longingly at the radiographs as if the teeth would come to life and spell out the name of their owner. Taylor turned away and sat heavily on a hard-backed chair, leaning her arms on a built-in desk. As she put her head down, her cell rang.

"Yeah?... Hey, Fitz... Okay, route it through." She turned to Sam. "Call came in for me. Some guy wants to talk to me and me alone. Won't give his name. Oh, hello." She listened to the other end of the phone, her eyes growing wide. "Can you... Damn, he hung up."

"What the hell was that?"

"An anonymous call from someone who claims to have done a pregnancy test on Jill Gates. Six months ago."

"Wait a minute. Jill Gates is pregnant?" Sam's astonishment was catching.

Taylor nodded. "According to this guy, she was six months ago. He wouldn't tell me anything else."

"Taylor, if it's true, and she didn't abort or miscarry, Gates could be at least seven months pregnant, maybe more. With all the emphasis on babies with this freak, I think you may have a bigger problem."

"What's that, Sam? Spit it out?"

"At thirty-four weeks, that baby can live on its own. Sometimes earlier, if they're lucky. Assuming all's gone well, she's twenty-eight weeks at a minimum, and could be as much as thirty-two, depending on how far along she was when she had the pregnancy test."

Realization of what Sam was trying to tell her finally sank in. Taylor flipped open her phone and called back to Price's office. No one picked up the phone. She hung up and dialed Baldwin's cell. The voice mail came on almost immediately, and she left him a message that felt as desperate as it sounded.

"This body isn't Jill Gates. She might still be alive, Baldwin. I think our killer is after her baby."

49

Baldwin had been sitting in Price's office for half an hour. He knew exactly what this conversation was going to be about and just wanted to get it over with. Yes, he was fine. Yes, he was interested in the case. No, he didn't have any answers yet, only overblown theories.

His mind was chewing the tidbit of information Taylor had just passed along. The fact that the killer wasn't the father of the child was of great importance to him. Though he didn't know the motive behind Shelby's killing, it was entirely possible that Jordan had been killed *because* of the pregnancy. It had been known to happen: a man being inordinately jealous of a woman who had cheated. The theory played into several aspects of her murder as well; Sam had told him that some of the stab wounds were postmortem. Baldwin could see the scenario easily. *He gets mad, stabs her in the chest, kills her, then in a fit of rage goes out of control and thrusts the knife into her flesh viciously, punishing her over and over again.* But why the aconite? And the herbs? Why such a huge difference between the murders of Jordan and Shelby? And, most important, where was Jill Gates, and who was the woman at the morgue?

"You're losing your touch, man." He looked around sheepishly to make sure no one had heard him, but the offices were deserted.

It was time for him to start making some leaps, maybe try to get a little faith in himself back. He pulled out his notebook and started trying to tie things together. He muttered aloud as he wrote.

"Gotta assume this is the same killer. There's no way all of them are coincidences. Okay. So we have the same guy. He kills Jordan because she got pregnant with someone else's child. It was definitely an intentional murder. But Shelby, maybe she was an accident. If he was having an affair with both of them, maybe Shelby found out about Jordan and confronted him, told him Jordan's baby wasn't his. Is he having an affair with Jill, too? Is this a close-knit group, and jealousy has crept in, or is this guy just a serial rapist who was close to being caught and had to shut the girls up?

"There's a thought. Rapists do escalate; he could have graduated to murder. Shelby's positioning could explain that. Maybe she was the first one he murdered and he felt so bad about it that he tried to treat her with respect. But no, it looked as if Jordan was killed first, and there was no respect there. Why poison Jordan if he was going to stab her? Did she fight back? Was he trying to give her the easy—yeah, ha, easy—death that Shelby was given, and she fought him? That could be…

"Step away from that for now. The victims at the church. What in the hell was that about? He kills a priest and another woman, using fire. The priest is easy to explain away, he could have just gotten in the way. But why take her to a church to kill her? We've got the church, the river, and the Parthenon. Church, river, Parthenon. God, this just doesn't make any sense.

"What's the most logical place to find this guy? All the girls are students at Vandy. Assuming the fire victim is as well, we're up to four students, and a possible priest of opportunity. Gotta be someone connected to Vandy. And what is he trying to tell us? River, Parthenon, church. Catholic Church. Poison, stabbing, fire. Trial by fire? Cleansing by fire? Damn it, this is crazy."

Baldwin slapped the notebook down on Price's desk. An idea sparked, one so off the wall he almost immediately discarded it. No, there was something he was missing, something he wasn't getting. The locations could be the key; granted, the murders were incredibly diverse, but if the guy was trying to send a message, he certainly had picked the right places to garner as much attention as possible. And there was something about Jordan's pregnancy that was nagging at him. He stood up and stretched. He knew from experience that brainstorming, word association, throwing a jumble of thoughts together often forced an answer later on. Ideas were starting to form, but he needed to talk them out, run through them aloud with another person. Preferably Taylor. He sensed she was moving along the same lines as he was. He liked seeing how her mind worked.

Price walked back in while Baldwin was still mulling things over. He came around to his side of the desk and sat down heavily. As he did, the phone rang. He stared at it a moment, as if he really didn't want to pick it up.

"I could get that for you, if you'd like. Let them know you're not here?"

Price gave him a smile.

"A magnanimous gesture, but that's okay, I'll get it. I'm just sick of putting out fires." He picked up the receiver. "Price."

Baldwin watched him listen to the person on the other line, wondering at the emotions that passed across his face. Good news or bad? Baldwin couldn't tell.

Price sighed and spoke again. "Yes, Julia, I can reach her. One hour? Okay. Bye."

Holding up his finger in a signal to wait, he hit the speakerphone and dialed Taylor's cell phone. She answered immediately.

"I was trying to call you."

"Good. Julia Page just called. The grand jury wants you in an hour."

Taylor let out a huge groan. "No, no, no, not right now. Please tell me you're kidding. Can't you get me out of it?"

Price chuckled. "You know I can't. Just get it

over with. We'll mark you off the rest of the day. Give us a call when you're back on the grid."

The annoyance in her voice was barely concealed. "Damn it. Fine. I'll let you know when I get out. But I have other news for you. The remains from the church? It isn't Jill Gates."

Price and Baldwin shared a look. The relief was palpable, yet tempered with concern. Price jumped back in first. "I take it you don't have an ID for us?"

"No, I don't. But we may have a much bigger problem. I got an anonymous phone call a little while ago. Jill Gates is pregnant. Assuming she's still alive, very pregnant. According to Sam, she's far enough along that if she had the baby now, it might survive without her."

Price sat straight up slowly, staring at Baldwin while Taylor continued.

"But I have to go testify in front of the grand jury instead of handling that little detail. I'll leave that up to you guys. My suggestion would be to get Baldwin working the pregnancy angle. He might have an idea of what this guy is up to. He didn't answer his phone when I called a few minutes ago."

"I'm right here, Taylor. Sorry, I must have turned off the ringer accidentally."

"Okay then. You guys have a fun afternoon. I'm outta here." She hung up before they could wish her luck.

Price hung up and stared at Baldwin, who didn't look terribly surprised by the news Taylor had just sprung on them. "Who was in that confessional?"

Baldwin sighed at the rhetorical question. "I

don't know. This is such a departure from the earlier killings it is possible that it's not related."

"You don't think that's the case, though, do you?" Price asked.

"I'm that easy to read, huh?" He frowned, shaking his head. "No, I don't. This is all connected somehow, but I haven't figured it out yet. It's not common, but killers do shift their patterns, especially when they're trying to communicate. I think there's a message in this church burning, and the victims were doubtless chosen for a specific purpose. I'm not sure what it is, though. And now, with Jill Gates having a late-stage pregnancy combined with Jordan Blake's pregnancy… Have there been any more missing person reports?"

"Lincoln is our guy there. He's outside, still working, though Taylor sent him home to sleep." He went to the door, called Lincoln in.

"What's up, Cap?"

"We just got off the phone with Taylor. The remains from the church aren't Jill Gates. But we have to find out who this woman is. Do you have any other MP reports?"

"Nothing that hasn't been resolved. The only outstanding one was from a former pro missing from Magdalene, but she turned up this morning floating in Old Hickory Lake."

"Think you can do some trolling, see if there are any others out there?"

"Yeah. I think I need to expand out the area. I was already running statewide. I'll go over the entire Southeast, see if anything else pops up. Check ya later." He turned to go, shoulders slumped with weariness.

Price leaned back in his chair, propped his feet up on his desk, and gazed at Baldwin, saying nothing. Baldwin waited him out. He had no intention of volunteering anything more without a good, long think about things.

Price dropped his feet off the desk. "C'mon. Let's go get something to eat."

50

Baldwin was too surprised by Price's invitation to do anything but agree.

They made their way out of the building, across the courthouse parking lot, and onto Second Avenue, his mind churning with possibilities. Price didn't speak much as they walked, lost in his own thoughts. He stopped in front of a restaurant with a red neon sign in the window that read SATCO. The San Antonio Taco Company was something of an establishment in Nashville. Their main restaurant was over by the Vanderbilt campus, servicing the students with beer and cheap food on the oversize deck. The small offshoot they were entering didn't have the ambiance, but the food was still quick and delicious.

Price held the door for Baldwin. "Hope you like Mexican," he said in a tone that told Baldwin he didn't give a crap whether he liked Mexican or not. Lucky for him, he did.

The restaurant was set up like a cafeteria. They ordered tacos and enchiladas, retrieved their food, and made their way to a private corner. The restaurant wasn't full, so they had plenty of privacy.

Digging into their meals, they were silent for a moment. Price took a long drink of his soda and eyed Baldwin, finally giving the younger man a smile.

"So how are you finding our little operation? Anyone giving you any trouble? Taylor keeping you in the loop on everything?"

It wasn't the beginning Baldwin expected, but he rolled with it. "Actually, everyone has been very gracious and helpful. Taylor especially."

They stared each other down. *Aha*, Baldwin thought. Maybe this wasn't about him after all.

"Son, I was a little dubious about letting you in on this case. But your boss and I go way back. Way back. And when he asks me a favor, I'm quite likely to comply. That's why I agreed to let you come on board and gave you the option of whether you could handle yourself enough to participate. You seem to be doing fine. But I'm wondering just how committed you are to this case. You know what I mean?"

Baldwin suppressed a grin. He felt sure Price was going to ask his intentions toward his lieutenant, like an overprotective father. It hit him that everyone was a little overprotective of Taylor, though he couldn't see any reason for them to be so concerned. Her anxiety attacks aside, the woman seemed to have steel fused in her backbone. He was debating how exactly to answer when Price continued, almost reflectively.

"The stuff that's been happening around here

is unusual, to say the least. We don't have a lot of high-profile cases, at least not this many in so short a period of time. I've been doing this for a long time, since before you were running around in short pants. I'm inclined to agree with you—my gut's telling me these murders are related and that we're dealing with one killer. You said you think he's trying to send us a message. You're the profiler on this case. Time to earn your pay."

Exam time. Baldwin decided to go for it. He felt Price was sincerely asking for his opinion. Perhaps it was time to trust him and show his worth to the man.

"I'm not 100 percent perfect yet, so I'm going to think aloud here, okay? We aren't dealing with a serial killer, not in the accepted sense of the word. This guy is on a spree—a very calculated, very organized spree. Each death has a meaning to him; each placement of the body is intentional. He hasn't left many physical clues besides the semen from Shelby Kincaid. And I think that was deliberate. It's part of the message. Shelby had been raped, but placed at the Parthenon and shrouded in herbs, which strikes me as a loving gesture. Jordan Blake was pregnant. Now we find out Jill Gates is pregnant as well. There is a fatherhood theme going on here. One interpretation—he feels protective toward them, he wants to be a father figure. Or, he desperately wants to be a father. *The* father. Look at the church fire. He kills a 'Father.'" He made air quotes with his fingers. "He places the bodies in a house of God, the *Father* of Christ. There are so many interpretations out of that alone that we could be puzzling it through for months."

Price was staring at him openmouthed, then laughed. "That's the craziest thing I've ever heard. But you're the profiler—you guys are paid to think differently than the rest of us. So profile this guy for me. The University Killer, I guess he's being called. Creative name, huh? Lee Mayfield at her best. Not the brightest woman, that one, thinking she can take on Taylor Jackson and win. She hates Taylor's guts."

"I heard about their issues. Mayfield may not be too bright, but she hit on something I doubt she realizes. We are dealing with someone who's smarter than average."

"Which holds true for most organized serial and spree killers."

"Yes, but this one keeps breaking his profile. Three girls and one man are dead, with three separate and distinct methods of killing. Another girl is missing. He's not leaving them in a secret dumping ground—he's placing them where we'll find them quickly. Even finding Jordan on the banks of the river was calculated. She could have easily been washed downstream, but I think he weighted her down right there in the area she was found, came back to her body after Shelby's was discovered, and released her, knowing with the slow current she wouldn't go far. A coincidence, finding them both in such a short period of time? There are no coincidences, not in this world." He sat back and steepled his fingers under his chin. "You know what they say, 'Coincidence is God's way of remaining anonymous.' So unless God ordained that Jordan was going to be found within twenty-four hours of Shelby, it was planned."

He broke off, taking a sip of his soda. "I think we need to be looking for someone a little older than the standard profiled age. Middle-aged even. And where do you find middle-aged men on a college campus?"

Price smiled. "Professors."

"Exactly. I think Shelby, Jordan, Jill, and our unidentified burn victim have all had contact with him in a controlled environment on campus. How the priest fits in, I don't know yet. There are no indications the girls were religious or attended St. Catherine's."

"Let's leave Father Xavier aside for the moment. He might have been in the wrong place at the wrong time. Focus on the girls. You think they've all had contact with the suspect one way or another. Are they taking classes from him?"

"That's the most obvious explanation. He could be a counselor, or a doctor, or a janitor for all I know. But he definitely has access to them, and I'm inclined to think he's in a position of authority over them. We've surmised they were all dating someone, Jill and Shelby perhaps on the sly. If they were all seeing the same man, and that man is the one who is killing them, it makes it simpler to understand their connection. He's having affairs with his students, which is a major no-no."

"So why kill them? They found out about each other? Might talk and turn him in?"

"I don't think so. One explanation for Jordan's death is her pregnancy. We've learned that the DNA of the fetus didn't match the DNA left at Shelby's crime scene. It's possible he was furious that she had gotten pregnant by another man. And Shelby... well, she was raped, repeatedly. Maybe he was trying to get her pregnant. With Jill's pregnancy... I can't be certain, but the father angle is the best thought I have for right now. The guy has a God complex."

Price gave him a long look and wadded up his taco wrappers. "You are scaring the hell out of me. Let's get back to the squad. It's time to kick this into high gear." He stood and took their trays to the trash can. His excitement was palpable; cases broke on less cogent theories. They started back to the office, walking quickly. Just before they reached the door, Price turned to Baldwin.

"And, son? You hurt Taylor, and I'll rip your balls off. Got me?"

Baldwin didn't miss a beat. Apparently their body language had been enough to give them away. He wasn't sure how she felt, or where it was going, but he did know he wanted to get to know Taylor much, much better. But he didn't hesitate or play around. He looked Price in the eye, unflinching.

"Yes, sir." And he meant it.

51

Taylor pulled up in front of the Washington Square building on Second Avenue. She looped into the parking lot and took the first open space. She locked her car, walked the twenty yards to the door, and entered the building.

She was prepared for this meeting of the grand jury. She wasn't thinking about guns. Or the coppery scent of blood. Or the slight sense of satisfaction she had felt when she realized who she had killed. None of those things were going through her mind at the moment. She was totally focused on an image of twelve-year-old Tamika Jones, lying in a puddle of blood on her grandmother's kitchen floor.

Taylor was so intent on her purpose, she walked right past Julia Page.

"Hey, Lieutenant. Over here." Page trotted after Taylor, an engaging grin on her rotund face. Taylor stopped dead and looked over her shoulder, realizing she had missed seeing the Assistant District Attorney. Granted, ADA Page was maybe five feet tall on a good day, so she wasn't automatically in Taylor's line of vision, but she shouldn't have missed her totally.

She started back up the hall. "Sorry, Julia. Lost in thought. We all set?"

Page tried to keep pace with Taylor's strides, her brown curls bobbing with the effort. "Yes, we're all set. Are you ready?"

Taylor stopped, realizing the shorter woman was practically running to keep up. "Ready as I'll ever be. I want to get this over with."

ADA Page pursed her lips and looked her over, as if to gauge whether Taylor was telling the truth. "I don't blame you. The grand jury is in room 502. They're waiting for you. You know I can't go in there with you." Her pug nose twitched, and her demeanor became all business. "And you know how important this is."

"That almost sounds like coaching, Julia. I've got it covered. I'll see you after, okay?"

With that, Taylor strode away, catching the elevator at the last moment. She shoved her hand in between the closing doors, and they slid back open. There was only one other passenger. He sighed loudly in annoyance. She gave him her brightest smile and fingered her Glock. He blushed and looked at the floor.

The ride was quick. The elevator stopped at the second floor. Taylor watched the man's pudgy ass waddle off the elevator. *Should have taken the stairs, buddy.*

She got off at the fifth floor. Following a black-and-white diamond-patterned corridor, she stopped in front of room 502. She didn't hesitate. She rapped three times, almost amused that it seemed like a secret knock. The door was opened immediately by the foreman of the jury, and she was ushered into the room.

Twelve members of the grand jury were already seated at the table. Taylor recognized the faces. She'd sat in front of them just a few weeks before. She had testified on her own behalf, explaining the shooting of Detective David Martin as self-defense. Thankfully, the grand jury had agreed with her assessment and did not indict her. Now they had to decide the rest of the case, the one Taylor had blown wide-open.

She took her seat at the head of the table. The thirteenth juror, the foreman, a sweet gentleman with a thick southern accent and black glasses, held the chair for her. She thought he looked a bit like the colonel from the fried chicken chain. When she was seated, he took the chair to her left and cleared his throat.

"Ladies and gentlemen, you all know Lieutenant Jackson. Lieutenant, could you state your name and occupation for the record, please?"

Her voice cracked when she answered. "Certainly. My name is Taylor Jackson, lieutenant, Criminal Investigations Division, Homicide Unit. Badge number 4746. Let me apologize up front for my voice. I've caught the Tennessee Crud. I'll try not to sneeze on you." That drew a few smiles and laughs from the room. Taylor relaxed. It was better to work with an audience that was at ease.

"Thank you, honey," the colonel replied, his courtly southern demeanor overshadowing his professionalism. He addressed the room. "We're here today to gather information relating to the alleged criminal activity of Ray Alvarez, Tom Westin, and Nelson Sanders, all employed by the Nashville Metro Police Department, working in the Vice squad, and David Martin, of the Homicide Unit." The contempt in his voice was apparent. Handing down indictments of officers of the law was not taken lightly.

He continued. "Now, we've read a summary of the case. Lieutenant Jackson, we understand that you were called in to investigate a suspicious death, a young girl named Tamika Jones. And the investigation led you to uncover information that implicated four fellow members of the Metro Police—David Martin, now deceased, Ray Alvarez, Tom Westin, and Nelson Sanders. These men were complicit in a black-market scheme that was ultimately profitable for them. Am I correct in this summary?"

Taylor nodded.

The colonel smiled and leaned back in his chair. The business end was over. It was time to hear Taylor's version of events. "Now then, let's discuss Tamika Jones. Could you go over it for us, please?"

Taylor surveyed the room. Here were thirteen very powerful people. They had the mission of deciding who and what got prosecuted in Nashville's criminal courts. They met in secret, were basically a self-governing body. No lawyers or district at-

torneys were allowed. It was just the person who
had been subpoenaed to appear, and the thirteen
jurors, like a lopsided cabal. Yet for all the seriousness of their job, the spirit in the room was conge-
nial, friendly even. This particular meeting held the
futures of three men in the balance, but the atmosphere was reminiscent of a book club gathering.

Taylor cleared her throat and took her notebook out of her pocket. She didn't need to open it.
"Of course, Mr. Foreman. On October second of
this year, I was called to the home of Clementine
Hamilton, 453-A Moore Street, Nashville, Tennessee. It was coming on ten o'clock in the evening.
When I entered the premises, I found the woman's
twelve-year-old granddaughter, Tamika Jones, on
the kitchen floor. She was lying on her right side,
curled in the fetal position. There was a pool of
blood under her body."

Taylor quickly lost herself in her narrative. She
couldn't have imagined how investigating Tamika
Jones's death would change her life forever.

*Moore Street was one of Nashville's nastiest
projects. Many of the city's homicides happened
there. Some were fueled by drugs, most others by
desperation. Whatever the cause, the effect was
tangible—the Moore Street projects accounted for
nearly 30 percent of all the murders in Nashville
in a given year.*

*In the gloaming dusk, Taylor exited her vehicle
to the usual catcalls. In these projects, men and
women of varied ages roamed the streets aimlessly*

at all hours of the day and night, talking, watching, being. The typical crowd had gathered when they heard the news. She ignored the rude gestures, the propositions, and threats. She walked through the manufactured similitude of the run-down buildings to the complainant's front door. The screen was cut. The wooden door stood open. Taylor could hear the sound of crying and smell the blood. Though there were other police around as well as EMTs, she instinctively put her hand on her gun.

A pale-faced EMT saw her looking through the screen and came over to the door. He opened it silently. His motions were sluggish. He looked as though he might be sick. She gave him a look of concern, then continued into the cramped house. The walls were paneled with dark walnut, lending the depressed air of the room a morose tone. Attempts had been made to keep the walls clean, but it seemed halfhearted. Lace curtains, yellowed with cigarette smoke, hung limply over the window. Taylor could see a bullet hole in one pane. The carpet was orange shag, about a million years old, and it didn't quite reach the four corners of the room. The home was squalid. The fetid stink of despair hung from every corner like a blanket.

She stepped through to the kitchen. She immediately realized why the home was such a mess—the woman sitting at the tiny, unstable kitchen table was blind. Her eyes were milky white, made more opaque by the contrast with her blue-black skin. She was old, very, very old. Taylor bit back a curse.

The woman should be in a home with people to take care of her, not living on her own.

There were tears leaking ever so slowly from the woman's blind eyes. For a moment, it seemed she and Taylor were alone, just the two of them in the putrid little kitchen, and she looked right into Taylor's soul. Taylor got a chill down her spine. Then the old woman's head turned and Taylor spotted the body of the girl. All other thoughts left her. She stepped carefully, avoiding the pooling blood.

The girl's skin was lighter than her grandmother's, and unmarred by the ravages of age. Her hair was braided into tiny rows, each held in place with alternating blue and white beads. Though dispatch had said the girl was twelve, she looked older. Taylor guessed that came from living hard.

She threw off all the cloaking of compassion and became a cop. She turned to the EMT leaning against the counter.

"What's the story here?"

"Tamika Jones, twelve years old. Seems she had an abortion today. Came by to check on her grandmother, collapsed on the floor. I'm assuming something went wrong with the procedure, and she bled out."

Taylor gave him a sharp look. Assuming wasn't allowed.

"You know for a fact she had an abortion?"

A voice, deep and rich, drifted toward Taylor's ears.

"She told me she was. That's how I know. Honeychile told me she was riddin' herself of the child.

I told her it was a sin. She didn't care. Never listened to old me anyways."

Taylor turned and saw Tamika's grandmother looking her straight in the eye. Taylor shuddered, and the woman laughed. "Don't take sight to see, girl. I know you're right there in front of me. Honeychile's been acting stupid for a while now, whoring around, taking drugs. I told her it would come to no good. She don't listen to her gran, though. I told her that man would kill her, one way or the other." The woman turned away, and Taylor stood, frozen, as if Medusa had glared out of the woman's sightless eyes.

"Ma'am, what man are you talking about? Does she have a boyfriend?"

"Haw," the woman spit out. "Boyfriend. Girl, child like that, she got herself a pimp. A sugar daddy. He whores her out, gives her the drugs."

"Do you have his name, ma'am? Any way I can contact him?"

The woman made the guttural noise again. Taylor understood it was a mirthless laugh. She got quiet, then seemed to shrink in on herself, drawing into the collar of her stained dressing gown like a turtle. The interview was obviously over.

Taylor took a deep breath and stared down at the little girl. The story was all too familiar.

52

"The medical examiner's autopsy report found the girl had in fact procured an abortion within the past twelve hours. You were able to contact the doctor who performed the abortion, one Carl Murray?" asked the foreman.

The question yanked Taylor back into the small room. She nodded and licked her lips.

"Correct. I was given his name by one of Tamika's friends. The girl only identified herself as Annya, wouldn't give me her last name. She was the one who confirmed that Tamika had seen Dr. Murray earlier that day. I visited Dr. Murray, and he denied ever seeing the girl. There was no way to confirm either story. Unfortunately, even if he had performed an abortion on Tamika, I couldn't prove it beyond a reasonable doubt.

"That's when Annya called again. She asked me just how stupid I really was." Taylor shook her head. "She told me about the setup. The word on the street was if you needed an abortion, you could go to Dr. Murray. He would do an abortion without parental consent for only a hundred dollars a pop. There was one catch. You had to bring as many boxes as you could of an over-the-counter decongestant known as pseudoephedrine hydrochloride with you. One hundred dollars and several packs of Sudafed? It was the deal of the century for these girls.

"Recognizing a possible criminal enterprise, I brought Annya on board as a confidential informant. With her contacts, I started seeing a trend. It wasn't just the poor black girls going to Dr. Murray. It seemed everyone who Vice would have interest in was seeing him as well. Strippers, prostitutes, drug addicts—all of them were being funneled to Dr. Murray for abortions."

"Which in itself is not necessarily illegal, is it, Lieutenant?" The foreman smiled at her gently. The grand jury knew all of the details of the case from their summary documents. For legal purposes, they needed to hear it from Taylor's own mouth.

"No, sir, it isn't. Incredibly unethical, but not illegal. I had a better chance of busting Dr. Murray for doing abortions on underage girls, but even that was tricky. If they show him an ID saying they're sixteen, he's covered.

"Something felt wrong to me. Rumors were swirling. Word on the street was there were other people involved, people in the police department, and drugs were playing a role. I didn't want to make any unfounded accusations, but I needed to separate the truth from the rumors.

"I set up a loose surveillance on Dr. Murray's

office. It quickly became apparent that he had a very successful practice. Almost too successful to be handling a patient load that large. If I hadn't been clued in about what he was doing I would have assumed he was just a very popular neighborhood doctor.

"That's when I was contacted by Detective David Martin."

The knock on the window of her unmarked vehicle made Taylor jump a mile. She looked out to see the grinning face of David Martin, one of the detectives in Homicide. He was blowing her cover, damn it. She put down her window in annoyance.

"What's up, David?"

"What's up with you, Taylor? Sitting on a house?"

She just smiled. "What can I do for you?"

He smiled back. "We need to talk about what's going on with the esteemed Dr. Murray. I know you're looking at him, and there's something going on that may involve the department. I've got some information for you. Let's go get something to eat and talk about it."

Taylor's first impression was that David had gotten information and was there to help her bust whoever was involved. She couldn't have been more wrong.

She followed him as he drove to the Shoney's across the bridge from police headquarters. Taylor noted that they were well away from Dr. Murray's office.

They went inside. Martin ordered coffee and eggs from a robust waitress. Taylor asked for Diet Coke. Her appetite had left her back at the stake-out.

Martin leaned back in the booth and gave her a lazy grin. "So, Taylor. Whatcha been up to lately?"

"David, I just want to talk about what's happening at Dr. Murray's. What information do you have?"

"Ah, c'mon now, sugar britches. Tell me you don't want to catch up with me."

Taylor started to fume. "I told you never to call me that. What the hell is your problem? You think being condescending is going to win you any points with me? You're an asshole, you know that?"

He started to laugh. "Oh, struck a nerve, did I? You need to lighten up, Miss Loo-tenant."

"I get it. You're still pissed I got promoted and you didn't. Tough shit, David. I earned this job."

"Whatever you say, sassafras."

That was the last straw. Taylor stood up and threw a dollar on the table. "Fuck you, Martin." *She turned to leave but he grabbed her wrist.*

"Oh, c'mon now. Sit back down. I know you're pissed at me, but you need to forget about it for a while. We need to talk about the doctor."

Taylor yanked her wrist out of his hand. Turning slowly, she sat back down. "Talk," *she spit out.*

53

"Detective Martin offered to cut me in on the deal. Dr. Murray was producing and selling the drug methamphetamine in the back room of his offices. He would do an abortion for a cut rate as long as the woman provided him with a certain quantity of pseudoephedrine. Since ephedrine, one of the main ingredients in meth, is a controlled substance and difficult to procure, meth cooks can produce ephedrine by processing large quantities of pseudoephedrine. It seems that once the laws on selling pseudoephedrine over the counter in Tennessee changed, when they put it back in the pharmacies where it couldn't be shoplifted, the meth makers were having a hard time producing the quantities to meet their demand. They needed a legitimate way to get their hands on the pseudoephedrine. Detective Martin was working with the three previously mentioned Vice squad detectives—Ray Alvarez, Tom Westin, and Nelson Sanders.

"According to Detective Martin, each man received a monthly 'reward' for funneling women and product to Dr. Murray. They had put the word out on the street that he was doing abortions cheap, and not looking at the IDs too closely as long as you brought the drugs with you. All the Vice guys had to do was tell the pimps and strippers that Dr. Murray would take care of them.

"In compensation for my efforts, I would receive approximately $15,000 a month. It was less than the others because I wasn't going to be doing any of the work. I was simply to keep my mouth shut and not pursue the matter.

"The money was large, and the detectives were getting rich. As many of you know, meth production and distribution is one of the biggest problems facing law enforcement in Tennessee. There always seems to be money in illegal drugs."

Taylor shifted in her chair and crossed her legs.

"Unfortunately, we have not recovered Dr. Murray's files."

The foreman consulted the sheets of paper in front of him. "That would be because allegedly, David Martin killed Dr. Murray, then burned all the files. Is that correct, Lieutenant?"

"That is correct, sir. Allegedly, Detective Martin made a visit to Dr. Murray the same evening he broke into my home."

"Which is the night you shot and killed the detective, isn't that right, Lieutenant?" A small woman with gray hair and piercing eyes glared at Taylor. Word on the street, meaning lawyers' gossip, was there had been a holdout in Taylor's case. Someone on the grand jury had actually voted to indict Taylor for homicide in the death of David Martin. But the grand jury had issued a "no true bill" in her case. It only took twelve of the thirteen jurors to issue a "true bill"—a yes to indict—or "no true bill"—a no to indict. The holdout had been effectively silenced in that final round. Taylor wondered if this was the one who voted to indict her, and felt an unexpected fury take hold. She bit the inside of her cheek and forced herself to be civil.

"Yes, ma'am, you are correct." Taylor did not continue. No sense in answering questions that weren't asked.

"That's enough, Inez," the foreman shot at her. The woman shuffled some papers angrily. "Now, Lieutenant Jackson, is there anything else we need to know?"

"No, sir. I believe that is all I can give you. I recused myself from the investigation after I...um, upon Detective Martin's death. That is all the information I have for the grand jury at this time."

There was throat clearing and paper shuffling. A few members stood and stretched. They were finished with her. Taylor stood as well. She smiled at the foreman. He gave her a wink. Nodding to the rest of the room, she left them to their next witness. She had done all she could. Maybe now she could finally put all of this behind her.

54

Jill didn't know if she was awake or dreaming. It looked as though there was light coming through the window of her room, but she couldn't be sure. Couldn't be sure of anything. She could vaguely understand she was being drugged, and that a man she thought she knew kept coming into the room, whispering crazy stories in her ear while he held her. She felt his voice inside her head constantly, saw glimmers of his face, hovering, concerned. Was she sick? In a hospital? She had a momentary vision of her parents: her mother crying, her father pacing. Were they worried about her? Was the baby okay?

Her thoughts drifted away again, and she felt herself slip into the darkness. The hallucinations were becoming more complex each time the drugs were injected into her arm. Jill felt herself walking on clouds, skimming over the earth, flying through the sky. She felt the wind in her hair and it brought her joy. She knew she had died, that she was flying to heaven. She was excited, thrilled, but a little frightened. What would God be like?

She drifted higher and higher. She started passing what she knew were angels. One looked at her, a blindingly beautiful girl with flowing blond hair. Jill saw she was crying, and frowned. Angels aren't supposed to cry. She heard the weeping then, multitudes of whimpering, sadness all around. The blond angel turned to her and reached out a hand, and Jill felt the touch in her soul. A word breezed through the air; she couldn't make it out. She strained, but the wind took the word and cast it aside before she could grasp its meaning.

She had stopped flying and was walking on the clouds. There were thousands of lights around her, celestial fireflies flitting through her. As they surrounded her, the voices became louder and louder, and she became frightened but was unable to stop, to turn back. She realized she was entering some sort of room, and the voices quieted. There was no sound; even the wind whipping through her hair was silent. The lights became people, men and women, all shimmery and gossamer thin. The people's mouths were moving, but no sound came out. She was terribly confused. She didn't know heaven was going to be a silent place.

55

Sam returned to her office after finishing the autopsies of the two burn victims, popped open a Halloween-size box of Milk Duds and tossed them in her mouth. She was exhausted; there had been so much happening in the past few days that her entire schedule had been disrupted. She was thankful she had four other medical examiners on the staff; they had been dividing up the normal duties between them to keep Sam free for Taylor's ever-growing list of bodies.

Though the sensational string of killings was getting all the media attention, there were still other people dying whom the medical examiner's office had to process. There were death certificates to be signed, meetings to attend, and piles of paperwork to be dug through. All the regular day-to-day aspects of working in an office had been languishing from Sam's lack of attention. Full of sugar, she reached into her in-box, pulled out the week's accumulated stack of death certificates, and opened her Montblanc fountain pen.

She'd been working for about an hour and making actual headway when Dr. Thomas Fox, one of her youngest MEs, stuck his head in her office. "Hey, Sam, can you come down into the autopsy suite for a minute?"

Sam wasn't taken aback; it wasn't unusual to have requests for a second on posts. But she didn't have the time, and asked Dr. Fox if he could round up one of the others.

"Actually, everyone is already down there. We have something you need to see on the woman pulled out of Old Hickory this morning."

Sam felt her heart sink. She followed Dr. Fox through the biovestibule, put on a smock and grabbed gloves and a shield, and joined the group of MEs standing over the body on the table.

The woman was young, probably barely into her twenties. There was a lot of damage to the skin, and she was bloated like a distorted puppet. The standard incisions had been made, she was laid open, her breastplate was set aside, her lungs had been excised, and the typical autopsy procedures had been followed. Sam didn't see anything obvious that would be enough to drag her away from her work.

"What's the problem?" she snapped, instantly sorry she sounded so bitchy. No one seemed to notice.

"She didn't drown," Dr. Fox volunteered. "She died of ventricular fibrillation."

"So she was dead before she went into the water.

C'mon, Fox, dazzle me! You dragged me all the way down here for that?"

"Look at her liver, Sam."

Sam looked at him long and hard. *Oh shit* was the only thing running through her mind. She leaned in and looked carefully at the woman's liver, then hastily examined the rest of the organs. When she looked up, her face was ashen.

Dr. Fox explained his reasoning, though he could tell Sam had just confirmed what all of the other MEs had been speculating. "I went back and looked at the pictures and slides from the Blake and Kincaid autopsies. The organ composition and liver necrosis match. I think this woman was given aconite prior to her plunge into Old Hickory Lake."

Sam's thoughts spun. What in the name of hell would a black ex-prostitute have to do with the University Killer? It didn't make sense. But that was Taylor's problem. Right now, she had to get positive confirmation that aconite was the cause of death for this poor woman.

"Fox, consider me dazzled. You deserve a raise. Pull all the blood work and get it over to Simon Loughley at Private Match. He's been handling the rest of this, and he's the best equipped to get the results ASAP." She had a thought and almost didn't voice it because it seemed so outlandish. But she trusted science, and science would give them the answers they were looking for.

"I want you to go back to the burn victims and pull their liver samples. They presented completely different, because of what the fire did to their bodies, so maybe we missed something. Send them over to Simon, and tell him to look for aconite in them as well."

Dr. Fox was surprised. Sam saw the look and understood perfectly. It didn't make any sense to her either. "Why poison someone, then go to the trouble to burn them to a crisp?" he asked.

"I know it's probably unlikely, but if there's a chance that aconite's present, that will tie everything together for Taylor's investigation. Also, find out what Tim Davis got from St. Catherine's. He said he was running the tea he found in the priest's office there. If it's got trace aconite in it, we at least have our delivery method. Go to it."

He nodded and went to work. Sam headed back to her office to grab her keys. She wanted to go to the squad room and tell them in person what was happening.

56

The conference room looked like a hurricane warning center—bedlam mixed with excitement and a sense of purpose. Pictures of all the victims had been hung side by side on a huge whiteboard with as much information about all of them as they could put together. There was one photo missing from the lineup: the face of the female burn victim from St. Catherine's. Instead, a shadowy sketch with long hair had been drawn, with a question mark under the distorted outline. Laptops were plugged in and lined the long table. File folders, computer printouts, and soda cans littered the room. The piles of paper had been sorted and lined up under corresponding title cards with headings representing "ViCAP" through "School Records." It was organized chaos, akin to the investigation itself.

Baldwin and Taylor stood in a corner, talking quietly. He ran through his theory with her, and she agreed, between sneezes, that Vanderbilt's staff held the key. Taylor was getting sicker by the minute and looked like a limp dishrag that had been wrung out too many times and was ready for the trash. She'd refused the repeated admonitions to go home; she wanted to get some sort of break in the case before she cut out.

Lincoln was seated at one of the laptops, blurring through cyberspace. He was running missing persons files from Georgia, Kentucky, Florida, North Carolina, and Virginia. He had open access to these databases; he was waiting for linkups to South Carolina, Alabama, and Mississippi. Fitz was back, floating in and out of the room; some new information had come in on the Lischey Avenue murder. He had managed to get Terrence Norton into an interview room and was trying to get him to give up his buddy, Little Man Graft. Terrence was consulting with his lawyer at the moment, trying to figure out how to save his own ass. It gave Fitz some time to check in with the University Killer investigation.

Marcus was sitting at the end of the table, trying to be inconspicuous. He was getting impatient to get started but didn't want to intrude on Taylor and Baldwin's conversation, so he put up his feet and waited. To his relief, the phone next to him rang.

"Homicide… Yes, she is, but we're in a meeting, can it wait?… Oh. Let me get her." He signaled to Taylor. She shook her head, but he covered the phone with his hand and said, "It's Shelby Kincaid's mother. She called the main number looking for you and said it was important."

Taylor blew her nose and took the phone. She

croaked a hello, then listened intently. "Can you hold on a moment? I need to get to another phone." She punched the Hold button, told them to start without her, and practically ran from the room.

She went into Price's office and shut the door, then punched the line to connect her back with Mrs. Kincaid.

"Mrs. Kincaid? I'm back, sorry about that. You were saying?" She could tell Mrs. Kincaid had been crying and could hear traffic in the background. *She's not at home*, Taylor thought, pulse speeding up.

"I'm sorry I didn't call you before now. I've been having a hard time, and the doctor has kept me sedated. I just couldn't take it, you know, losing my Shelby. But I needed to talk to you, so I made an excuse to go out, and I'm at a pay phone. I couldn't call from the house. There are too many people around."

Taylor was leaning forward in the chair, her cold forgotten. Whatever would drive a preacher's wife out of the house to call her when she was in seclusion and mourning had to be big.

"I understand completely, Mrs. Kincaid. What do you need to talk to me about?"

"It's about Shelby. She called me the weekend before she was killed. She told me something, swore me to secrecy. Her father wouldn't understand. He's a good man, but he just…well, that's neither here nor there."

"Go on, ma'am."

"You have to understand, Shelby was a good girl.

She never gave us any trouble. She was such a loving child, a wonderful daughter. I can't imagine this happening to her—she's always so levelheaded."

Taylor was getting fidgety, but realized she needed to let Mrs. Kincaid tell her story her own way. "I've been told by many people what a lovely young lady Shelby was. I am so sorry this happened, Mrs. Kincaid."

"I know you are, dear, that's why I'm calling. I knew you'd know how to handle everything. You have to promise me no one will know about this. It would kill my husband if he found out."

"Absolutely, Mrs. Kincaid. You have my word that I will keep this limited to the people working on the investigation."

"Thank you, Lieutenant." Taylor heard her take a big breath, steeling herself. "Shelby called me when she knew her father would have already left for church—he always goes in early on Sunday mornings. She was crying so hard, completely hysterical. I finally got her to calm down, and she told me she had been…" Mrs. Kincaid was sobbing uncontrollably. Taylor made sympathetic noises until the woman calmed down. She finally got herself together and finished the story.

Taylor hung up the phone in shock.

57

Taylor was walking back to the conference room when Sam appeared at the end of the hall.

"T!" she called.

Taylor held up, and Sam jogged down the hall to her. Taylor could see this wasn't going to be good news. Sam's face was drawn, and she looked tired. Little wonder, they were all burning the candle at both ends. But there was something else in her look that sent a shiver down Taylor's spine. Sam grabbed her arm and pulled her into Price's office.

"Have you heard anything about the floater that was pulled from Old Hickory this morning?"

Taylor thought for a moment. "Oh yeah, the prostitute. Lincoln said he's given you a positive ID. Why?"

"Better sit down, Taylor. You're not going to believe this."

"What? You already called off the wedding?" she joked halfheartedly.

"No, I'm serious. We've got a big problem." Taylor sat down, and Sam started in with the details.

"The prostitute didn't drown. She was poisoned. Her liver presented just like Shelby's and Jordan's. Fox caught it and called me down. She was dead before she went into the lake."

Taylor's thoughts were spinning, and her chest tightened. "Aconite again? What the hell? A black prostitute completely breaks the pattern. Why would he...oh, wait a minute. Could she have been a test case? Was he trying out the poison on her to see how it worked?"

"Girl, I don't know, but this thing is getting really screwy. Whoa there, are you okay?"

Taylor was having a hard time catching her breath. "He's been out there doing this for fun. Just to see what would happen. My God, I can't stop him. None of us can stop him." She was wheezing and losing her focus on Sam's face.

"Head between your knees. Good girl, now breathe. C'mon, T, give it a shot. There, that's right." Sam was smoothing her hand along Taylor's back. It was comforting, but Taylor couldn't seem to get a grip on herself. This was the second one she'd had today, damn it all.

She'd just started to catch her breath when Baldwin came into the room.

"Hey there, Sam, have you seen... Jesus, Taylor, are you okay?" He rushed over to her and knelt down beside the chair. "Is it like this morning?"

Taylor gave him a dirty look. She didn't want anyone to know about this. She hadn't hidden it from Sam; her best friend knew she was riding on the edge, but now Baldwin was on board, and Marcus and Fitz. And she suspected Fitz might have said something to Price, too, damn his eyes.

Sam leaned back against the desk. "Second one today? You had one earlier?"

Taylor had her voice back and was feeling a little more in control. "It was nothing, Sam. I saw Jill's posters and got upset. I spent two hours with the grand jury this afternoon, and I'm just worn out. I feel like crap. I need some antibiotics and a good night's sleep, and everything will be just fine. Okay? So back off, both of you. Baldwin, Sam has another poison victim." *Good job, girl*, she thought. *Focus their attention elsewhere.*

"What?"

Sam pulled up her legs and sat cross-legged on Price's small desk. "We had a floater this morning. Black prostitute named Tammy Boxer, alias Mona Lisa. We thought she had drowned, but the post showed the same necrosis that was present in both Shelby's and Jordan's organs. This may have been your very first victim." She held up a hand, anticipating Baldwin's next question. "And yes, I'm having the tox run on the fire vics. Maybe that's your commonality, I don't know."

Baldwin was shaking his head. "Wow. This guy is getting around. How long had she been in the water?"

"At least a couple of weeks. Taylor suggested she might have been a test case."

"That's an excellent thought, given the timing. This case is so screwed up." He turned to Taylor, who was enthusiastically blowing her nose. "Better?" She nodded, blew out a breath. "Good. How was your conversation with Shelby's mom?"

Taylor tested her voice and found it working properly. "She wanted us to know Shelby had been date-raped. More than once, according to her mother. She called and told her the weekend before she died. She wouldn't tell her who had done it; she was scared to death of the guy. But she promised that she was going to go to the campus police and report the rape. That's probably why her roommate was so evasive when we asked if she was seeing anyone. I got the sense she suspected Shelby was involved with someone. She was involved, all right, with some son of a bitch who was forcing her to have sex with him. Bastard!"

"There's our motive for Shelby's murder. She tells him she's going to the police, and he has to kill her to make sure he's not found out." Baldwin's eyes drifted off, and he was silent for a moment. His eyes came back into focus, and he gave them a huge grin. "That's it. That explains the herbs you found on Shelby. They *were* burial herbs."

Both Sam and Taylor were looking at him blankly.

"You don't get it? Okay, roll with me for a minute. He left her at the Parthenon. The ancient Greeks, hell, most of the ancient cultures used herbs during a burial to ensure that the spirit of the deceased made it into the spirit world without problem. That's what he was doing. In his mind, he *was* giving her a proper burial. I'll be damned. And I'll bet he put her at the Parthenon so we would understand, that we would pick up on the connection and know that he was reluctant to kill her but had no choice. That he gave her the most proper and sympathetic burial he possibly could. And the aconite. The aconite!"

Taylor and Sam were staring with their mouths agape. Either he was right on target, or he'd gone round the bend. He shook the hair out of his eyes and launched back in.

"You know Socrates was unjustly sentenced to death and was forced to create his own execution? So in order to maintain his dignity, he drank hemlock, effectively committing suicide?"

They still looked confused, but Taylor motioned with her hand. "Go on, Baldwin."

"Man, didn't you guys ever study the classics? Anyway, there's always been some debate over whether it was actually hemlock that he drank. The descriptions of his death weren't completely consistent with hemlock poisoning. In some circles, they believe it was aconite."

"Wait a minute. So you're saying that the herbs were a burial rite, and the aconite was to symbolize Socrates's death?" Sam was shaking her head, looking at them like they were crazy. But Taylor took it a step further.

"I see where you're going, Baldwin. The guy knows the classics. Plato, Socrates, Aristotle, the fathers of modern logic. The ancient Greeks and their rash of poisonings. This MO was logical to him. If he gave the girls poison, they would be purged, cleansed, right? You said early on that he was sacrificing them. Socrates had to sacrifice himself to save his dignity, to make sure no one thought he was a coward. What better way to sacrifice them than by following the lead of one of the greatest philosophers in the world?" She trailed off.

He took her hand and squeezed it. "In his world, Taylor. In his world. We've got him."

58

Jill began to wake. She had been dreaming of something, but she couldn't remember it exactly. She felt peaceful and happy, so it must have been a good dream.

She started to get out of the bed and realized where she was. Locked in a room by a man she thought cared for her. She started screaming his name as loud as she could, desperate to know what was going on.

"Hello? Hello? Are you here?" There was no response. She yelled louder. "Is anyone there? Help me, please, help me! He's holding me prisoner. Please, somebody help!"

She heard footsteps running down the hall. The locks turned and the man came into the room. He was disheveled and looked ill. There was sweat dripping off his brow, and his face was gray, as though no blood was reaching it. He came over to the bed, breathing heavily. Jill scooted out from under the covers and tried to back away, but he was too quick. He grabbed her and nearly threw her back onto the bed.

"Don't do that again, Jill. I'm warning you."

She had never heard that tone from him. It was angry, threatening. His body was tensed, and she feared for a moment that he would hit her. She cowered on the bed.

The man reached in his pocket and drew out a syringe. His entire demeanor changed. He smiled sweetly and transformed into the man she knew. But she was afraid now, afraid that he was actually going to hurt her.

Jill began to beg. "Oh God, please, no. Don't give me any more of that. I swear I'll be good. Please, just let me go home."

He shook his head sadly and chucked her under the chin. She flashed to an old memory of her grandfather—he used to ball his fist and gently bump her under the chin just the same way. "Chin up, girl," he always said.

He grabbed her hand, and his touch made her shudder. His hand was cold and clammy, and she tried to yank hers back. But he held fast, caressing her fingers one by one.

"Oh, my sweet, darling girl, I wish I could let you go. But there is a bad world out there, a world that is conspiring to hurt you. There are men who want to take you away from me, but I need to keep you close, by my side. I need to know my son is safe. They will take him away from us, away from me. I am his father. I need to show him the way. I'm the only one who can help him, guide him. He has so many things to do to save us, and it is my responsibility to let the world understand his importance. Don't you understand? I have taken all the steps I know of to keep both of you safe. But it's better for you not to fight. I hate to see you anxious, and it's not good for my son. You just need to stay calm and relaxed. I won't let anything bad happen to you."

Jill started crying. She knew he was crazy, and what he was saying made no sense. His son was going to save them? Save them from what?

"Please, I don't understand. Let me go home. I know my family's frightened to death. I don't even know how long it's been since you brought me here." She saw she wasn't getting anywhere and decided to try a different tactic. She was willing to tell him anything to make him let her go. She pitched her voice low, seductive.

"I love you, you know that. I'll always come back to you. I'd never take your child from you. Why have you changed so much? Please, just let me go, or let me call my parents and tell them I'm okay."

Her pleading was having no effect on him. He held the syringe up to the light, checking for air bubbles. "Soon, love. Soon, you'll be able to see them. After my son is born." He pulled her arm straight and injected the drug into her vein. "You rest now, and be a good girl. I'll tell you a bedtime story." He fluffed up her pillows and pulled the blanket up around her chin, stopping briefly to put his hand on her growing belly.

"Do you remember Plato?"

She nodded weakly; whatever drug he was giving her was already taking effect.

"Then you remember the story of Plato's Allegory of the Cave. Where all of humanity was kept underground, in the dark, chained to their seats, their heads immobilized? And the only things they were allowed to see were the shadows on the walls. Remember the puppet masters? Those who controlled the images of what humanity was allowed to see? They'd show humanity the shadow of a woman, or a chair, or a mouse, and that was the only representation they would ever know as a woman, or a chair, or a mouse. But one man was strong enough to break the chains, and he snuck out of the cave into the real world. The sunlight was so strong his eyes teared and stung, and when he could finally adjust to the light, he saw what a real woman looked like, and a real chair, and a real mouse. And he ran back into the cave to tell the others, to let humanity know they were being tricked, duped into believing what the puppet masters wanted them to believe."

He ran his hand lovingly across Jill's cheek. She didn't resist, and he could tell she'd fallen under the spell of the morphine he had given her. He felt himself stir, but it wouldn't be right. He couldn't take the chance that he would harm the child.

She was so lovely, her mouth slightly open as she slipped into sleep. Oh, just a moment or two of that softness couldn't hurt. He'd be so gentle and sweet.

He loosened his pants and pulled down the blanket. Jill was naked in the bed, and he stretched out beside her. As he entered her unconscious body, he whispered the rest of the story in her ear.

"And the man returned to the cave, but humanity was stupid and didn't believe him. They finally got fed up with his lies and killed him. But no, my darling, that won't be the fate of our son. He will be strong, strong enough to lead them all out of the cave, into the light, and let the lives of all those worthy begin again."

59

After an hour of arguing, Taylor relented and agreed to head home for the night. The whole crew had ganged up on her, insisting that she was too sick to go through another all-nighter. They'd all had rest, and she hadn't. Marcus and Fitz had taken it upon themselves to secure a warrant for the records of all the professors from the classics and theology departments at Vanderbilt, and were on their way with a court order to drag Vanderbilt's dean out of bed to gain access to the names of their possible suspects. Lincoln was setting up to run the names they retrieved through his databases and look for past indiscretions that would help solidify their case. Price had practically forced her out the door, handing her jacket and purse to her and walking her to the stairs that led to the parking lot.

Baldwin drove her into the night, stopping briefly at the Walgreens drive-through to pick up a prescription for antibiotics Taylor's doctor had called in for her. He followed her directions and got her home.

Taylor lived in a remote, rambling log house with lots of windows, perched on several acres of land. She loved watching the animals, kept the bird feeders full all year and salt licks out for the deer. The inside of the house was as comfortable as the outside, with a soft leather sofa, throw rugs, and a big fireplace with logs stacked perfectly on the brick hearth. A second-story loft overlooked the open living/dining room, and Taylor made her bedroom up there, along with her precious pool table. She was as dependent on the table as she would have been on a drug to help her relax in the middle of her sleepless nights. It was a great pastime for an insomniac. She had an office set up in the bedroom downstairs, with inset bookcases filled with everything from hardbound classics to paperback mysteries. It was lived-in, comfortable, away from the world she had to deal with day in and day out. It was a little lonely at times, but she wouldn't trade it for the world. It was a casual and comfortable lifestyle for her.

Seeing Baldwin in her space confused her. He fit so well. As if he'd been a part of her world from the beginning.

Baldwin got Taylor laid out on her couch, a mug of steaming green tea sitting on the coffee table next to her. Taylor was impressed by his domesticity and bedside manner. He had been clucking over her like a mother hen since they got to her place, and was currently in her kitchen, using her pots and pans to make her an omelet. Normally, she would have been uncomfortable having him wait on her hand and foot, but she felt so lousy, she didn't have the strength to argue. She relaxed a little, letting herself enjoy his ministrations. She heard him humming to himself as he put together her food, then laughing and scolding the cat for trying to get into the eggs.

As he came back into the living room carrying their dinner, he couldn't help but notice that despite being sick, run-down, and sleepless for two nights, Taylor looked beautiful. She'd changed clothes when they'd gotten there, and was casually dressed in cutoff jeans and a long-sleeved University of Tennessee T-shirt; her bare feet revealed toenails polished hooker red, which surprised him a bit. She didn't seem the type. He was surprised to find himself wondering how he could fit into the sanctuary Taylor had created for herself.

He shook his head, laughing quietly. Man, he was getting the cart before the horse. But he recognized he was finally coming back to life, and he liked how he felt when he was with her. As strange as it was, he sensed that it was right.

They ate together in silence, both anticipating their next moves. Baldwin finished his eggs, pushed the plate away, and gave Taylor a smile.

"You want me to make a fire?"

"Aren't you just the little domestic?" she teased. "Yes, that would be nice. Thanks." She settled in deeper, grabbed her cup of tea, and watched him. She was drawn to him in a way she couldn't understand. It was more than lust: Though he was a very handsome man, he was still much too thin and had dark circles under his eyes. But she could sense the change in his energy. The sense of purpose he carried with him was palpable.

He got the fire lit and returned to the chair facing the sofa. "Can I get you anything else? More tea? More food? Soup? You have some nasty canned stuff in the pantry. I could heat it up for you?"

"Nasty canned stuff? Thanks for the commentary on my taste. No, I'm fine. I just want to sit here and relax. It seems like weeks since I even sat down."

"It has been a crazy couple of days."

"Do you think Fitz and Marcus have found anything yet?"

"Taylor, they told you they'd call the minute they had anything worthwhile. There have to be thirty or so professors for them to look at, and the school is still closed after the storm. It's going to take them some time. They're good cops. They won't miss anything."

"I know. I just feel so stupid lying here doing nothing." She coughed.

"Like you coughing and sneezing all over the faculty at Vandy is going to help things? C'mon, Taylor, give yourself a break. Let's give them some time, and we'll call and check on their progress later. Why don't we just talk about something other than the case for a bit?"

Taylor gave him a sidelong glance. "Like what?"

"How about these panic attacks you're having? You want to tell me about that?"

"Not particularly. Want to tell me how things are going with you?" she challenged.

Baldwin looked off into space and gave a big sigh. "Okay, if I talk then you have to. Fair enough?"

"No, but I'll think about it."

"Great, thanks. So what do you want to know?"

She looked him frankly in the eyes. "I want to know why you were busy playing with your life when I met you."

He snorted. "You are direct, aren't you?"

"C'mon, Baldwin. I'll show you mine if you show me yours."

He sat back in the chair. "If I tell you this, you may feel you need to get involved, and I don't want that."

"I'm already involved, Baldwin," she said softly.

He met her gaze with a long look. "That's not exactly what I meant, but it's good to know. I'm feeling involved myself. Very involved." He smiled at her, then his lips curved down in a frown. "You know the whole story about the shooting in Virginia, right? How I got three good men killed for no reason?"

"I've heard some. You went into a suspect's home—he came back unexpectedly, drew down on you, and you shot him. But he got off shots and hit the three you were with. It shook you up, and you left for a while. That's what I know."

"That's the official story, but it was a little more complicated than that." He got up and went to the fire, throwing on another log and using the poker to mess with the hot embers.

"Tell me, Baldwin. Is that not the whole story?"

He gave her a rueful smile. "No. It's not the whole story. Harold Arlen was a bad man, Taylor. Evil. We just didn't have the evidence to sink his ship. He was raping and killing little girls, and we couldn't get him for the murders. There was no evidence at his house except tons of child porn, which wasn't enough. We couldn't find any other properties he may have used to rape and kill them. Nothing. But I knew it was him. Knew it in my heart. I knew if we let it go, he'd just kill again. I couldn't let that happen."

"What did you do, Baldwin?"

He turned to her. "No one knows this, Taylor. At least not officially. Have you ever done something you know in your heart is wrong, but it's the only way you can see to resolve a situation?"

Taylor was getting an idea of what he was talking about. "You planted evidence," she said flatly.

He hung his head, turning back to the fire. "Yeah, I did. I know it was wrong, but I had to get this guy. There was blood evidence in the case— enough from one of the girls that could be slipped out and used. I took a handkerchief and put some of the blood on it, broke into his house, put it in one of his dresser drawers. When we went in with the warrant, one of the guys found the handkerchief. We had him, and he was going away for a long time."

"God, Baldwin. How could you do that?" Taylor

knew she sounded judgmental, and tried to change her tone. "You just weren't thinking, right?"

"I don't know what I was thinking. I was in a pressure cooker situation, with other…" He stopped abruptly, as if he'd changed his mind about telling her something. "It seemed like the only course of action I had left. I knew he was responsible. But I did something really stupid, and it got three guys killed. That day… Arlen got off the shots before I could react. I hit him and he went down, but it was too late." His eyes were welling up; he shook his head sharply to stop them from spilling over. "But that's not the worst of it. It all worked, for a while. Arlen was dead and the case was solved, right? A few weeks later another little girl turned up. She'd been dead for at least a couple of weeks and was majorly decomposed. But there was no way to know for sure if it was another one of his victims that we had missed or a copycat killer. The scene was in close proximity to where we found the other girls. The body was placed in the same position as the others. There was no discernible DNA. It looked just like one of his. But there were a couple of unfamiliar hairs found on the girl. They ran them for DNA, but it wasn't a match to Arlen.

"I could tell by the way everyone looked at me that they knew what I had done. They knew it was my fault. I just couldn't handle it. So I ran, and when I couldn't live with myself anymore, I decided that not living was a much better choice than living in the hell on earth I had created. I just didn't have the guts to flat-out do it."

To admit aloud what he'd done was too much for him, and he felt the despair creeping back. He went to the window, stared out into the black forest. He was shocked when he felt Taylor's arms around him, holding him from behind.

"Baldwin, what you did? There's no excuse. You knew in your heart it was Arlen, that he was doing the killing. You stopped a horrible person from committing even more crimes. You have to find a way to forgive yourself. You made a terrible mistake, Baldwin, but you made it for the right reasons. That's good enough for me."

The relief washed over him, a waterfall of cascading emotions. He turned in her arms, and before he could stop to think, kissed her deeply. She kissed him back.

He didn't know how long it had been when they finally came up for air. Taylor was smiling but turned away, suddenly shy. Though every fiber of his being cried out to hold her again, to feel her soft lips on his forever, he knew he couldn't push.

Taylor sat back down on the couch, but when he moved toward the chair she patted the seat next to her. He joined her with a sigh. Taylor caught the sound and put her hand on his arm.

"I know you've been through a lot, but it's over now. And you're here. With me. Do you think you can make a go at this? Living your life, I mean."

Baldwin leaned over and kissed her forehead tenderly. "I think I may have enough reason to, now."

"Good. 'Cause I'd kinda like you to stick around

for a while." She smiled. "Even though I probably just gave you my cold."

He kissed her again, slower this time, memorizing the feel of her beneath his hands, then folded her into his arms. "I don't care if I get pneumonia. I'll be here for as long as you want."

"Good. That's good."

Taylor suddenly felt too exhausted to keep her eyes open. The emotion of the case, Baldwin's confession, her feeling like crap, was all catching up with her. She felt safe in his arms, and drifted off to sleep.

60

Bullets were flying in the darkened sky. She heard them whizzing by her head, felt the heat as they ripped through her hair. She saw him go down. She was screaming, clawing at him, trying to get away from the hand that reached up and grabbed her by the throat. She fell beside him. He was dead. She could see the entrance wound, glistening silver in the moonlight. Her hands were slick with blood: It covered all of her, drowning her in its viscous blanket, dragging her down into the weeds as they curled and spread over her body. There was no hope. There was no pain. She gave up her struggle and lay serenely next to the empty soul beside her, waiting for the strangled vines to drag her into the earth to decompose along with him. She raised her hand, only mildly revolted as she watched the flesh fall off the bone. She turned to the skeleton beside her and saw the mandible smile, heard his disembodied voice. And then she was back

*on solid ground, walking away from David's
body, and she could see Baldwin in the distance, his hand held out, beckoning to her...*

"Taylor! Taylor, wake up!" Baldwin was shaking
her. She fought her way out of the dream to find
him standing over her, eyes wild, hair disheveled.
She looked at him vacantly, still caught up in the
remnants of the dream.

"I was dreaming," she murmured.

"No, you were having a nightmare. You were
yelling to someone named David, telling him to
get down. Are you okay? Who is David?"

Taylor stood up, spilling the afghan and the cat
onto the floor.

"What time is it?"

Baldwin looked at his watch. "Almost five in
the morning. Taylor, what was the dream about?"

A few hours of sleep had made her feel better.
She ignored Baldwin for the moment and wandered
into the kitchen. She pulled a Diet Coke from the
refrigerator, gulped it down, and grabbed another.
Setting it on the counter, she opened the antibiotics and popped three in her mouth.

"Taylor, you're not going to get better any faster
ODing on Keflex."

"I feel better already. How long was I out?" She
made her way back into the living room and collapsed on the couch. Jade jumped into her lap and
made a nest, purring heavily. Taylor ran her hand
absently along her silky back.

"About five hours. You zonked out so hard, I just let you sleep."

"Thanks." She gave him a sad smile. "You know the best thing about not sleeping for the past couple of days? I didn't have any dreams."

"What's up with the dreams? Is David the detective you shot?"

She nodded slowly. "David Martin. Dirty as they come. And I came this close to getting indicted for his murder. Murder, Baldwin. He breaks into my house, attacks me, and I'm the one who nearly takes the fall. I don't know how he could do that to me. How he could put me in the position he put me in. Trying to bribe me to let him go on his happy little way." She snorted in disgust, shaking her head.

"There's more, isn't there, Taylor?" Baldwin reached over and took her hand. She wanted to pull away, but resisted the urge. It was time to get it off her chest.

"Yeah, well, we were lovers, briefly. No one but Sam knows, though I think Fitz suspects."

Baldwin felt a pang of jealousy and shoved it aside. The man was dead, for God's sake. He had no business being jealous of a ghost. But this was a ghost who was haunting his woman's dreams.

He understood, though. Ghosts visited him as well. Every night since the shooting, the three men who had been shot came and sat on the foot of his bed, watching him. He shook off the memory. "So you dream about him?"

"I dream about his death. Same dream every night since I shot him. He gets shot, goes down, and I go down with him. He's decomposing, so am I. His skull turns to say something to me, and then I wake up. It's expanded recently. All the victims I haven't saved show up, too. This massive field of graves, and they're all talking to me."

"What do they say?"

"*'Help me. It's your fault.'* I thought I heard something different this time. He said, 'Go on.' I don't really know what that means."

Baldwin sat next to her and took her other hand. "I think it means he's telling you he doesn't blame you for shooting him. Were you in love with him?"

Taylor shook her head. "That's what's so awful. I wasn't. I was lonely, and he was there. It didn't even last very long. It was a casual thing for me, but, yes, he loved me and wanted more. I broke it off, then he approached me to keep my mouth shut about his little venture, and I just snapped. I felt like he'd betrayed more than just my body, you know? He put my whole career on the line. If I turned him in to Internal Affairs, I might have taken the brunt of it. He could have said that I was in on it from the beginning, made it a 'he said/she said.' IA doesn't like to see their cops embroiled in illegal doings, you know? Especially the female cops.

"But the worst of it was the satisfaction I felt when I saw him lying dead on the floor. I felt like he deserved it. And that's just so wrong."

"That's a lot of guilt to be carrying around, Taylor. It wasn't your fault you had to shoot him. He did attack you. These things happen."

"'These things happen,'" she echoed. "That's

what I just don't get. I don't know why these things 'happen.' Why do they happen?"

"If I could tell you that, Taylor, I would be God. And I'm not."

She looked at him. "After all you've seen, you still believe in God?"

"I never said that. I just don't understand. But I have a confession to make. Earlier tonight, when I kissed you, I thought I might have a glimmer. When I realized you understood what happened in Virginia, that you didn't judge me, I felt like I had been forgiven. By whom, I'm not sure. I wasn't looking for it, but it's there. I don't know what to do with it, and I don't know if it changes anything, but it's there."

Taylor felt tears in her eyes. She had asked for forgiveness a million times, and she never felt as if she'd gotten it. But as she looked at Baldwin, she realized that it had happened a long time ago. She just wasn't willing to forgive herself.

They both jumped as the phone rang. Taylor lunged for it. "Fitz?"

Baldwin could hear his voice booming through the phone. "How'd ya know it was me?"

"I was hoping. Did you get anything?"

"Yeah, I think we did. Are you coming in?"

She gave Baldwin a smile and squeezed his hand. "We're on our way."

THE
SIXTH
DAY

61

Sam walked out the main doors to the parking lot, only to see Dr. Gerald Peterson hailing her down.

"Hey, Dr. Owens, I came by to check out your burn vic. You got a minute?"

Sam felt a brief rush of annoyance. Peterson was the backup forensic odontologist on contract to Davidson County to do dental identifications. He was a small, graying mouse of a man, interminably cheerful. His pink nose twitched with allergies, and he had a wide smile that rose to watery blue eyes behind round, wire-rimmed John Lennon glasses. He was prone to seersucker, and even this late in the fall sported a salmon stripe with a wadded white linen handkerchief bulging from his breast pocket. The man was nice enough, but he was a little erratic, sometimes impossible to reach for weeks at a time. It was his practice to drop in on Sam at his leisure, citing his booming dental practice as his number one priority. Thankfully she didn't need his services terribly often. Dr. Michael Tabor was their main guy, and he was almost always available, except for when he was out on major cases, on loan to other jurisdictions.

Sam had called Tabor's office, found out he was in New York on a case, and had been forced to ring Peterson. He'd been surprisingly quick to respond. It was amazing what a little press coverage could do. Everyone wanted their name in the paper, especially on a case that was rapidly turning into a colossal citywide panic.

"Hey, Gerald. Come on in. I didn't expect to hear from you so soon."

Sam swiped her card, and the security doors unlocked. They entered and made their way through the lobby and the security door, then headed right into the clinical area and through the biovestibule.

Sam stopped and swung open a door, allowing the dentist in before her. The body had been taken to the anthropology laboratory, which was used primarily for the examination of skeletal remains. Just like the main autopsy suite, it had a skylight, but was much smaller, with a single stainless steel table resting against the wall.

The body was housed in the small refrigerator unit in the room. They brought her out and set her on the aluminum table. Sam turned on the large overhead spotlight, and Peterson settled in to work, pausing briefly to pull a clipboard with the National Crime Information Center dental form from his briefcase.

Sam sat back and let him work, helping as needed.

The female they were trying to identify was most likely on a missing persons list. She'd had at least ten thousand dollars of cosmetic work done on her teeth. Veneers, bonding, a well-done root canal, wisdom teeth extractions. Taylor had set Lincoln to work looking for a young female who would have gone missing within the past two months, just to cover all the bases. If there was any chance of finding the identity of this girl, it would be through her dental records.

Dr. Peterson was humming, marking his coded chart, and clucking to himself occasionally. He finally looked up.

"Someone is missing this girl. She's had a lot of work done, and someone had to pay for it. As young as she is, I'd bet anything on parents."

"Care to hazard a guess at her age?"

"You really should talk to your anthropologist to be completely accurate, but the lack of wear, the condition of her bone, I'd give it a guess at twenty to twenty-five years old."

"Yeah, she put it there, too."

He handed her the dental chart he had completed. "I know it's a long shot, but eventually that damn NCIC database is gonna make a match. Give this to Taylor, and let's see how lucky we are."

"I'll fax it up there right now. Are you going to be available if I need to get in touch?"

"Of course. I'm always available for your calls." He gave her a winsome smile, nose twitching, and they walked back to the lobby together.

"Thanks so much for your help, Gerald. I really hope we can find out who this girl is."

Sam walked him out, then swiped her card and went back inside, stopping in the reception area.

"Kris, could you fax this over to Lincoln Ross in Homicide? Tell him it needs to go in the dental database right away. If by the grace of God something matches, tell him to call me on my cell."

"Certainly, Dr. Owens. I'll do it right now." As she spoke, she was already out of her chair.

"Thank you," Sam said then headed to her office, saying a prayer as she went.

62

"Forensic Medical, can I help you?"

"Can I speak to Dr. Owens, please? This is Lincoln Ross with Homicide."

"I'm not sure exactly where she is, but if you would hold on, I'll forward you to her cell." There was a brief moment of silence, then a click as the phone was transferred.

"Yes?"

"Sam? It's Lincoln. I just finished talking to Taylor. She asked me to give you a call. You are never in a million years going to guess what happened when I ran the dental records."

"Yeah, sure, Lincoln. You got a match. Now tell me what's really going on."

"No, Sam, seriously, we got a match."

"You're full of crap." Sam spun in her chair, watching her office walls fly by.

"I swear by all that's holy that I have your girl. Her name is Mary Margaret de Rossi."

"Are you sure it's her? I mean really, that frickin'

database hasn't ever made a match. How can we be sure it's correct?"

"I'm sure. Can you come on over here? Taylor wants to call her parents, but she needs you to make a positive on the records."

"Hell yeah, I'm on my way."

63

An hour later, Sam was staring at Mary Margaret de Rossi's antemortem radiographs on the computer screen. Her mind was crowded with a future image of the poor girl's parents, bravely sitting in the family waiting room at her office, waiting to fill out the paperwork. There was no reason to show them the body; it was burned beyond recognition, and Sam didn't want them to have that image of their daughter.

Mary Margaret's parents had told Taylor the sad story of their runaway daughter. They had only recently found out that she was alive and living in Nashville. They were so proud she'd gotten her life together, kicked her demons, was in college, and had found her own way back to the real world. They'd forgiven her, and she'd forgiven them.

When she first went missing, several years earlier, they didn't know she had simply run away from home. They had filed a missing person report with the Atlanta police. The police investigation turned up nothing. Because of her age and background, they chalked it up to a runaway situation and dropped the case. But a year or so ago, a young detective had contacted them. He was looking at all the missing person cases for the past ten years, and asked if they were still looking for their daughter. When they admitted they still didn't know where she was or if she were alive or dead, the young cop suggested they provide her dental records for him to put in his new database. He had warned them that finding a match was unlikely, but wanted to give it a shot.

He was excited to learn about all the work that had been done on her teeth. Braces in her youth hadn't fully corrected a large frontal gap, so her parents had spent even more money, ten thousand dollars, to have veneers put on, which even they agreed took their daughter from ugly duckling status to elegant swan. The detective was certain the work done on her teeth would differentiate her radiographs, and give them a better shot at finding a match should her body ever be found.

When Mary Margaret finally contacted her family, they had forgotten to let the detective know she'd been found. The records languished in the system until Lincoln made his triumphant match.

Sam used the slides from the database to make her final confirmation. The veneers were a dead giveaway. The antemortem records showed the gap in the girl's teeth. The records were a 100 percent match.

Based on Mary Margaret's distraught parents' information, Lincoln had called over to Aquinas and found one of the nuns who had been close to her.

Sister Agatha sounded a hundred years old, but despite her quavering voice, she seemed sharp as a tack. Lincoln told her the nature of his call, and the old nun broke down. Lincoln heard her saying a rosary in the background. She finally pulled it together and apologized.

"I am so sorry for that poor girl. I think she'd had a hard life. I didn't know much about her. She had the look of a young girl who's seen too much of the world. But she was lovely and studied so hard."

"You say you don't know much about her past. Can you tell me what you do know? Her parents are trying to fill in the gaps."

"Of course. She came to us from the Sisters of the Covenant out in Colorado. Wonderful women, they run a small hospital up there in the mountains. Let me see here, I've got her record right in front of me. She was getting straight A's, the poor lamb. Taking a full load, too, and working in the Student Center. My goodness, it shows here she was also auditing classes over at Vanderbilt last semester. Working so hard. Oh, this is just too much."

Lincoln's heart beat a little faster. He motioned to Taylor and wrote on his blotter *MM audited at Vandy last sem*.

Taylor knocked her knuckles against the desk. There it was. There was the link between the girls.

Lincoln dragged his attention back to the old nun. He had missed some of what she was talking about, but a name caught his ear.

"I'm sorry, Sister, can you say that again?"

"You need to pay more attention, young man." Lincoln immediately had a vision of a stooped old nun smacking his palm with a ruler and nearly laughed aloud. "I was saying that I don't think there is anyone else here that she was very close to, but she spent a lot of time with the priest who was killed. Such a good man, such a loss to the church. We have a hard time bringing in the younger people these days. Boys just don't want to be priests anymore. I'm getting off the subject. She was friends with him. With Father Xavier. They spent quite a bit of time together. I believe he was tutoring her in Latin. She wanted to attend the Latin Mass, you know. Such a good girl."

"Sister, thank you so much for your time. I have to let you go now."

"God bless you and keep you." She hung up before he could answer.

He turned to Taylor, who was impatiently tapping her fingers on top of the filing cabinet.

"Got another tidbit for you."

"Yeah? Well, if it's as good as your last one I'm going to kiss you."

"Ooh, baby. Then get over here and pucker up. Guess who Mary Margaret spent all her time with?"

"Who?"

"Father Xavier."

Taylor started grinning. "Damn good job, Lincoln. C'mere." She grabbed him and laid one on him, then ran off down the hall, shouting for Baldwin.

64

Armed with her team's hours of work, Taylor and Baldwin went to the Vanderbilt campus. The storm damage was extensive, but the cleanup had gone very well, and all the roads through downtown were back open, as was the campus itself.

It was a beautiful morning. The sun shone on the quad, the grass had been freshly mowed, probably for the last time before the bitter cold of winter hit. There was just a hint of the smell of burning leaves wafting through the air; most had been blown off the trees during the heavy storms. The scent reminded Taylor that the nights would soon turn frigid and warm fires would be needed to chase away the fingers of winter.

Students milled about, happy to be back to school, enjoying the unseasonably warm morning. Two boys played with a football, showing off for three girls in bikini tops and cutoff shorts on a blanket nearby.

There were two professors they needed to talk to from the classics department: Edward Lear and

Barry James. Fitz and Marcus had gone through Shelby's, Jordan's, and Jill's records since their arrival at Vanderbilt. By intersecting their schedules, they had come up with the names of two professors all three had taken classes from. After the conversation with the nun in administration at Aquinas College revealed that Mary Margaret de Rossi sometimes audited classes at Vanderbilt in the classics—a program not offered at her school—they found she'd audited several classes, including one each from each professor.

The net was closing.

Baldwin had found the girl who had put together the flyer campaign to help find Jill. Her name was Susan Davidson, and he thought it would be smart to speak with her first, before the professors. If they knew a little more about Jill, they might be able to piece the rest of the story together.

Taylor and Baldwin made their way to the Student Center, and Susan met them at the door, escorted them inside, and found them a table.

Taylor started the interview with a few niceties, asking about the girl's study and major. Then she started in.

"So, Susan, tell us how you know Jill Gates."

"We met at a sorority rush party in the first week of school. She wasn't thrilled to be there, which surprised me. I mean, she had the looks, the body, the whole package the sororities look for. I also heard she was a Tri-Delt legacy, so I figured she'd be snapped up quickly. I really wouldn't have paid a lot of attention, you know, except she took off in the middle of rush. Just left. I thought it was strange, but I had my own stuff to deal with, you know?"

"But you met her again, right? You said on the phone that you two had a class together."

"Yeah, last semester. I added it in the second week. I didn't like my psychology class, so I trans-ferred into this classics class, you know, mythol-ogy and all that? One of the girls in my dorm told me the prof was totally cool, and he was. Went off all the time on these weird tangents, but he was so into the gods and their roles shaping our lives that we couldn't help but get interested. And he has the grooviest eyes, you know. Sort of this sea green, like yours, Agent Baldwin, though yours are much prettier."

Taylor smiled and shot Baldwin a look, but inter-rupted the girl's daydream. "Susan, let's get back to Jill Gates. You and she were in the class together?"

Susan snapped back to reality. "Yeah, we sat next to each other. She knew so much about this stuff already, you know? She sat glued to his every word, and I always saw her go talk to him after class. It was weird, though. She'd ask him ques-tions she already knew the answers to, 'cause I'd see her write them down before she went up to him. But whatever, you know? Everyone thought he was hot. She seemed really into him."

"Did you ever talk to her about it?"

"She blew me off as soon as I brought it up. Said she wanted to go on and get her doctorate in the classics, and it would be really helpful if she had such an influential teacher to back her up. Yeah, whatever, like I bought that."

"Did you know Shelby and Jordan?"

"Well, sure. They were in the same class with me and Jill that first semester."

Taylor felt a bump of adrenaline. "Who was the professor, Susan?"

"You didn't already know? Dr. Lucas, of course."

"Dr. Lucas?"

"Yeah, Gabriel. Gabriel Lucas. He's not a prof here anymore, though. I don't know where he went."

Gabriel Lucas wasn't one of the two professors they had come to speak with. She'd never even seen the name. Taylor made a mental note to call Fitz the second they finished and ask about him.

"So you thought they may have been involved? Romantically?"

Susan shook her head, staring over Taylor's shoulder. A little frown started in her forehead. "I don't know if she was sleeping with him, if that's what you mean. It was almost like they had this strange link, like they had a secret that no one else knew. I always assumed there was something going on, but I never saw them together outside of his office, where there were always people around. They'd be in these deep conversations about Plato and stuff. We studied the Allegory of the Cave for two weeks, and she really got into it. That's really all I know. I need to get to class, so is there anything else?"

Baldwin finally spoke up. "Susan, we'll handle your absence from class. I want to know more about Jill. What was she like?"

Susan shrugged. "Well, she was totally gorgeous, but it was like she didn't really know it. Never got dolled up for class and stuff. She was really natural. Not a granola, but pretty laid-back about her looks. I guess that's what I noticed in the first place. It's not like I'm some kind of beauty queen. Then when she gained some weight this year, I guess I felt even more at ease with her, you know? Some of us just aren't meant to be perfect."

Susan wasn't exaggerating. She was plain, with unfashionably large, pink-rimmed glasses and a slight overbite, making her look like an overeager chipmunk. When she smiled, her cheeks puffed out as if she were holding a large store of nuts in her mouth. Baldwin smiled gently, catching Taylor's eye. The weight gain. That must have been the pregnancy.

"So she was nice to you?"

"Yeah, most of the time. I'd hang around some, asking her to get coffee and stuff. Most of the time she'd come, but sometimes she just blew me off with this look in her eye, like she found me disgusting. But then she'd smile and be really nice, bring me a muffin from Starbucks or something. Anyway, whatever. I liked her."

Both Baldwin and Taylor were starting to get the idea that Susan may have felt more than "like" for Jill Gates, but neither of them pushed the issue.

Baldwin continued trying to draw a mental picture of Jill. "So what did you guys talk about when you hung out? Class? Professors? Anything you can think of would be helpful."

Susan teared up. "I don't know anything else. Do you think Jill is dead? All of us were in class together with Dr. Lucas. And Shelby and Jordan are dead. Am I next?"

65

Taylor's heart was galloping in her chest. They needed to wrap this up and go investigate who the hell Gabriel Lucas was.

"Susan," she said soothingly, setting a hand on the girl's pudgy arm. "I'm sure you're fine. But we need to get an idea of what Jill was like, to see if there's anything we need to look into. Did she ever go off like this before, without telling anyone where she was headed?"

"Well, sure, every weekend. She said she had a boyfriend down at Sewanee, and they met there every Friday afternoon, and she stayed until late Sunday night."

"Did anyone else know about this?"

"No, she swore me to secrecy. She really didn't talk to anyone else about her personal life, you know?" Susan's chest had puffed with a small sense of pride, and Taylor felt for the girl. The secret keeper always was made to feel like the most important person in a woman's world, especially if the person was a shade too nerdy and harboring some more-than-friendly feelings toward her friend. Women could be used that way, and it was starting to look like Jill Gates had been taking advantage of Susan's affections from the beginning. Taylor realized Susan was still talking.

"…Jill was kind of intense, you know? Like when you're talking to her, she like leans into you, like she really cares about what you're saying. There was this time…" Susan reddened, and both of them could understand completely her embarrassment.

"It's okay, Susan. I think I'm starting to understand how you felt about Jill." Taylor handed the girl a tissue. She accepted it gratefully and hid behind it for a moment.

"Yeah, well, she wasn't into me like that, but I didn't mind. I think she knew, but she was good enough never to mention it, you know. Like she didn't hold it against me or anything." Susan's voice had gotten bitter, but she smiled and went back to her story.

"I don't really know how to explain it. She was so intense, so interested, that sometimes it was a little creepy, you know? Like she wanted to turn my mind inside out. She just looks right into you. And I told her things I'd never admit to anyone. Dreams, feelings. Not about how I felt for her, but about dealing with life feeling different. And she understood so much. I know she'd never felt like she didn't fit in, but she made me feel like she understood it completely. So I poured out my deepest darkest secrets, my biggest fears, like about my parents finding out I'm not their perfect little girl. And she understood, you know, she really understood. I know she really cared about me in her own way."

Baldwin was starting to get the picture. "Susan, think carefully. Was she like that with anyone else?"

"Well, she was like that with a lot of people. I guess I'd like to think that she was special friends with me alone, but she was, you know, kinda *intense* with a lot of people."

"Was she *intense* with Shelby Kincaid or Jordan Blake?"

"No, not Shelby. That girl was a little mouse. But she did hang out with Jordan, partied with her some. They went their own way after a while. Jordan got picked up by Tri-Delt, and Jill just wasn't into the sorority scene. Me neither."

Taylor gave the girl's hand a quick squeeze. "Susan, you've been a huge help. Thank you so much for your time and for being so honest with us." They stood to leave. Susan looked back.

"Will you let me know if you find Jill? I just want to make sure she's okay, you know?"

Baldwin gave her a long look. "We'll do our best."

She smiled sadly and hoisted her backpack on her shoulder, half waved good-bye, and wandered off toward the food court.

Taylor and Baldwin sat back down.

Taylor spoke first. "What do you think?"

Baldwin was running his hands through his hair. "I don't know. There's definitely a link with all the girls through this Gabriel Lucas character. Mary Margaret audited the same classics class Susan was talking about. But Lucas isn't on our list, right?"

Taylor was already dialing Fitz's cell. He picked up quickly.

"Hey, it's me. I need you to check a name for me. Gabriel Lucas." She was quiet for a moment, listening. "Okay. Find him. We'll check it out."

She hung up and pulled out a cigarette. Baldwin gave her a look that she waved off. She lit it and stared off into space, coughing a little.

Baldwin was getting impatient. "Well?"

"Gabriel Lucas wasn't on their list because he's taking a sabbatical this semester. He's taken some time off to write a book of his experiences with the Greco-Roman culture."

"You're kidding."

Taylor took another drag, then squashed the butt under her shoe. She raised an eyebrow at him.

"An expertise in Greco-Roman culture fits our profile about a person intimately familiar with the ancient customs," he said.

"It sure does. The way Susan talked about him, and the connection he had with Jill…we need to find this guy and have a nice long talk with him. Fitz is tracking him down. Also, Sam called in to tell us there was aconite in the teacups found at the church. Definitely the same killer, Baldwin."

Baldwin's mind was spinning. Shelby, date-raped. Jordan, pregnant with another man's child. Jill, at least seven months gone and having a secret affair. So where did Mary Margaret, the priest, and Tammy/Mona Lisa fit into all of this? He didn't know the answer, only knew they had to find Jill.

66

Their interviews with Professor Lear and Professor James yielded nothing. Professor Lear was physically incapable of committing the crimes. A paraplegic since birth, his wheelchair would have made it difficult to manage the stairs at the Parthenon, at the very least. Though he did remember all of the students, he couldn't say he knew anything about them outside of his classes.

Their interview with Professor James hadn't gone any better. Though young and physically fit, he was openly gay. Much to Taylor's amusement, he had flirted his way through the entire interview, going so far as to ask Baldwin for his phone number, which Baldwin genially declined.

They asked both men about Gabriel Lucas. Lear had nothing but kind words for the man. James, on the other hand, made his dislike clear, but couldn't give any solid reasons for it. Taylor couldn't help but wonder if he'd been turned down and was harboring a grudge.

Taylor and Baldwin sat on the grass under a huge

oak tree and talked it through. Either man could have hired a killer, but that scenario didn't make sense. Baldwin was sure their suspect was on a personal quest; the murders were too intricately woven, too symbolic to have been committed on contract. Between Professor Lear's infirmities and Professor James's sexual orientation, neither man fit what Baldwin was looking for in their suspects.

Taylor's cell rang. It was Fitz, eager to share their latest discovery.

"Taylor, we just ran back through Mary Margaret's records. Two of the classes she audited were taught by…ready for it? One Professor Gabriel Lucas."

Her heart was pounding. "Excellent. This has to be our guy. But where the hell is he?"

"I'm looking. Got one more little morsel for you. Our priest, Father Xavier? The rector at St. Catherine's called. Didn't know if it would help the investigation at all, but since it was related to Vanderbilt, he thought we should know that Father X conducted the community breakfast there last month."

"There's our last link. We're on it. Thanks, Fitz!"

She gave Baldwin a huge smile, her teeth flashing in the sunlight. "Check this out…"

Taylor and Baldwin barged into the office of Vanderbilt's dean of the College of Arts and Sciences. His secretary hedged when they walked in the door, telling them that the dean was out of the office on business, but she didn't know exactly where he was. She was trying to talk them into an appointment much later in the afternoon when the dean walked through the door. He had two men with him, both dressed elegantly and wearing grimaces on their faces. Taylor could tell they were simply being polite while he jovially tried to amuse them. He stopped short when he saw Taylor and Baldwin.

Taylor stuck out her hand. "Dean Royce? Lieutenant Taylor Jackson and Dr. John Baldwin. We need to speak to you about—"

He cut her off. "Oh yes, my dear, I know all about it. If you would give me a minute here." He addressed his secretary. "Janet, please see Ms. Jackson and Mr. Baldwin into my office and get them something to drink. I won't be a moment."

He turned and put his arms around the shoulders of his reluctant companions. "Gentlemen, I can't tell you how much we appreciate all you've done for Vanderbilt. I'll be in touch as soon as I can. If there's…"

Taylor lost the conversation as she entered the dean's office.

He came through the door a moment later, mopping his brow with a handkerchief. Taylor had taken an instant dislike to the man. He was all smiles and handshakes. He politely offered to pour the tea, prattling about the overwhelming support the college was receiving from their donors, segueing into his distress over the fate of his students. But Taylor read the look in his eyes as he got himself settled behind his desk. He was not happy to see them. Homicide detectives and FBI agents combing his campus for murder suspects was not good publicity for the school.

Taylor started fidgeting in her chair, trying to find a good place to interrupt. Baldwin wasn't as polite.

"Dean Royce, please. We need to speak with you about one of your professors. What can you tell us about Gabriel Lucas?"

"Gabriel? Great man. Entirely devoted to the school. Came to us several years ago from New Mexico, I believe. He'd finished his doctorate in ancient and modern Hellenistic and Greco-Roman cultures. Had a stunning dissertation on Plato, argued that Plato's philosophy was the first true divine revelation. Made an excellent case for Hellenistic philosophy as the basis for the Bible. Absolutely amazing work. I read all the dissertations of our professors personally, you know," he puffed. "Something of a hobby for me, that's why I remember it so well. We grabbed him up as soon as we talked with him. Took him after the first interview. Brilliant man, Gabriel, simply brilliant. Why, he was—"

Baldwin cut him off again. "We understand he's taking a sabbatical this semester?"

The dean sat back in his chair for a moment. "Certainly you don't think he had anything to do with these murders? That's preposterous. Gabriel is a gentle soul. And I know how much he loves his students."

Taylor raised an eyebrow at him. "Any students that he loved in particular?"

Royce started sputtering. "Ms. Jackson…"

"You can call me Lieutenant, Dean Royce."

He flushed and took a deep breath. "Lieutenant. Vanderbilt University holds its students and faculty to the highest standards of conduct. Dating a student here isn't simply frowned upon, it is grounds for dismissal. So to answer your little insinuation, no. Gabriel was not involved with any of his students. It simply wouldn't be allowed."

Baldwin smiled. "You've never seen anyone break the rules, Dean? I mean, really, in this day and age? A bright young professor, whom we've heard was quite handsome, wouldn't have any social contact with any of his female students?"

"No, Mr. Baldwin, he wouldn't. Especially not in the past months."

"Oh? Why's that?"

"Because Gabriel is ill. Very ill. He's taken the semester to…recuperate."

67

Taylor stood and went to his window. "Dean Royce, we talked with two of your professors, Edward Lear and Barry James, from the classics department. They weren't aware Professor Lucas had any physical problems. They were under the impression that he was taking a sabbatical to work on a book."

"No, they wouldn't know the whole story. Gabriel and I decided to keep it from as many people as we could. It was such a shattering blow to him, and he wanted time to sort things out. Such a shame. Incredibly bright man. Though he was starting to act a little erratic. He'd had a revelation, he said. Kept talking about the revelation that was changing his life. Wouldn't tell me what it was, though. I told him to write it down. You know how it is, publish or perish," he chortled. "That's why we decided it was best for him to simply take a sabbatical. Didn't want the students to see him that way, see him acting different, if you know what I mean."

Baldwin was getting a little fed up by the dean's

dance. "Dean, what exactly is the nature of Professor Lucas's illness?"

"Really, officers, you can't think that Gabriel is involved in these crimes in any way." He started to get out of his chair, but Taylor snapped at him.

"Sit down. Of course we can. We know that Jill Gates, Jordan Blake, and Shelby Kincaid all took his classes. We know that Mary Margaret de Rossi audited two of his classes. That's four of our victims that Professor Lucas was at the very least *familiar* with. That's a lot for us to go on right there. So I suggest you start cooperating before I haul your ass into the station and charge you with obstruction of justice. Now, what is wrong with Lucas?"

"Fine. He has cancer. Brain cancer. A tumor of some sort. He took the semester off to have it treated. Are you happy now? I've broken the confidence of a man who begged me to make sure no one at the school found out about his condition. Thank you for forcing me to compromise my morals. I've told you all I can. Now, I think you should leave."

Taylor ignored him. "Have you spoken with him lately?"

The dean was red in the face and looked close to blowing a gasket. "No, I haven't spoken with him in about a month. He came to the monthly community breakfast. He told me he would be out of touch for a while, and was talking about having a new experience. I just assumed it was a medical advancement that he couldn't receive here in town and he was seeking treatment elsewhere. We only spoke for a few minutes. The speaker started moments after we greeted each other, and after the presentation he was gone."

"Would that speaker have been Father Francis Xavier from St. Catherine's Church?"

The dean's face crumpled. He put his face in his hands, and all the defensiveness left his body. "Oh my God. It can't be. He couldn't have done any of this. It has to be a coincidence."

Baldwin spoke quietly. "There are no coincidences, Dean Royce. We need to speak with Professor Lucas. Can you get us his address and phone number?"

"Janet!" he bellowed. The diminutive woman came scurrying into the office. "Janet, I need you to give the detectives Professor Lucas's address."

Janet was obviously a little afraid of her boss and squeaked her answer like a mouse. "I'm sure I have it around here somewhere. I think he moved recently. I'll probably have to call down to records, and Melinda is out sick today, so there's only a student working the desk. It may take a little while."

"Ma'am, go on down to records yourself and pull the address for me." Taylor scribbled her number on the back of a card and handed it to her. "The minute you have it, I want you to call me on my cell phone. Do you understand?"

The woman nodded and started to bustle away. Taylor grabbed her arm. "Hold on a second. Do you have any pictures of Professor Lucas?"

"Well, of course, dear. We have the annuals right here." She motioned to the bookshelf behind her boss. Taylor went to the bookshelf and pulled the most recent annual. She looked in the back for Lucas's name, found he was pictured on several pages. She started flipping through until she found one of him alone.

Taylor had to admit he was a handsome man. Square jaw, heavy silver hair, green eyes, full mouth, three days of stubble. A rebel-without-a-cause attitude spilling from his smile. She could see why some of the girls would want to take his classes.

Baldwin turned back to the dean. "Mr. Royce, do you happen to know which doctor was treating the professor?"

The dean had gathered himself and was a little more willing to cooperate.

"Surely, surely. A doctor named Hoyt, I believe. Steven Hoyt, over at Vanderbilt University Medical Center. Great man, loves the college. Did his undergrad here, I believe. Before my time, though."

She stood and stuck out her hand. "Thank you so much for your time. Can I take this with me?" She pointed to the annual.

"Of course, of course, anything I can do to help, just give me a call. Though I'm sure you'll find our poor professor has had nothing to do with all this tragedy. At Vanderbilt… I'm sure you understand that we cannot be held responsible for any actions any of our students or faculty take outside of campus. We're terribly upset by these deaths and want to cooperate however we can." Taylor rolled her eyes at his spin as he saw them to the door, then shut it behind them.

Taylor and Baldwin made their way back to the car. Taylor lit a cigarette, a grimace on her face.

"Smarmy old dope. He gave me the creeps."

Baldwin started laughing. "Gave you the creeps, huh? He wasn't the friendliest person I've ever met."

"Ick. Didn't you love his quick CYA? Always gotta cover your ass." She picked up her phone and called in to the office. "Hey, it's me. Is Lincoln there?" She waited a moment. "Linc, I need you to do your magic. Get a number and address on Gabriel Lucas... Right... Cool. Let me talk to Marcus... Hey, puppy, how ya holdin' up?... Oh, you poor baby. Do me a favor. Get on the phone with a doctor named Steven Hoyt. He'll be with the oncology unit at Vanderbilt. We need all the records he has regarding treatment of Gabriel Lucas. Brain cancer. See if he has anything we can use for DNA. Yeah, we have a live one. Thanks." She hung up and lit another cigarette.

"Lincoln will get the records a sight faster than Miss Mouse back there. Hopefully Marcus can find this Dr. Hoyt. Let's get back over there and see what we can find out." She realized she was walking alone. Baldwin was standing stock-still ten feet behind her.

"Baldwin? What's wrong?"

He gave her a look, his eyes shining. "I think I know what's going on."

68

"Wake up, love. That's right. Sit up a little now. You need to drink this."

The cool water slid down the back of her throat. Jill realized she was awake, and felt Gabriel's arm around her shoulders. She tried to gulp. She was thirsty, so thirsty, and choked on the water. Sputtering, she opened her eyes.

Gabriel was sitting next to her. She saw he had brought some food, and realized she was starving. She reached out for the tray, but he grabbed her hand gently and set it back in her lap.

"No, my darling, let me." He reached for the plate, broke off a piece of bread and gave it to her. She took it and started chewing.

"Gabriel, what is going on?" she mumbled through the bread in her mouth.

He just looked at her, got off the bed, and picked up a sheet of paper. Clearing his throat like an actor on the stage preparing for a great soliloquy, he began reading aloud. "'A Call to Arms' by Jill Gates."

Thoughts thrash and tumble
like lions crashing
through the cresting waves.
No movement, no action
lost in the abyss they call my mind,
fleeing like sandpipers
chasing ghost crabs
on the milky white powder expanse.
A calm breeze blows harmless
smiles and stabbing glares
wash away the tumult.
And I lie
in dreamless death,
suspended in my cage.

He finished with a flourish, bowing to his audience. Jill put the bread back on the plate, staring at him. He was absolutely crazy. She could see it in his eyes. And he looked even sicker than earlier, pale and drawn. She had a vague memory, some rumor about him leaving school because he was ill. But that couldn't be. He was writing a book. He would have told her if there was something wrong.

She tried to access the memory, but her mind was so muddled from all the drugs, and she just couldn't grasp the memory. And now he was reading her old poetry?

"What, you don't remember this glorious ode? You wrote it for me. For *me*. When I read it, I knew. I knew you would be the one. You would never betray me, Jilly. I knew it in my heart that we would be together forever. 'And I lie in dreamless death, suspended in my cage'? When I read this, I wept. I knew I had found you, the one who could help me become immortal. I knew you would bear a child, a son, who will live on forever. A son who will be strong enough to lead all of us into the afterlife, who will bless us and make us pure."

Jill was crawling backward on the bed. This man in front of her was not Gabriel. This was not the wonderful, seductive professor she had found so incredibly attractive. This man was a raving lunatic. She hadn't written the poem for him; it was an assignment from another teacher in another class. She couldn't even remember showing it to him, which meant he must have gone through all of her old things. But how…oh, that was it. She remembered asking him if she could store some old boxes of work in his attic months ago, after their affair began.

"Oh God, what have I done?" she groaned aloud. It had seemed so simple, so fun. An older professor, so smart and sexy. He had shown so much interest in her from the minute she met him, always wanted to hear her thoughts and opinions. Remarks she made to the boys her age in class were often met by blank stares or derisive giggles. They weren't interested in talking about philosophy and religion. They just wanted to get in her pants.

But Gabriel, oh, he was so different. He encouraged her crazy questions, made her feel so intelligent. He'd treated her like an equal from the day she met him, pushed her to think about the world in ways she'd never dreamed possible. And when

they'd finally consummated their intellectual court-
ship, she'd never felt anything had been so right in
the world. She didn't think for a minute that she
was the only woman he was sleeping with, but it
didn't matter to her. He was sharing his life with
her, and when she became pregnant he was overwhelmed with joy, promised to take care of her
and the baby forever. No, this wild-eyed thing before her was not the man she'd known. The man
she knew.

She swung her head around frantically, trying
to find some way out of the room he'd been keeping her prisoner in. The door was open, and she
lunged for it, but he was quicker and threw her
back on the bed.

"No, no, no, not like that. You need to stay here
with me, love. I need to take care of you and our
son. I've put everything in motion and done all I
know to secure his way."

She continued to squirm, and he screamed, "You
must listen to me. Listen!"

"No. Let me out of here, Gabriel. Let me out of
here right now, or I swear to God I'll kill you." Her
venomous threat made him laugh. He knelt on her
chest, threw her hands over her head and secured
them with handcuffs. He slid down her body till
he was off the bed, then took each of her thrashing legs and tied them to the foot of the antique
bed frame.

"Jilly. My beautiful, lovely girl, don't you see?
You can't escape me. You can't escape our destiny.

You were given to me to bear me a son. You are carrying the Messiah."

"Gabriel, let me go. Undo these handcuffs!"

Gabriel just smiled serenely and reached for her arm. She felt the prick of the needle and started becoming woozy. Gabriel patted her on the head and started out the door.

"God damn you, Gabriel!"

He was back to the bed in a shot and slapped her across the face, hard enough she felt blood filling her mouth.

He spoke quietly, gently. "Don't ever say that again, Jilly. God will not damn me. He will welcome me to heaven with open arms, thankful that I have given His Son back to the world. I will be rewarded, Jill, not damned. I will be His righteous angel, and I will watch by His side as His Son, our son, saves the world. Do you not understand?"

He left the room and locked the door behind him, ignoring Jill's shrieks of protest. She heard the phone ringing in the background, but before she could summon the energy to scream, her mind swirled into a blank, and she fell back into the pillows.

69

Price motioned Taylor and Baldwin into his office. "What do you have? Lincoln told me he's looking for property records for a professor who didn't make the initial list."

Taylor threw herself in the chair. "His name is Gabriel Lucas. Professor of the classics at Vandy. He wasn't on the list because he's taken a sabbatical. The dean told us he has brain cancer."

Marcus came into the office. "And pretty bad brain cancer. The doctor at Vandy? Hoyt? He didn't want to give up any information, doctor-patient confidentiality. I showed him the warrant and threatened him with an accomplice-to-murder charge. He started talking."

He looked at his notes. "Lucas, Gabriel, forty-eight. 3802 West End Avenue. Presented eight months ago with headaches he thought were migraines. A neurologist did an MRI, which showed a large tumor in his brain stem, something called brain stem glioma. Pretty heavy-duty cancer. The neurologist sent him to Dr. Hoyt, but it was too late.

The tumor was inoperable, and a biopsy showed it was stage four, as bad as it gets. The cancer was already moving into other parts of his brain. Because of the size of the tumor and the location, there was nothing that they could do. They offered to try radiation and chemo, but Lucas decided he didn't want to go through all of the motions with such a small chance of it actually working. They gave him prescriptions for pain medication, which he has been filling; they had to renew the prescription last month. Publix Pharmacy in Bellevue.

"Dr. Hoyt was surprised that he's made it this long. He gave Lucas an optimistic estimate of six months, and didn't think he'd make it over four. He's living on borrowed time."

Baldwin was fascinated. "A tumor like that, in that position, could easily alter his personality, his speech. Hell, it could make him a completely different person. He could go off the deep end. Whether he already had a propensity toward violence, and the tumor brought it to the surface, or he was a genuinely good guy and it's altered him into madness, we may never know. But I'm willing to put money down this is our guy. I need to go look some stuff up. Before I go, did Hoyt give you any DNA samples?"

Marcus beamed. "Yep. He had pathology pull the slides from the biopsy. I called Sam, and she met me at Private Match. She and Simon are going to try and match it to the semen we found on Shelby."

"Brilliant job, Marcus. Okay, I'll be back in a minute." He raced off.

Taylor watched Baldwin's back disappear out the door. "We need to get a team over to the address from the prescription refills right now. If we—"

"Taylor, I've got the address." Lincoln came into the room, waving a piece of paper over his head. "Lucas has a house on Granny White Pike, right near the Lipscomb Drive crossroads. Got it off the voter registration rolls. A good old-fashioned registered Democrat. Bought the house in 1996."

Taylor reached for the sheet of paper. "Wait a minute. The doctor's office had him living on West End. What the hell?" Her cell phone rang, and she looked at it. *Vandy*, she mouthed to Price as she picked it up. "This is Lieutenant Jackson. Yes, Janet, thank you for getting back to me so quickly. Okay, let me write that down. 6002 Hillsboro Road? That's his new address? Do you have a record of the old address? Ah, 3802 West End. Okay, I've got it. Thanks." She hung up and looked at Price.

"Looks like he moved from West End to Hillsboro recently."

"How recently?"

"Six months ago."

"So what's with the Granny White address?"

"Hell if I know," Taylor said. "He had multiple addresses—one listed for the school, one for the doc, and one for the state."

"How does a professor, on a professor's salary, end up owning three houses?"

"An excellent question. Family money, maybe. Who needs three houses in one town?"

Price twisted the ends of his mustache, thinking. "One to live in, one to kill in, and one to hold his victims?"

Taylor was on her feet. "I don't know, but it doesn't matter what he's doing with his finances. We need to get teams to all three of these houses. Can you call in Officer Bob Miller and Officer Keith Wills? They're SWAT trained, so they can take Granny White. Fitz and Marcus can take West End, and Baldwin and I will hit Hillsboro."

"Good plan. Let me make the calls. A little privacy, if you please?" The team went back to the bullpen.

"Damn, this just couldn't be easy, could it?" Taylor said. "Oh, wait a second. Marcus, call the pharmacy in Bellevue. Confirm what address he has on his prescription, and see if they'll tell you what it's for."

Marcus grabbed the phone and called information for the number. They sat and watched while he dialed. Taylor was tapping her foot nervously against the corner of her desk drawer. Lincoln noticed and reached over, touched her knee and stilled the shakes. "We're cool, T. We've got him. We just need to find out where he is, and we've got three places to look. Relax."

She gave him a grateful smile and winked. He was right—they had him. Now all they needed was Sam's DNA match and the right address, and maybe, God willing, they would find Jill Gates alive. She looked over her shoulder. Where the hell was Baldwin?

Marcus hung up the phone and nodded. "The pharmacy has the Hillsboro address, and he's taking injectable morphine. They filled the prescription for the drugs and syringes a few weeks ago."

Fitz strolled in. "Got us a real live suspect?"

Taylor smiled and raised her eyebrows. "Think so. He has three addresses, but one of them, a house on Hillsboro, has come up twice. Marcus here earned his pay and threatened to arrest a doctor at Vandy if he wouldn't give up the info."

Marcus sat with a Cheshire cat grin. Fitz looked at him and couldn't help but laugh. "Good job, son. There's more good news, if you want to call it that."

"What?" Taylor asked, shoving her chair over to make room for Fitz.

"Three things. Arrested the father of your seventeen-year-old suicide. Though as you suspected, he wasn't a suicide."

Taylor's mouth fell open. "You're kidding? What happened?"

"Guy waltzed in here this afternoon and announced he did it. It was just like you thought, LT. They were fighting, he was drunk, and when the kid got up to leave, he grabbed the gun and shot him. The guilt finally got to him. Got him down in night court being booked right now, and he's got company."

"Who?"

"Little Man Graft. Big bad Little Man. Your kid gave a statement. His mama found a job out of state, so they packed up all their stuff and stopped by the station on their way out of town. Kid gave me the whole story. He saw Little Man shoot Lashon Hall, no question about it. I videotaped a statement and let his mom take him to their new home. She gave me a cell phone number where I can reach her if we need him again. Then the planets aligned. Central sector called to say they'd picked up Terrence Norton after they'd gotten reports he was involved in a shooting on Charlotte Pike. Seems he took a shot at one of the homeless guys who've been breaking into cars down by the Exxon station.

"He was singing my name the moment they cuffed him, asking to talk to me before they booked him. They brought him in, and I sat down with him. Lo and behold, Terrence suddenly remembered that Little Man shot Lashon Hall, just like we thought. We have Little Man sitting in a cell, and we'll get him for this one, what with two witness statements and all. I promised to drop the accessory charge on Terrence in exchange for his testimony."

"Well done, Fitz. Thank you."

"It gets better. The homeless guy, God rest his soul, died on the way to the hospital. Central has the gun Terrence was carrying when they picked him up. If the ballistics match we finally have Terrence dead to rights for murder."

Taylor pumped her arm in the air. "Yes! Get both

those thugs off the street in one fell swoop." She got up and gave him a huge hug.

He hugged her back. "Ah, it was nothing. Anything for you, love. There's one more thing, though."

"What's that?"

"Your dad's in the lobby."

70

Taylor rolled her eyes and sank back in her chair. "What the hell does he want?"

"I don't know, honey, but you'd better get out there and find out so we can go arrest Gabriel Lucas."

Taylor sat for a moment, trying to gather herself. Of all the times to come barging into her life. How dare he?

"Fine. Fine, I'll go talk to him. But you're coming with me."

Fitz hesitated for a moment. "I think you'd—"

"I'm pulling rank. Come on." She grabbed his hand and dragged him into the hallway. They walked the hallway down to the lobby door. Taking a deep breath, Taylor flung the door open and strode purposefully into the lobby.

She saw Win immediately, his back turned to her as he laughed it up with the desk clerk. Typical.

"Win," she said quietly. He wheeled around and broke into a huge grin.

"Ah, my little girl! How are you, sweetheart?"

He rushed to her and enveloped her in a hug. She stood stiffly with her arms at her sides until he got the hint.

"Still pissed at your old man, I see."

"Win, what do you want? This isn't the best time."

"Well, I've been trying to reach you for days. Come on, sugar, cut an old man a break." He noticed Fitz standing behind Taylor.

"Why, I'll be damned. Pete Fitzgerald. You're a sight for sore eyes." He reached out to shake Fitz's hand, but Taylor cut him off.

"Win, we're really tied up at the moment. Just say what you came to say, and let us get back to work."

"Jeez, Taylor, just trying to say hello to an old friend."

Fitz rolled his eyes. "An old friend who put your sorry ass in jail. What do you want, Win?"

"Ah, Fitz, I'm willing to let bygones be bygones. What's it like, working for my little girl?" The remark was meant to sting, but Fitz laughed instead.

Taylor was getting more frustrated by the minute. "Spit it out, Win. Now!"

He quickly became serious. "I just wanted to let you know that I'm engaged."

Taylor felt like a rock had hit her in the chest. "What? To who? Does Mom know?"

Win was grinning like a jackal. "You remember Lori Westerson?"

Taylor felt her head spinning. "Lori Westerson

that I graduated from Father Ryan with? Are you kidding me?"

"No, honey, I'm not. We've been together for a while, now. She's the most wonderful woman. I just wanted you to hear it from me, sweetheart. I know this is hard to hear, but I'm so happy, and I want you to be happy for me." He reached out as if he was going to hug her again, but Taylor took a step back.

"I'm thrilled for you, Win. Now I have to go back to work. Congratulations." She turned on her heel and walked back to the lobby door.

"Taylor, wait. Please, honey, can we just get together for dinner and talk about this? Talk about anything? Please. I'm still your father."

His pleading only made her heart tighten and her throat constrict. "Win, I can't deal with this right now. Maybe later. I'll call you." She swiped her card and disappeared through the door.

Fitz watched her slam through the door. He turned back to Win, whose smile was gone. He looked a bit ashen, almost as if he were going to be sick. Fitz felt a moment of pity for the man. He quickly shoved it away. Taylor was like a daughter to him, and he knew the pain Win's antics had caused her over the years. Taylor was a woman who dealt with the world in black and white, and Win Jackson got off exploiting all the shades of gray he could find. Fitz knew it tore her to pieces, having a father who was dishonest, a criminal.

"Listen, Win, I think you'd best leave now. We're real busy, you know?"

Win hung his head. "Yeah, I know. Just tell her… tell her I love her. Will you do that for me?"

"Yeah. When the time's right. See ya, Win."

Taylor didn't know whether to laugh or cry. The absurdity of the whole situation, her father marrying one of her old classmates, was so sick it was almost funny. Lincoln and Marcus were eyeing her, but she assiduously avoided their looks. She saw Fitz come back into the squad room. She knew he wasn't going to let her fall apart, or dwell, or worry. That's what she loved about him.

He came over to her, put an arm around her, and bellowed, "So, are we gonna arrest this guy or what?"

She gave him a grateful smile. "Damn straight."

"So, let's do this." He yelled into Price's office. "Captain, where we at?"

Price slammed the phone down and came out of his office. "Okay, I just called us in some backup. Here's how this is going to go. Taylor, I want you and Fitz to take the Hillsboro address. Take Officer Wills and Officer Miller with you. The pharmacy and the school both list it as his address, so it may be the best shot for finding him, and they'll have your backs.

"I want Baldwin at the Granny White address with Marcus. Lincoln and I will take West End. I'll get four officers to back the rest of us up at the Granny White and West End addresses. Keep your radios on channel twenty. I don't want the media picking up on this before we get there and putting ghetto birds in the air. Full suit and everything, and I don't want anyone getting hurt. You hear me?"

He was talking to all of them, but he was looking directly at Taylor. She squirmed in her chair but nodded dutifully. She was glad Baldwin hadn't heard the remark. It seemed as though Price was saying, "Hey, guys, be really careful. You're heading out into a dangerous situation with two cops who have gotten four people shot between them, so be sure to watch your asses."

She felt her chest tighten but shook it off. *Not now. Please not now.* She knew in her heart that Price didn't mean a thing by his comment; it was a standard warning. But the self-recriminations were building up on her. She hadn't gone into a situation knowing she would have to draw her weapon since that awful night she had shot and killed David, and she had to admit to herself, she was a little scared.

When Price had finished his briefing, she got up and went into the ladies' room. She splashed cold water on her face and toweled it off. Her chest was still tight, but she was breathing easier. She had it under control. She looked in the mirror and was surprised at what she saw. There was no little girl with scared eyes staring back at her. The woman standing in the mirror was strong, and her jaw was determined. The panic was gone, her breathing was calm, and she realized that she was back. Taylor was back. And she would have Baldwin in her life, no matter what happened.

She gave herself a smile and looked at her watch. Five o'clock. It was starting to get dark. The streets of Nashville would be filled with people heading home to their other lives, students making their way to their favorite watering holes.

She walked back into the squad room, saying a small prayer under her breath. *Please, God, let us find her. Let us find Jill alive and catch this guy.* She stopped herself short of promising to go to church on Sunday if they did. She knew enough not to make promises she wouldn't keep.

Baldwin came bounding back into the office with a book in his hand.

"What do you have there?" Taylor wandered over to him and stood close, happy to have him back near her.

"King James Bible."

"That was quite a conversion. Are you going to start preaching to us now?"

"Naw, it'll wait. I'll tell you about it in the car. Are we ready to rock?"

"Actually, I'm heading to Hillsboro and you're headed to Granny White with Marcus. Can you call me on the cell and tell me about it while we ride over?"

"No problem."

Taylor looked at Price, who gave them a thumbs-up, then addressed the entire squad.

"Keep in touch, and I mean *really* keep in touch. No heroics here today, kids. If you find the Gates girl, call everyone in to that location. If she's alive, we can go from there. You find this Gabriel Lucas, and you get him whatever way you have to. Am I clear?"

Taylor was surprised, but tried not to show it. "We have clearance to use deadly force if necessary?"

"Yes. Now let's go. Lincoln, you ready?"

"Sure thing." He gathered up his vest. "LT? Be good, girl!" He gave her a brief hug.

"Okay, guys, let's go catch us a bad guy."

There were backslaps and high fives. They all knew the case was going down tonight. The excitement was building in her chest. She was pumped, ready to roll, ready to save Jill Gates. She just hoped Jill was at one of the three addresses.

They made their way into the parking lots. Patrol cars paraded like ants along Third Avenue. Taylor got in her car and rolled down the window as Fitz climbed into the passenger seat.

Baldwin leaned in her window for a brief moment. He looked her straight in the eyes. "Just so we're clear? No worries, okay. I'm up for this."

Taylor felt her body melt. "Baldwin, I wouldn't let you go out if I didn't think you were. Now, get in that car with Marcus, watch his back, and call me on the cell. I want to hear your theory."

She leaned out the window, kissed him full on the mouth, and heard cheers and honks from the cars around her. She just smiled, put the car in gear, shot them the bird out her window, and peeled out of the lot. Man, it felt good to be back.

71

Taylor was trying not to kill any of Nashville's finest citizens as she drove toward Green Hills. She concentrated on the road, had her cell phone on Speaker, listening to Baldwin explain why he'd rushed off in search of a Bible.

"It was something that jerk-off Royce at Vanderbilt said. Lucas told him he'd had a revelation. It got me thinking about the prayer breakfast Lucas had gone to, the one where Father Xavier spoke? I called Royce and asked what the topic was. Get this. It was basically a modern-day interpretation of the Apocalypse. All of the problems the world is having. The war on terror, the religious fanaticism driving suicide bombers…he was sermonizing that if we all came back into the Church, it would all end."

"Yeah, like that's going to happen. I know it sounds naive, but I've never been able to understand why we all can't just get along. Really, I don't get it. All religions have a God. Buddha, Krishna, Mohammad, Christ. Everyone is praying to something they think has control or worships a word that represents what they believe in. Can't they see that everyone, regardless of what religion they call themselves, is looking for that spiritual meaning? Does it really have to be so complicated? We all want to think that something is out there giving us strength and guidance. Who cares what you call Him? Sorry, I don't mean to get on my soapbox. But most of what I see, the violence and greed and hatred, day after day, could be wiped out entirely if we'd only accept people's differences, instead of attacking them for it."

"No problem, preach away. I'd love to discuss it further, because you make an excellent point. But let's get back to the Apocalypse."

"Yes, let's. So the world is going to end in a fiery crash, huh?"

"Perhaps. This sounds crazy, but this is what I think Lucas is up to. Shelby Kincaid. Jordan Blake. Mary Margaret de Rossi. Father Francis Xavier. Tammy Boxer, known as Mona Lisa. These are our victims, right?"

"Right. Don't forget Jill."

"I'm not, I just don't think she's dead. I think she's holding the key to all of this."

Taylor turned onto Hillsboro Road. "You'd better hurry it up. I'm going to be at the address in less than ten minutes."

"Okay, let me back up. The dean at Vanderbilt said Lucas kept telling him that he'd had a 'revelation.'"

"I'm not following you, Baldwin."

"The Book of Revelation. It's about the Apocalypse. Look at the aconite. All the victims were given aconite. We agreed that they were being sacrificed, right? He was giving them the aconite to purify them, to allow them passage into the next world in preparation for his apocalypse. Follow?"

Fitz's cell phone rang, and she asked Baldwin to hold on a minute while he answered so she could hear the news. "Fitz here… Hey, Sam… Really?… Okay, I'll tell her… Yeah, we will." He hung up the phone and picked up the police radio.

"What did she say?"

"That the DNA isn't back, but they've matched the blood type from Lucas's tissue sample to the semen from Shelby. It's gotta be him, Taylor. It's gotta be Lucas."

As she relayed the information to Baldwin, Fitz called in on the radio. He squelched the button. "Gentlemen? We have a positive ID, repeat, positive match."

Voices filtered back through the static, excited 10-4s riding the airways.

Taylor went back to her cell phone. "Okay, Baldwin, we're still about five minutes out. I follow you so far. Finish your explanation."

"Okay. The pregnancies are the key. He's been date-raping Shelby, trying to get her pregnant against her will. She threatens to go to the police. He doesn't want to kill her, but he can't be found out, so he gives her aconite and a symbolic burial, one full of love. He thought Jordan was pregnant with his child, but she tells him it's not his, and he kills her in a fit of rage. Jill is pregnant, and he's probably just trying to get her somewhere safe so nothing will happen to this child. He wants this baby, Taylor."

"So where do Mary Margaret and Mona Lisa figure into this? And why kill the priest?"

"The Seven Seals. The Apocalypse. The end of time. When a Messiah will come again and lead those worthy to the kingdom of heaven? The killings are representative of the seals. He's creating his own version of the Apocalypse. Maybe he got the idea from the lecture Father Xavier gave at the community breakfast. Maybe it had been brewing in his head all along."

She could hear paper rustling in the background.

"I realize this isn't perfect, and as far as I can tell he didn't go through all of the Seven Seals, but this makes sense to me. If he's trying to create a messiah, doesn't there have to be an end of the world?"

Taylor gave him an exasperated laugh. "Baldwin, it's been a long time since I went to Bible study."

"Me, too, so this may be all wrong. But here goes. Shelby Kincaid was killed at the Parthenon, the figurative lap of Rome. She represents the whore of Babylon, the fall of the seven hills. She is poisoned and purified, ready for the Lamb of God. Jordan Blake was stabbed and thrown in the Cumberland, the blood from her stab wounds turning the rivers to blood. Mona Lisa was poisoned and thrown into Old Hickory Lake. She has AIDS; she poisons the water, and the seas die. Mary Margaret de Rossi gave her life over to the church and was purified by fire; she becomes the Last Martyr. Father Francis Xavier was a physical representation of heaven—by killing him, he silences heaven."

Taylor was silent. This was quite a theory. Baldwin continued his explanation.

"The tornado was just an added bonus. I would say it represents the winds being unleashed from the four corners of the earth. He certainly didn't have any control over it, but it fits nicely, don't you think? It would affirm his path, a true sign from God."

"I think you're out of your ever-loving mind, is what I think. I know this guy is a nut, but why in the world would he go to such lengths to create an apocalypse?"

"Because he thinks he is creating our Messiah. He needs the Apocalypse to fulfill the ancient prophecies. He needs the Apocalypse to legitimize his son. He believes his unborn child is the Messiah."

Taylor started slowing the car. They were getting close to the address, and in the heavy dusk it would be easy to shoot right past the driveway. Most were discreetly hidden in this part of town.

"So by creating life, and putting the proper sacrifices in order, he thinks he's created all the steps of the Apocalypse, and his son will be the Messiah. He is one seriously screwed-up dude."

"Yes, he is. And Apocalypse or not, right now, let's worry about saving Jill Gates's life. I hope to

God she's still alive. Marcus and I just pulled up to Granny White."

"Roger that. Fitz and I are almost at the Hillsboro address. Be careful, okay?"

"Right. You be careful, too. Bye."

Price's disembodied voice crackled from the radio. "We're at site three, and we have renters on the property. Repeat, this is a rental, and the checks go to site two. This site is clear. Copy?"

Fitz spoke into the radio. "Fourteen copies. Eighteen, what's your twenty?"

Marcus logged in to the conversation. "Eighteen at site two. We're about to go into the house now. We'll be radio silent for a few minutes while we check this place out."

"Copy that, eighteen. Fourteen out." Fitz put the mic back on the hook. "Okay, sunshine, you ready to rock this?"

Taylor looked over at Fitz and gave him a smile. "Absolutely."

72

Marcus and Baldwin walked carefully around the perimeter of the small Cape Cod on Granny White Pike. A real estate agent would call it charming; buyers in their right mind would see a fixer-upper. Even in the faltering light, they could see the white paint needed refreshing. Ants foraged in the windowsills. Several unkempt azalea shrubs grew wild around the base of the house; while they would be spectacular when they bloomed in the spring, now they just looked sick and straggly. There were no lights on inside.

Baldwin went carefully up the stairs and onto the front porch. The boards creaked and he froze, signaling to Marcus to take the route leading to the back entrance. He waited until the younger man disappeared around the corner, then stepped as softly as possible to the front door. He took up a sheltered position to the right, where he could stand out of the line of sight, keep his weapon drawn, and still open the door freely. He reached for the doorknob and carefully started to turn it. It moved easily, and he stopped. The front door was unlocked.

Marcus appeared silently at the edge of the porch. Baldwin pointed to the knob and nodded. Marcus made his way carefully to Baldwin, then whispered to him.

"The back door is boarded up from the outside. Looks like it's been that way for a while. I don't think anyone is here."

"Okay," Baldwin whispered back. "The front door is open. Let's do it."

Marcus nodded and drew his weapon. Baldwin counted off one, two, three on his fingers, then he and Marcus burst into the open foyer. A stunning antique rolltop desk greeted them, and an Oriental runner led down a close hallway.

Baldwin took the lead and walked silently down the hall. It ended in a large kitchen, white cabinets and counters gleaming in the dark. A combination eat-in kitchen and great room was on their left. They could see the room was empty. Another dark hallway led off the kitchen to the right. Two doors were visible, closed. Another was open. Bedrooms.

Baldwin motioned to Marcus. They moved into the hallway, listening for any noise. They reached the open door. Baldwin stuck his head in and saw a neat bathroom. He pulled back into the hallway as Marcus opened the next door. The room was empty; a shell night-light plugged into the wall illuminated a bed made up with a hand-sewn quilt. It struck Baldwin that this house didn't look like it belonged to a young college professor; it was the sort of home you'd expect from a retired grandmother.

Baldwin reached the next door and silently turned the knob. The door swung open, and the coppery scent of old blood assailed his nose. This room was a duplicate of the first, but the nightlight spun dark shadows on the bed and walls. It smelled of death.

Marcus whispered a quick "We're clear." Baldwin nodded, holstered his weapon, and turned on the light with the back of his hand. The bedspread was black with blood, the wall to the right of the bed sprayed with an arc of dark red. Cast off. The knife had swung away from its target, blood flying off of it, creating a Pollock-esque pattern on the wall. An expert would be able to tell them every tiny detail of how the blood got there, every strike into flesh. Baldwin immediately thought of the autopsy photos of Jordan Blake. The gaping stab wounds in her young body must have been the ultimate cause of the stains.

He turned to Marcus and shook his head. They'd definitely found the killing house. He made his way back to the kitchen, snapping on extra lights as he went. When the room was fully illuminated, he started opening cabinets and drawers. In addition to the usual kitchen accoutrements, he found a large white-and-green bottle with a stopper top. The label read Aconite, and had directions for use. It looked as if it came from a store, like any other vitamin or supplements. Baldwin remembered Lincoln mentioning that aconite could be bought over the internet from many different sources. How convenient.

He opened it and took a whiff of the contents. He couldn't smell anything. Marcus came into the kitchen, looking pale. Baldwin showed him the bottle. "Bastard bought it from somewhere. Man, that's spooky. People can get anything online these days. The internet isn't helping our jobs, is it?"

Baldwin gave him a sad smile. "No, it's not. Time to call this in."

Leaving all the lights burning, they retreated carefully, out the hallway to the front door, down the creaking porch steps to their car. Their backup was pulling up in their squad car. Marcus waved to them, then slid in the driver's seat and keyed the microphone.

"This is eighteen at site two. Evidence galore. Bottle of something that starts with an A."

They were being as cryptic as possible in case one of the media radios had accidentally been tuned to their frequency.

"Eighteen, is that our COD?" Fitz answered brusquely.

"Yes, fourteen, it is. We have biologicals in a back bedroom, too. Otherwise site two is clear. Nobody home. Copy?"

"Copy, eighteen. Request you call Sam's team to site two, then meet us at site three, please. Copy?"

"Copy that." Marcus turned to Baldwin. "Let's get the Crime Scene techs out here and head on to Hillsboro. I've got a bad feeling about this."

The Hillsboro address was their last chance. Baldwin sent up a silent prayer Taylor and Fitz would find Jill safe.

73

Taylor slowed and shut off her lights, pulled into the long driveway of the single-story rambler. There were no cars in the drive, and the lights weren't burning. She looked around for better cover and saw a small road forking off to the right. It was unused and unpaved, overgrown with weeds.

"This place must be worth a fortune." Fitz was looking at the land greedily. "Even though the house looks small, the land would go for half a million, at the very least. Man, I'd kill for a spread like this."

Taylor raised an eyebrow and gave him a smile. "You're probably right. Look at this road. Must be the track to an old barn. Lots of horse country out here before they built it all up. Lucky us, it's the perfect place to stash the car."

She pulled down the path and almost rammed the car into a police cruiser. Officer Miller and Officer Wills must have had the same idea. She stopped behind the first car and popped the trunk so they could grab the gear stashed there. She and Fitz stepped out into the cool night air.

The two officers stepped out from the front of their cars. They looked dangerous, dressed head to toe in their black SWAT gear, guns pointing from every angle.

"Good of you to join us," Miller said. "Didn't see any cars in the drive when we pulled in, thought we'd just duck in here." He flashed Taylor a smile, his white teeth flashing in the moonlight. "Heard your transmissions. You guys matched DNA on this one, huh?"

"Close—there's a blood type match between this guy and semen found at the first scene. Enough to go on. His other two addresses are clear. The West End property is a rental. You heard Marcus's transmission—looks like he was killing the girls at the Granny White address. Which leaves this spot as his hidey-hole. Marcus and Baldwin will be showing up, so don't shoot them. You've seen the picture of the girl we're looking for?"

"Yeah, Jill Gates. We also got a shot of this Gabriel Lucas character. How do you want it to go down?"

Taylor was shrugging into her bulletproof vest, and Fitz was checking the shells on a shotgun he'd gotten out of her trunk. "Fitz and I will take the front. You guys get the back. When you hear the door break in, get in the house. We'll start looking for Jill. You start looking for Lucas. Clear?"

"Clear." Their combined voices made the word echo in the darkness.

"Good. He's going to protect Jill and the baby. He'll probably think we're trying to hurt her and will do anything to defend her, but he's sick and may not have the physical power to fend us off. Keep an eye out for weapons."

After conducting one last press check on their guns, they stole silently into the night.

The house was set back far from the road, on at least a few acres of land. Though there were other houses around, they were far enough apart that nosy neighbors wouldn't see them sneaking through the grass.

They crept to the house to take up their stations. There was a flicker of light coming through the window on the east side of the house. Taylor reached the window, stuck her head up quickly, and saw it was the kitchen. She couldn't see anyone inside. She signaled to Miller and Wills to head around the back. She and Fitz made their way to the front of the house, then to the porch. She felt Fitz tug lightly on her shirt. She pulled up short and turned to him, brows raised. He whispered, "Easy, now." She blew out a deep breath and nodded. They made their way to the front door.

Taylor had a momentary thought of simply ringing the bell, and grinned to herself. Surely a rational man like Gabriel Lucas would invite them in to make their arrest. She sent up a last silent prayer as Fitz stepped in front of her, lifted his fingers in a silent one, two, three, then shouted, "Metro Police," and kicked in the door.

They were met with no resistance. They saw

Miller and Wills come in the back door. It was unlocked; they had simply turned the knob and it opened. Both entrances opened into a dark great room. Two hallways shot off opposite sides of the room. One led to the kitchen; the source of the meager light she'd seen from the window was the backsplash light on the stove. The other hall was dark.

Fitz jerked his head to Miller, who tapped Wills on the shoulder and gestured toward the kitchen. He nodded at Taylor and pointed down the darkened hall. Taylor went first; Fitz followed, guns at the ready.

There were two doors down the hall. The door at the end was open. The one at the beginning of the hall had a slide lock bolted to the door's exterior.

Taylor figured if Jill were in the house, this would be the best place for her. She stopped and put her ear to the door as Fitz continued down the hall. He swept into the other bedroom, then signaled her it was clear. He came back up the hall.

Quietly, gently, Taylor slid the lock on the door and turned the knob.

It opened into darkness. Letting her eyes adjust, Taylor saw there was little in the room besides a bed. Fitz touched her on the shoulder and signaled to the light switch. Taylor reached for it, gun pointed into the middle of the gloomy room.

She flicked on the light. There was a woman tied down, spread-eagled, centered perfectly in the middle of the bed. Her stomach was rounded with an advanced pregnancy.

"Jill? Jill Gates?"

The woman didn't answer immediately and didn't move. *We're too late, damn it, we're too late.* Before she could move, Taylor heard a small moan. Jill was alive. Relief coursed through her, and she rushed to the girl's side.

Jill was strapped to the bed, hands handcuffed to the headboard, ankles tied to the foot. She seemed barely conscious, but as Taylor bent over the girl, murmuring soothing nonsensical words, she opened her eyes and looked at Taylor. The tears started down her face.

"Is he gone? Gabriel? Is he gone? Did you kill him?"

"Shhh. We're going to get you out of here."

"Are you the police?"

"Yes, honey, we are." She unlocked the handcuffs and reached down to untie her feet.

Jill cried, "Thank God. Thank God you're here. He's going to kill me—he's insane. Please, get me out of here."

Fitz moved beside the bed and helped Jill sit up. She was obviously a little woozy, but they needed to get as much information out of her as possible if they were going to find Gabriel.

"Do you know where he is, Jill? Is he in the house?"

"I don't know. He's kept me locked in this room the whole time. How long have I been here?"

"We think at least five days, maybe more. But you're safe now, honey—we've got you. Can you stand?" He got her to her feet, eyeing the swelling in her belly. "How far along are you, Jill?" he asked.

"Eight months. Are my parents here? Are they okay? Oh, they must be freaking out."

Taylor patted her on the shoulder. "They're here in town, honey. They came as soon as they heard you were missing. They're gonna be real glad to see you. Can you tell us any more about Gabriel Lucas?"

Jill lost her balance when she got to her feet and toppled against Taylor.

"Oops, here you go, sit back down."

Jill plopped back on the bed, embarrassed, and gave Taylor a smile. "I'm okay. My feet are just asleep. My parents are going to kill me when they see I'm pregnant."

"Trust me—your parents are going to be thrilled to have you back, you and the baby. Tell me what you can, okay?"

Jill shook her head. "I'm having a hard time remembering a lot. I've been trying to think. I know it's been a while since he was here. I've been awake since right before dark. Usually he comes in and gives me a shot of something the minute I wake up and he hears me. He tells me stories while I'm drifting off, nutty stuff I can't really understand about these women and their 'representations,' stuff about the Bible. Whatever is in the shot makes me fall asleep almost immediately, and I kept having all these weird hallucinations. When I was awoke he was talking crazy." She put a hand protectively over her stomach. "He kept telling me I was carrying the Messiah. He's out of his mind."

Taylor nodded and looked at Fitz. "The injectable morphine." She turned back to Jill. "We think he was giving you morphine. Did he tell you he has cancer?"

"What? No."

"He has brain cancer. We think it's affected him to the point where he's not thinking rationally. He's hurt a lot of people in the past couple of weeks."

"Brain cancer? Giving me morphine? My God, what was he planning on doing to me?"

Fitz held out a hand. "We think he was planning on keeping you safe. He wasn't going to let anything happen to you or his baby. Do you think you can stand up now?"

He got her to her feet, and they made their way into the great room. Between the room and the kitchen was a small breakfast bar with stools. He got her seated, checked in with the rest of their force.

"You find anything?"

Wills was keeping watch by the front door. "He's not here, and there's nothing much to go on. Doesn't look like he's living here—it's just a safe place for him to hold the girl. We'll keep looking around."

"Okay. I want you guys to be ready for anything. He'll come back for her at some point. When he sees we've found her, he's liable to go nuts, and I can't predict what he'll do. I want you to be ready."

They nodded and melted into the background. Fitz watched them for a moment as they set up their defensive positions. Satisfied they wouldn't be ambushed, he turned his attention back to Taylor and Jill.

Taylor was on the radio. "Fourteen to base. We've got the package. She's a single, repeat, no one else found. Copy?"

"Copy that, fourteen. Eighteen is on the way, ETA five minutes."

"Copy. Base, we need a bus sent here. No ME. Copy?"

"Copy, fourteen, bus, no ME. Got it. Out."

Taylor smiled at Fitz. An ambulance was on the way for Jill. Marcus and Baldwin had found enough evidence at the Granny White address to sink Gabriel Lucas. But they couldn't celebrate yet. They were only halfway there. Now they had to find Lucas.

"It doesn't look like he's living here, just has some bare essentials to keep Jill fed. Didn't find any drugs or syringes either. He must keep them with him," Taylor said.

Fitz started opening drawers and cabinets in the kitchen. Taylor went to the window. From this angle, she could see a large shed about one hundred feet away from the house, backed up to the woods.

She turned to Fitz, who was ministering to Jill, getting her a glass of water. "Hey, Fitz, there's a shed out here. I'm going to go check it out."

"Miller's out there. Make sure he knows it's you."

"Gotcha." She went out the front door and whistled sharply. Miller stepped out from the side of the house, and she pointed at the shed. He nodded and melted back into the darkness.

She crossed the hundred feet or so to the shed. It was old and rickety, didn't look like it would stand a good storm. Miller slid around the side of the shed from the back, and they took up standard positions on either side of the door.

Taylor nodded at him, then kicked it open.

74

The interior of the shed was about ten feet by six, and smelled musty, like old mulch left to rot through the fall. Taylor flashed her Maglite from corner to corner and saw nothing to excite her. A few rusted garden tools, an old lawn mower, a bag of birdseed ravaged and emptied by scavengers. She shook her head to Miller and closed the door behind her.

"Go on back to the house. I'm right behind you."

She took advantage of the relative calm to congratulate herself. They had found Jill safely and had identified where Lucas was doing his horrific crimes. Now they just had to find Lucas himself, and they could wrap this up with a neat little bow.

She started back to the house, and a shadow flitted out of the corner of her eye. She felt every nerve ending start to tingle. Her heart thumped hard in her chest.

He was here. She could feel him now. He must have been hiding in the woods behind the shed. She drew her Glock and went into a crouch, trying vainly to see in the darkness. She swung the sight of the gun left, then right, started to move forward. She heard a twig snap and spun around, then a loud grunt. It was too dark to see—was that Miller? She was afraid to call out, didn't want to draw attention to her spot.

She took a cautious step forward, and something shoved her backward. She fell hard on her butt, her gun jolting out of her hand as she tried to catch herself. She caught her breath and scrambled up. *The gun, where is the gun? Where is Miller?*

Gabriel Lucas stepped out of the shadows and stood in front of her, a wicked long chef's knife held in his right hand.

"Did you hurt her? Did you hurt Jill?"

Breathe, Taylor. Talk him down.

"No, Professor Lucas, Jill is fine. She's inside with some of my men. Why don't you drop that knife and we can go in and talk to her."

Taylor could see the fright in his eyes. "You said you didn't hurt her? You're lying, I can tell you're lying. Jill!" he screamed.

"Professor Lucas, stop right there. Drop the knife. If you don't drop the knife, you can't talk to Jill."

Gabriel's mood shifted, and he smiled at her. His voice was calm now, gentle. "I am Gabriel. Only Gabriel. I have changed the universe. You can't hurt me." He took two steps backward, never taking his eyes off Taylor.

Taylor tried to keep his line of vision to the kitchen blocked. "Gabriel. I told you Jill is fine.

Now put your hands on your head, and turn around, very slowly." She stepped back, saw the outline of her Glock four feet away to her right. She'd have to dive for it if she needed to use it. She needed to distract Lucas, get him to put down the knife.

His eyes were roving, searching, looking behind her, almost as if he was trying to get her to turn her head away from him, and then he'd tackle her. She wasn't falling for it, kept her eyes locked on his.

When he feinted a move toward her, she stepped to the right. One step closer to her Glock.

"Gabriel, it's all over. We know what you've done."

He started to laugh. "You know what I've done? How can you possibly know what I've done? I've saved you. I've saved all of you! I have created the perfect One, He who will reign forever, the spirit of humanity, the one true God. His path has been cleared. His way will be followed. The signs have been fulfilled! *'And there shall be no more curse: but the throne of God and of the Lamb shall be in it; and his name shall be in their foreheads.'*" He was screaming now, arms thrown to the heavens, his face a mask of ecstasy.

Taylor was thankful for his episode; surely his screaming would bring some backup. *Keep him distracted, step to your right again. Pick up the damn gun.*

Gabriel continued howling. "*'And there shall be no night there, and they need no candle, neither the light of the sun; for the Lord God giveth them light: and they shall reign for ever and ever.'* Don't you see? Don't you understand? I have created the light!"

Taylor spoke calmly. "I know what you think you've done, Gabriel. I know you think you can create the Messiah through Jill. But you haven't, you can't. All you've done is get a young girl pregnant and murder five other people. You're sick, and we want to help you. Now turn around and get on the ground. Get on the ground now. Now!"

Gabriel ignored the command. He was looking over Taylor's shoulder. She caught it, realizing that Gabriel must have seen Jill somewhere behind her.

The transformation was amazing. He was suddenly calm, the joy on his face shining like a beam of light. Gabriel held out his arms.

"Oh, my love, my sweet. You're okay now. I won't let anything happen to you. Come to me, my dove."

His eyes were glazed, and he had a smile on his face, one so yearning that Taylor almost felt sorry for him for a moment. The man was seriously ill, and it was possible his illness had robbed him of his ability to think competently. But they had him now, and he would pay. She'd make sure of it.

She gave a quick look over her shoulder and saw Jill standing with Fitz in the back door of the house. The light radiated behind her, and she shone like an angel.

Taylor turned back to Gabriel. She saw something in his eyes that frightened her. She shouted over her shoulder. "Fitz, get the girl back inside. Now!"

Gabriel's face was suffused with love and hatred. Taylor watched him warily as she heard the first of the sirens pulling into the drive. He was going to go after the girl; she was certain of that. She couldn't let him get past her.

Fitz was yelling now, and Taylor saw Miller out of the corner of her eye, down on the ground. She didn't know if he was alive or just knocked out. She knew she was in the way; Fitz couldn't take a shot, but she couldn't move, couldn't take the chance that Lucas had a gun and would try to kill everyone to get to Jill.

In that moment, Gabriel launched himself at the house, screaming wildly. Taylor met him with a punch to the chest, and he staggered for a moment, not expecting resistance. She launched a kick at his abdomen, connected solidly, heard the breath go out of him in a groan. She stepped in to take him down, but he managed to get his feet under him and plowed into her. He started toward the house again, his arms locked on her shoulders.

She fought him, and they grappled for a moment, until his weight and frenzy started to overpower her. A step closer, another, and the gun was finally within reach. She shoved Gabriel backward with all her strength and swung her hand down. Caught the grip of the gun on the first try, whipped her arms up. "Stop. Don't take another step."

With a roar, Gabriel charged, the knife flashing in the light from the back door. She reacted as quickly as she could, spinning around him, out of reach, the Glock pointed at his chest. He kept coming, the knife high, lunging at her, and she spun away again, pulling the trigger, once, twice, three times. He went down, hard, and suddenly, she couldn't breathe.

75

Marcus pulled into the drive at speed, and Baldwin caught sight of the fight in the headlights. He saw a flurry of blond hair, the flash of a knife, heard the shots. He jumped out of the car as a wash of red spurted into the air. He froze. Taylor was facing him, standing stock-still, and looked confused, as if she couldn't understand why she'd discharged her weapon. A small smile played on her lips, and her hand rose to her throat, then she crumpled to the ground, next to the body of a man.

Baldwin felt as if he was watching the scene underwater. Every motion was sluggish, unhurried, casual. He stared for a moment in disbelief, then snapped back to real time. Gabriel had landed neatly at Taylor's feet, three shots to the chest, his tainted blood mingling with Taylor's where she'd fallen. It was all over in a second, but Baldwin felt a lifetime had passed. He could hear his own screaming, but it was simply a background noise to the commotion that ensued.

"Officer down, officer down, get the EMTs in

here now!" Fitz was on the walkie-talkie screaming for help, Marcus was on the radio in the car yelling for assistance. People were rushing around in the background, yet Baldwin couldn't identify them. More sirens wailed closer and closer, and suddenly the yard was full of people babbling, yelling.

Taylor was down, one booted leg bent, hands to her neck. He dropped by her side. Her eyes were closed, her face pale. Bright red arterial blood spilled recklessly from her neck.

He pressed his hands against the flow, and her eyes opened, briefly, full of pain. "You're going to be okay—just hang in there. Don't try to talk."

The eyes closed again, and Baldwin felt his heart stop. Had he just seen her eyes for the last time? *No, don't think it, don't think it, man.*

"Come on, Taylor, open your eyes for me, come on, sweetheart, open them up."

But she lay still as marble. He was pulled back off her, and fell into the dirt. The EMTs had arrived. They hustled her onto a gurney and slapped a pressure bandage on her neck. The doors to the ambulance closed, and it screamed away.

Baldwin was on the ground next to Gabriel; he couldn't move. He stared at their suspect. The man was dead, head cocked toward Baldwin, his eyes open, a small smile on his lips. Baldwin sat paralyzed, almost as if Gabriel's mythical death gaze had turned him to stone.

He thought of Taylor's dreams, her nightmares. He couldn't lose her. He couldn't stand it.

Then he was up, on his feet. Fitz pulled him toward the car.

"Don't give up on her yet," he said grimly, and started the engine.

They followed the ambulance in Taylor's car. Surreal, it was all so surreal, so fast and unthinkable. She'd been on her feet, had shot Lucas, and suddenly was down, on the ground, bleeding out, the knife calmly resting in the dirt by her head, just out of reach of Lucas's outstretched hand.

The ambulance screamed down Hillsboro, blowing by all the cars and trucks. Fitz drove without speaking, though Baldwin could see his lips moving in silent prayer. Baldwin was still in shock, not seeing the trees, the cars and signs as they sped through the neighborhoods toward Vanderbilt University Hospital, the closest available trauma emergency room.

They arrived at the hospital in record time, less than ten minutes after they had left Gabriel's lair. In the emergency bay, the ambulance doors opened. Taylor's limp body was pulled out and rushed into the hospital.

Fitz screeched to a stop behind the ambulance. "Go, go. Go with her."

Baldwin gave him a tight smile, then ran, right on the heels of the stretcher. Taylor was so pale, so pale; they were pumping air into her, the EMT perched on the stretcher, doing chest compressions, the pressure bandage dark and wet.

Someone in blue scrubs grabbed his arm, shouting, holding him back.

"Sir, sir, you have to wait here—they're taking her into surgery. I'll go check and give you an update. You can't go in. Sir, sit here." She pushed him hard into a chair. Baldwin felt his world shrink to pinpoint depth. All he could hear in his head was his own prayers.

And Taylor was gone, through the honey-colored wood doors, a hand trailing off the edge of the bed, her blond hair red with blood.

76

Two interminable hours had passed since the doctors had taken Taylor up to surgery. It seemed every cop in Nashville had arrived at the hospital. Price and Sam were in a corner, Sam crying her eyes out. Simon stood at her elbow, helpless, tears running down his face. Marcus and Lincoln slumped in two chairs opposite a coffee machine, contemplating the linoleum floor.

Fitz found Baldwin staring at the door to surgery, not seeing, overcome with his internal dialogue, which he didn't realize he was saying aloud. "Dear God, don't let her die. Dear God, don't let her die." The mantra seemed to be comforting him somewhat, but Fitz could tell the man was in shock, and was furious no one had attended to him.

"C'mon, Baldwin. Sit down here. Good, good, that's more like it. Here, drink this." He handed Baldwin a cup, which he drank automatically. It was brown and bitter; he assumed it was supposed to be coffee.

"She's going to be okay, Baldwin. Taylor's the

toughest chick I've ever seen. She's going to pull through—you just watch. She's too stubborn to die on us." His words thickened, and Baldwin noticed he was wiping tears from his eyes.

"What the hell happened? I couldn't see— she was blocking my view of him. I sure as hell couldn't shoot, didn't want to hit her. All I could see was Miller, down on the ground, like he'd been coldcocked, which I guess he was, since he's over there." He pointed across the room, where Miller had a bandage on his forehead. "Baldwin, what did you see? Did Lucas attack Taylor? She tried to stop him and got cut?"

Baldwin shook his head, searching for words. "I think, well, I'm not sure exactly. I just saw flashes of it as we pulled up. They were fighting. It looked like Taylor had the gun between her and his chest. She spun away from him to get a clear shot, but Gabriel had the knife up, and he lunged at her. She was moving around him. It just caught her in the neck as he went down. Freak thing... Then Taylor collapsed, and I was frozen. I didn't move to do anything, I couldn't, I... I just don't know." He fought back the tears. A strangled sob came from his throat, and Fitz held him like a little boy, murmuring words into his hair. They stayed like that for a moment, Baldwin trying to pull himself together, to be strong.

"You weren't frozen. You were right by her side. You had your hand on her neck. You probably saved her life. Don't you remember?"

He did, but it hadn't felt real. He looked at his

hands; though he'd washed them, there was still blood around the edges of his nails.

"Come on. Let's get some air." He guided Baldwin from the waiting room, down the pea-green hallway and into the ambulance bay. He leaned against the railing and pulled the ever-present cigarette from behind his ear. "I think a little toke is called for about now, don't you?"

Baldwin stared at him blankly. "Could I have one of those?"

Fitz looked around, then fished a pack of Camels out of his front pants pocket. "Don't tell anyone I bought these, okay? Taylor'd kill me if she knew."

Baldwin sucked smoke into his lungs. "Ah, hell, I might've got her killed. She was a sitting duck."

"It wasn't your fault."

"It was, Fitz. I think I distracted her. When she was about to shoot Gabriel she hesitated, just for a second, because she saw me come around the corner of the house."

Fitz took a deep breath. "That's not what I saw. She hesitated because she didn't want to take Gabriel's life if she didn't have to. She was being a good cop, assessing the situation, whether to use deadly force. She was doing it right. She always does it right."

"If she hadn't hesitated, he wouldn't have been able to slap at her with the knife."

"Buddy, listen to me. Everything happens for a reason. And we saved a girl. Jill is okay. She's with her parents upstairs somewhere. Docs say she'll be fine, and the baby's doing well."

"I'm glad. I am."

Fitz raised an eyebrow. "I heard some of what he was saying before Taylor shot him. He really thought he could create the Apocalypse and his son would be the Savior. The son of a bitch certainly succeeded in creating his progeny. A son to raise the world and to lead us to salvation. The guy's a whack job. Too bad he didn't survive. I hear we have enough evidence from the Granny White house to fry the son of a bitch."

Baldwin took a long drag on the cigarette, then flicked it over the edge of the railing. "I just... I need some time to sort through all of that. I think, no, well... Fitz, we need to go back in. They may come out anytime to let us know how she is."

Fitz put his arm around the younger man, and they walked wordlessly back through the ER.

As they rounded the corner to take them to the waiting room, Lincoln came flying down the hall, grinning, shouting to them, "She's gonna make it! She's going to be okay!"

He smashed into Fitz, hugging him and pounding him on the back.

Baldwin barely registered his knees buckling underneath him as he pitched headfirst into the linoleum floor.

EPILOGUE

Taylor and Baldwin were sharing a beer, holding hands, watching the sun set. The air was pink and chilly; the fire pit at their feet put out a steady heat.

After a time, the sky turned purple and the shadows around them disappeared. She finished off the beer and grinned at him.

"Want some dinner?" Her voice still sounded like sandpaper, and the scar that traversed her neck stood out, a stark red reminder of how close he'd actually come to losing her.

"Yeah, but I'll cook. You just sit here." He stood and bent to her, giving her a long kiss. When he went inside, whistling, Taylor felt the absence of his lips sharply, pulled her scarf closer around her throat.

Her survival had been nothing short of miraculous. She'd only been out of the hospital for a few days. It had taken three weeks of advances and setbacks, plus two more surgeries, until she had been cleared for release. She would be in therapy for several more weeks, but the prognosis was excellent. She'd always had a raspy voice, but now it was deep and husky. She thought she sounded awful; Baldwin found it incredibly sexy.

He'd been by her side the whole time, and she was so grateful. There'd been an attraction between them from the beginning, certainly, but it had grown into more, much more, in the weeks since they'd met. In the hospital, through the pain and agony and recriminations, every time she opened her eyes, he was close by, reading, working on his computer, sleeping. He talked to her, read to her, kept her spirits from flagging when the pain threatened to overwhelm her.

She should have told him to leave, to go live his life, but she couldn't. She didn't want a life without him in it.

When she'd been discharged, he'd driven her home. She'd asked him to come in, and he hadn't left. She was so very glad. Having him in her life, in her house, banished the demons she'd been facing. She felt right again, as if she'd come back to herself. She knew he felt the same way.

Baldwin opened the refrigerator door and pulled out the steaks. He set them on the counter, pulled out a pot to cook the corn. Her home was easy to be in, relaxing, restful. He hadn't felt this comfortable in years.

Taylor had saved him, and nothing would keep him from her side ever again. He thanked God

every day for bringing her into his life. And Garrett
Woods, and Mitchell Price, and the whole Nashville
Murder Squad, for forcing him back to the land of
the living. Nothing in his past mattered anymore.
Taylor had forgiven him, and he'd forgiven himself.
He'd have to go to Quantico at some point, grab
some of his things from his apartment up there. He
didn't want to go back to the BSU full-time. Not
yet. Woods had agreed he could work out of the
Nashville field office. Baldwin might be healing,
but there were still people who would never forgive
him. Staying away seemed like the best course of
action for now.

There was also the added bonus of the blond
goddess out on the deck, the fire making her skin
glow.

His stomach flipped as he watched her. The cat
hopped in her lap, settled in by the fire. She stroked
her soft head, kissed her between the ears. Gentle
and strong. Loving and fiery. Capable, yet vulnerable.

Mine. She's mine. Yes, staying put was a very
good thing.

He put the corn in the water, was carrying the
steaks to the grill when the phone rang. He picked
it up.

"Hello?… Yeah… Oh wow. Okay, I'll tell Taylor… Yeah, she's doing well. Thanks for calling."

He left the food in the kitchen and went out to
the deck.

"Was that the phone?" She started to sit up, but
he put a hand on her shoulder, dipped down, and

gave her a small kiss on the forehead, a longer one on the lips.

"It was Fitz. Jill delivered the baby an hour ago."

Taylor nodded. "We knew this day was coming. Jill finally fulfilled Gabriel's prophecy."

He took her hand. "Sort of. It's a girl, Taylor. Gabriel's Messiah is a girl."

* * * * *

AUTHOR NOTE

Thank you for taking the time to read *Field of Graves*. I hope you enjoyed seeing Taylor and Baldwin meet and fall in love, and of course, how Taylor got her remarkable scar.

This novel was my very first full-length work. Written between 2003 and 2005, in a complete and utter vacuum, it is the novel that landed me my agent but didn't sell to the marketplace. On my agent's advice, I went on to write *All the Pretty Girls*, continuing the Taylor series, which was my first sale.

I put *Field of Graves* in a drawer, jokingly calling it my 80,000 words of backstory. Over the course of the Jackson series, I stole from it on occasion, referred to it often, making it a living, breathing document, a real part of the series, though unseen by readers' eyes until now.

It has been lightly edited, and I've done this on purpose. First, seventeen novels later, I am now a better writer, with a more solid grasp of story and a more distinct voice and style. Second, there were some scientific and forensic mistakes that have now been corrected. Third, since I did steal some scenes verbatim for later books, I needed to smooth over those sections. I apologize for any repetitions I've missed.

But I didn't want to change the book too much. It is my first novel, with the flaws inherent to a debut effort. It was rather fun to revisit the book and see these flaws. Some I've left; others, where egregious, I've fixed.

The Nashville setting represents the city at the time I wrote the book; there are places, restaurants, and cultural situations no longer familiar to our town.

The biggest issue I found was how to deal with Taylor's cat, Jade. In the current series, beginning with *All the Pretty Girls*, she does not have a pet. Between the books, I realized the demands being placed on her character would preclude the time and effort needed to care properly for an animal. Having someone at home who needs you to show up, feed, water, and love does take time away from catching bad guys.

But in *Field of Graves*, Taylor has Jade.

Some of you may recognize the name, and the description of the cat. The Jade in this book is my baby, Thrillercat. For those who don't know the story, let me share it with you.

She came to us as a replacement cat, after we suffered the loss of our nineteen-year-old Siamese,

Jiblet. (All names in my family start with *J*—from parents to siblings to animals to husband). When I first saw her at the pound, she was five weeks old, suffering from a bad cold. So bad that they were going to put her down. They can't afford to have sick kittens in the cages; disease spreads too quickly.

We took her to the vet next door and insisted he patch her up. He did. When we brought her home, we named her Jade for her intense green eyes.

Having just moved to Nashville, I couldn't find work in my chosen field, so I was happy to accept a position with the vet who healed little Jade. I thought I'd be working the desk, but he wanted me as a tech in the back. Bad. Bad. Bad. After my first neutering, I was done. But before I could quit, I picked up a large golden retriever and herniated a disc in my back. That led to surgery, and recovery time, and library books, where I discovered John Sandford. The rest, as they say, is history. I sat down and wrote a Jackson novella, then took what I'd learned and created *Field of Graves*.

Sadly, Jade passed away in 2012 from pancreatic cancer. It took years, but we finally adopted again—this time, sisters, also shelter kittens. How Jameson and Jordan came to live with us is a story for another time, but I will share that Jade was a huge part of the process. And it's not lost on us that we needed two kittens to fill the void Jade left behind. She was a magnificent cat.

Though it is a departure from the rest of the series, I've chosen to leave Jade in this story to honor her spirit. I miss my little furry muse terribly, and I simply couldn't erase her from the book that she gave me. It wouldn't be right.

Thank you for reading, and for being a part of my writer's journey. Please forgive the book's rawness. We all need to have a first.

J.T. Ellison
Nashville, Tennessee

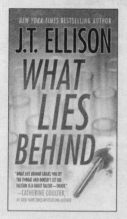

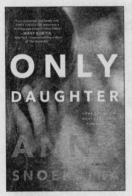

Turn your love of reading into rewards you'll love with
Harlequin My Rewards

**Join for FREE today at
www.HarlequinMyRewards.com**

Earn **FREE BOOKS** of your choice.

Experience **EXCLUSIVE OFFERS** and contests.

Enjoy **BOOK RECOMMENDATIONS**
selected just for you.

PLUS! Sign up now
and get **500** points
right away!

Earn
FREE
REWARDS
Join
Today!
HarlequinMyRewards.com

MYR16RTALL

J.T. ELLISON

32093	ALL THE PRETTY GIRLS	___ $9.99U.S. ___$11.99 CAN.
31764	WHAT LIES BEHIND	___ $7.99U.S. ___ $9.99 CAN.
31710	WHEN SHADOWS FALL	___ $5.99U.S. ___ $5.99 CAN.

(limited quantities available)

TOTAL AMOUNT	$ _____
POSTAGE & HANDLING	$ _____
($1.00 for 1 book, 50¢ for each additional)	
APPLICABLE TAXES*	$ _____
TOTAL PAYABLE	$ _____

(check or money order—please do not send cash)

To order, complete this form and send it, along with a check or money order for the total above, payable to MIRA Books, to: **In the U.S.:** 3010 Walden Avenue, P.O. Box 9077, Buffalo, NY 14269-9077; **In Canada:** P.O. Box 636, Fort Erie, Ontario, L2A 5X3.

Name: _____
Address: _____ City: _____
State/Prov.: _____ Zip/Postal Code: _____
Account Number (if applicable): _____
075 CSAS

*New York residents remit applicable sales taxes.
*Canadian residents remit applicable GST and provincial taxes.

MIRA®

www.MIRABooks.com

MJTE1216BLTALL